TIDES OF MARITINIA

Also by Warren Hammond

KOP
Ex-KOP
KOP Killer

TIDES OF MARITINIA

WARREN HAMMOND

HARPER
VOYAGER
IMPULSE
An Imprint of HarperCollins Publishers

EPub Edition DECEMBER 2014 ISBN: 9780062389251

Print Edition ISBN: 9780062389244

10 9 8 7 6 5 4 3 2 1

For Mom

PROLOGUE

Dear Reader:

Nine years before the publication of this text, after several months' worth of contentious debate, the University of Maritinia made the decision to convert the voluminous journals of Jakob Bryce (also known as Colonel Kell) to a form more easily understood by the Maritinian peoples.

Please know that any and all fictionalizations were made for the sole purpose of enhancing the narrative's readability. Absolutely every effort has been made to preserve historical accuracy.

Danii Mmoro
High Chancellor
University of Maritinia

CHAPTER 1

I was an assassin.

And a virgin.

I didn't mean to say I'd never had sex; stabbing flesh with flesh was the best kind of stabbing there was.

I was a virgin because I hadn't knifed for real. Never put blade to skin and loosed a river of blood. Never sliced through muscles and organs. Never drove a blade deep to the core.

Never put my lips to the flame and blew out another's soul.

Never until Maritinia.

Kneeling on the restaurant's rooftop, I scanned the watery horizon until I spotted a few slivered strokes of brown against the endless sprawl of rolling emerald and gold. The boats came from the Empire's Ministry, sunlight glinting off five domes at the horizon's edge.

This was the last flotilla of the afternoon. *He* would be on one of those boats. My target. Colonel Drake Kell.

My throat was dry. Strange that it could get so dry on a world that was nothing but water. I tried to tell myself it wasn't fear. But it was.

I wiped sweat from my forehead. Again. Pol must have noticed. <You need to relax, Jakob. You've trained for this.>

<I know,> I replied, my words traveling down the little channel in my thoughts. That was how I communicated with the consciousness living inside my skull. Pol was what I called him. Short for Political Officer.

<You're ready for this,> he said.

I sucked in a deep, calming breath and tried to believe he was right. He should know. He'd been through this before. Countless times. For centuries, he—or one of his many duplicate consciousnesses— had been coaching operatives like me. More than a coach, though, he was a companion and a comrade. A confidant. A source of strength.

No way I could do this without him.

Crouching to stay hidden, I moved away from the wall, shoes crunching on broken tile. From the corner of my eye, I spotted a crab disappearing under a roof shingle. This planet was infested with the damn things.

A few more steps, and I'd moved far enough that

nobody would see me if they looked up from the quay. I stood straight and stretched my arms to the cloudless sky, muscles gleefully unknotting.

I paced back and forth. Had to get the blood pumping. Get the circulation circulating.

Feeling refreshed, I moved back to the whitewashed wall, dropped back down to my knees, and checked for crabs before propping my elbows on the stone.

Chin resting in my right hand, I looked to the east. The flotilla was closer but still a long ways off. <You see how slow they move, Pol?>

Of course he did. He saw through my eyes and heard through my ears. <You must be patient.>

<How can they stand to move so slow? How do they ever get anything done?>

<You know they have no choice.>

I knew. The Sire's wisdom had been drilled into me all my life. I was from Korda, home world of the Sire. A world at the center of an empire of ten thousand worlds.

I'd traveled a long way to get to Maritinia, an ocean-covered planet on the farthest fringe of the Outermost Ring. Like all the other worlds in the Outermost Ring, it was too far from the Empire's Core to be controlled at gunpoint. The Empire was far too vast to station armies and fleets in every corner.

A more clever solution was required: population control by means of technology control.

For the Maritinian people, that meant *no* technology. None at all. No plastics or metals. No electricity.

No computers or robots or engines. Nothing beyond wheel, pulley, and lever.

Assert technological control and with it came political control. Such was the wisdom of the Sire.

<But look at them, Pol,> I said with a grin. <Couldn't we just slip them a couple outboard motors?>

<You say that because you're impatient. The Sire's wisdom is long-term. Besides, they have the squids.>

Yes. They had the squiddies. I supposed that was better than paddling. Not much faster, though.

A small contingent of roughly one hundred of the Empire's finest soldiers and administrators could manage a tech-restricted world like this one. It led to a remarkably stable system. It had worked since the Empire's founding three thousand years ago.

But not anymore. Not here. Maritinia had gone rogue.

And one of my mission's numerous goals was to find out why.

But first the traitor had to die.

If only those boats would hurry up. Infuriating things moved like drugged snails.

The waiting was the worst part. So much nerve-wracking, hair-pulling, crazy-making time to fuss and worry. Fourteen months since the Eyes and Ears of the Empire gave me my orders. Fourteen months. Maritinia was that far.

But those fourteen months were the easy part—I was training. I was *doing*. I'd made landfall eight days ago, though. Eight days with nothing to do but wait. And watch the tide go in and out. And think.

A sharp pinch made me jerk my elbow away from the wall. I rubbed the sore spot and looked down to see a pair of pincers retreating under a stone. Damn crabs got me again.

<You got too close. You have to be more careful.>

<Oh, there's a helpful nugget. I wish you could feel pain, Pol. I really do.> I unbuttoned my sleeve and reached inside to rub the skin near my elbow. <I hate this place.>

I missed Korda. Illustrious home of the Sire. A civilized world. We'd tamed that fickle Mother Nature millennia ago. Smothered her by blanketing the globe with so many cities that they'd merged into one enormous metropolis that wrapped the entire planet in stone and steel. It was a beautiful place. A testament to the engineering skills of the Empire.

Looking to the setting sun, seeing the swaths of pink and purple sweeping the sky, I supposed this place had some natural appeal. But as far as I was concerned, it was the kind of appeal best appreciated in a painting.

Turning my gaze eastward, I saw that the flotilla of skiffs was finally getting close. Wouldn't be much longer now.

I felt the tension in my gut, springs winding tighter and tighter.

To distract myself, I turned my attention to a pair of barges coasting in from the north. They rode low in the emerald water, their holds pregnant with kelp. Gliding to a stop, the barges were boarded by sweat-soaked Jebyl dockhands, who began the tough work of wrestling sopping bails of kelp down bamboo ramps to the pier, where woolly mammoths flapped their ears while awaiting their cargo.

I always knew that life in the Outermost Ring was different, but this world, with its winds and rains, and its rotten-fish stench, and its disfigured beggars, and barefoot children was so . . . so . . . crude.

At times, I wondered if the Empire should even bother retaking this planet. But all the ten thousand worlds served their purpose. The Sire smiled upon those who contributed, no matter how small. How these people could've shunned Him, I didn't know.

The sun dropped below the watery horizon, the cool of dusk already on the air. Me, I was still sweating.

Sun departed, the rolling swells of the sea had lost their sparkle, and emerald water faded to a mosslike green. The golden kelp fields could hardly be called golden anymore. More like brown mustard now. And the domes of the Empire's Ministry in the distance had lost their luster, brilliant silver dimmed down to the dull gray of concrete.

It was as if the sun had pilfered this world's only riches on its way out.

Only the skyscreens still shone brightly, the stern-faced Admiral Dii Mnai—the self-appointed ruler of Free Maritinia—looking down on Maringua, his capital city. The man was a mystery to us. After seizing control, he'd severed communication with the rest of the Empire, and we'd not had much information on him beforehand. For a world like Maritinia, there had never seemed a need.

The voice came from deep inside my head. <Jakob? You're going to miss the colonel.>

I jerked my eyes back to the docks. <I know. I know.> Eyes on the docks.

<Do you see him?> asked Pol.

I did. Colonel Kell was easy to spot, his walking pace seemingly twice as fast as anybody else's. Of course, to me his bustling stride was normal. Kell was from Korda just as I was, his internal metronome forever swinging at a citified tempo. I watched him and his two guards move along the quay, coming in my direction.

<Are you ready, Jakob?>

Dread welled up from deep inside. Brittle nerves felt ready to snap. But I swallowed hard and answered in the affirmative. I can do this, I told myself. I can.

My knees creaked and cracked as I stepped across roof tiles and down a set of stairs that led to a meandering marketplace. I strolled past the first two fish stalls before turning right and exiting onto the quay just in time to fall in step about ten feet behind the colonel and his guards.

Kell moved with authority, head up, shoulders square, each step perfectly placed. His bootheels clacked sharply on the stone, precisely the way you'd expect of a lifelong military officer, one who clearly still knew how to handle himself. He was a real man, this Kell, a decorated veteran of the Secession Skirmishes, commander of dozens of ops, a true leader, and later a diplomat.

I was no match for Kell. My training wasn't good enough or long enough. What in Sire's name had I gotten myself into?

Until fourteen months ago, I was just an Analyst Second Class, a fancy title for a simple bureaucrat. A pastry-eating, coffee-and-cream-drinking, clock-punching pencil pusher complete with a wardrobe full of nothing but dark-toned suits that needed to be let out an inch per year.

A lifelong slacker foolishly trying to live up to Daddy's expectations.

I was a pretender. A fraud . . .

<I wouldn't get too close, Jakob.>

<Right.> I slowed down, taking one step for every two of my hyper heartbeats. Letting Kell reel out a ways, I allowed the crowd to swallow every bit of him except for his cap, which bobbed regularly into view.

From experience, I knew early evening was a busy time on the quay. Tethered boats would take on supplies. Wheelbarrows full of fish would head for the markets, eel tails hanging over the edges. Herds of mammoth would be shepherded into their stables by gangs of young boys adept at the most deaf-making whistling I'd ever heard.

But tonight all that commotion was invisible to me.

The only thing I could see was the traitor's cap.

The only thing I could hear was the insistent hammer of my heart.

The time was near. Time to do the job I was sent to do.

Assassinate the colonel.

Nobody could see me do it. Nobody could ever find his body. Because once he was dead, I was going to take his place.

Meet the new Colonel Drake Kell.

CHAPTER 2

"My firstt ru le for killing a man: Dont call it
murder. Finnd a word that will go soffter onthe
consceincce."

–JAKOB BRYCE

The crowd was thinner here. I could clearly see Kell
and his guards now. I watched their backs, the traitor
and his protectors. The guards were in full uniform,
dark blue with turquoise piping, a sharp contrast to
Kell's beige-and-gold livery. Kell had some nerve don-
ning the official uniform of the Empire, defiling it further with the emerald green scarf of the Free Maritinia
Republic wrapped about his neck.

The quay angled slightly away from the sea, thus
becoming a street. As far as I could see stood block after
block of squat, stone buildings, the entire city resting

atop a broad stone platform raised over the sea. So focused on my quarry, though, I was barely aware of the restaurants and bars lining both sides of the avenue, their pitchmen hawking good eats and better prices.

The trio turned left and approached a two-story residence with a tiled roof and white walls—white except for the bottom third of the first floor, which was painted blue in the style of Maritinia's capital city.

As was their routine, the guards took up positions on either side of the entry while Kell went inside.

<Everything is going according to plan, Jakob. I see no reason not to proceed.>

<I agree,> I said, trying to sound certain, willing it to be so. It had taken me a day to get my bearings, but for the past six nights, I'd been spying through Kell's bedroom window from a neighboring rooftop.

Six nights straight, the colonel had followed the same routine. He'd appear in the upstairs bedroom shortly after entering his home. He'd settle down on his sleeping mat with a drink, and nap for ninety minutes before waking up, downing the remainder of his drink, and heading downstairs, presumably to shower and shave. Soon thereafter, I'd see him exit the house to go to the club for dinner.

I was nearing the residence myself now, acutely aware of the firerods slung over the guards' shoulders. I continued past the residence without making eye contact, half expecting crackling purple fire to electrify my back.

Eyes straight ahead, I kept moving, short breaths

puffing in and out until, a few minutes later, I arrived at a set of stairs that led down to a dock.

I strode up to Beleaux's boat and gave it a kick, startling the Jebyl fisherman out of his nap. Seeing me, he smiled, his face striped with wrinkles. "I didn't touch your things as you ask-ed," he said, his voice thick with provincial charm, always enunciating the "ed" at the end of a past-tense verb as if it were a separate word.

"Where's the squid? I told you I didn't want to row."

"Yes, of course you did. I think she's eating." Leaning down, he rapped on the boat's hull several times. "I rent-ed you the best squiddie of the school." He knocked again, and a rust brown tentacle appeared over the boat's rail, then another on the opposite side. More tentacles came stretching up out of the water, briefly exposing their tight-packed rows of suckers before slithering down the boat's sides and across the floor like fast-growing tree roots. The boat creaked as the tentacles, eight of them now, squeezed down. "See? She's a strong one."

"Good."

Grinning with a set of dingy teeth, he said, "You must bring a guide. Beleaux will take care of you."

I shook my head no.

Beleaux complied with a shrug and climbed up to the dock. I hopped down into the boat, careful not to step on the cablelike tentacles. Checking first to make sure my supplies were indeed on board, I told him to untie the boat, then I poked my head over the prow to look at the beast, a broad dark shadow just under the surface. I looked into the creature's white eye. "Go."

The skiff lunged forward, then slacked for a moment before kicking ahead again. Like a slow rowing stroke, the cephalopod moved the boat ahead in regular spurts. It was the damnedest thing, this living motor.

When I looked back, Beleaux waved good-bye. I returned the courtesy.

<Why did you wave, Jakob?>

<No need to be unfriendly.>

<Be careful of getting attached to people. The closer you let them come, the more likely they'll have to be silenced later.>

A chill tickled my spine. <We have nothing to fear from Beleaux. He won't even recognize me when I change my appearance to match Kell's.>

<Yes, but my point still stands. The locals are not your friends.>

<It was just a wave. Now can we please move on? I have a boat to pilot.>

<Proceed.>

Turning my attention to the task at hand, I took hold of the rudder and steered the shallow-bottomed craft alongside the quay. Undulating waves slapped at the thousands of stone stanchions that held the city above water.

The squid whooshed the boat forward while I looked up, searching until I spotted the dangling glowgrub. I'd left it there an hour earlier, tied it to Kell's water sluice with a silk thread, and tossed it over the platform's edge as a marker.

Navigating up to the glowgrub, I tapped one of the

squid's tentacles twice—the signal to stop—and reached high to cut the worm loose and dropped it into the sea.

Needing a better light source, I fumbled for the paper globe I'd placed on board this morning. Giving it a good shake, I woke the fireflies inside, and the globe lit with a shimmering phosphorescent glow. Navigating into the dark shadow cast by the city, I scanned the platform's underside, having little problem locating Kell's trash chute.

Through a series of stop-and-go single and double taps, I coaxed the squid next to a heavily barnacled column and wrapped it with kelpstalk rope.

I pulled another rope from my supplies, this one with a large fishhook carved of mammoth bone on the end. I made quick work of wrapping the hook in silk. <You sure this will work?> I asked Pol.

<Yes. The cloth will deaden the noise.>

I took my first shot at throwing it up into the chute. Missing, I pulled the rope and hook out of the water and tried again and again until I finally succeeded in landing the hook over the chute's lip.

Next, I strung a leather-strapped machete over my shoulder, so the blade would hang on my back. Taking up a filleting knife, I tucked it into my belt. I untied the boat, pulled up the rudder, and gave the squid a single tap. "Go on home now."

As the skiff lunged forward, I took hold of the rope and started up, hand over hand, pulling myself into the rotten-fish stench of the short chute, barnacles slicing my knuckles, pincers nipping at my wrists. Keeping focus, I threw up a hand and caught hold of the chute's lip. Pulling hard, I lifted my torso into the opening, my shirt shredding as I scraped over the shells. With a final scramble, I pulled up my legs and stood.

I was inside. Standing in a small supply closet, the chute I'd climbed through rested at my feet.

My heart pounded like it was trying to club its way out of my chest. Desperate lungs huffed thirstily at the air. Blood dripped from my hands. Blood seeped from the scrapes on my chest, a single droplet rolling slowly from rib to rib to rib.

<Excellent work.> Pol's voice was soft like velvet. <You're doing great.>

I gripped my weapons, machete in my right hand, filleting knife in my left, both blades carved of mammoth bone—no technology meant little metal for weapons. I squeezed the handles tight inside my fists.

<For the Empire, Jakob.>

<Sire and Empire.>

Feeling strangely brave and determined, I moved forward, my hands and feet tingling. I passed quietly by the entryway, the guards' feet visible below the curtain that posed as a door. I crept through the dark room, avoiding chair silhouettes, feeling the ripple of sea-bamboo mats through the thin soles of my shoes.

Afraid to blink, my eyes began to water. Scared of being heard, I sucked air through my nose.

I climbed the staircase slow and deliberate, stone

to stone to stone. At the top, I found myself in a small room. A sleeping form lay on a sponge mat on the floor. A flicker of candlelight danced across his face.

I approached, my fists squeezing painfully down on the weapons' handles. With the machete raised over my head, I skulked up to him undetected. I stopped close. Watched his bare chest move up and down to the rhythm of a gentle snore. I put my eyes on his neck. Targeted my swing.

One clean chop was all it would take.

One. Clean. Chop.

I brought the blade down with full force . . . but my aim was wide, and the blade struck his chin with a bone-on-bone crack, warm blood splattering up my hand and wrist.

He sat up, machete embedded in his lower jaw, his eyes stunned and confused.

I missed. I fucking missed! Fingers of panic squeezed down on my throat. Claws dug into my heart.

<Again,> Pol said, no emotion in his voice.

Pol's command brought me back to the situation at hand. The knife. I drove it into his shoulder.

He grunted as I pulled the two blades free. He knew what was happening to him now, eyes completely wild. Savage. Yet also alert—the look of a trained warrior. His destroyed jaw kept him from making a sound and calling for the guards, but not from attacking. He lunged for me. I met his reach with the machete, and severed fingers fell to the floor.

I drove with the knife. Chopped with the machete.

Again with the knife. Again with the machete. He tried to fight, but I wouldn't let him. I kept hacking and stabbing until there was stillness.

I backed away from the body, letting the weapons fall from my fingers. He lay half-off his mat, a bloody mess of cleaved and pierced flesh.

Still moving backward, I bumped into a wall and let myself lean against it. My knees buckled, and I collapsed, my back sliding along the stone until my tailbone struck the floor with a jolt.

I leaned over to vomit, and the twisted muscles in my gut heaved bile onto the stone.

<You've done a great deed, Jakob. He was a traitor and a threat to the Empire. You mustn't let yourself feel guilty. Your cause was, and always will be, just.>

Wiping my mouth with a quaking hand, I saw Kell move. With a jerk of his left leg he managed to roll himself off the mat. Horrified, I watched him inch slowly forward, heading for the staircase.

<Oh, Sire, what have I done?>

<Finish him, Jakob.>

<I can't. Don't make me.>

<Jakob. You have to finish him—for the Sire. Now!>

For the Sire, I thought grimly. I stood and walked over to the machete. Looking down at the handle, I refused to pick it up. Picking it up, I refused to take another step. Taking another step, I told Pol I couldn't do it, I just couldn't.

Chopping downward, I said I couldn't over and over and over.

CHAPTER 3

"Why must teh Empirre recapture ths world?
Because Maritinian kelp isrich in, of all things,
vitamins."

—JAKOB BRYCE

I stopped reading the mission report right there. This had to be a joke. "Vitamins?"

<Say it in your head.>

Right. I kept forgetting. This was fourteen months before arriving on Maritinia. Fourteen months before I slaughtered Colonel Kell.

It had been only a few days since they'd implanted Pol's consciousness into my head. Just the first of many surgeries I'd have to suffer over the coming months while in transit to Maritinia. Soon they'd carve my pear stomach into a washboard. Then they'd hone the sloping curves in my face. Slim my eyebrows and reshape my stumpy fingers. They'd work me up and down with scalpel and surgical saw until I looked like Kell.

\<Say it in your head, Jakob. You have to practice.\>

I lay back on my bunk, the only furniture inside the small cargo hold, and tried to concentrate. I conjured the rabbit hole in my mind, the small opening through which conversation was possible. The trick was to drop an imaginary spider silk into the hole and send the words vibrating along the invisible thread.

\<This is about vitamins?\>

\<The Eyes and Ears of the Empire wouldn't send us if it weren't important.\>

\<That's all this backwater planet has to offer? Vitamins?\>

\<Maritinian kelp is also used as a thickening agent in jellies and toothpaste.\>

\<I'm supposed to risk my life for toothpaste?\>

\<The Empire needs toothpaste, Jakob.\>

\<Why can't we get our toothpaste thickeners from somewhere else?\>

\<An entire world has spurned the Sire. That isn't a small thing. Now please allow me to read the rest of the report.\>

\<How am I going to get onto the planet?\>

\<Not now. Let me read the report.\>

\<Can't you just tell me?\>

He responded after an annoyed sigh—which was impressive considering Pol didn't have lungs. \<The de-

tails are still being worked out, but I suspect you'll get a cover identity to gain entrance. Some kind of merchant perhaps.>

<I thought Maritinia had cut itself off from the rest of the Empire.>

<It has. But the governors of some of the worlds in that sector tell us the Maritinians still sell kelp on the black market and to The Beyond. That means the black marketeers must be sending supply shuttles down to the surface. It won't be hard to hitch a ride.>

<But what if they don't allow foreigners on their world?>

<If they're doing commerce with other worlds, there must be at least a few people passing in and out. Now, can I please read the report?>

I stared at the screen, letting him read through my eyes, scrolling down when asked.

Maritinia. I knew I couldn't have expected to land the choicest assignment, but I'd sacrificed the next three years of my life for this mission. I'd been hoping for something a little more consequential than the Empire's dental health.

Mundane facts scrolled by. *Population: 700,000 (approximate). Biota: piscine with chlorophyll-based ocean vegetation. Economy: agrarian.*

The statistics painted a simple picture. Maritinians were kelp farmers. No wonder I'd never heard of the place. The only thing remotely interesting about it was how those simple kelp farmers had managed to overthrow the Empire's appointed governor.

<The news of this rebellion must never reach the wrong ears,> said Pol.

<You're referring to the Secessionists.>

<I am. A story like this will make it easier for them to convince people on the streets that revolution is possible.>

I nodded, realizing that this mission had a symbolic importance that far outweighed vitamins and toothpaste. <You think the censors can keep a lid on a story this big?>

<They'll do their best. Don't you want to watch the video file?> Even in this short time, I'd come to realize that most of Pol's questions were more like firm suggestions. I told the video labeled *Maritinia's Final Broadcast* to play. Several screens worth of legalese scrolled in front of the E³ seal before the screen flashed to Maritinia. I saw five domes of polished silver resting on one side of a ring-shaped island of weathered stone.

<That must be the Ministry of Maritinia,> said Pol.

<Yes.> The Empire's outermost worlds were each ruled by a governor who, along with a small contingent of diplomats and soldiers, resided inside a ministry, where technology was allowed.

The sun rose from the emerald ocean. Bright morning rays made the sea sparkle as if it had been sprinkled with gold dust.

The quintet of silver domes were small by Empire standards, but they were pretty in their way, the bulbous, onion-shaped structures each tapered into a point at the top. Quaint.

The island was a man-made atoll, a slate gray circle set in an ocean of undulating green. The ring was broken in places, collapsed stone visible through shallow water that channeled into the inner lagoon. The lagoon itself looked like an inlaid emerald lassoed by granite. Patches of purple, blue, and orange coral showed through the seawater like squirts of paint pressed under aquamarine glass.

The camera zoomed in on one section of the atoll, where a crowd of people stood surrounded by Maritinian soldiers holding firerods that must've been seized during the coup. Inside the circle of guards, about a hundred prisoners stood lined up in military-style rows. Some in uniforms, others wearing civilian dress, all of the men and women standing with hands bound behind their backs.

<The Empire's contingent?> I asked.

<I assume so.>

The camera continued to zoom until it focused on Admiral Dii Mnai, the coup's leader and self-appointed admiral of a rebel navy. Standing on a dais, his ample frame loomed behind a podium. An emerald-colored cloth hung over the spot where the five-pillared logo of the Empire would normally show.

He looked into the camera, his harsh eyes intimidating the lens. *Let it be known that the peoples of Maritinia have been free-ed from the grip of the Empire.*

I upped the volume, his provincial accent hard for me to grasp.

Admiral Mnai jabbed a finger at the heavens. *The*

Empire's hold on our flow has been shatter-ed! Maritinia is free! Today is a day to remember. A day to rejoice.

Look at them, he said. On cue, the camera panned over the prisoners. *For millennia, they have steer-ed our currents, and they have stolen our resources, and they have murder-ed our children. They have jail-ed and torture-ed our Interpreters, but no more.*

The camera returned to Mnai, who pounded the podium with his fist. *No more! They are parasites, these so-call-ed representatives of the Empire. And today, they will pay for their sins, and the sins of their predecessors. Tomorrow, we will build a new Maritinia, but today . . . Today, we will feed the angry souls they have wrong-ed!*

The camera moved to the right and settled on Colonel Drake Kell. He wore the Empire's uniform, colonel's bars on his cap. Draped around his shoulders was an emerald cloth, the new Maritinian flag worn like a stole.

Kell stepped to the water's edge, waves lapping against the pitted stone. A woman was escorted by a pair of guards to where he stood. Her eyes were puffy and red, her hair straggling and flapping in the wind. She had the look of a career civil servant whose frumpy clothes hung wearily on a body fattened by years of sedentary work.

She reminded me of me.

Colonel Kell grinned through the corner of his mouth and lifted the machete he held in his right hand. Mortified, I watched him give the woman a swift chop on the shoulder. She screamed and fell to her knees, blood already seeping through her blouse.

Get in the water, he said.

No, she wailed. *No!* She tried to stand and run, but tripped and fell on her side. *Please, please!*

Lifting his leg, he put his boot in the center of her back and rolled her off the edge. With barely a splash, she disappeared, reappearing a second later, desperately gasping for air. She sank out of view again, and I thought she'd sunk for good until she resurfaced. Over and over, she sank under and bobbed back into view, each time sucking what I thought would be her last gasp of air.

Something appeared from the corner of the screen. It looked like a tiny silver sail gliding through the water. A fin. Now I saw several. It seemed they were everywhere, all of them swiftly moving in. She came back up one last time before the water went wild with thrashing fish tails and sleek silver bodies that jumped and flipped amid violent splashes of sea spray.

Dry-mouthed, I looked away, my stomach turning over.

<Jakob. I can't see.>

I turned back to the screen, hoping it would be over, but it had only just begun. The guards were shoving people in the water, beating them with firerods, kicking and dragging and tossing them in, dozens of them. One made a break, getting twenty yards before the purple lightning of a firerod caught his leg and dropped him to the ground, smoke curling up from his charred limb.

Some of the doomed swam for the coral, their numbers dwindling one by one as the fish—these silver needles of death—overtook them in a swarm of frothing water that took on a pinkish hue.

\<Are you okay, Jakob?\>

I couldn't believe this was real. Those poor souls ripped apart and eaten alive. Eaten.

\<Talk to me,\> said Pol. \<I can't read your mind.\>

\<Colonel Kell is a monster.\>

\<Yes. You see now this is about more than toothpaste.\>

I saw.

Maritinia had to be liberated.

The Empire could've sent an army. But, instead, they were sending me.

Me.

Kill Kell. Take his place and subvert this new regime of monsters and madmen. Foment discontent and sabotage their defenses.

Pave the way for the Empire's return.

That was my mission.

CHAPTER 4

> "A machete isn'ta weaponn. Not by designg. But
> It can dkill. Such is our way. alwaysy turning
> tools intoweapons."
>
> —JAKOB BRYCE

The butcher lay at my feet.

Dead.

My hands were covered in blood. I could feel it on my face, my neck, speckled and smeared. Kell's blood.

<It's done,> said the voice in my head.

I nodded. Speechless. Ghostly candlelight flickered over the corpse. The machete in my hand cast a menacing shadow.

<You have to hurry.>

Yes. Much to do.

I wrestled the corpse onto the blood-drenched

sleeping mat and dragged it across the floor, sliding it behind the hanging blanket that served as the closet door.

I rushed downstairs and tiptoed past the front door, where the guards' feet were still visible below the curtain. Hurrying into the kitchen, I found a scrubbing brush and a bucket. Hustling to the sluice, I dipped the bucket directly into the stream, filling it with seawater. Back upstairs, I dumped the whole bucket onto the bloody scene and went to work scrubbing until my arms were spent before forcing water toward the back wall, where I could channel it into a small gutter that dumped into the sea.

<Don't forget the wall.>

I didn't. Splashing the wall with half of a second bucket of water, I brushed left and right, up and down.

Unable to gauge the quality of my work by candlelight, I eventually had to call it good. Kell's usual nap time was already over, and the guards outside were certainly expecting the colonel to go to the club for dinner.

But I couldn't go out until another critical task was completed. Nabbing Kell's glass of imported whiskey from the small stone block on the floor, I hurried back downstairs to the bathroom. I set the whiskey glass on the washbasin, then thumped the paper globe hanging from the ceiling. Fireflies brightened the small space with their fluttering glow. Despite a full week on planet, I still couldn't help but recoil at the sight of the toilet, a stone-carved basin with two footholds and a hole through which you could hit the ocean below. How could people live like this? How could *I* live like this?

I looked at the mirror. My face didn't entirely match Kell's. Not yet. For the last eight days, I couldn't exactly walk around looking like Kell's long-lost twin without attracting the wrong kind of attention.

Until now, I'd been known as George Barnes. A black marketeer who was seeking a good price for kelp. I hadn't been allowed to enter the capital city until I'd successfully arranged an appointment with one of Free Maritinia's new officials. Lucky for me, I wouldn't have to keep that appointment since it was still a week out. Poor George would be a no-show.

I felt for the sewing needle I'd neatly stuck through the leather of my belt. Locating it, I extracted the slender sliver of fishbone with my fingers.

I dipped the needle into the whiskey and, squeezing it tight between my quivering fingers, lifted the pin past my eyes to my forehead.

At the moment, my cheeks were too puffy to be Kell's. Brow too pronounced. Same for my cleft chin.

My hand froze where it was. I didn't like needles, dammit.

<You're already running late, Jakob.>

<Give me a break, will you? You're not the one who's going to feel it.>

<You must hurry.>

Biting my lip, I gave myself a poke and winced at the sharp sting. Having punctured the skin, I'd driven deep enough to run a hole into the implant underneath. Warm fluid squirted free, a mixture of saline and blood dribbling down my face. Holding my breath and clenching my jaw, I launched into a needle-poking frenzy, jabbing each of my cheeks, piercing the bump on the bridge of my nose, lancing both sides of my cleft chin. My face smarted all over. Protesting nerves chanted and throbbed.

But the hard part was done.

Like a water balloon that had brushed too close to a cactus, my face had sprung a half dozen leaks. Liquid ran down my face and dripped off my chin. The implants under my skin deflated, and overstated features sank and tamed.

My face became his.

I massaged irritated skin with my fingers, squeezing my implants empty. My Neanderthal-like brow had shrunk until it lay against my surgically restructured skull. Flabby cheeks had disappeared. The cleft chin cleft was no more.

I wiped the blood and saline off my face with my sleeve and checked the mirror. The pinholes were small, barely noticeable. The skin hung a bit loose where the implants had been, but I'd been assured that the skin would tighten up after a few days.

I worked for some clever folks.

I took another moment to study my newest face in the mirror.

<You look good, Jakob.>

I did. I was fully Kell now. Or at least a haggard version of the colonel.

Hurriedly, I stripped off my clothes and showered under chilly seawater that trickled from a bamboo showerhead caked with salt deposits. I gave myself a good rinse, this body still feeling strange under my soapy hands—firm biceps, trim stomach, thick chest hair, and muscular legs.

Quite an improvement over the original.

I dried with a coarse, mammoth-wool towel, then hustled back upstairs, where I pulled the Empire's uniform out of Kell's closet with barely a glance at the dead heap on the floor.

I dressed myself, the uniform a nice fit. My body had been perfectly tailored to fit his clothes—perfectly tailored to be Colonel Kell.

I applied the finishing touches, cap on the head, flag wrapped around my neck.

I *was* Kell.

It was time.

I marched back downstairs and to the front door. The guards stood just on the other side of the curtain. I reached for the drapery but stopped before taking hold.

What was I going to say?

I had the right face and the right body. My scraped vocal cords were a perfect match.

But I couldn't breathe. The reality of what I was about to attempt clamped down on my throat.

What if they didn't believe I was Kell? They'd cut me and drop me in the water and let the cuda fish have me. An entire school of them would nip and gnaw at my arms and legs before tearing me apart in bite-sized chunks.

<What are you waiting for, Jakob?>

My legs felt heavy. I wanted to sink to the floor.

<Jakob!>

My nerves had stretched to the breaking point. "What?"

<You said that out loud.>

The guards heard me and came through the curtain. "Are you okay, sir?"

I fought to keep my legs under me. "I'm okay. Just feeling a little under the weather."

The one on my left studied me in the dim light. "You don't look well. Perhaps you should retire for the night."

"No. I'll be fine. Just need to walk a bit."

"Very well, sir. Where to?" asked the one on the right.

"To the . . . um the—"

"The usual?"

"Um, yes." The guards nodded and stepped outside. I wobbled through the doorframe. My feet felt numb, like I was walking on stumps.

<You're doing fine, Jakob.>

I fell in step with Kell's protectors. My protectors now.

Darkness had taken the city, our path lit by a drizzle of faint moonlight. Pedestrians ambled about, their indistinct black shadows moving to and fro. Feeling more sturdy, I breathed deep of the cool, saltwater breeze ruffling the flag wrapped around my neck.

We turned left, and the smell of a mammoth stable swamped my nostrils. I could hear their snorts. The ruffle of flapping ears. The slurp, slurp, slurp of lapping tongues. I wanted to gag, the stench of matted wool was so bad.

We took another left, and a narrow alley with a raised water sluice running down the center closed around us. Tiny homes stood on either side, with paper lanterns hanging from the eaves. Jebyl children ran and chased, ducked and dodged to the sound of squealing laughter. Men sat in their windowsills, and women hunched over small fire pits, the air thick with the smoky aromas of roasted fish and stewed kelp.

Exiting the long alley, our destination stood dead ahead, the doorway surrounded by a string of glow-grubs, the yam-sized creatures wriggling as the string blew in the breeze.

Before I could reach the door, a Jebyl ducked through the curtain only to be backed out a moment later by a Kwuba doorman. The Jebyl dropped to his knees before beginning to beg. "Please, sir, I only need a bite. Just a bite for me and my children."

Spotting me, the Kwuba doorman welcomed me with a smile before touching his heart with one hand, a common greeting on Maritinia. "Sorry, Colonel. You shouldn't be subject-ed to trash like this," he said, with a swat at the Jebyl.

The Jebyl rose to his feet but stayed bent at the waist as he backed away.

The doorman crossed his arms. "You believe these Jebyl? Somebody needs to teach them a lesson, I say."

Standing opposite him, I shook my head in that what-can-you-do way. He pulled aside the curtain, and the mistreated beggar disappeared from my mind.

I had no idea what waited inside.

With nervous tingling in my fingertips, I stepped past the doorman.

My eyes scanned across leather chairs and wine racks. To my left stood a Jebyl workman, who turned a six-foot eel on a spit. Red-hot embers cast a deep glow across the workman's bare chest and face. The eel turned round and round, its browned flesh sweating out juices that sizzled and steamed.

No wonder that Jebyl wanted inside. A rare posh oasis on this backward world.

I studied the faces in the room, wondering where Kell usually parked himself. My guards abandoned their position on my wings and took posts in an out-of-the-way corner, while I stood paralyzed by the thought of choosing the wrong location, or the wrong people to join.

<Don't just stand there, Jakob.>

<Where do I go?>

Of all the eyes that had looked my way when I came through the door, there was only one pair still meeting mine, a heavy man, his broad face bathed in firelight.

Everybody else appeared to be ducking for cover. Targeting the lone pair of friendly eyes, I weaved through tables of foreigners in business suits and Kwuba elites, who wore formal silk robes that hung past their knees, their feet in sandals.

Tense nods of greeting came from every direction. These people were scared of Kell. Terrified. Broadcasting an image of yourself committing the vicious murder of a hundred civil servants will do that.

I took a seat on an eel-skin wingback, the quilted leather soft and supple from years of wear. I faced my new . . . friend? Coworker? Business associate?

"Good to see you, Colonel."

"Same here," I said.

A bottle of wine appeared with two glasses. From his pocket, the waiter pulled what looked like a leather shoelace with a knot on one end and wormed the knot between the cork and the glass, shoving it past the bottom of the cork with a filleting knife. Wrapping the lace around his hand, and giving a long, sustained pull, he uncorked the bottle.

"So have you thought over my offer?" asked my new drinking partner.

<What's he talking about, Pol?>

<No clue. But I believe he's from The Beyond.> The Beyond. A renegade collection of worlds well outside the Empire's immense reach.

<How do you know?>

<You see his ring?>

I did. A colorful band of cloth tied around his pinky.

Catching me looking, he rubbed the cloth with a thick thumb. "The red stripe is for luck. The yellow for prosperity." He took a glass from the waiter. "I've brought this special bottle of wine from my home world. Accept my offer, Colonel. Let's toast to a deal."

I took a glass for myself. "I've, um, been giving your offer serious consideration."

"And?"

"Must we start with business? Can't we just chat a bit first?"

He stared at me, this stranger with cheeks so fat they sagged like soggy slices of bread. He twisted in his seat, the chair's sturdy arms only affording his sprawling hips a few degrees of leeway. "I'd love to chat, Colonel, but I'll be much better company when our business is concluded. You're not going to find a better price."

\<Dammit. Now what do I say?\>

\<Don't ask me.\>

I lifted the wineglass with an unsteady hand. "I think your offer is um . . . a pretty good one."

"Ah, I thought you would," he said. The corners of his smile disappeared under fleshy cheek overhangs. A gold tooth glowed in the candlelight. He held up his glass. "It's a deal then?"

We clinked glasses. "Deal," I said.

I took a sip tasting of tart grapes and bitter tannins. \<What did I just do?\>

\<I don't know, but look at him. He doesn't suspect you're not Kell.\>

"You're doing the right thing," he said. "These people you've become so enamored with, they need protection."

"Yes."

"And you, too, Colonel. If the E^3 ever caught up with you, I can't imagine what they would do to you."

"I can," I said with a sober tenor.

He gave me a thoughtful look. "I suppose you can, can't you? You spent enough time in the Empire's employ to know their ways."

Chop-chop, I thought, as a sick twist wrenched my gut.

"Why did you do it?" he asked.

A simple question was all it was. But through the filter of my guilty conscience, it sounded like an accusation. "Do what?" I asked tentatively.

"Don't be coy, Colonel. Tell me why you did it."

I wanted to say that I was following orders. That I meant for him to go quick. I didn't mean for him to suffer.

Instead, I said nothing.

"Come now," he said. "Look at all the people in this room who came to do business like me. Besides the pursuit of profit, you know what they all have in common? They all want to know why you betrayed the Sire and helped Admiral Mnai capture the Ministry."

I reduced pressure on the teeth I'd been clenching. The question was a good one. One I needed to find an answer to. "I had my reasons," I responded.

He frowned, his jowls sagging halfway down his

neck. "No problem, Colonel, you don't have to tell me. They say you converted, you know."

"Do they?"

"They say you're a Falal now."

I lifted my brows. The Falal were a local cult.

"Hey, Colonel, don't get upset," the man said. "Your spiritual life is your business. I'm just trying to make conversation."

I chugged the rest of my drink, my tongue awash in harsh flavors. His people were sorely mistaken if they thought they'd made a decent wine. As I refilled my glass, the waiter brought a bowl of food, the smell absolutely intoxicating.

I peered into the bowl—some kind of shellfish in a thin brown sauce. Smelled like butter.

My new business partner pinched a shell between his stubby fingers, then brought it up to his lips and sucked the creature down before returning an empty shell to the bowl.

<You better eat,> said Pol.

<I don't like shellfish.>

<You do now.>

<I do miss butter.> I picked a shell from the bottom of the pile, making sure to scoop up as much of the sauce as I could. Ignoring the purple flesh and the wilted eyestalks, I pulled it up to my mouth. With a suck, butter splashed over my tongue. More oily than the butter at home. My mouth was instantly slick with it. I bit into the snail-like creature, a bizarre flavor bursting forth. Not that bad.

My dinner partner was getting in the groove now, slurping them down as fast as he could with one hand motoring back and forth between the bowl and his mouth, his lips shiny with buttery grease.

I picked up another shell, marveling over the simple wonder of butter. No idea what animal's milk they'd made it from, but I didn't care.

"What is that on your forehead?" asked my dining partner.

The fingers of my free hand went to my forehead and came away wet with saline.

"Sweating," I said, trying to sound nonchalant. "Is it hot in here?"

"Not really," he said, deep-set eyes searching my face. "You don't look well. I didn't notice until now, but what are those marks on your face?"

"I have been feeling a little feverish. Must be coming down with something."

"That explains why you're sweating but not the marks."

"What kind of marks?" I asked, trying to keep the mounting panic out of my voice.

"Little red marks."

I brushed his concern away with a wave of my hand. "Those are just bug bites."

He gave me a long stare, eyes boring into me from deep sockets.

I sucked down a snail and reached for another. Next, I took a hearty swig of wine. "See, I'm fine. Nothing to worry about."

He relaxed into his seat. "You must take better care of yourself."

My blood pressure eased. "All this fine food and drink will fix me up."

"That it will." He refilled his wineglass. "It's hard to believe we used to be enemies, eh?"

"That was a long time ago," I said because it seemed like the right thing to say.

"That it was, my friend. I like to think that if we had met back then, you'd have seen I wasn't really your enemy. I'm just a good businessman, that's all. I had no stake in the Secession Skirmishes."

"I suppose not."

"You were great for my bottom line, Colonel. The rebels were so scared of you, I could've sold them anything. Could've sold them rocks if I'd called them projectile missiles."

<An arms dealer? Is that who he is?>

<Apparently so,> said Pol.

He reached for his wine, and the glass was swallowed in his big mitt. "Wait until you see the system I got for you. The Empire better bring a fleet if they want to retake this world."

<Oh, Sire, what did I buy?>

CHAPTER 5

"There atre times to be a gentleman, and ther are
timmes not to."

—JAKOB BRYCE

Daybreak was coming. Weak gray light came through
the windows to gradually erase the room's darkest
shadows. I'd been awake all night. Perhaps dozed a
little here and there, but I was too hopped up to get
any serious sleep. The best I could do was lie here and
try to relax.

My back hurt. So did my hips. These bed mats offered little comfort on the stone floor although I should
probably count myself lucky I'd found a spare, considering the state of the previous one.

I looked over at the closet. Disposing of the dead

colonel was a must. But if I dropped him through the trash chute, I couldn't guarantee the cuda fish would dispose of his body. The smart move was to make sure he would sink. For that I needed more rope. Lots of heavy stones. But a late-night search of the entire residence yielded neither.

I still couldn't believe I'd done it. It felt like a dream now. My father would be proud. Finally living up to the family name.

I heard voices outside. Holding my breath, I tilted my ear in the direction of the sound. "Go on in," I heard one of the guards say.

My breath caught in my throat. <Pol?>

<Somebody's coming in.>

<No kidding. Who?>

<I don't know, but don't panic.>

Too late for that. <There's a dead body in the closet!>

Whoever had entered was already on the stairs.

<Pol?>

<Keep your cool. You can handle this.>

I was frozen, my back glued to the mat. Cotton-mouthed, I tried to swallow. Footsteps came closer and closer, sounding like the dwindling ticks of a time bomb.

A figure appeared in the doorway. She wore a loose-fitting white shirt over a silky yellow wrapped skirt that hung to her ankles. "Hello, Drake. I'm home."

I croaked out something unintelligible.

"Did I wake you?" She was short, even by Maritinian standards. Five feet at best. But she stood tall, her chest held out front, her chin raised in defiance of some unseen power. She dropped her bag and approached me with sturdy steps. "I'm exhaust-ed."

"Sure you are," I replied though she looked anything but.

She stopped at the sleeping mat's edge. "You're on my side."

"Just keeping it warm for you." I scooted over.

She dropped down with an audible exhale, then curled into me and draped her leg across my boxers.

<It appears you have a girlfriend, Jakob.>

My cheeks flushed, and I suddenly felt hot all over. She nuzzled into my shoulder, curly hair tickling my cheek.

<We watched him for six fucking days, Pol. How could we not know about her?>

<Since the coup, Maritinia has been a blind spot to the Empire. We could only know what we observed ourselves.>

"Don't ever let me do that again," she said. "I can't handle Mother that long."

"How long is too long?"

"The first day was nice. The other thirteen were torture."

Gone for two weeks? I couldn't believe the timing. <I knew we should've watched him longer. This is your fault.>

<Even the best operational plans rarely survive contact with the enemy.>

I turned my head toward the closet, her hair tickling my nose. I could see the body through the gap between the curtain and the floor. She'd see him, too, if
she only rolled over.

I wanted to scream. Wanted to scream and run away.

She breathed quietly, her fingers raking through
my chest hair. I told myself not to fight it. She couldn't
tell I wasn't Kell. We were an exact match. Kell had
been through body scans all his life. The Empire knew
every last detail.

Her index finger stopped on the scar near my shoulder, and she traced the war wound all the way down to
the bottom of my rib cage, then slowly back up. He'd
earned the scar in the Secession Skirmishes.

"You ready for the ceremony?" she asked. "We leave
this afternoon, remember?"

"Of course, I'm ready." <What's she talking about?>
<I don't know.>

She gave my bare chest a pat before sitting up.

"Where are you going?" I asked.

"I need to wash. I've been wearing these clothes for
four days." She stood and stepped over to her bag.

<She must have clothes in the closet,> said Pol.

I was up in an instant, hurrying to put myself between her and the corpse, my heart pumping erratic
beats. Dammit, I hadn't seen any women's clothes in
there last night. But it was dark. And I was looking for
rope.

The bag was in her hand. She watched me with
puzzled eyes. "What are you doing?"

"You must be tired," I said. "Let me take care of that."

"Really, Drake, I think I can handle it."

"No, you've had a long trip." I reached for her bag. "Let me unpack for you."

"What are you talking about?"

"Please let me do it." I grabbed the leather handle and yanked it from her hand.

"Ow. What's your problem?"

"Just trying to help."

"Why are you always such a bully?"

I stayed silent as I stood my ground, the bag's itchy wool rubbing against my thigh.

"I'll be downstairs," she said, but she didn't move, her eyes focused on something behind me. "What is that?"

I looked over my shoulder. At the wall, up near the ceiling. Blood.

My stomach plummeted like a stone sinking to the ocean floor below. <Oh, shit.>

Pol's voice slipped into my mind like a dagger between shoulder blades. <Kill her.>

<What!>

<You can't let her ruin your cover.>

She moved to the wall to get a better look. "Is that blood?"

<Smash her head into the wall, Jakob.>

<No.>

<DO IT NOW!>

"Crab," I blurted. "He was on the wall last night,

and I went to grab him so I could toss him out the window. Nipped me good." I showed her one of the gouges on my knuckles.

"You didn't think to clean up?"

"It was late. I'll tell the guards to clean it later."

She turned to stare at me, intense eyes probing and penetrating, like she was trying to detect the imposter inside. "Why are you acting so strange?"

<End this, Jakob. You know what you need to do.>

I ignored Pol and volleyed her question back at her. "Strange? What's so strange?"

"Why are you so damn cranky? I've never seen you like this."

"Maybe that ceremony is getting to me after all."

"You're nervous about it?"

"I guess so. Couldn't sleep."

"I see it in your face. You look terrible. Are you sure you're ready for a long trip?"

"I'll be fine," I said.

She smiled. "Good. It's not like we can cancel when the whole world will be watching. I'm going to take my shower." With that, she was heading down the stairs, pulling her shirt over her head.

I watched her go, pulse pounding in my ears, sweat breaking on my forehead.

<I told you to kill her. You've jeopardized your mission.>

<Not now.> I was in the closet, staring down at the hacked-up corpse on its sleeping mat.

I tossed her bag into the corner and grabbed hold of

the mat. Squatting low, I walked backward, pulling the body along while I kept my eyes glued to the stairwell, willing her to stay downstairs.

<Where are you taking him?>

<To the window.>

<Somebody will see.>

<Can't bring him downstairs. No other choice.>

<I gave you a choice. It's not too late to do your duty.>

<I'm not going to kill her. She's innocent.>

<She's a rebel. All Maritinians are rebels.>

Reaching the window, I swept the hanging cloth aside and poked my head out, eyes searching left and right. Neighboring balconies were empty, except for one. A woman drinking tea, her gaze aimed out at the water.

I checked for boats. None were close, but several rode the golden waves a ways out. Fishing boats and a kelp barge.

<This can work,> I said. <After he hits the water, the current will take him under the platform.>

<Too risky.>

<It will work.> It had to.

I took hold of the body, hooked my arms under his armpits, his flesh cool on my forearms. With a heave, I tried to lift him off the sleeping mat, but the body slipped from my fingers, and his head clunked back down.

<Stop this now, Jakob. It's too risky. You have to kill her.>

I stopped trying to lift the body, so I could gather my thoughts. <No. If I make her disappear, that will just bring more suspicion.>

<You can tell people she's late getting back from her trip.>

<But the guards already saw her. And she said the whole world will be watching this ceremony, whatever it is. You really think nobody's going to notice that she's not there?>

<Fine,> he said. <Do it your way. But remember what I said about the locals: Don't get too close.>

I grabbed Kell again and had to suppress a chill as I found a better grip by sinking the fingers of both my hands into a pair of deep wounds.

Another heave, and I had him off the floor, then out the window.

I watched the body descend, five, ten, twenty feet until he struck the water in a violent explosion of sea spray. Waves emanated outward, then rebounded back, foamy green water washing over his back.

I looked at the woman on her balcony. She'd heard it. Her back was straight, her head lifted high like a cat listening for danger. I ducked under the cloth, one eye still peeking.

<Somebody's going to find the body,> said Pol.

<The cuda fish will take care of him.>

<What if they don't? If they find him, they'll recognize him.>

<Not after he floats awhile. You trained me to know water does nasty things to a body.>

The woman on the balcony stayed in her chair, the noise not loud enough or unusual enough to investigate further. Soon she was back to drinking her tea. I checked the boats. None changed course.

I nabbed the blood-stained sleeping mat along with Kell's severed fingers and sent them out the window. I went to the water bucket, still half-full from last night, and gave the windowsill a quick wipe down, same for my bloody arms and hands.

Leaning out, I watched for cuda fish, watched for fins slicing through the water. Didn't see any, but the body did drift under the platform. Out of sight. Elation surged inside me. <See, nothing to it. I'm better at this than you think.>

I felt a hand on my back. "What are you doing?"

Startled, I wheeled on her. "Nothing."

She was in a towel, her forearm pinning it to her chest. "You're all sweaty."

"I was just—"

"Were you doing your push-ups?"

I nodded.

"A little early for that, isn't it?"

I tried on a nervous smile. "Never too early to exercise."

She dropped the towel. "Never too early for a lot of things."

My gaze wandered downward, her bare skin kissed by the sun's early rays. I caressed her curves with my eyes. Then my hands.

For Sire and Empire.

CHAPTER 6

> "KWuba and Jebyl, Maritinias' two castes. One
> the ariastocaracy. The other teh worker bees. All
> know their place. Such is the wisdon of the Sire."
>
> —JAKOB BRYCE

I looked at my guards, who sat across from me, facing sternward, firerods on their laps. The guards were new. A shift change must have come at some point during the night. Based on the silk scarves neatly folded in their pockets, both were Kwuba, their faces fixed in soldierly scowls.

Looking past them, I could see the Ministry. On the water for ten minutes already, and it was still a long way off. The boat lunged and slacked, lunged and slacked to the beat of three squids jetting in unison.

I relaxed into the rhythmic motion, my mind

swinging to a similar rhythm, the sweet memory of a passion-filled sunrise.

I'd forgotten it could be that good. Forgot what it was like to have a physique I wasn't ashamed of. There'd been no need to hide under the sheets, or subtly direct probing hands away from my flabby parts.

It was like I was young again. Reinvigorated.

She was an aggressive lover, and fearing I'd give my identity away by doing something Kell wouldn't, I'd succumbed to her greed. I'd let myself be molded into whatever she needed, let her position my hands. My hips. My mouth.

I let her control the pace. The ebb and flow. She was the moon, and I was the sea whose tide rose at her command.

And I'd reveled in every second. Unburdened by the mission. Unshackled from my responsibilities.

The things she made me do . . .

Unbelievable.

It was strange at first, knowing my political officer could see and hear all, but I got over it. Fourteen months since I'd touched a woman? I got over it in a hurry.

I looked up at the sun and let its hot rays bake my face. For the first time since arriving on Maritinia, I didn't mind the open water or broad sky. I was finally getting used to being outdoors.

It was a gorgeous day, really. A warm breeze textured the rolling water with millions of tiny ripples. Vast fields of golden kelp swayed just below the surface with a natural grace that was totally foreign to my home world of all-encompassing structures and enclosed spaces.

High over the water, Admiral Mnai's face shone brightly on a massive skyscreen, his austere gaze aimed at the city. His forehead tall and imposing as a prison wall. His cheekbones high as towers. Eyes like searchlights.

The skyscreens were supposed to serve as the Empire's voice. They surrounded all the major population centers to act as the conduit through which the Sire lavished praise when kelp yields were high or meted out criticism when quotas weren't met.

But after transmitting the video of the contingent's slaughter, Mnai had severed all communication with the Empire. He'd taken control of the skyscreens and used them for his own purposes. Used them to scowl upon his population one long day after another. A stifling reminder of who was in charge.

Soon, I lost sight of him as we passed underneath, the boat coasting between a pair of sturdy concrete stanchions that held the skyscreen and surrounding speakers more than three hundred feet in the air. Safely out of reach of the prying fingers of a technology-deprived population. Such was the wisdom of the Sire.

For the first time since I'd defied his order to kill the woman, the voice in my mind spoke. <We need to talk.>

A stir of dread soured my stomach. I didn't respond. Didn't want to.

<Jakob?>

Turning to my right, I watched as we lunged our way past another boat, the deck no more than a broad leather tarp stretched between pontoons made from bundles of sea bamboo. The Jebyl crew—three of them—bowed in our direction and touched their fingers to their hearts. Moving my gaze down past the water's surface, I spotted tentacles sprouting from long, tube-shaped shadows.

<Jakob?>

I craned my neck to look back at my boat's captain. "Can't we go any faster?"

"I can ask, sir, but the squiddies are a fickle lot."

"Ask."

Reaching for a tentacle that stretched across the hull, he gave the taut skin a triple tap—code for giddyup. Didn't do much good. Best I could tell, our forward lurching continued at the same sluggish pace.

The captain gave me a bow of apology. "I try-ed, honor-ed sir. But the squiddies have chosen to heed only Falal today. Please forgive my inadequacy."

My ears perked at the word Falal. Some kind of cult according to the reports I'd read. I wished I could go back and surf the database more closely, but I'd had to ditch my comm unit when crossing into tech-restricted space.

<You questioned the advice of your political officer.> Pol's voice was tight as a violin string. <When we establish communication with the E^3, I'll have no choice but to report this to your superiors.>

I dropped my chin into my left hand. I didn't want to disappoint my father, and I knew he'd be reading my mission reports. The old spy was proud I'd finally decided to take the challenge of being an operative. Finally followed in his highly decorated footsteps.

We were a family of spies. Generation after generation of the Empire's eyes and ears. Read an E³ org chart, my father would tell me, and you might as well be reading the Bryce family tree. We were the Empire's first family of spies. We had a reputation to protect. Even a minor blemish on my record would be sure to earn his ire.

<Listen, Pol, you don't need to report this, do you? You couldn't expect me to kill that woman when there was a better way.>

<It's not your place to question your political officer.>

<But it all worked out, didn't it? In the end, you agreed with my decision. Killing her would've brought more suspicion.>

<Yes, I did agree. But avoiding suspicion wasn't your original rationale for sparing her. First, you said she was innocent.>

For the guards' benefit, I struggled to keep signs of emotion off my face. <It's true, isn't it?>

<So what you're telling me is it's not okay to kill an innocent woman, but it's perfectly fine to kill her lover and take his place between her legs?>

The accusation stabbed straight into my heart, outrage spilling from the wound.

A voice, a real voice said, "Are you okay, sir?"

"What?"

"Are you okay?"

"Yes, of course," I said to the guard. "Just thinking."

"You look ill. Perhaps we should take you back home. Let Sali take care of you. I'm sure you missed her. She was gone so long."

Sali. That was her name. "No. I'm fine. Really."

"Very well, sir." The guard's eyes went back to the sea.

<Jakob, you must keep your face blank when we talk.>

<Hard to do when you're accusing me of rape.>

<You're not a rapist, Jakob. If you hadn't returned her affections, you would have jeopardized your cover. But I won't let you fool yourself into thinking you did the moral thing by sparing her life. You've still wronged her in a very meaningful way. The high road you think you've taken is an illusion. Your very existence here is a lie. You understand? You are the embodiment of deception.>

I closed my eyes to let the words sink in.

<You're not a schoolchild. And I'm not a teacher who cares about your feelings. This game is for grown-ups.>

He'd taught me this lesson many times before. I thought I'd understood. Thought that when the time came, I could do anything the Sire required of me. Anything.

<You must eliminate thoughts of right or wrong.

There is achieving the mission, and there is failure. That is all the right or wrong you can afford.>

I wanted to argue that, given the circumstances, I'd made a smartest decision possible. But even if that was true, he and I both knew that the original reason I'd balked at killing her had nothing to do with tactics. I'd let my conscience get in the way. I opened my eyes and sat silent, knowing I'd screwed up. Knowing I'd been weak. Knowing I had no choice but to take my medicine.

<More than a half million people on this planet are being deprived of the Empire's leadership. They've fallen into the hands of a despot. What's one life compared to so much pain and suffering? You can't build a glorious garden without sticking your hands in the dirt, Jakob.>

I didn't speak. My eyes were trained on the approaching domes of the Ministry.

<Your mission is righteous. You're serving the greater good, the greatest good that is your Empire.>

<Yes, Pol. You're right.> And he was.

<Tell me you're ready to rededicate yourself to your mission.>

<I'm ready,> I said. <Absolutely ready.>

CHAPTER 7

"the scariest smotion for a spy? Surprise.
Surprisse can't portend to anythng good."

—Jakob Bryce

The squids gave one last push, and the boat surged forward. Tentacles disengaged and slithered away, disappearing over the bamboo rails while the boat glided the last few feet to the Ministry dock. The guards were off the boat first, one of them taking a kelpstalk rope and tying off. I followed sure-footedly. Couldn't let them think I didn't have my sea legs.

I let the guards lead me along the pier at a leisurely pace. Reaching a pair of weather-beaten stairs, I stepped up to the island proper. Constructed from slabs of granite, the ring-shaped island provided a broad walking surface. To my immediate right was a collapsed stretch, sunken stone tipped at awkward angles, green water flowing freely between the lagoon and the sea. To my left stood the five bulb-shaped Ministry domes. Evenly spaced, they sat directly on the atoll, like freshly pulled onions left on the ground.

Straight ahead, I laid eyes on the lagoon where the Empire's contingent had been executed. Civil servants and administrators. People who were simply doing their jobs. Doing their best for this world and its people.

Murdered.

Dumped into the water to be ripped apart, bite by barbarous bite.

I skimmed the water with my eyes and saw no sign of the terror perpetrated here. No screaming souls or silver torpedoes of death.

Instead, the still, green water peacefully lapped at the stone.

We walked along the pool's edge, my eyes transfixed by bountiful blossoms of bright coral and so many schools of little fish—colorful gemstones dancing and darting in a luscious kaleidoscope of amethysts, rubies, and sapphires.

I told my guards to wait, so my eyes could feast some more.

Below the surface, translucent amoebas the size of my hand floated about, the shapeless creatures forming improvised arms as they stretched for food, several with tiny undigested fish trapped like flies inside their gelatinous bodies. Lime-colored creatures resembling corkscrews spun their way to the surface, then slowly sank back down. Striped eels moved from one branch of coral to the next, coiling and uncoiling while vast clusters of purple and red anemone tentacles swayed to an unheard melody.

Much as I hated to admit this world had anything worthwhile, the lagoon was beguiling. Even the five Ministry domes couldn't resist its bewitching trance, their reflections forever trapped in the pool's emerald-tinted mirror.

<The Empire holds many wonders,> said the voice in my mind.

<Wonder indeed.>

I tore my gaze away and turned it on Dome 3, its outer shell covered with many thousands of teardrop-shaped silver tiles that fit together like the scales of a fish, the lowest ones dusted by sea salt and peppered with air barnacles.

Moving again, we headed for the entryway. Flanked by guards, the tall arch mimicked the dome's onion shape. When I approached, the guards touched their fingers to their hearts while my detail peeled off to head back to the pier.

I marched past the guards and into the dome with purpose in my gait, as if I'd done it a thousand times before, heels clacking on polished granite, the sound echoing around the inside of the rotunda. The walls were painted cerulean from foot to shoulder, then whitewashed the rest of the way up, tapering to a point forty feet overhead.

The dome was vacant, except for a shrine dedicated to the Sire, His image in statue form. Raised on a column of rough-hewn stone, He was surrounded by four shorter columns topped by statues of adoring Kwuba and Jebyl kneeling and bowing.

The Sire Himself had been defaced, the royal robes around his crotch chiseled away. Castrated.

Passing the shrine, I found the stairs exactly where the blueprints I'd studied said I would, a small doorway cut into the dome's back wall, the staircase angling down out of sight. The domes were just for show. The bulk of the Ministry was down those stairs.

At the bottom of the ocean.

I started down, my hand running along the dewy steel rail. The walls were alive with mossy growths sprouting from black trails of slimy seawater. I took the stairs slow, the thought of tunneling below the water weighing heavy on my mind. <I don't know about this, Pol.>

<This structure was built many centuries ago. It's not about to collapse today.>

A glance at the rust-eaten seams told me it just might. The air began to taste stale, and I swore at the architect who designed this death trap. I didn't care what the reports said about an underwater construction being impervious to attack. In the end, it hadn't proven so impervious, had it?

Ten steps down, I reached a landing and stepped through an open bulkhead where I faced another set of neck-breakingly steep stairs carved directly into the reef.

Deeper and deeper I went, more bulkheads with open hatches followed by more staircases. My ears felt the pressure of pumped air that reeked of mildew, and my skin turned tacky with the damp of deep ocean.

I reached the bottom, one hundred feet of impossibly heavy water pressing down from above. With fluorescent bulbs lighting the way, I headed down the steel-walled corridor, supports spaced every two feet. I avoided the puddles. Puddles where there should be no damn water.

<I don't like this, Pol. Shouldn't this place be watertight?>

<That's what the water pumps are for.>

I marched ahead despite the tug of fear pulling at my back. Arriving at a T, I knew the arched corridor to my right would lead to the main rotunda. My feet splashed into inch-deep seawater, and soon the splashing turned to sloshing as the chilly water rose past my ankles. Passing over a floor drain that was barely visible under the black water, I asked Pol if he was sure the water pumps were working.

<They must be, or you'd be swimming.>

The water was up to my knees now. <I might as well be. It's getting deeper.>

<The pumps are likely in need of servicing. It has

been more than a year since they slaughtered the Empire's engineers.>

<Surely, they must've put somebody new in charge of the pumps.>

<Agreed. But what do the natives know of machines?>

Not a comforting thought.

A soldier waded from the other direction, his face calm and collected. I hated him. I was tempted to scream at the levelheaded bastard.

A staircase lifted me up out of the water. At the top, the main rotunda opened before me, a broad space with tall video screens lining the far wall, some of them dipped in seawater, but amazingly still working. The screens' moving images hazily reflected off the water. On my side of the rotunda sat many semicircular rows of desks and tables, all of them facing the front, auditorium style. Some were populated by soldiers, many by Kwuba in their formal silks.

A drop of water struck the top of my head, and I looked up at the leaky ceiling, great panes of reinforced glass and riveted steel standing high overhead. I tried to stop myself from picturing the glass giving way, a crush of seawater bringing a watery death.

"We've been waiting for you." Admiral Dii Mnai stalked up to me, weighty in both size and gaze. "You're late." His hair was short as a two-day beard, his tone shorter still.

I swallowed the clamshell in my throat. "Sorry."

"Come. We must start our morning briefing."

With water squishing in my boots, I followed his uniformed frame through a door and down a long hall. He walked large, shoulders held high, his rounded girth that of somebody who never denied himself.

I trailed him into a conference room. The floor was dry except for a rusty puddle fed by a streak of water seeping from under the window frame. The table appeared to have been made from Karthedran redwood. A crater of splintered wood sat where the Empire's seal should be. A crime against the Empire. An even greater crime against a fine piece of wood on a world that had so little.

I surveyed the attendees. Based on the bars sewn on their chests, I counted a captain and two lieutenants seated at the table, their navy blue uniforms meshing nicely with the emerald flags wrapped around their necks.

I took a seat at the table, directly across from the admiral.

"Did you come to a deal?" he asked, his moon-shaped face watching me expectantly.

"What?"

"A deal. Last night."

I nodded. "Yes."

His face lit with a wide, gap-toothed smile. "Good. Most good."

"The price?" asked the captain.

"I had to take his offer."

"I thought you were going to bargain him down."

I shrugged. "He wouldn't budge. Tough bargainer."

The disdain on the captain's face was painted on thick. "I told you we couldn't pay his price."

I cringed on the inside. <I screwed up, Pol.>

<No. Let them overpay. Let them exhaust all the funds they seized.>

Mnai laid a heavy hand on the table. "Captain Mmirehl has a point, Colonel. Our funds are limit-ed."

<Don't let him intimidate you, Jakob.>

I leaned forward in my chair, forced my voice straight as a firerod. "You wanted a good weapons system, and I got it for you."

Mnai pinched his lips and moved his penetrating stare from person to person in order to gather silent opinions from the group. Captain Mmirehl gave him an eye roll. The two lieutenants shook their heads in disapproval.

<Pol, this is not good.>

Mnai turned his big head back on me. "You're sure this is a good system?"

<Say yes, Jakob. Sell it.>

Wringing some confidence from Pol's voice, I said, "The best." For all I knew, it really was.

Mnai folded his arms and rested them on his ample stomach. "Do we have the funds, Captain?"

Mmirehl roasted me with a flaming glare. His face was narrow with hollows for cheeks and a beak for a nose. He spoke through his teeth. "We do, but—"

Mnai didn't let him finish. "Buy it."

"But—"

"We must pay it. Air defense is critical."

"But one missile platform will hardly stop a fleet."

"They won't send a fleet."

"You can't be sure."

My thoughts hustled to incorporate the new fact. I'd bought a surface-to-air missile platform. <That's going to complicate things, Pol.>

<Indeed.>

Captain Mmirehl stabbed the tabletop with an insistent finger. "We kill-ed their contingent. They will seek retribution."

The admiral brushed the captain's argument away with one of his big mitts. "They won't send a fleet. Explain it to him again, Colonel."

I twisted in my seat, my mind scrambling for the right response. "That's not necessary, is it?" I smiled at the captain. "You remember perfectly well, don't you?"

He sneered at me, but answered the question, the words squeezing through his teeth like meat from a grinder. "I remember."

Relief washed over me. <Close one.>

"No," said the admiral. "Explain it to him."

"But he just said he understands."

Mnai lifted a fist over his head and slammed it down on the table. My heart jumped along with the water glasses, the sound echoing off the steel walls like he'd fired a cannon.

"I told you to explain it to him!" he shouted, spittle spraying from his mouth, a droplet clinging to his chin. "Explain it until the shit-for-brains understands."

Captain Mmirehl's jaw dropped in disbelief. I thought he was going to protest, but his mouth closed, and his face tensed up like he was prepping for a serious lashing.

I looked to the lieutenants, who both sat with their heads bowed, suddenly very interested in their laps.

<You better start talking, Jakob.>

I fought to keep my voice from cracking. "They won't send a fleet. Maritinia is too far from the Empire's Core. Many in the Empire believe the Secession Skirmishes were a precursor to something bigger. They believe war is coming. It could break out at any time, and if it does, they can't afford to have warships sitting a year away from where the action is."

"Yes," said the admiral. "Go on."

My fingers hurt from strangling the wad of pant leg in my fist. "The truth is this world isn't strategically important. They'll send a ship with a new governor and a new contingent, some extra soldiers. But no fleet."

"You hear that, Captain? You understand now, or shall I have him go over it again?"

Captain Mmirehl gave a reluctant nod. "I understand."

The admiral's gap-toothed smile was back. "And how can they be sure to succeed in retaking this world with a single ship, Colonel?"

<How much did Kell tell him?> I asked Pol.

<The traitor likely told him everything.>

"Colonel?" repeated the admiral.

"The E³ will send their agents first," I said, my fingernails digging into my thigh. "They'll try to infiltrate this government and sabotage it."

Mnai stared at me, a smile frozen on his face.

I met his stare, unable to escape the feeling he'd noticed something different about me, that he was trying to put his finger on exactly what it was. I could practically feel that thick finger of his probing and prodding me, trying to find what was real and what wasn't.

He lifted his hand, stuck his index finger in the air. "One ship," he said to Captain Mmirehl. "Just one ship, and when it comes, I shall shoot it out of the sky."

I let out the breath I hadn't realized I was holding. Let it out slow through my nose.

"Yes, Admiral," responded the captain. "As you say."

Apparently deciding the captain was sufficiently humbled, he turned to one of the lieutenants. "Tell me of the Jebyl."

"We have reports of two demonstrations yesterday, a thousand people in Mmangu, three hundred in Selaita. There were no overt displays of dissension in the capital, but we heard several reports of unrest. Gangs of Jebyl delinquents have begun vandalizing Kwuba-owned stores, spilling salt and knocking over shelves. Anything they can do to make themselves a nuisance. Among other things, they keep griping about being exclude-ed from the new government."

Mnai hmmphed. "Tell me, what other things do these ingrates whine about?"

"I'm afraid you won't like it, sir."

"Proceed, Lieutenant."

"They claim the Kwuba are hoarding all the wine and tea."

"Nonsense. Haven't they heard of the Empire's embargo? The price of all imports is up. I can't control who can afford to buy wine and who can't."

"The Jebyl are ridiculous," Mmirehl scoffed. "What do they expect? Are we suppose-ed to buy their wine now? How about the lazy freeloaders learn to work for it?"

"Anything else, Lieutenant?" asked the admiral.

"They say people who speak up disappear."

Admiral Mnai rolled his eyes. "And what do you think about these claims?"

The lieutenant fidgeted in his seat. "What do I care about the claims of traitors?"

The admiral took a few seconds to measure the response before finding it worthy and turning to the other lieutenant. "What have we heard from the Falali Mother?"

"Nothing yet. I expect-ed a response by carrier already, but the easterly currents are strong this season. The messenger mantas have to fight them all the way back from Selaita."

Mnai nodded. Turning to me, he asked, "You ready for your departure."

"Departure?"

"Must I ask everything twice?"

"Yes. The ceremony. I'm ready."

"Good," he said. "The boats go this afternoon. Captain Mmirehl, you will write up a story about it. I want it running on all the skyscreens a half hour before he departs. Keep it on a continuous loop. I want the departure film-ed and broadcast live, understand?"

"Yes, sir," said the captain.

"Are you sure you're up for it, Colonel?"

"Of course," I said.

"Good. The Jebyl need to be mollify-ed. I hope to get a positive response from the Falali Mother when the mantas arrive, but if not, it will be up to you to convince her to come back with you so she can make a statement and end this unrest."

"You think she'll do it?" asked one of the lieutenants.

Mnai nodded, a second chin appearing on his big head with each downstroke. "If anyone can convince her, the colonel can."

How, exactly, I was supposed to do that I didn't know. "I'll do my best."

A woman appeared at the door, her hair braided with silk ribbons, her robes the color of the sea, with an embroidered eel spiraling round and round. Her thin-soled sandals were strapped to her feet with silks that snaked around her ankles.

"The businessmen have arrive-ed," she said. "They're waiting for you to greet them topside."

Mnai didn't respond.

"Did you hear me, husband? Answer me when I talk to you."

"I heard you, woman. Now leave us be."

"What shall I tell them?"

"I do not care. Now go."

"Fine." With a rustle of silk, she spun around and stormed out. From down the corridor, I heard her call, "Limp-dick bastard."

Mnai closed his eyes, lids going down slow. "Sometimes I swear I don't know why I chose to remarry. She's got a dirty mouth."

"Come on, Admiral," said one of the lieutenants, grinning broadly. "You have to admire a woman who's willing to get dirty with her mouth."

Mnai chuckled. "You're so right, Lieutenant. Now I remember perfectly how she snared me. She's got strong knees, that one."

"You think she found out about last night?"

"Probably," said the admiral. "Little escapes that woman's notice." To one of the lieutenants, he asked, "You brought the girls down the Dome 2 stairs, didn't you?"

"I did," responded the lieutenant. "But sneaking fifty girls around this complex is difficult without anybody's noticing."

With conversation safely drifting away from business, I relaxed into my seat. <We did it, Pol.>

<Excellent job, Jakob.>

Satisfied with myself, I sat quiet as details of last night's lustful excess began to unfold. I breathed easy, happily allowing the conversation to continue flowing away from me and deeper into the gutter. They were like a group of excited schoolboys, all of them reliving a night of fantasies come true. Even Captain Mmirehl was enjoying himself, his laugh sounding like the caw of a crow.

I stayed silent, still marveling over the fact that I'd done it. I'd actually infiltrated their inner circle.

My insertion was complete. I was Colonel Kell.

I smiled as they ribbed and teased each other. I chuckled as they swapped salacious details of nubile pleasures, each of them mounting ever-taller tales of their sexual prowess until the escalating to-and-fro finally culminated in a release of deafening laughter.

Spent, they sat quiet. Gratified. Just like me.

One of the lieutenants turned to me. "Sorry you had to miss it, Colonel."

"Think nothing of it," I responded. "Sali came home this morning, and she was in a hungry mood if you know what I mean. She wore me out." With an exaggeratedly high-pitched female voice, I gave my best imitation. "Faster. Faster."

It took me a moment to realize nobody laughed.

Nobody.

The two lieutenants squirmed uncomfortably in their seats, every single laugh line wiped clean from their faces. Captain Mmirehl watched me with brows raised high over his eyes.

My insides clenched up tight. <What did I say?>

Mnai was up out of his chair, coming my way, his mouth twisted in a snarl. He stepped straight up to me, so close he eclipsed the rest of the room. He snatched my hand, his meaty digits squeezing until my bones rubbed in searing pain.

"If you ever talk about my daughter like that again, Colonel, you shall find yourself supervising your own execution."

CHAPTER 8

"I can'te imagine a place lonelier than THe
bottom of hte ociean."

—JAKOB BRYCE

As he stood over me, my hand trapped in his bone-
crushing grip, the admiral bent my hand backward.
Screeching nerves fired up my arm, and I came out of
my chair, twisting my back and shoulder to keep my
wrist from snapping.

He leaned close, lips brushing my ear. His whispered voice burrowed down my ear canal. "Your use-
fulness won't last much longer, Colonel."

He let go and walked out, sandals scuffling down
the corridor.

The pain quickly faded but not the grimace on my

face. Sali was his daughter. My teeth gnashed on the bitter realization.

Sali was his daughter. <Seems like information we should have had beforehand, no?> I asked Pol.

<We knew nothing about this so-called "admiral" until the rebellion. The Eyes and Ears had no file on him—there was no reason to.>

Once again, I was reminded how I had only fourteen months to prepare—clearly it hadn't been nearly enough time.

I hugged my aching hand to my chest and looked at the two lieutenants, who bowed their heads to keep from meeting my eyes. They stood and slinked out, one of them giving me a comforting pat on the shoulder as he passed. Captain Mmirehl stayed put, pencil-thin lips elongating into a wicked smile. His delighted eyes met mine. "That was most entertaining, Colonel. Thank you for that."

He rose from his chair, his short frame so incredibly lean that his uniform jacket looked like it had been tailored to man twice his size. "You pay-ed too much for the missile system."

I rubbed my wrist. "I thought that matter was settled."

"What's your cut?"

My brows cinched. "Cut?"

"You can fool the admiral, but you can't fool me. You and that arms dealer are overcharging us. So what's your cut? Are you splitting the difference with him?"

I shook my head no. "I'm not getting a cut." At least I didn't think I was.

"Don't lie to me. What's your plan, Colonel? Take us for everything we're worth and move on to the next world?"

I leveled a serious stare. "No. I'm doing my best to help us defend ourselves."

He shook his head and screwed up his face like he'd just found a hair in his dinner.

"If the Empire retakes this world," I said, "we'll all be executed, and that includes you, Captain. And *me*."

He pointed a bony finger. "You'll never leave Maritinia, Colonel. I'll promise you that. Even in death, you'll never leave Maritinia." He marched past me and ducked his head through the bulkhead. "You won't be bury-ed in dirt."

I stayed where I was, alone in the room.

Pol's voice sounded in my mind. <I don't think he likes you.>

I wiped a sleeve across my sweaty forehead. <Could that have gone any worse?>

<They could've discovered your true identity.>

<You think they'd like me any less?> Exhausted, I dropped myself into a chair and tried to shake the aches out of my crushed hand.

<You know what we have to do next, don't you?>

<Can't it wait?>

<We don't know how long you'll be gone for this mysterious ceremony. We may not have another chance for a while.>

<At least let me rest a minute, will you?>

He went silent.

I blew out a sigh, and the last of my composure went with. Water welled in the corners of my eyes. A drop leaked free to be swiped away with my sore hand. Events were moving too damn fast. I couldn't keep up with the lies stacking high all around me like giant towers of rounded stones. One wrong move, they'd topple and crush me to dust.

It hadn't even been a full day since becoming Kell, and so much had happened. So much I couldn't begin to process it all.

<You can't just stay in here by yourself, Jakob. It will begin to look strange.>

I wiped another tear, smearing the moisture across the cheek that wasn't mine. It was time to go. But where? I tried to think, but couldn't. My mind was too busy ducking from the fragmented thoughts shooting around my skull in a cacophonous cross fire.

<Jakob?>

I blotted my other cheek with my sleeve.

<You mustn't allow yourself to feel overwhelmed. You remember what I taught you to do at times like these?>

My drowning mind reached for the lifeline he'd tossed. He'd taught me to focus on the next task. To be like a gambler placing his next bet. To be like a stray searching for his next meal. My focus had to be singular. Unwavering.

<What matters is what's next,> he said. <You have to let everything else go.>

He was right. Reflection was a luxury I couldn't

afford. Not while I was in the field. I could debrief all I wanted on the year-plus trip home.

The next task was all that mattered.

The. Next. Task.

<We have to report in.>

I stood against the back wall of the main underwater dome, arms crossed, trying to look important. The clock on the wall said I'd been waiting for twenty minutes.

Waiting to make my move.

I kept an eye on an open bulkhead wedged between a pair of video screens on the far side of the rotunda. I could see the soldier inside. Sitting at a desk. Staring at the wall.

I needed some alone time in that cabin. I had to send a message to the Empire. Much as I feared the likelihood that Pol would report how I'd let my conscience get the better of me this morning, the E^3 *had* to know my insertion was successful or they wouldn't send their new contingent to retake this world.

It would be so much easier if the political officer in my head had come with a transmitter, but even a microscopic antenna would've blown my cover when I passed through the spaceport scanners on my way into tech-restricted space.

As it was, Pol couldn't communicate with anybody but me. Restricted to a lump of my own gray matter, his only contacts with the outside world were the verbal channel we shared and the taps into my optical and cochlear nerves, which allowed him see and hear everything I did.

So if I was going to get a message to the Empire, I had to get in that cabin.

But the soldier wouldn't leave his post.

So I waited.

The lowest tiers of the auditorium-style workspace were still completely swamped by black seawater. Deep as a swimming pool, the water level didn't seem to be rising, but disconcerting drops of water continued to plink, plink, plink from the ceiling. The walls leaked, too, seeping water leaving slick patches on the floor and severe doubts in my mind.

I rested a hand on the steel wall at my back, taking strength from the solid surface. I hadn't come here to drown, dammit.

Nobody seemed to think it strange I was standing here. Not the soldiers who occasionally passed by nor the half dozen Kwuba sitting at computer terminals with hands in their laps. I hadn't seen a single one of them touch any of the equipment, which was probably wise since I doubted any of them had any clue how to operate the systems.

They were just keeping up appearances. Trying their best to look like a legitimate government. But they were pretenders.

Just like I was.

I scanned the video screens yet again. Many, like the skyscreens outside, displayed the accusing eye of

Admiral Mnai. I could feel his cold stare coming at me from every direction. Daring me to talk about Sali again, just so he would have an excuse to kill me.

Weather screens showed stretches of blue space mottled by weblike swirls of wispy clouds. Other screens tracked geothermal activity with a mind-numbing assemblage of fluctuating graphs and numbers. The screen on the top right monitored the underwater complex itself with a series of stats, several of them flashing red to signify the sections that had been completely flooded due to poor maintenance of the pumps.

To the left was a group of screens with live feeds of Maritinia's cities taken from cameras atop the skyscreens. Shot from a distance, I had to admit the cities were quite pleasant on the eye. Densely packed rooftops clustered to form stepped fields of thatch or tile. City walls were painted white, with occasional splashes of cerulean or amber or coral depending on the city. Each had its official color.

For such a primitive world, it was quite a marvel the Empire had provided: entire cities raised off the water, lifted on the heads of rank upon rank of stone columns lined up in the water like a vast armies standing at attention.

<It's getting late, Jakob.>

It was. I looked through the open bulkhead into the communications center. The soldier still hadn't left. No guarantee he would before I had to leave for the mysterious ceremony. <Time for plan B?>

<Definitely.>

Summoning my resolve, I walked along the outer wall, the circular path leading me around the rotunda. I took a quick glance at the so-called technicians. None of them paid any attention to me.

I passed in front of the first few video screens, my body bathed in radiant color.

Reaching the gap between screens, I high-stepped through the bulkhead to enter the small cabin. Racks of electronics rife with blinking lights and cascading tangles of cable stood against one wall. Against the opposite wall was the desk, the uniformed soldier staring up at me from his chair.

He touched his heart with his fingers. "Good to see you, Colonel."

"Captain Mmirehl asked for you."

He slid his chair back. "Why?"

"He needs help preparing a message for the sky-screens."

"Very well." He stood, and I let him pass.

I took his seat, heart drumming with nervous energy. Had to hurry. I touched the communications-system display. I entered the Empire's backdoor password and was greeted with graphs and controls. With Pol's expert coaching, I navigated the interface and quickly located the setting that had disabled the off-world link.

I turned on the link and opened a channel, stealing a quick peek over my shoulder before putting my mouth up to the microphone.

I spoke fast as my double-timing pulse. "Jakob Bryce. Mission number 6728394. Insertion successful. Warning, enemy has antiair-defense system. Do not land until threat can be assessed." I asked Pol for his code of authenticity.

He recited an impossibly long string of numbers, my voice echoing one after the next into the microphone.

<Do you have anything to add?> I asked with a hopeful tone.

<No. Send it as is.>

Relieved that my record would, for now, remain clean, I sent the message, closed the channel, and shut down the offworld link. Another glance over my shoulder.

Still alone.

I called up the Eyes and Ears' secret in-box to see if anything came in while transmitting. One message. Opening it, I stared at the page-long chain of numbers. Code for which only Pol knew the key.

I kept staring so Pol could get a good look through my eyes. <Got it?>

<Not yet.>

I couldn't resist taking another glance over my shoulder. Captain Mmirehl and the soldier were on the far side of the dome. Walking this way.

Eyes back on the message. <Done yet?>

<Not yet,> he said. <A little longer.>

<Hurry.>

My hammering heart thumped against my rib cage. I was afraid to blink for fear of slowing Pol down.

<Done. Get out.>

I stabbed the screen with my index finger to delete the message. Another stab to close out. I spun my chair to face the hatchway, leaned back, and crossed my arms. Nothing to see here.

Mmirehl and the soldier arrived an instant later. The captain stepped inside, ducking low to get through the hatch. He stood over me, his brows creased, his beak of a nose ready to strike. "I did not send for this man."

I smiled my sweetest smile, my voice drenched in honey. "I thought you could use some help. It's almost time, Captain. The skyscreens should be touting my virtues by now, don't you think?"

He gave me a long, heated stare. "Get out." His voice was on a low burn. "Let me do my work."

He didn't step back as I stood. I looked him in the eye and broadened my smile, gave him enough sugar to choke on. Stepping around the man, I walked out, back into the main rotunda.

<Well done, Jakob.>

<Bastard wants a rival, I'll give him one.>

I walked around to the other side of the rotunda and took a different corridor from the partly flooded one I'd used to get here. Finding the stairs to Dome 2, I hustled up one staircase after the next, climbing out from under the sea. Reaching the top, I stepped into the second of five above-water domes, where the sound of my heavy breathing was easily overwhelmed by the unhealthy sputter of a motor. Near the wall was a rattling collection of rusty pipes and gauges, the engine's sickly whine echoing around the inside of the dome. Water pumps.

I was amazed by how out of place the clacking grind of machinery sounded on this world.

Ugly.

Standing near the pumps was a team of Jebyl, their rough, kelp-fiber clothes stained with black grease, all of them watching the strained pumps. Spotting me, they tried to look busy by fiddling with tools or reading gauges. One of them started rubbing the machinery casing with grease as if it were a magic salve.

Kell and the admiral had made a huge blunder killing the Empire's entire contingent. Clearly, they should've kept one of the maintenance engineers alive long enough to train these men.

<More proof they need the Sire's benevolence,> Pol said, as if reading my mind.

I walked past them and the pumps, following the path of a pair of thick power cables that ran from the pumps, across the floor, and out the door.

Exiting the front side of the dome, I traced the cable's path with my eyes until it ran into the jewel-like lagoon. From there, it presumably ran to the north side of the atoll, then down to the underwater turbines that powered the Ministry.

Moving toward the lagoon, I exited the dome's shadow and let the sun heat my face. Looking to my left, three more onion domes curved around this side of atoll. Dome 1 stood to my right. Beyond it was the pier where three large boats were moored, and a small platoon of soldiers loaded supplies.

The young soldier from the communications room appeared at my shoulder. "The captain sent me to film the departure."

Facing him, I saw his cheeks were round, belly, too, like he'd never shed his baby fat. Sparse patches of whiskers grew like weeds on his chin and upper lip. His cheeks stretched like big arid fields that led to long, silo-shaped sideburns. He pulled a comm unit out of his pocket.

"Know how to work that?" I asked.

"Not really. But I know how to work the camera. I found dozens of these things in a box inside the communications room. I wasn't sure which one to take."

I held out a hand. He passed it to me, and I made a quick check. Decent camera resolution. Plenty of storage space. A full charge. "It will work."

"Um, sir, I was thinking that when the time comes, you could walk out of the central dome with your detail, and I could shoot from over there." He pointed to where the pier intersected the atoll. "That way, I can get you with the domes and the sun in the background. That would look good, wouldn't it?"

"Sounds perfect, soldier."

He flashed a smile full of big teeth. "Then when your boat shoves off, I'll ride on a bundle of sea bamboo tied to the stern and keep shooting until the sun sets."

Before I could respond, speakers crackled to life in the distance. I turned to the closest skyscreen just in time to see the still shot of Admiral Mnai disappear, leaving a few seconds of black before footage of Kell appeared. Kell standing before the lagoon. Kell standing before a crowd waving the Free Maritinia flag. Kell with bloody machete in hand.

A voice boomed, the newly familiar sound of Captain Mmirehl.

Come, brothers and sisters. Come and gaze upon a true hero of the Maritinian people. Look to the skyscreens, and you will see a great man. A warrior and a thinker. His current is strong, my friends. The spirit of Falal flows inside him. Come, brothers and sisters, and you will see the. . .

The platoon on the pier had stopped loading goods. The Jebyl team responsible for the water pumps exited the dome to join the young soldier and me. I glanced at Maringua, Maritinia's capital city standing in the distance, and I imagined the people coming out to the street or standing on rooftops to watch the nearest screen.

You all know the story of Colonel Drake Kell. An honored war hero who was brought to our fair world to be a minion of the usurpers. But Colonel Kell is a man of honor! A minion to no one. He came to Maritinia with his eyes open, his ears ready to listen, and he found a people needlessly suffering. Face-ed with the gross injustices impose-ed by the invaders and occupiers, he join-ed the Free Maritinia movement. He join-ed Admiral Mnai, the hallow-ed father of Free Mari-

tinia. Without his fearless bravery, this planet would still be in the grip of the usurpers and colonialist enslavers.

Total propaganda. But good propaganda. Watching the glorified footage of Kell before adoring crowds, I understood for the first time the allure he must've felt. The power of facing down an empire. The intoxicating temptation of becoming a hero and an icon.

A great man, Colonel Kell. A man who rebell-ed against his own people because he saw the evil that reside-ed in their hearts. He peer-ed behind their false smiles and saw their greed, and their cruelty, and their arrogance, and he cut them. Yes, he cut them, and he fed them to the angry souls they'd wrong-ed!

And now, my brothers and sisters, he wishes to become a true Maritinian. He wishes to be one of us. Soon, he departs for Selaita. Tomorrow night, he will take the sacred rites.

Tomorrow, he will brave the ocean depths, and tomorrow, he will ask the cuda fish for mercy.

Cuda fish?

Tomorrow, they will smell his blood, but they will also smell the purity in his heart. Sensing the strength of the spirit flowing within, they will spare him.

My heart dropped like an anchor. Not for the first time, I couldn't help but think: What in Sire's name was I in for?

CHAPTER 9

"The most peacful waters hide the deadliesst undrecurrents."

—Jakob Bryce

After voyaging through the night, I sat on the prow, watching the sun peek over the portside horizon to cast morning rays that glistened off the rolling emerald sea. My booted feet dangled over the water, catching splashes of sea spray as the boat cut through the waves.

Unlike the Jebyl crew, I wasn't going barefoot. Not until I knew for a fact cuda fish couldn't leap.

Ahead, I could see gray shapes below the surface, a team of ten yoked squiddies dragging the boat forward in regular spurts. They were fascinating to watch, the way their tentacles would snake randomly about like hair gusting in the wind until the next jet forward, when all those stray tentacles would suddenly converge in a coordinated thrust. All ten squids in unison. With every burst, kelpstalk ropes would snap taut, and the boat would lunge forward in time to a lazy waltz.

The squids were an invention of the Empire. A genetically engineered gift to the peoples of Maritinia. Same with the mammoths, the mantas, and many others, all of the creatures intended to increase kelp production without machines.

Like all who were born into the Empire's aristocracy, I'd learned all about the technology restrictions in school. It was too dangerous to provide machines to worlds so far from the military and economic controls of the Empire. Provide a machine, and you have to provide expertise to operate and repair it. Offer that knowledge to a populace, and you give them the tools they need to rebel.

Repeat after me, children, "Knowledge is the enemy of stability."

And stability was the Empire's greatest strength. The stability for all to know their place. The stability for all to accept their roles and live their lives to their fullest.

Such was the wisdom of the Sire . . . even if there were those, like the people of this world, who would try to deny it.

A hand touched my shoulder, and I looked up to see Sali, a damp breeze fanning her hair. "Sleep well?" she asked.

"I did." It was the best night of sleep I'd had since arriving on this watery world. Rocking the night away in a fishnet hammock was far superior to sleeping on stone.

She squeezed in next to me, her feet hanging over the water, our hips and elbows touching. "You saw my father yesterday?"

"Yes."

"You told him I was back from my trip, didn't you?"

I'd told him more than that. Idiot.

"Didn't you?" she repeated.

"Yes. I mentioned it during our briefing."

"Then why didn't he come out to see me before our departure? He knew I'd be there."

I didn't know. But I was glad they hadn't talked. Glad the admiral didn't have the opportunity to share what a fool I'd made of myself.

I looked into her eyes, saw the sparkle of hope, and watched it extinguish when I said I had no idea why he hadn't bothered to see her. I knew how she felt. Knew what it was like to not be a father's top priority. "He probably didn't want to be filmed," I said.

I felt her tense beside me. Her voice grew thorns. "Don't patronize me. Didn't want to be film-ed? That man loves cameras. His image is plaster-ed all over this world."

"You know you could've gone into the Ministry to see him."

"And risk running into that witch he married? Why would you even suggest that?" Her eyes were tight slits.

I wanted out of this bramble of father-daughter dysfunction. When it came to her and me, I had no clue what I was doing, a fact that became more evident every time I opened my mouth. Rather than entangle myself any deeper, I decided it was time I offered silent support. So I reached for her hand, but she dodged my grasp and pinched my forearm. Hard.

"Ow." I stung from the shock more than the pain.

"Don't try to pick a fight, Drake. You know how I feel about that woman."

I stuttered out a syllable or two but couldn't find any complete words.

She gave me a disapproving shake of her head, her brows angled downward like the corners of her mouth. She swung herself around, a sharp elbow poking me in the side. Then she was up, bare feet padding across the bamboo decking.

I craned my neck, watching as she reached the stern and began to pace left and right, probably frustrated she'd reached the end of the boat and couldn't get any farther away.

Pol's wry voice sounded in my mind. <I bet you regret not killing her now.>

I suppressed a chuckle and faced forward. She was quite the complication.

Off the starboard side coasted the other two boats in our group, each boat running on several pontoons that cut wakes in the emerald water like rakes. Atop the pontoons were decks made of sea bamboo, and atop the decks stood small lean-to-style cabins, with roofs made of dried kelp leaves. Above the cabins, each boat had a second story made of several fishnets strung between a dozen or more vertical supports, the nets drooping with supplies.

<We should be there by midday,> said Pol.

<Yes, just a few more hours. Any guesses what this ceremony is about?>

<Other than the sparse details provided by Captain Mmirehl, I have no idea. The Falali are cultists, so you must be prepared for anything.>

<We can safely assume the Falali Mother is their leader, can't we?>

<I believe so.>

As if I didn't have enough to worry about, the admiral had also tasked me with convincing the voodoo priestess to come back with me. Something about needing her to calm tensions with the Jebyl by making a statement.

<Jakob, I finished decoding the message we received from the Eyes and Ears.>

<And?>

<The new contingent will debark now that they know your insertion was successful. They've assembled a fine team, Jakob. The new governor has ruled three other worlds in this sector.>

<Where is the new contingent debarking from?>

<Miravalla.>

<What is that, six weeks away?>

<Approximately.>

<Military capabilities?>

<As expected, they will carry an assault force of fifty soldiers.>

Fifty well-armed, well-trained soldiers. Plus one well-placed undercover assassin. Together, we'd decapitate the illegitimate regime. Together, we'd take back the Ministry and reclaim this world in the name of the Sire.

A surge of pride swelled my heart. For the first time since I'd arrived, the mission seemed possible. Achievable.

<This is good news, Pol.>

<Not all is good, Jakob.>

Of course not. My inflated heart sprung a leak. Always another complication.

<They've commissioned a civilian transport vessel to bring them here.>

Civilian transport. As in no defensive capabilities. <The missile platform I bought . . . >

<We'll have to disable it ourselves.>

I still sat on the boat's prow, noonday sun beating on the top of my head. Selaita's city platform had eclipsed the horizon twenty minutes ago. Another five minutes, we'd be docked.

I put a bite of stewed skate in my mouth and chewed on the mealy flesh. It had no flavor whatsoever. <How can they stand to eat like this? Of all the ten thousand worlds, none are in more need of spice than Maritinia.>

<This is a good thing, Jakob. It proves the Empire's

embargo has depleted their supplies. When the Empire returns, they can trade their kelp for all the spice, wine, and tea they want.>

But they wouldn't be able to trade for money. Give them money, and there was no telling what they might buy. Give them consumable goods, and they'll keep producing kelp. Such was the wisdom of the Sire.

I swallowed the last bite and dropped the kelp leaf I'd been using as a plate into the water, and, conquering my fear of leaping cuda fish, I reached way down to rinse my fingers in the sea. I let my hand dangle in the water for a few seconds to enjoy the feel of kelp leaves dragging across my skin before pulling my hand out and shaking it dry.

Not far off the starboard side, raised on columns high over the water, almost as high as the skyscreens, stood a round, stone platform with a large square punched into the floor's western side. Centered under the four-sided hole was a smaller platform, this one made of bamboo. Twenty feet above water level, the bamboo lift moved slowly upward, carrying bales of dried kelp. Swaying from ropes, the lift was powered by a group of five circling mammoths turning a big stone winch connected to a series of pulleys.

The cargo shuttle that brought me to Maritinia landed on a similar platform. And I'd ridden a similar lift down after debarking. This platform was one of Maritinia's eight landing points for cargo shuttles to lift kelp up to orbiting space barges.

Despite the Empire's embargo, a handful of shuttles

continued to come and go every month. Some of the kelp was shipped to the worlds of the Beyond, but the majority of the harvests went to the Empire's black market.

A voice sounded over my shoulder. "I think we could use a shot of this, Colonel."

Turning around, I found the eager young soldier and filmographer. The other soldiers called him Dugu.

"Yes, of course," I said. Standing, I smoothed my uniform and straightened the Maritinian flag I wore around my neck.

"Hang on," said Dugu as he fiddled with his comm unit. "I'm trying to hook up to the skyscreens."

My eyes went to the screen standing off the port side, the constantly watchful eye of Admiral Mnai bearing down. He disappeared in a blink, replaced by a jerky picture of the water.

"Got it," said Dugu before aiming the camera at me.

My image appeared on the giant screen. I stood on the boat's prow, one hand lifted high, with fingers grasping the netting overhead. I looked good on screen. Bold. The Empire's uniform appeared crisper than it felt. The slight grin on my face projected confident authority. I was the Hero of Free Maritinia.

The bobbing image of Selaita served as my backdrop. Balconies filled with people, and rooftops overflowed with flag flappers. I turned around to face them and waved with my free hand, the crowds waving back, cheers skimming across the waves to my delighted ears.

I was learning to enjoy being Kell.

A pair of Jebyl deckhands stepped past me. Wearing nothing but wraps around their waists, they jumped the prow's rails and tumbled into a fishnet strung between the two pontoons that extended beyond the boat's decking. Crawling to the net's edge, they took hold of the harness ropes and dropped into the water. Pulling along the ropes, they dragged themselves toward the first pair of squids, their human torsos momentarily disappearing in twisting, twining tangles of tentacles.

The Jebyl ducked their heads underwater and unfastened the yokes around the first two squids, who peeled off to the sides. Yoke by yoke, the Jebyl worked their way forward until there were only two squids still tugging the boat slowly along.

The pier approached. Jebyl stood along the edge, ropes in hand, behind them a crowd thick with smiles. The last two squids were set loose, and the boat coasted the last few feet. Ropes flew back and forth between the boat and the pier, the Jebyl beginning to tie off.

I jumped the short gap between the starboard rail and the stone pier, feet landing to thunderous applause. I walked forward, and the crowd closed around me. Hands grasped at my clothes and touched my face. Voices rang in my ears, rousing cheers and shouts of joy. The sweep of excitement invaded every pore, and my every last nerve hummed with electricity.

From somewhere far off, a chant started, and the cacophonous voices around me shaped into a chorus.

One of us.

One of us.

One of us!

Soldiers arrived from one of the other boats, and they jostled into position around me, carving a small bubble of free space. Dugu shouted in my ear. "Please, don't move ahead of security again. You need to wait until we're in position."

I heard his words but didn't let them dim the moment. Such adulation. Such adoration. I understand why you rebelled, Colonel Drake Kell. I understand.

As a group, we moved toward a trio of mammoths standing just ahead. My guards ushered me to a ladder propped against the second animal, and I climbed the bamboo rungs, each step taking me higher up a wall of wool, the air smelling of damp must.

My hands arrived at the top rung, and I reached for a braided-silk hand rope that rested on the beast's back and led a short distance to the canopied howdah. A figure sat inside, a woman on an embroidered-silk mat. Her headdress was made of hundreds of tiny seashells carved to look like fish scales. Her sarong was a deep green silk with embroidered leaves of golden kelp.

Going hand over hand along the rope, I climbed toward the peak of the beast's back, my shoes sinking into the wool as if I were stepping across a mattress. Pulling myself into the howdah, I took a seat next to her.

She touched her fingers to her heart. "We meet again, Colonel." Her voice was firm, somehow loud enough to be heard over the crowd without yelling. She wasn't old, but she wasn't young, either. Her eyes were perched on high cheekbones, crow's-feet forming in the corners when she smiled.

<The Falali Mother, I presume.>

<Yes, Jakob. It must be her.>

I touched my heart. "The honor is mine."

I turned to my left just in time to see Sali reach the top of the ladder. She'd changed her clothes. Her dress was silk, fuchsia with gold trim, her hair pulled up and tied with gold ribbons that curled down her neck. She made a quick transition from the ladder to the hand rope and pulled her way up with a most unladylike efficiency. The dress didn't suit her, and the sour expression on her face said she knew it.

I reached out a hand to help her with the last step, but she waved it away and settled behind me. "Dearest Mother," she said with a touch to her heart.

"Sali," said the Falali Mother. "You look well."

"And you as well."

A pair of guards reached the top of the mammoth in front of ours and took a seat under the pointed canopy. Dugu joined them and sat facing us, his legs hanging out the back of the howdah, his camera raised. The mammoths began to walk, crowds cheering all around.

The city was classic Maritinia, the usual mosaic of whitewashed walls with Selaita's unique accents of amber. Between the buildings ran a vast network of sluices, some made of stone, others of bamboo. Some carrying salt water, others fresh. Ahead was a water-wheel, powered by mammoths, the wheel cranking slowly around, the rising buckets raining with over-flow.

We turned off the pier and onto a street. Every door-way, every window, every balcony was jammed with onlookers. The Falali Mother and I put our waving hands on a constant swivel. Our mammoth labored forward, the howdah listing left, then right. People threw handfuls of powdered dye, the air filling with drifting poofs of turquoise and ruby and gold.

The Falali Mother said, "Thank you for accepting my invitation. I have great hope this gesture will im-prove relations."

"As do I. Have you received the admiral's mes-sages?"

"That he wishes me to calm the Jebyl by making a statement? Yes."

"Will you?"

"The Jebyl are frustrate-ed they've been shut out of Admiral Mnai's government. Statement or no state-ment, that fact remains."

"He just wants to calm tensions. He wants you to let them know their concerns will be heard."

She looked me in the eye. "Will he actually make concessions?"

"I can't speak for the admiral, but he asked me to invite you to the Ministry after the ceremony. If you're willing, you can express your concerns in person."

She seemed to chew on it, painted lips squeezed

tight. "I've express-ed my concerns many times before, and it has made no difference. He refuses to acknowl-edge that the Jebyl cannot be ignore-ed. They are citi-zens of Free Maritinia, and they require a voice. They are the majority caste, after all."

Frustrated, I bit my lip. I couldn't go back without her. I was already on the outs with the admiral, and I had little doubt Captain Mmirehl would make maxi-mum use of my failure. I had a missile-defense system to disable as well as a government to undermine, and I couldn't do either unless I kept my place in the inner circle.

"I can't promise much," I said. "But I can promise you a fair hearing."

Craning her neck to look at Sali, she said, "Your father is a stubborn man. I've never known him to listen to anybody."

"I'm aware of how he is," Sali said with a shrug.

"Did he say he would negotiate?"

The air smelled of chalk as wafting clouds of color-ful powdered dye mingled. Bright dust covered people on the street. The crowded sea of mottled hair and clothes looked like fields of wildflowers.

<You have to make the Falali Mother agree,> said Pol.

I had to.

I would.

"He'll listen to me," I said with certainty. "Me and Sali, we'll confront him with you. He won't be able to turn us all down. We'll see to it he listens. Really listens."

The Falali Mother looked back at Sali, who nodded, and said, "We can assure you he'll listen."

Ahead, I saw one of the guards lean out of the lead mammoth's howdah and signal the team of soldiers marching below. Catching their attention, he pointed to a man on an approaching balcony. The man was holding a white banner. The black image of a cuda fish had been painted on the cloth in a rough scrawl. The cuda's mouth was open wide, jagged teeth drawn to resemble a saw's blade.

<What does that flag mean?> I asked Pol.

<I don't know.>

The Jebyl man on the balcony began to wave the banner. Wearing nothing but his waistwrap, his gray hair hung over his shoulders in knotted braids. A pair of soldiers stormed into the tiny residence, disappearing as they headed for the stairs.

I looked at Dugu. He'd put the camera down. I turned to the Falali Mother. Her jaw had dropped, a deep worry line standing between her brows. She grabbed my arm, fingernails digging into my biceps. "Stop them."

I waved with my free arm and shouted, my vocal cords straining to cross the gap, but my voice was helplessly swept away, like a paper airplane in a windstorm.

Two soldiers.

On the balcony.

Taking aim.

The old man's eyes went wide like eggs cracked

into a sizzling skillet. Purple fire struck, and the man toppled over the balcony wall and crumpled to the pavement in a cloud of multicolored dust.

She dropped my arm. "I will go." Her voice dripped with disgust. "The admiral must answer for these outrages."

CHAPTER 10

> "The ocean is made of compeitng tiides and
> currents. Sme as a person."
>
> —JAKOB BRYCE

I'd left the parade two hours ago, but I still felt it all around me. Felt it in my ears, the crowd's chants running in a constant loop. Felt it in my nose, the dank reek of mammoth wool still clinging to the insides of my nostrils. Felt it on my skin, powdered dye covering every last inch. And I felt it in my heart. The old man. Killed for an act of defiance I didn't even understand.

The rest of the parade went without incident. And without conversation. The Falali Mother did her duty, a smile fixed on her face, but I could feel the hostility in the way she held herself so stiff, her eyes refusing to meet mine.

The parade route had ended at another set of boats, and those boats had taken us across the short gap between Selaita and the sunken volcano named Primhala. And there I stood. In the caldera.

Water lapped against the stone near my feet. The floor of the volcano's crater was flooded by seawater flush with kelp. Enclosing the water on three sides, the volcano's C-shaped caldera crested the sea with black rock carved into bleachers and terraces and stairs.

<You sure this volcano is dead?>

<Yes, Jakob. We read about it several times. I'm surprised you don't remember.>

<I remember, but our information has been wrong before.>

<When?>

<The databases said the Falali were cultists.>

<They are.>

<You saw those crowds, Pol. They weren't all there to see me. The Falali Mother is leading a full-blown religion.>

<The number of followers is irrelevant. They are extremely misguided in their beliefs. Therefore, they are extremists.>

<Just because they worship Falal instead of the Sire?>

<Indeed.>

I chose not to argue the point. A few days ago, I couldn't have imagined wanting to, but seeing all those people today, so many with such joy on their faces—dockworkers and street sweepers, seamstresses and fishermen, young mothers and fathers—they couldn't all be cultists and extremists.

As I looked east, the faint pinpricks of stars were beginning to show through the dark blue velvet of the dusk sky. To the west, the last sliver of the sun's giant orange orb was about to squeeze out of sight.

<Why aren't there any skyscreens here?> I asked.

<Seriously, Jakob, do you remember nothing of the reports we read? The Empire did not build this place. The Jebyl and Kwuba did it themselves.>

<How long ago?>

<From what I recall, they started carving the rock two centuries after the Empire populated this world two thousand years ago.>

The stadium was almost full, yet people continued to spill over the rim and down the steep insides of the caldera. The ceremony would happen here. Soon.

I pushed against the fear nibbling up my spine. Captain Mmirehl had announced over the skyscreens that I'd have to face the ocean depths and ask the cuda for mercy. Whatever this ceremony was, I told myself it couldn't be as dangerous as it sounded. These people loved Kell. They surely didn't come to watch him die.

A hand grasped mine. Sali. "The musicians will start shortly. They won't play long before you take the rites. The Falali Mother is ready for you. Her assistants need to get you prepped."

"Very well."

Hand in hand, we stepped onto a bamboo walkway that barely cleared the high-tide seawater. Bamboo planks creaked under our weight as we approached a Jebyl woman with a wicker basket full of black dirt. Fishing through the rich soil with her hands, she pulled out a glowgrub and ran a needle through its thickest part. The needle was tied to a silk cord, which she wrapped around a post. The wriggling grub—one of several— was now suspended in the air between posts. When we stepped over her basket, she touched her heart and smudged the breast of her sarong with the yellow glow.

We reached the main platform, suspended over the center of the small inlet. The round stage was crisscrossed with ropes hanging overhead, from which Jebyl suspended paper lanterns filled with fireflies. We made our way to the far side of the stage, where three small tents stood. Sali led me to the one in the center and kissed my cheek. "Good luck, Drake."

Her smile was surprisingly soft. Looking into her eyes, I felt I was looking into a deep well of compassion. Quite a change from the prickly woman I'd come to know over the last day and a half, starting when her father failed to greet her at the Ministry.

I knew what it was like to pine for a father's attention. And now I knew to look past the urchinlike spines to see the soft soul inside.

I gave her hand a squeeze before lifting it to my lips. "Thank you, Sali. I'll be fine."

"I know you will." She turned around and walked away.

I watched her stroll down a walkway that led to stairs. Watched her gather her dress as she climbed to the raised balcony, which appeared to be reserved for Kwuba elites and Falali priestesses. I waited until she found a seat and turned to face me again. I gave her a wave and won a new smile for my efforts.

Buoyed by our first genuine moment, I lifted the tent flap and stepped inside. The Falali Mother sat on a three-legged stool. "Colonel," she said. No touch of her heart this time.

"Dearest Mother," I replied.

"Sit."

I ducked under the paper lantern and sat on a stool resting on the other side of the tiny tent. With the back of my head and back pressed against the tent wall, I leaned to my right to see around the pole standing between us. She'd taken off her headdress, revealing dark hair with little touches of gray.

"I talk-ed to your soldiers," she said. "They claim they were acting under Captain Mmirehl's orders."

Without hesitation, I said, "Captain Mmirehl is an overzealous ass."

She smiled. "He is that, Colonel. What I need to know is if his overzealousness was order-ed by the admiral."

"I don't know."

She crossed her legs, and her bare foot bobbed up and down. "Can I count on your support with the admiral?"

"Like I told you, Sali and I will make sure you get your say."

"I'm seeking more than that from you, Colonel."

I worked to keep the surprise off my face. It hadn't occurred to me she might need something from me. "Like what?"

"This crackdown on free expression must stop."

"Is that how you'd describe what that old man was doing waving that flag? Free expression?"

"What else would you call it? He was no threat. This Jebyl resistance the admiral frets about doesn't exist. There are no cabals, no Jebyl militias. Only regular people with legitimate complaints. Admiral Mnai promise-ed schools for every child. He promise-ed medicines and liberties. Instead, he gives us soldiers and false conspiracies."

Pol spoke in my mind. <She sounds surprised it turned out poorly. What did she expect when they shunned the stability of the Empire?>

I didn't have time to respond before she spoke again. "Through fear, he may be winning their obedience, but he's lost their hearts."

I nodded my understanding.

"The admiral needs to be convince-ed this crackdown is unjust. But I can't convince him alone. I need you to argue alongside me. I need you to marshal support within his navy, convince as many officers as you can to come forward." She leaned toward me, her eyes zeroed in on mine. "Together, we can remind him this is suppose-ed to be *Free* Maritinia. What do you say?"

I rubbed my jaw, searching for the right answer. I didn't want to anger her by refusing. No, I didn't want to do anything that would make her renege on her pledge to accompany me back to the Ministry. But I also couldn't let myself become an agent of her agenda. I had my own agenda to execute.

"I understand your reluctance," she said. "You remember what I told you the first time we met?"

"Of course," I lied.

"I told you your tide was strong. You were blessed by Falal, Colonel. Your kind is rare. Few are given the gift of such a mighty current. You don't just draw people in and make them want to follow, yours is a current so powerful it can sweep history right along with it."

I wanted to believe her. Wanted to believe she was talking to me. To Jakob.

She batted the paper lantern, and the tent suddenly brightened with awakened fireflies. "You mustn't allow yourself to become the admiral's show toy. It was through your courage and strength we cast off the chains of the Empire. The admiral didn't engineer the coup. That was you." She pointed a finger at the spot between my eyes. "You."

That wasn't me, I said to myself. That was Kell.

"Mistake me not," she continued, "we will be forever indebt-ed. But Maritinia needs you again. All over this world, people are suffering. Kelp is the driving force of our simple economy, and thanks to the Empire's embargo, so many have lost their livelihoods. The young and strong can fish for themselves, but the weak and elderly are in crisis. Our churches are overflowing with the frail and malnourished. People are dying, Colonel."

I listened quietly while she continued. "This is a time for people to pull together, but Admiral Mnai insists upon tearing us apart by stoking old tensions to pit Kwuba against Jebyl. We are a strong people, capable of caring for one another, and this is a bountiful world in which no one should ever go hungry. We need leadership that will foster the bonds of family and clan. Instead, he stokes fear that encourages hoarding instead of sharing. We desperately need a unifier. You must convince the admiral to become that person. And if he won't, then you must be that person."

My eyes widened in surprise. "Are you advocating another coup?"

"Those words won't leave my lips," she said. "But I fear the path we're on."

"I will take your thoughts into consideration," I said with all the false earnestness I could. I didn't need to get involved in this world's internal politics, especially not to help heal any breaches. All I needed was time, just six more weeks of the status quo. Six weeks before the Empire made its glorious return.

"Very well," she said with a slight bow of her head. "I will afford you time to consider. The ceremony will begin very soon." She stood and clapped her hands.

Two attractive young women entered the tent, dressed in traditional Jebyl sarongs, their hair tied with thick ribbons made of eel skin.

"Wash him," said the Falali Mother before exiting.

Stepping up to me, one unwrapped the flag around my neck while the other worked the buttons on my shirt.

Outside the tent, I heard the slow beat of a lonely drum. Then a voice. A coarse, grating wail.

> Oh, Governor
> You better run
> Run for the sea
> Cuda goin' get you
> Fly for the sky
> Sky goin' poison you

Coaxing me upright, the women took off my shoes. My pants. My underwear. Resisting the urge to cover myself, I kept my eyes looking straight ahead.

Outside, more drums joined in, each beat a unique pattern, all the patterns interlacing into a textured whole. I felt the vibrations in my eardrums. Under my feet. In my rib cage. The voice again. I'd never heard anything like it. So harsh. So abrasive.

> Oh, Governor
> Run, governor, run
> Run for the rocks
> Rocks goin' crush you.
> Run and hide
> Machete goin' cut you.

I spread my arms wide as I could in the cramped space as the women ladled water over my head and shoulders, causing my skin—still caked with powdered dye from the parade—to streak with rivulets of inky water. They scrubbed me with wet cloths, excess water draining back into the sea through the bamboo slats underfoot.

The drumming stopped, followed by the same haunting voice, its scraping wail sounding like a throat full of broken glass.

Governor goin' burn
Governor goin' burn
Governor goin' burn

Voices joined in, thousands of them, the crowd bellowing the repetitive chorus. A chill tickled my wet skin as the gravity of their animosity toward the Empire sank into my bones. Perhaps the Empire's return wouldn't be so glorious.

One of the women pulled a waistwrap from a bag on the floor. Silk the color of thunderclouds. They wrapped the cloth around me, once, twice, then tied it in place with a cord of cobalt blue. A second song started, and the young women left.

Alone, I tipped my stool forward to run the water off the seat and noticed the carvings in the bamboo. Fish swimming through kelp fronds. I tapped the lantern to get more light and ran my fingers over the etchings, remembering a time when I was a boy, a time when I used to carve birds and turtles, a time when I wanted to be an artisan.

A time before I fully understood the trappings of family expectations.

The etchings were expertly done, the rounded surface of bamboo adding to the difficulty level. Hard to imagine how such fine carvings were created without metal gouges or chisels.

One of the young women poked her head in. "We're ready for you."

I ran my finger across the carvings one last time, across the fins and fishtails, the scales and teeth.

So many teeth.

It was time to face the cuda.

CHAPTER 11

> "A mission like theis requires tyou commit all
> theway."
>
> —JAKOB BRYCE

I knelt at center stage, my waistwrap hugging my
thighs, a sleeping mat under my knees. Dugu watched
from a few feet away, his camera transmitting a live
feed to the skyscreens. The Falali Mother stood before
me, her voice firm and sturdy. "Falal weaves our hearts
into one cloth."

Nearby, a man echoed her words, his voice a sharp
holler that triggered the holler of another and another
and another, her words traveling on the breath of one
crier to the next until they reached every ear around
the caldera.

The Falali Mother lifted her hands to the night sky. "Falal weaves our hearts with the souls of every creature on this world. She threads us through the spirit of the sky and the spirit of the sea. She stitches in the souls of our past and the souls of our future. All of us part of one fabric that spans the centuries."

I looked past her to the crowd, patchy lighting from glowgrubs and paper lanterns casting a hazy glow over faceless silhouettes.

She bowed her head in my direction. "Today we honor a soul of our present." Touching her heart, she said, "And we honor Mmasa. A soul of our past. Mmasa was a great diver, the greatest diver our world has ever known. And like all the great kelp harvesters of his time, he was invite-ed by the governor to participate in the games. But these were no ordinary games. These were the games of Governor Greyson the Blacksoul."

The name traveled around the crater, and the crowd hissed with displeasure, the earsplitting sibilance making me wince.

<Do you remember reading about Greyson?> I asked Pol.

<Yes. He served for fifty years in the Empire's twenty-fifth century.>

<That was six hundred years ago.>

<These people obviously have a long memory.>

"Mmasa," she said, "thrill-ed the spectators who sat where you now sit. He enchant-ed the governor, who stood where I now stand. He made them cheer by diving deeper than the squiddies dare, and by staying under long past anybody thought possible. His feats were so spectacular that even his fiercest competition could do nothing but watch and applaud with respect.

"But like so many of the Sire's governors, Greyson the Blacksoul was a cruel man. A man who enjoyed others' suffering. He order-ed Mmasa to dive even longer. Even deeper. And when Mmasa did as he was told, Greyson order-ed it again. And again. Always deeper. Always longer. He made Mmasa dive until his lungs could take no more, and he curl-ed up in pain from depth illness."

<Is this story true?> I asked Pol.

<Does it matter?>

Perhaps, I thought. Perhaps.

The Falali Mother's voice turned somber. "Governor Greyson's spirit was black, black like smoking ash. He watched Mmasa writhe in agony, and still, he order-ed him to dive. And do you know what Mmasa said?"

She paused to drag out the moment. "He ask-ed, 'Is there no limit to your cruelty?'"

Again, she waited for the words to ripple from crier to crier, waited until she was sure every ear had heard. "Mmasa wasn't just speaking one man to another. He was speaking to the Empire on behalf of us all. He was asking: Is there no limit to what you'll take from us?

"Greyson the Blacksoul did not like to be question-ed, but he was devious enough to react with a polite smile. Then he wave-ed to the crowd, calling for all who were members of Mmasa's family. He trick-ed them by telling them he want-ed to honor them. Mmasa's performance was so brilliant, he said, they all deserve-ed to share in his glory. And the unsuspecting came forward. Twenty-three of them, including his wife and child. And when they did, Greyson the Black-soul had them all bound."

Slowly, her words spread around the crater, kicking off a barrage of hisses and catcalls. From somewhere offstage, the Falali Mother's two assistants appeared carrying a small pedestal topped by a large conch shell. They set the pedestal next to the Falali Mother, who beckoned for me to stand, and when I did, one of her assistants passed me a mallet of stone with a handle of mammoth bone.

"And once his family members were all bound," she said, "the Governor order-ed Mmasa to break the shell."

She gave me a nod.

I stepped up to the pedestal and hefted the weighty hammer. With a quick swing, I brought the hammer down and shattered the shell with a loud crunch fol-lowed by the scatter of pieces skipping across the bamboo stage. I lifted the hammer off the pedestal and revealed a jagged collection of rough shards and sliv-ers.

The Falali Mother silently watched as her assistants selected fragments from the pedestal and pinched the shards between their knuckles. I watched, too, my eyes riveted, my confused mind racing through the possi-bilities of what was to come next.

Taking the hammer from my hand, the Falali Mother dosed her words with venom. "Then Greyson the Blacksoul cut Mmasa until his body ran red."

My skin went cold, and I gritted my teeth as one of the women dragged the shells down my arm, a trail of scraped skin beading with blood. I braced myself against the sharp pain as shells sliced down my back. Across my chest. Down my calves and across the tops of my feet.

Dugu came forward, camera in hand, coming for a close-up. I wiped the grimace off my face, my glassed-over eyes staring straight ahead as shells ran down my thigh and across my stomach. I clenched every muscle against the pain, shells dragging over my chest, nipples oozing blood.

Dugu circled around me, biting his lower lip, his camera lens soaking up every bloody drop. Sparing my face, the women dragged their conch claws over every inch of exposed skin, scraping side to side, up and down, over and over until my body was slick with seeping blood.

The Falali Mother put up a hand, and her assistants mercifully dropped the bloody shards.

My skin burned as if it were on fire, flames licking at every inch. Every pore.

Reaching into a bucket near my feet, the women retrieved a belt of glowgrubs, lifted it over my head, and draped it across my chest like a sash. I felt the grubs wriggling against my raw flesh, phosphorescent goo dripping down my stomach and mingling with blood.

Next, they tied two small fishnets to the belt around my waist and started filling the nets with round stones.

<The stones will help you sink,> said Pol. <And the glowgrubs will help you see.>

Help me sink. Help me see.

When I went underwater.

My mind swam in a black flood that drowned all hope. Sire, help me.

The Falali Mother called to the crowd. "Satisfy-ed that Mmasa was sufficiently bloody-ed, Greyson the Blacksoul beckon-ed the cuda."

I heard a creaking sound above me. Looking up, I spotted the dim outline of a Jebyl man hanging from the ropes over the stage. He was swinging to and fro, and the stage brightened as the movement woke the firefly lanterns overhead. Soon the entire area lit as dozens of other Jebyl shook the broad latticework of ropes spanning the inlet into a slow, flapping motion. Hundreds of dangling lanterns came to life.

A light breeze breathed across me, and the sensation of drying blood felt like the sting of an icy gust. A foul odor crept into my nostrils, and I turned to my right, where a pair of Jebyl stepped onto the stage, each carrying a large bucket that they promptly dumped into the black water. They left the stage and were immediately replaced by another pair of Jebyl with another pair of buckets ripe with the stench of rotten fish.

Soon, the water was bobbing with fish guts, making my own innards shrivel with dread. They couldn't expect me to get in that water, could they?

The crowd gasped at a silver fin the size of a hand cutting through the water. Moments later, a second fin, a second gasp.

"And the cuda arrive-ed," said the Falali Mother. "Carrying the souls of all those who were wrong-ed. All those who were deprive-ed or starve-ed. Those who were murder-ed or rape-ed. They all return as cuda."

More fins arrived. Five. Six. Seven.

"When the angry souls come back," she said with a stomp of her foot, "they come back with teeth."

The water was full of circling fins now, too many to count. Yet the infernal Jebyl kept chumming, bucket after bucket of fetid offal splashing into the water.

The women finished piling rocks into the nets on my hips, and the Falali Mother led me to the water's edge, netted rocks bouncing painfully against my tender thighs.

The water reeked of blood and rot, fins slicing through like razors. A cuda jumped out of the water, its body long and sleek and silver like a sword. It jerked its tail left and right, jaws snapping at the air, teeth like the points of nails.

More cuda jumped, and the water began to froth as they fed in a frenzy of flip-flopping fins and tails.

Shivers rippled up my spine, nerves sparking like live wires. I closed my eyes, wishing it all away. What was Colonel Kell thinking when he agreed to this madness? If I could, I'd kill the bastard again.

I opened my eyes to the sight of the Falali Mother

flipping the lid off a large bucket. She reached her hand inside, and a tentacle wrapped around her wrist. With a large spill of water, she pulled a creature from the bucket, suckered tentacles snaking up her arm.

<What in Sire's name is that?>

<Octopus. We read about them. Remember?>

I didn't. Not at the moment anyway. Panic had such a stranglehold on me, I doubted I could've remembered my name.

Hands grasped me. Jebyl workmen took hold of my wrists and ankles and squeezed painfully down on my blood-slicked skin.

She carried the octopus to me, tentacles curling and uncurling, its skin the color of a bruise. She lifted it toward my face, and the tentacles stretched for me.

I tried to scream, but my voice had run away to hide. A tentacle slithered past my ear. Another twined around my neck as it pulled itself closer. It stared at me with a black, emotionless eye before it transferred itself onto my face.

My heart pounded, and my knees went weak, so weak I would've collapsed if not for the many hands holding me upright.

A tentacle slid under my armpit and wrapped itself around my shoulder so tight, it would take a saw to cut it loose. The octopus inched toward the top of my head, tentacles uncoiling and recoiling, unsqueezing and resqueezing in a coordinated, eight-way relocation effort.

It reached the top of my head, allowing me to see

again. It let me watch a tentacle creep down my face, this one different from the others. Pink and fleshy, it probed instead of grasped. Passing my left eye, it snaked its way alongside my nose to arrive at my mouth. It pressed hard against my lips. Worming. Penetrating.

I tried but failed to turn my head out of the foreign appendage's reach. I blocked it with my teeth and yanked with futility against the hands that held me firm.

<Relax, Jakob.>

I heard the words, but my ability to reason had run to hide in the same dark hole as my voice. I sucked air through my nose, but my lungs couldn't keep up with my triple-timing heart.

The Falali Mother reached a hand for my face, her eyes soft and brimming with compassion.

I screamed with my eyes. Get this thing off me!

She pinched my nose shut. I tried to shake my nose free, but the octopus immobilized my head by tightening its grip. I held my breath, the pressure quickly building in my lungs until my reflexes betrayed me, and my mouth opened to suck in a panicked breath.

The appendage was in, slithering across my tongue. I bit hard as I could but it was tough like a tree root, and it forced its way to the back of my throat. I choked as it entered my windpipe. My entire body jerked with each gagging cough.

<It's okay, Jakob. You're okay. Remember, they use the octopi to breathe underwater.>

I kept coughing, tears streaming down my cheeks.

\<Jakob?\>

I tried to breathe but couldn't stop choking.

\<It's breathing for you now. You need to relax.\>

I forced myself to stop fighting. Air blew into my lungs and slowly emptied back out. They filled again, the octopus on my head acting as a respirator.

I wasn't dead. Not suffocating. I was okay.

The Falali Mother stood close, waiting with concern on her face. "The first time is always the hardest," she said in a quiet voice that only I would hear.

I nodded as best I could with the added weight on my head.

She gave me a wink and stepped a few feet away to pick up a life-sized stick figure, which she held up for the crowd to see. The figure was constructed with bamboo arms and legs, fishhooked glowgrubs for hands and feet.

"Greyson the Blacksoul tie-ed Mmasa's family to rocks." She pointed to a large stone at her feet. "And he sank them." She pushed the stone off the edge, and a short coil of rope spooled out before the stick figure ripped out of her hands and disappeared into the blood-stained water. "All twenty-three of them. Parents and grandparents. Brothers and sisters. Wife and child."

She sank four more stones, and four more stick figures dropped underwater. "He sank them all and told Mmasa he had to dive to save them. Mmasa dive-ed. He had no choice. Sick and exhaust-ed, he fell below the waves with machetes in each hand."

Her assistants set machetes in my hands.

"The cuda smell-ed his blood, but they didn't feed. Weak as he was, Mmasa's tide was strong, and the cuda sense-ed the spirit of Falal flowing out of his veins. They didn't feed on him. Instead, they kiss-ed him on the cheek. They nudge-ed him with their noses, and nipp-ed him when he close-ed his eyes. They guide-ed him until he'd cut every single one of his family free."

Her words traveled around the caldera, cheers coming back.

"Since that day," she continued, "all divers take these rites. When they come of age, they dive with the cuda, not just to prove their courage and bravery but to prove they are bless-ed by Falal. And tonight, our honor-ed guest will take the rites. Tonight, my friends, Colonel Kell becomes one of us."

The chant started slow, but quickly built momentum.

One of us.

One of us.

One of us!

I looked down at the water. Cuda were everywhere, water roiling and frothing, the blood in my veins doing the same.

The Falali Mother came close and whispered in my ear, her voice soft but steady. "Soon the cuda will have had their fill. Dive deep and stay below until they move on."

I nodded and clumsily stepped to the very edge. Stones swung from my hips, and my neck worked to keep my overloaded head upright. My toes hung off the stage. I tried for a deep breath but couldn't suck air faster than the octopus's regular offering.

The crowd's chanting picked up pace.

One of us.

One of us!

The volume rose until the deafening chorus drowned my ears.

<Do it, Jakob.>

The speed of the chants continued to accelerate until the words rolled into one, the noise building to a crescendo.

It was time.

I stepped off.

CHAPTER 12

"When you thnk hthe limit o f human suffering
has been reached, that's when the unidverhse
reminds you theire is no limit."

—JAKOB BRYCE

My feet plunged into the chummed water, then my legs, hips, torso, and octopus-topped head. I kept my eyes open but couldn't see through the thick screen of air bubbles rising through the agitated seawater. Something bumped my foot, and I reflexively kicked at whatever it was. I swung the machetes, left then right, chopping at bubbles and kelp fronds, my heart pumping frantic beats.

I sank fast, my view clearing as I passed below the churning frenzy of cuda. Relief surged through me, but only for the briefest of seconds before the salt water attacked my wounds. Liquid pain flowed into every scratch. Every slice. Every crevice. Burning. Searing.

Dazed by shock, I barely noticed when the machete in my left hand fell from my grasp. I concentrated on my breathing. On keeping the second machete firm in my fist.

I descended through the warm surface water to the cool layer below, the chill helping me focus, helping me notice a different pain, this one stabbing at my eardrums, the pressure rapidly building until ice picks stabbed for my brain.

I squeezed my nose tight, sealed my lips around the octopus's breathing tube, and blew as hard as I could until my ears equalized. I blew again every few feet as I sank deeper into the kelp forest, shoulders bumping against stalks, my feet plunging through sprawling fronds and leaves the size of kites.

The salt chewed deeper into my lesions and ate from every scratch and cut before licking the length of each wound with urchin spines.

I swiped my free hand across my chest and stomach, thighs and shoulders, neck and calves, my hand moving fast, as if I were trying to tamp out a fire. But this was a fire that couldn't be extinguished, my body engulfed by flames of pain.

I wanted the cuda. Wished they would rip me apart and end this torture. I looked up, but my view was blocked by dense foliage. As promised, the angry souls must've stayed on the surface, sticking to the ample food being dumped into the water.

My feet touched the bottom and sank into the silt, the soothing chill of mud erasing the pain from my feet and toes. I wanted to bury myself in the silt, coast through it like a carefree ray. But I stayed where I was, suffering from wave after wave of throbbing, pulsating agony.

A voice came from the rabbit hole. <Are you okay, Jakob?>

I managed to send a response. <I'm alive.>

<Does it hurt?>

I closed my eyes. <Not. Funny.>

<I'm sorry. You must be suffering terribly.>

They gave the bastard my sight and my sound but spared him my pain. The unfairness of it was too much to take. <I hate you, Pol. I really do.>

<You have to get moving. The octopus can't provide the oxygen levels you're used to for long.>

I cracked my eyes open, the sting of salt mild compared to the wildfires raging over the rest of my body. <How long can I stay under?>

<With training, Jebyl divers can stay down for over twenty minutes. For you, I'm guessing half that.>

I had a job to do. Cut the stick figures free. Had to concentrate. Had to conquer the pain.

I gripped the machete tight and bit down on the tentacle in my mouth. I was ready.

My lungs went still. Dead still.

A momentary flash of panic gave way to annoyance when I realized I'd pinched off my air. Sire, must you rob me of every comfort? I relaxed my jaws, and air thankfully flowed back into my lungs.

<I want a medal for this. A whole chestful of medals.>

<Get moving, Jakob.>

I turned around, searching the dark. The glowgrubs strung across my chest afforded a short, murky range of view. Ignoring the pain, I pushed forward, machete first, my feet kicking against the ocean bottom as I ducked under a leaf as big as a tent flap and took hold of the kelpstalk's woody trunk.

I hefted the machete and chopped at the thin stem holding the lowest leaf. The blade didn't cut all the way through but did enough damage to make the leaf hang like a broken wing. Having marked my starting location, I slogged ahead, feet dragging through silt, my eyes straining at the black fog beyond the light.

The kelp forest slowly swayed with the soft current. Stalks, thick as my arm, reached for the surface, their broad leaves drooping like mammoth ears. Imagining cuda behind every leaf, I gently brushed the leaves aside with my machete. Slow. Careful.

I moved from stalk to stalk, counting as I went. Tiny fish swam in and out of view. Crabs dodged my footsteps.

No sign of the stick figures.

Reaching kelpstalk number ten, I stopped and turned back, eyes moving on a swivel as I worked my way back to the broken wing.

When I arrived at my starting point, I took a ninety-degree turn and set out on another foray into the bleak darkness while the salty ocean scoured my raw skin like a wire brush.

Ten stalks out.

Nothing.

Again, I returned to the broken wing and took another perpendicular turn. Four stalks out, I spotted a light behind a cluster of leaves. A dim yellow moon-glow against a midnight background.

Moving closer, brushing more leaves aside, I could plainly see the stick figure now. The quartet of fish-hooked glowgrubs hung from the figure's bamboo limbs, which stretched for the surface like the family of Mmasa the diver must've done so many years ago.

I grabbed the rope mooring the figure to the stone and raised my machete for a hack. I swung, but the drag of water slowed the blade until it harmlessly bounced off the rope.

<Use the sawtooth side.>

I turned the blade over and sawed back and forth, back and forth, until the rope cut free and the figure rocketed for the surface.

One down. Four to go.

Moving just a few feet in the same direction, I located the next stick figure and, like Mmasa, I cut it loose.

I found the next two with ease and cut them free. I imagined the cheers of the crowd above, pictured their mounting suspense as each stick figure popped to the surface.

The pain wasn't so bad now. Just a bunch of scratches. Nothing the Hero of Maritinia couldn't handle.

I located the fifth nestled between a pair of stalks. I took hold of the rope and waited. Had to wait as long as possible. Had to wait for the cuda to move on.

I'd done it. I felt a rush of euphoria, felt it tingle up and down my arms and legs. My eyelids felt heavy with contentment. I should lie down for a minute. Lie in this cool mud. Bury myself like a ray.

<Open your eyes, Jakob.>

<Not now.>

<You're running out of air. It's time to go.>

Right. Had to cut the stick figure free. Had to get to the surface. I'd get to it in a little bit.

<Jakob!>

My eyes snapped open. Alarmed heartbeats rammed my ribs. I tried to fill my starving lungs, but all the octopus could provide was a slow stream of weak air.

Where was my machete? Must've dropped it. I swept my fingers through the silt, once, twice, and struck something solid on the third try. Nabbing the machete, I went to work on the rope, the blade cutting rapidly through. The stick figure broke loose and soared for the surface. Exactly what I needed to do.

I jumped upward, but sank back down.

\<The rocks, Jakob. Dump the rocks.\>

That sounded like a lot of work. I jumped again.

\<Dump the rocks!\>

Another jump. Why wasn't I rising?

\<Jakob. You need to listen to me. You need to empty the rocks from the nets tied to your belt. You need to do it now.\>

I dropped the machete and reached for my right hip. Fumbling for the net, I dropped my hand inside and grasped a round stone. I lifted, but the stone slipped through numb fingers. Slippery little bugger.

\<Concentrate, Jakob.\>

I took hold of the stone, clamping my fingers tight and yanked it free. Dropping the rock, I nabbed another, and another, my feet lifting slowly off the ocean bottom.

I went to the net on my other hip and shed two, three, four more stones, my upward momentum notching upward with every dumped weight.

Sapped of every last morsel of energy, I rolled onto my back and let my arms and legs hang limp as I rose. Staring upward, I watched leaves drag over my face while starving lungs wrung foul air for every drop of oxygen.

The forest thinned, affording me a limited view of the surface. I stared at the hazy, ripple of light, watched it dance as I rose closer and closer.

Shadows coasted into view, dozens of them moving into the light. Long narrow torpedoes with fanned tails. I watched them glide, the entire school moving as one.

I was too tired to be scared. Too drained to care. The surface was close, just seconds away.

The cuda showed no interest in me, the school coasting slowly away. They'd had their fill as the Falali Mother had promised.

But then they turned.

All as one.

Time seemed to slow, milliseconds dragging into seconds, seconds stretching into lifetimes. They stared at me, heads like the tips of silver bullets, eyes black as abandoned mine shafts.

I glanced at the surface. So, so close.

Eyes back on the cuda. The slow billow of gills. Watching. Waiting.

Fishtails flicked, and the cuda charged like darts.

<SWIM, JAKOB!>

Fear jolted through me, my body going electric with desperate energy.

Time collapsed. Seconds compressed into each other.

Instinct propelled my arms and legs. Rapid strokes pushed for the surface. Cuda bore down, hinged jaws spiked with teeth.

My head and shoulders burst out of the water. I caught a glimpse of the stage, barely ten feet to my right.

I turned and stroked, knowing it was too far, knowing I wouldn't make it.

The cuda struck, needle noses punching my ribs and hips. The impact pushed me under, and I rolled, arms flailing, legs kicking. Fish tumbled over me in a blur of snapping teeth and slapping tails.

I forced my head out of the water and tried to scream for help, but the breathing tube in my throat snuffed my shouts. I spun around, fists swinging for cuda but failing to land. I spun the other way, and chopped at empty water with my hands.

Confused, I stopped fighting and bobbed quietly in the water. Where did they go?

I spotted a fin moving away from me, cutting for open water. It disappeared, replaced by two others heading in the same direction.

The octopus retracted its breathing tube. I gagged as it slipped out of my throat, then out of my mouth.

I sucked air. Sweet, sweet air.

The octopus disengaged and sloughed off my head and into the water. I watched it swim for the stage, tentacles fanning out like rubbery umbrella spines, then squeezing together in an eight-way thrust.

Lungs huffing, I noticed the cheers of the crowd, the sound muffled by the water in my ears. I looked to the stage. Sali knelt on the edge, hands beckoning for me to come. The Falali Mother stood behind her, a smile on her face. Dugu waited off to the side, filming as always.

I checked my hands. Ten fingers. I ran my hands down my chest. Didn't feel any bite-sized divots.

<What just happened?>

Pol didn't answer. There was no answer.

I swam for the stage, exhausted muscles straining with the effort. Reaching the stage, I lifted my arms like a tired toddler and allowed a pair of Jebyl to pull me out of the water. I tried to stand, but wobbly knees betrayed me. The Jebyl looped my arms over their shoulders and lifted me upright.

Sali's hands clapped onto my cheeks, her eyes staring into mine. "Are you okay?"

I tried to speak, but my heaving chest was still making up for lost time. Instead, I held her gaze and gave the slightest of nods.

"He's okay," she shouted, her words carrying from crier to crier around the caldera to a chorus of wild cheers. With a broad smile, she pulled her hands off my cheeks and looked at the palm of her left hand.

"What is it?" I croaked.

She held her palm up for me to see. Blood.

But she'd only touched my cheeks. My face hadn't been scored by the shells.

Sali turned to the Falali Mother and pointed at my right cheek. "He's been bitten."

The Falali Mother stepped close for a look. She touched my cheek with her finger, and I winced from a pain I hadn't felt until now. She studied the blood on her finger, then backing up a step, she dropped to one knee.

As did Sali.

As did everybody else on the stage except for the pair of Jebyl who held me.

And Dugu who kept filming.

The crowd hushed, silence descending like a burial shroud.

The Falali Mother bowed her head. "He wasn't bitten," she called.

I waited as her words circled the crater.

She lifted her face to me, eyes wide with awe. "He was kiss-ed."

CHAPTER 13

"Comfort isan illusiion. Find yourself a comforttable
place andyou'll eventually discvoer you were really
in a waiting room for rhte next disaster."

—JAKOB BRYCE

I hurt.

Everywhere.

Especially my cheek.

I remembered boarding the boat in the middle of
the night. Wrapping myself in silk cloths. Climbing
into this fishnet hammock.

Not much after that. Mustn't have taken long for
the bliss of sleep to take hold.

But I was awake now. And it was daylight. I could
feel the sun warming my exposed face, could feel it
soaking through my silk cocoon. I kept my eyes closed,

preferring to let everybody—even Pol—think I was out. I needed to rest. Needed to heal. Needed to let the boat's gentle sway rock away my pain.

A voice whispered near my ear. Sali. "You need to eat something, Drake. The Ministry is only an hour away."

An hour? I'd been sleeping all day.

Still, I didn't open my eyes. I didn't want to eat. Or talk. I didn't want to crack my little bubble of peace and solitude.

She put a hand on my shoulder and gave it a gentle shake. "Drake, you need to wake up."

I opened an eye.

A simple Jebyl-style body wrap came into focus, her curves hugged by long pink and green stripes. I angled my gaze up to her face, concerned by what I saw. She had bags under her eyes and a pair of black curls poked from unruly hair like springs from a smashed wrist-watch.

"Are you okay?" I asked.

"Just woke up myself. Couldn't sleep last night, so I took a little nap." She held out a bowl of boiled kelp shoots.

I fought stiff muscles to sit up. Silk cloths slid off my bared shoulders, which were crisscrossed with long scratch marks. I poked my feet out of the silks and dangled them over the side of the hammock.

Taking the bowl, I dropped my fingers in to pick up a kelp shoot, a pale yellow stalk with a curlicue of new growth on one end. Gingerly, I opened my mouth and bit off the end. To avoid my wounded cheek, I chewed on the left side of my mouth, tangy and salty.

"You're bleeding," said Sali.

I touched my cheek. Fingertips came away bloody. "Must've opened back up." I touched again. My cheek was puffed, like I'd stuffed my mouth with cotton. I ran a careful finger over the bite, a trail of puncture wounds, from chin to ear. I swallowed the kelp shoot and explored the inside of my cheek with my tongue, tasting blood where a few of the holes had punched all the way through.

Damn cuda kissed me good.

"You frighten-ed me," said Sali.

"Is that why you couldn't sleep?"

"Yes. Plus you know how I get before I go to see Father."

I didn't, but I could imagine. "I do."

Using one of my already bloodstained silks, I wiped my face and fingers, then put the thick end of the kelp shoot in my mouth.

She climbed onto the hammock and sat next to me, gravity mashing our hips together. "I've attended many of those ceremonies. The cuda don't normally stay after the chumming. They could've kill-ed you."

I took another kelp shoot, beginning to realize how hungry I was.

"The kiss was a powerful symbol," she said.

I stopped chewing. I wished I knew how Kell would have responded. Chide her as superstitious? Or was he a believer himself? "Felt like a bite to me."

"But only one. And it was on the right cheek. Just like Mmasa."

"Maybe the cuda didn't like how I tasted." I touched her knee. "Tell me the rest of Mmasa's story."

"You've heard it before."

"I want to hear it again."

She sighed and rested her head on my shoulder. "Mmasa cut them all free. Every last one of his sunken family. Some survive-ed. Others had already drowned. But he still free-ed them all. Nobody will ever know how he manage-ed to stay underwater so long. They say it was the kiss of the cuda that kept him going."

<Jakob, you're not believing this garbage, are you?>

<Of course not,> I snapped.

<A little defensive, are we?>

<No.> My pulse beat inside my temples. Sali was still talking, but I wasn't listening anymore. My entire focus was on the rabbit hole in my head. I sent the words through. One at a time. <What exactly are you accusing me of?>

<Believing your own hype. I know you had an eventful night, but you mustn't listen to these pseudospiritual interpretations. I can't have you entertaining delusions of grandeur. I need you focused on the mission.>

I kept my inner voice level. Professional. <I have no such delusions. Colonel Kell was the one caught up in all this foolishness. I simply need to know as much as possible to keep my cover.>

<Colonel Kell was a traitor. Your job is to imitate him. Not to become him.>

<I know what my damn jo—>

Sali bumped my ribs with an elbow. "Did you hear me?"

"Of course I did," I said. "Go on."

"I asked you if wanted some water."

"Um, sure." She started to rise, but I held her back. I didn't care how much Pol griped. I knew what I was doing. I was in control. "Finish the story first."

Sali gave me a quizzical quirk of her brows. "You've been acting strange lately. You know that?"

I tensed. "Strange how?"

"I don't know. It's like you're a different person."

I swallowed and shook my head at another conversation taking a bad turn.

"Relax." She put her hand on my thigh. "I didn't say that was a bad thing. Since I've known you, you've always been so driven, you know what I mean? Always so sure of yourself. You seem so much more uncertain now."

"Like I'm lost?"

"I prefer to think you finally found some humility."

I picked out another kelp shoot. "I'm just trying to understand."

"Understand what?"

"Everything."

"See. That's exactly what I mean. When did you get so deep?"

"About the time I met you."

She gave my leg a slap.

"Ow!"

With a chuckle, she said, "That's what you get for saying stupid things that aren't true."

I laughed and rubbed my thigh. "Tell me the rest of Mmasa's story."

"Where did I leave off?"

"Start where he gets out of the water."

"Well, he couldn't stand when he pull-ed himself onto the stage. His eardrums had burst, and he was suffering from the blinding pain of depth sickness." She pointed at my face. "And his right cheek was bleeding."

"Then what happened?"

"Mmasa had dropped his machete, but he had a smaller blade strapp-ed to his hip, and when Governor Greyson came to him, Mmasa beckon-ed like he wanted to say something. The Governor leaned down, and from somewhere deep inside, Mmasa summon-ed the strength to make one last harvesting stroke."

"He killed Greyson."

"He sliced his throat open. The monster die-ed within a minute."

I put the last kelp shoot in my mouth, this one bigger than the rest.

Sali let out a sigh. "Mmasa and his surviving family were execute-ed that same night. But he inspire-ed all of Maritinia. He struck the first blow in a revolution that took centuries to complete."

She put her hand on my chin, turned my face to

hers. "You finish-ed the revolution, Drake. You and my father. I've been thinking about it all night. That's the link between you and Mmasa. He start-ed it, and you end-ed it."

I chewed on a stringy knot of kelp, my mind chewing on a stringy knot of its own.

The symmetry of her interpretation was beautiful.

Except I hadn't ended their revolution.

Yet.

I jumped down to the dock and held up a hand to help Sali, my uniform scratching my scraped skin. She waved my hand away, making it plenty clear to all who watched that she didn't need any help.

Next came the Falali Mother, who did accept my assistance. The shells in her headdress rattled as she made the short jump down.

Together, the three of us walked along the quay toward the Ministry's ringed island. Dugu backpedaled before us, his camera transmitting a live feed to the sky-screens. The Ministry domes stood ahead and to the left, silver tiles afire with the glow of the setting sun.

We stopped halfway up the quay, where a small welcoming committee waited. Admiral Mnai stood at the center. His wife—Sali's stepmother—on his left elbow, the beak-faced Captain Mmirehl in right-hand-man position. Standing off to the side were the two lieutenants I'd met in the conference room, and behind them a large man in an oversized business suit.

The weapons dealer. Still had no idea what his name was.

We touched our fingers to our hearts, our greeters returning the gesture. The admiral said some words into the camera. How honored he was to receive the Falali Mother. How proud he was to call Colonel Drake Kell, the Hero of Maritinia, a friend. He thanked us both for our dedication to the peoples of Maritinia and wrapped it up with promises of productive discussions.

Dugu lowered the camera to fiddle with its control screen. "It's off," he called.

The whole group relaxed. Except for Sali, her smile fragile as a quilt of rose petals. He hadn't even mentioned her.

"Come," said the admiral to the Falali Mother. "You must be weary after such a long journey. We must get you to your room. We can talk after you've had a chance to clean up."

They headed for the Ministry domes. Not even a hello for his daughter.

I searched for something to say to her, something that would make it okay. I opened my mouth but never got the chance to speak.

"Welcome back, Colonel," said Captain Mmirehl. "Can I borrow you for a bit?"

Biting off whatever I was about to say, I looked at the captain, a thin-lipped smile bridging the hollows in his cheeks.

"Certainly," I said.

"Walk with us."

By us, he meant him and the weapons dealer. I fell in step between the two men, the lean-faced, rail-thin Mmirehl on my left, the broad-cheeked, ample-bodied weapons dealer on my right. Cuda and blowfish.

I stole a look over my shoulder. The entire group had dispersed. Except for Sali. She stood in the same spot. All by herself.

A string tugged on my heart, but only for a second before Captain Mmirehl snipped it with his sharp tongue. "I quite enjoyed your little show last night. Am I right, Mathus?"

"I've never seen anything like it," said the arms dealer with a tentative tone. Probably trying to figure out if Mmirehl was trying to insult me.

The captain eliminated any doubt. "I love a good piece of theater, Colonel. Thank you for that."

My voice was cold. "That's not makeup on my cheek, Captain."

Mathus kept me from saying any more. "Mind if I take a look at that wound?"

I stopped so he could lean close, his nose speckled with dewy sweat.

"That's quite a bite, Colonel. But I suppose a decorated soldier like you has had worse. Like that hunk of shrapnel you took in the Secession Skirmishes. A bomb, right?"

"Land mine." So said the battle reports.

"Nasty little things, those land mines. I'd be happy to sell you some, but"—he swept his hands before the vast swaths of ocean—"I don't think you'll find a use for them here."

We started moving again. Silently.

Reaching the end of the quay, my eyes went to the lagoon. The quiet water flowered with abundant bouquets of coral. We turned right, moving away from the domes, but I kept gazing at the water. Sea snakes propelled themselves with a whiplike swim stroke. Cloud-shaped shoals of sparkly fish moved to and fro like shimmering mosaics constructed of living tiles.

"Speaking of explosives," said the weapons dealer.

I peeled my eyes off the lagoon to follow the direction of his pointing finger. A short tower stood on the far side of the atoll. I was surprised I hadn't noticed it already. Bamboo beams and struts supported a small platform with the beginnings of a spiral staircase attached to one side. A dozen or more Jebyl workmen hustled about. Not much time before they'd have to quit, along with the sun.

"That will be your launch tower," said the arms dealer. "Fifteen feet tall. When it's done, we'll mount the missile launcher on top. I'll have you operational by the end of day tomorrow."

"Excellent," I said, trying to sound like I meant it.

We reached a narrow bridge that crossed a gap of collapsed stone. I went over the bridge first, bamboo slats with rope railings. Below, shallow water channeled into the lagoon across jagged slabs of barnacled rock. Mmirehl came over second, the bridge bouncing with each long, lanky stride. Finally, the arms dealer started across. He went slow, worried hands on the ropes. The creaky bridge bowed and strained against his bulk but held.

When he stepped down to solid stone, he smiled broadly, his gold tooth glinting in the late-day sunlight. Reunited, we passed a group of well-armed guards and walked toward the tower, a barge moored next to it. One of the Jebyl workmen noticed our approach and gave his coworker an elbow. Another stopped sweeping. Yet another came out from behind the tower to watch our approach. Soon, the whole group had stopped their cleanup, every eye on us. On me.

I followed Captain Mmirehl onto the gangplank leading to the barge but stopped halfway across and turned to face the workers. "Please," I said. "Don't stop working on account of me."

They stared, tools of stone and bone in their hands, skin slick with sweat. The closest man dropped his tools and put one hand then the other over his heart, the skin on his weather-beaten face wrinkling and bunching around a bright smile. The others followed suit, hearts hidden under hands over hands.

Unsure what I was supposed to do, I touched my fingers to my heart and offered a smile that hurt my cheek. They seemed satisfied, so I left them to join Mmirehl on the barge.

The arms dealer appeared at my side. "You sure made an impression on them last night."

Mmirehl rolled his eyes. "Savages are easily impressed."

The dealer put his hand on Mmirehl's shoulder. "Savages? A word like that tells me you must not trust the Jebyl to behave themselves. You know, I have hundreds of firerods for sale. Grenades, too. Nothing will tamp a little unrest like a show of strength."

"We can't afford it," said Mmirehl.

The dealer raised his thick brows, and I couldn't escape the feeling that I'd just watched a pair of prey-seeking hawks lift into the vast sky of his forehead. "You haven't heard my prices," he said.

"The answer is no, Mathus. You've already taken us for everything we had."

The hawks landed with empty talons. "You and I both know that's not true, but do as you wish." To me he said, "Come, I'd like to show you your new missile system."

I followed the big man to a group of crates. Popping the lid of the closest, he waved me forward for a look inside. A control board. I leaned down for a close look. <Recognize it?> I asked.

<That's an incredibly new model.>

<Surprised to find it here?>

<Very.>

I pulled my head out of the box. "And the missiles?"

"Yes, yes. We have a full complement." He opened another crate. "Sixteen as agreed. Plus I threw in a spare."

I leaned over the box, the tangy smell of propellant

filling my nostrils. Two missiles. Each tube roughly six feet of shiny steel.

<This is impossible,> said the voice in my head. <Those are MG-877s.>

<Are they capable of downing the new contingent's transport vessel?>

<These things could bring down a military gunship. The Empire started manufacturing this model only three years ago. We have to disable this system before the new contingent enters our airspace.>

I didn't want to think about it. So I didn't. I stood up straight, gave the big man a slap on the back. "You've outdone yourself."

A grin spread, slow as a burning fuse. "I knew you'd be pleased." He lifted the lid off the next crate, and I looked inside to find more missiles and what appeared to be part of the launcher.

<A security breach of this magnitude is totally unheard of, Jakob.>

Not totally, I thought. I'd listened to enough family conversations to know the Empire wasn't as efficient as it used to be. The fact that this world had won independence, no matter how temporary, was proof.

<The man must have inside connections,> said Pol.

<Want me to ask where he got the system?>

<No. Let's not allow our mission to get sidetracked. Instead, we'll be sure to report this so the E^3 can follow up later.> After viewing the next crate of missiles, I turned to Mmirehl. "Has the admiral seen these?"

"He has."

"And?" I wanted to hear him say I was right to buy the system. It didn't matter if I'd had no clue what I was doing. I just wanted to watch the smug bastard eat his words.

He blinked his eyes. Twice. "The admiral was most impress-ed."

I smiled. And this time I felt no pain in my cheek. "Shall we?" With a quick about-face, I strode back to the gangplank, an extra bounce in my step. I stopped. The Jebyl. They were waiting for me. All of them down on one knee.

I knew I hadn't done anything to deserve such reverence, but I still felt a surge of pride filling my chest. A man could get used to this. I walked down the gangplank and stood before them.

One man rose and carried a small box to me. With a bow of his head, he undid the catch and lifted the lid for me to see inside. Five tools made of mammoth bone lined up in a row and fastened in place with worn silk ties. One tool had a V-shaped tip. The next a U. The third's tip was broad and flat. The fourth's was shaped like a scalpel. The fifth's like a fishtail. I knew what they were. Tools for wood carving.

"A gift," said the workman.

"You mustn't," I said. "You'll need these."

"We can find new tools. We only regret we didn't have anything else to offer."

I held a hand over my heart. Put a second hand over the first. "You are all most kind. I will treasure them."

Grins all around.

I took the box with a slight nod and turned around to find Mmirehl standing behind me. "Can we go now, Colonel?"

Mathus stood fast on the barge. "I'm staying to supervise the construction cleanup, gentlemen. I'll see you tomorrow."

After a final wave of thanks for the gift, I caught up to Mmirehl, who had already started toward the domes. A few steps out, the captain spoke up. "I'd like to show you something else. Something you'll find very interesting."

I didn't like his deadpan tone. I could feel the needle hovering over my good mood. "What would that be?"

"A dead body."

Pop it went.

CHAPTER 14

> "Abbove water, the Minstry is a jewel. Beleow is
> a dungeon."

> —JAKOB BRYCE

The cabin was cold, the chill of deep ocean pressing
in on the steel walls. Mmirehl was watching me, his
mouth and nose buried in the crook of his elbow. The
stench was powerful. Mold, mildew, and meat.

Spoiled. Rotten. Meat.

Before me was a table, my handiwork on display.

I stared at the cleaved jawbone, remembering the
first blow when I missed his throat and embedded my
machete in his jaw.

It was him. Kell had come back to haunt me.

What was left of him.

I squeezed the carving tools I'd been given in my hand and tried a deep, calming breath. I inhaled of his deathly odor, my nostrils filling with the stink of payback.

"Who is he?" asked Mmirehl from the opposite side of the table, his voice muffled by his sleeve.

\<Play dumb, Jakob.\>

\<You think?\>

I cleared my throat. "I was about to ask the same thing."

The dead colonel's face was unrecognizable. Eyeless and cheekless. His nose a craggy nub of exposed cartilage. He'd been gutted by ocean scavengers, his chest cavity an empty cage of bones. Patches of blistered and split skin still remained in a few places. Forehead. Elbows. Ankles.

And shoulders.

I could see Kell's scar. Starting at the collarbone, it ran for an inch before disappearing into a flayed strip of chewed muscle. It was only an inch, but it was a perfect match for the scar on my shoulder. The scar I'd shown to every person on this world last night.

Kell's revenge was upon me. I could practically feel his bony fingers wrapping my windpipe. Could see him grinning with his split jaw.

\<I tried to tell you this could happen.\>

\<Not now, Pol.\>

Mmirehl lowered his elbow to speak. "He's not from Maritinia."

I was slow to process the words. Slow to recognize the matter-of-fact tone. The bland lack of accusation.

\<The scar,\> I said to Pol. \<He hasn't noticed.\>

\<Or he hasn't made the connection that you could've replaced Kell. What does he know of the ways of the E³?\>

I forced my mouth to speak. "How do you know he's foreign?"

He pointed to the tattered piece of underwear on his waist. Elastic.

I put my hand on my chin and creased my brows in an attempt to feign curiosity. "Where was he found?"

"A pair of fishermen spott-ed him floating near Maringua around noon, and they tow-ed him here. I think he was a spy."

My gut twisted. "Why?"

"Who else could he be? We've had no reports of a missing foreigner."

The hatch opened, and Admiral Mnai ducked his head inside. Punched by the smell, the bridge of his nose wrinkled up, and his eyes rolled in their sockets. He shook his head and waved his big mitt of a hand in front of his face in a feeble attempt to wipe the stench away.

"You should've warn-ed me," he said to Mmirehl.

"Apologies, Admiral. The body is most ripe."

The admiral pinched his nose shut. "He was found near Maringua?"

"Yes. We believe he was the Empire's spy."

The admiral's eyes narrowed. "You agree with this assessment, Colonel?"

"I agree." My mind clicked into action. "The Empire has begun its infiltration."

<Good, Jakob. Time to point fingers and let them chase their tails.>

The admiral lowered his hands and took a position next to Mmirehl. "How did he die?"

"Look at the jaw," said Mmirehl. "He died violently."

"Who would've murder-ed him? And why?"

"I do not know. It is most troubling."

The admiral looked down at the corpse, his mouth contorting with anger, a twitch flickering his right eye. "A spy," he muttered, barely audible. Lifting his thick arms, he brought both fists down to pound the table with a loud slam.

Mmirehl and I both moved back a step as if the extra distance would protect us from the admiral's sudden outrage. Mnai turned and snatched hold of Mmirehl's shoulder, pulled him close and put a finger in his face. "I want an investigation, you hear me? Find out who this man was. Find out who kill-ed him. I demand answers!"

"An investigation. An excellent idea."

"That's not all, Captain. I want foreigners rounded up. Anybody who sympathizes with the Empire, get them off my planet!" The admiral released him with a little shove. "Get to it."

"Right away, sir." Mmirehl spun on his heels and made his escape out the hatchway.

The admiral watched him go, mouth hanging open like he had more orders to shout, but then his jaw slammed closed like a prison door, and he turned that massive head on me. His brows were as twisted as barbed wire. Eyes like white-hot irons.

I battled the urge to bow my head and run. Instead, I met his gaze, standing tall against whatever bluster was about to blow my way.

<This man is not stable,> said Pol.

<No kidding.>

Mnai sniffed air in and out his nose, the edges of his nostrils flaring with the force. His eyes moved, just enough to tell me he was studying my wounded cheek.

"It will heal," I said in an attempt to change the subject.

Ignoring the comment, he looked down at the body and rested his hands on the table's edge. "The Empire's spies are working with the Jebyl, aren't they?"

I had no idea why he wanted to take that particular wrong turn, but I wasn't going steer him back. "Spies will use anybody they can."

"The resistance must be crush-ed." His voice was deep and bleak as the ocean bottom. "The Jebyl are a menace. You see what they're doing, don't you? They'll lend their assistance to the Empire, and when the Empire takes back this world, the Jebyl traitors will take their place as the new ruling class."

I nodded as my mind incorporated the new fact: He fears the Jebyl as much as he does the Empire.

Mnai leaned forward. "I don't understand this soft spot you have for the Jebyl. It's like a blight on a piece of fruit. A stinking, rotten blight that has to be cut out before it spreads."

"If that's how you feel, then why did you send me to participate in the ceremony? I thought we were trying to bridge the gap between us and them. Isn't that why we're going to meet with the Falali Mother?"

With a toss of his massive arms, he flipped over the table. I jumped back and bit the inside of my swollen cheek, which shouted in pain as the table hit the floor with an earsplitting crash. Kell's body struck the floor with a wet thud.

I stared at the admiral, my heart pumping with abandon as I tried to keep my eyes from going wide with shock.

He returned the stare with a slight, self-satisfied grin tugging at the corners of his mouth. "I didn't ask for your opinion."

I rested my hand over my smarting cheek while blood spilled across my tongue.

Without another word, he turned around and walked out. I watched the empty hatchway for a long time. <He doesn't trust me, Pol.>

<Agreed, but you did well. Although your influence over him is limited, we must do our best to stay in his inner circle or risk becoming completely uninformed.>

I nodded before looking down to the floor.

Once again, Kell lay at my feet.

Dead.

Sitting side by side, Sali and I watched Admiral Mnai enter the conference room. After a brief nod at the Falali Mother, he walked behind a seated Captain Mmirehl to the table's head. Dropping his bulk into a chair, he put his hands together on the table's well-polished surface, his knitted fingers stacked like fire-wood. "Tell us what you know of the resistance."

The Falali Mother sat at the opposite end of the table. Same place I'd sat the first time I was in this con-ference room. "There is no resistance," she said.

"Then who was that agitator harassing my soldiers yesterday?"

"What agitator?"

"You know very well my soldiers were force-ed to tame an agitator at the parade."

The Falali Mother dropped her jaw and widened her eyes in dumbfounded disbelief. "That was no agi-tator. That was an old man with a flag." She looked to Sali and me. "Tell them."

"She's right," I said at the risk of angering the admi-ral. "He didn't pose a threat."

The admiral gave me an icy stare. "He was waving the flag of the resistance."

"The flag of the Jebyl," corrected the Falali Mother. "You once wave-ed that same flag when you sought Jebyl support after your coup."

Captain Mmirehl poked his beak into the conver-sation. "I debrief-ed my soldiers while you were all having dinner. The old man was a subversive with ties to the Empire."

"Ties? What ties?"

"He was identify-ed as an ex-dockhand at Selaita's landing platform. According to his former coworkers, he was very chummy with the foreign pilots. Clearly, he was an Empire sympathizer."

Admiral Mnai leaned back in his chair and rested his hands on his rounded stomach. "How do you respond to that, Dearest Mother?"

"This just happen-ed yesterday, and you already interview-ed his former coworkers?"

"I did," said Mmirehl. "One of our soldiers work-ed with him before enlisting in our navy."

"One? You said coworkers." She emphasized the plural with a drawn-out Z.

Mmirehl shrugged his shoulders. "One is enough."

The Falali Mother shook her head, the shells of her headdress rattling against each other. "This is an injustice. The man is dead. Kill-ed for nothing more than expressing pride in his people, and the best you can do is sully his character with ridiculous accusations?"

The admiral's voice was straight as a knife blade. "He was an enemy of Free Maritinia, and enemies will be dealt with harshly."

The Falali Mother threw up her hands. "This is pointless." Looking at me, she said, "Can you please talk some sense into this man?"

I reluctantly opened my mouth to talk, but closed

it when I saw Sali inch up in her chair. Her head was bowed, brows shading her eyes. "Father?"

"Yes, child."

She lifted her gaze and met her father's eyes. "We promise-ed her you would listen."

"I have listen-ed," he said dismissively.

"You haven't listen-ed at all."

He leaned forward and grasped the armrests with his meaty hands. "What did you say to me?"

She put some granite in her voice. "I said you haven't been listening."

His lips slowly curved into a joyless smile. "Why must you defy me at every turn? You truly are your mother's daughter."

"The Jebyl are dissatisfy-ed," she said. "You need to listen to her."

The soulless grin stayed frozen on his face, his thoughts unreadable. Sali did her best to mirror his gaze, but her mirror had cracks forming in the corners of her mouth and eyes. I reached for her hand under the table, felt it quiver as I grasped hold to give it a squeeze.

"Fine," he with a wave of his hand. "I keep my promises. Speak your mind, Dearest Mother."

The Falali Mother cleared her throat. "The Jebyl support-ed you because you promise-ed them change. Schools and medicines. Freedom and liberty. But they've seen none of these changes."

"They need to be patient."

"Patience comes in limited supply, Admiral. They

celebrate-ed when they broke free of the Empire's fist, but now they feel like fools. They see the truth that they've simply exchange-ed one set of chains for another."

"I must stop you there, Dearest Mother. They didn't cast off the chains of the Empire. They didn't do a damn thing. I was the one who cut them loose." He pointed a finger at his chest. "*Me*. I risk-ed my life. My family. You'd think they'd show some appreciation for my sacrifices."

She gave a slight bow of her head to acknowledge the point. "Yet the problem remains. The Jebyl demand representation in your government. They need advocates who will make sure these travesties of justice don't continue."

"You want me to let them into my government?"

"Yes—into the government of a free Maritinia. They need a say in our future. They need a voice. That's what this unrest is about."

"The unrest must stop."

"Exactly. When they gain inclusion in this government, the unrest will cease."

"No. It will stop when you calm them with your words. Tell them their concerns have been heard. Tell them to be patient."

"I won't say anything of the sort until I see you're willing to make some concessions."

"By inviting Jebyl spies into the Ministry? I don't think so."

"Spies? Are you mad?"

"You think I can't see what you Jebyl are up to? I know the resistance is conspiring with the Empire to topple me."

Her forehead creased in bewilderment. "What, pray tell, are you talking about?"

"Don't deny it. Who do you hate more than the Empire? Us. The Kwuba. You'll welcome back the Empire with open arms if it means you can take our place as the ruling class."

"You can't be serious."

"Admit it," he said with flames dancing inside his eyes. "You Jebyl won't rest until we become your slaves." The accusation hung in the air like the blade of a guillotine. He slapped the table with an open palm, his voice booming from deep inside his gut. "I won't allow it."

The room fell into stunned silence. I pulled my eyes off the admiral and moved them from person to person around the table. Mmirehl's head was cocked to one side, gears cranking behind his eyes. The Falali Mother's face was a mixture of puzzlement and disgust. Sali bit her bottom lip and slowly shook her head side to side like a person who couldn't believe what she had heard but knew the futility of arguing.

<This is great news, Jakob. As long as Kwuba and Jebyl stay focused on one another, our task becomes easier and easier.>

Pol was right. My mission was to foment discontent, to create chaos and anarchy. The Empire's contingent was coming on just a single transport vessel.

Fifty soldiers and another fifty administrators was all the Empire could spare for this far-flung world. I had to make sure they didn't face an organized defense.

And the admiral was falling into right into my hands.

I should've been elated. Head-over-heels happy. But that wasn't what I felt.

Instead, I was disturbed. Disturbed to the core. I was in the presence of true madness. And if I didn't watch my step, I'd soon be caught in the flood of unrestrained paranoia.

The Falali Mother broke the quiet. "How can you sit there and accuse us of sympathizing with the Empire? It's the Kwuba who have been doing the Empire's dirty work for the last two thousand years."

The admiral sat up straight, causing the shirt of his uniform to pull free from his beltline. "All the more reason the Jebyl want their revenge."

"But that's crazy."

The admiral nodded as if his large head were a boulder teetering on a cliff above us all.

Captain Mmirehl jumped to the admiral's defense like the toady he was. "Nothing crazy about it. In fact, we found the body of a spy earlier today. The Jebyl resistance wants to destroy our independence. They'll bring back the Empire and impose their will upon the rest of us."

"Shame on you both," she said, stern eyes attempting to stare them down. "I'll hear no more of this hateful talk."

Mmirehl clucked his tongue. "And why do you deny the truth? Could it be you yourself are part of—"

"Enough of this," interrupted the admiral. "Tell me, Dearest Mother, will you make a statement or not?"

"Are you willing to admit Jebyl into your government?"

"No."

She crossed her arms. "Then I won't make a statement."

The admiral stood and pulled his uniform shirt down where it had crept up his belly. "We are done here."

"Shall I send her back to Selaita?" asked Mmirehl.

"No," he said with another of his grim smiles, teeth lined up like gravestones. "Lock her up until she changes her mind."

CHAPTER 15

> "Starat a fire and there'sno telling where it might spreadr."
>
> —Jakob Bryce

Sali passed me a drink before setting the bottle on the floor and taking the chair next to mine. I tapped the paper globe over my head, and firefly light slowly seeped toward the edges of the small rooftop patio atop Kell's house. My house.

I looked to the sky, a vast black canvas spray-painted with a sparse coat of sparkling pinholes of light. I turned my gaze northward, where the pinpricks thickened into a spotted mass. The heart of the Empire. I stared into the thick swath of suns and felt the burdens of duty and home staring back.

For Sire and Empire.

I took a whiff of the unidentified liquid in my glass, my nose wrinkling as the burn of alcohol tingled up my nostrils. I put the glass to my lips and took a long, flavorful draw. I didn't need my cheek bite getting infected, so I steeled myself against the sting as I swished the alcohol around my mouth.

"You better enjoy it because it's our last bottle," Sali said with a bitter edge. She'd been like this since we left the Ministry, her needle-tipped tongue shooting poison darts. A glance at the bottle told me a good portion had already disappeared.

I took another sip. The booze tasted silky and smooth, as good as anything from home. "We can buy more tomorrow."

"There's no more to buy. They stopp-ed importing it months ago. Haven't you seen how few ships drop to the surface now? I'd be surprise-ed if more than one lands each week."

I stayed silent and took another swig. Fruity undertones put the alcohol in the brandy family, and the satiny finish said it had been aged a good long time.

"You lie-ed to me," she said with the harshness of cheap bootleg.

I took another look at the bottle on the floor and measured the empty space with my eyes. She had to be three or four drinks in. "Lied about what?"

"You said over and over that independence would bring opportunity. You said it enough, I believe-ed you. But look what's happen-ed. Kelp exports are down 80 percent. Tea and wine are so expensive that only the richest Kwuba can afford them."

"It will take time."

"You should've seen what I saw when I went to visit my mother. Kelp farmers don't know what to do with themselves. Half of them still harvest because it's what they've always done even though most of their harvest rots in place. The other half rot their brains trying to get high off fermenting puffer-fish fumes."

She downed the rest of her glass and poured another. "You knew the market for kelp would dry up without the Empire, didn't you?"

<Kell had to know,> said Pol.

Pol was right. And I might as well admit it. "I knew."

"That makes you a liar. How could you do that to me? How can you call yourself Hero of Maritinia?"

I tried to shrug off the accusation, knowing it was Kell who had told her that particular lie. But I was a liar, too. Everything I'd done since I met her was a lie. "I never called myself that. Others did. I did what I had to do."

"Is that all you have to say?"

"It's the truth."

"You lie-ed to the Falali Mother. You lie-ed to fool her into coming."

I turned to her. "You think I knew your father planned to lock her up?"

Her eyes shone intensely under the dim light. She leaned in my direction, her hands gripping her armrests tight enough to make the wicker creak. "You tell me."

I downed the rest of my drink before responding in a sober tone. "I thought he was genuine in wanting to reach out to the Jebyl. I wouldn't have gone through the ceremony if I'd known it was all for show."

She stared at me for a few seconds, apparently trying to read my face. Finally, she relaxed into her chair. "He use-ed us."

"He did." I reached for the bottle and poured myself a second drink. Putting the bottle down, I startled a crab into scuttling for the roof's edge. "I was proud of you the way you stood up to him earlier."

"A lot of good it did. He can be so difficult."

"Why is he so obsessed with the Jebyl?"

She shook her head slow. "Captain Mmirehl is the real problem. He's always planting hateful seeds in my father's mind."

<I don't trust this one,> said Pol. <You see how she blames someone else for her father's failings?>

<Give her a break, Pol.>

<You mustn't let yourself get too close.>

<I know, dammit.>

<I don't think you do.>

I slugged my drink down. <I've got it under control.>

<You can't fool me, Jakob.> His tone was cold. <I see through your eyes. I see when you stare at her.>

I reached for the bottle. <So what if I look at her? There's nothing wrong with watching.>

<Enough with the excuses, Jakob. Get your head on straight. Or else.>

<Or else what?> Frosty silence took hold. <Or else what, Pol?>

Nothing. The rabbit hole in my mind had iced over. The chill crept toward my heart. Pol was supposed to be my closest ally. My only ally. <Pol?>

"More?" asked Sali.

I threw my drink down my throat and gladly held out my glass.

"Sorry," she said, as the bottle's neck wavered over the glass. "I may have had too much." She spilled a few drops down my wrist but managed to get the rest into my glass.

I sat back in my chair and defiantly kept my eyes on the sky, so Pol couldn't see me take her hand.

I tried to push him out of my mind. He was over-reacting. While I might not have followed every one of his directions down to the minutest detail, the success of the results were speaking for themselves. It was time he started trusting my abilities.

Speakers crackled in the distance, and the sky-screens lit with a live shot of Admiral Mnai's grim face. He wore a tall green cap on his head, its straight black brim forming a triangle with his downturned brows. A billowing emerald scarf wrapped his neck and disappeared beneath his uniform jacket.

He stood inside the Ministry's control center, a sprawl of video screens flanking him on both sides. When he spoke, his voice was firm. Somber.

People of Free Maritinia, I come to you with disturb-

ing news. There are spies among us. He sneered at the camera. *Spies.*

Thanks to the vigilance of some honorable fishermen, we've capture-ed our first spy. A series of interrogations have reveal-ed plots of staggering dimensions. One of the most insidious was a plot to assassinate our revere-ed Falali Mother. Fear not, because this scheme has been foil-ed, but as a precaution, the Falali Mother has chosen to go into hiding.

I bowed my head. The man had no shame.

You see what is happening, don't you? The Empire seeks to subvert our freedom. They plan to destroy the new world we are building together, and they want to punish us for our defiance.

We cannot let this happen. He dropped a fist into his palm.

We must resist with all of our might. That is why I've install-ed a missile-defense system. When the new contingent arrives, we will blast their ship out of the sky and joyously watch its fiery remains fall into the sea.

But spies are another matter. They cannot be defeat-ed through force. They hide among us, posing as friends and family. They pretend to be our brothers and sisters, mothers and fathers, wives, husbands, and lovers. But they are not true Maritinians.

They are parasites. They latch onto our skin like lampreys and suck our blood. They are leeches who hide in the crevices, and they must be eradicate-ed.

That is why I've order-ed the creation of a new branch of government, the People's Protection Force. Tomorrow, we begin the process of appointing officers in every city and every village. *We seek all able-bodied patriots who want to help their world stay free. And for all other lovers of liberty, I beseech you to report any and all suspicious activities.*

The screens blinked out. I looked left and right at the people on the neighboring rooftops. I could see them talking, but I couldn't make out the words. I looked at Sali but couldn't see her eyes.

I looked inside myself and couldn't believe what I'd started.

I reached for the bottle. It had no chance of lasting the night.

CHAPTER 16

"Stay onne stepahead of your enemy. Easy to do
when you know whre they're goingg."

—Jakob Bryce

Flanked by two guards, I walked up the pier. The sun
continued its slow descent, now just four fingers from
dipping into the salty bath. Bright rays reflected off
the Ministry domes and drilled into my pained pupils.
This hangover had been dragging me down the entire
day. <Don't ever let me drink that much again,> I
told Pol.

Still no response.

On one level, I understood why he was so upset. He
felt my affection for Sali was causing him to lose control

of me. But I knew better. He didn't understand people. How could he when he wasn't a person himself?

I waved good-bye to my escort and turned for the missile platform. The tower wasn't any taller than it had been yesterday, but its skeletal frame was now fleshed into a sturdy structure. The launcher had been mounted on top, its two arms stretching left and right like the wings of a giant eagle feathered with missiles.

Approaching the section of collapsed stone, I stepped onto the makeshift bridge, lagoon to my left, open seas to my right, the two kissing under my feet. I marched past the guards as the barge set sail, workmen waving from the railings.

A voice called at my back. "Colonel!"

I looked over my shoulder to find Dugu hustling up. His face was perfectly round, a crescent-shaped smile cupping his nose. I'd forgotten what he looked like without that camera covering his face.

"How's the cheek, sir?" he asked.

"Getting better."

"My family wait-ed up for me to get home last night. They couldn't believe I was actually onstage for the ceremony. Everybody's talking about it."

I smiled as best I could.

"Do you think the angry souls really kiss-ed you?"

"I have no idea." And I didn't. "You know what, Dugu? I was wondering if you wanted to take a permanent post with me?"

"Sir?"

"I want you to be my guard as well as my personal assistant."

"Really?" His chest puffed to equal the girth of his belly.

"Absolutely."

"When do I start?"

"Right now. I'll leave it to you to tell my regular detail they've been dismissed."

I headed for the tower with my new assistant in tow. <See that, Pol? I'm accumulating assets now. Just like you taught me.>

Captain Mmirehl stood in front of the tower, watching me approach. Cocking his chin in the direction of the departing barge, he said, "They're all done. The platform is totally operational."

"Good."

"Where have you been all day?"

"Home. Where's Mathus? I need to talk to him."

"Why?"

"I want to see what he thinks of a tent."

"A tent for what?"

"We need to cover this tower," I said. "When the Empire comes, we don't want them to see it from space."

"They can see from space?"

I nodded.

Mmirehl rubbed his chin. "I'll order it done."

"You don't want to talk to Mathus first?"

"Mathus is gone. His work here was finish-ed."

<Why the tent, Jakob?>

The voice in my head took me by surprise. <Talking to me again?>

<Yes. Why the tent?>

<While you were off pouting, I've been making a plan.>

We passed another hatch with a sign hanging on the wheel lock: *Flooded*. It seemed that almost half of the underwater structure had been abandoned to the sea. When the Empire returned, the engineers would have to make fixing the water pumps their top priority.

Dugu pointed a finger down a long corridor. "I think they lock-ed her up somewhere down there."

We marched forward, our shoes slapping at the thin film of water on the rusted-steel floor. Another left, and we found a pair of guards standing outside a hatch. Stepping up, I waved them aside.

"No, sir," said the one of the left. "I'm afraid I can't do that."

I straightened my spine and leveled an authoritative stare. "Excuse me?"

"Captain Mmirehl's orders," said the one on the right.

"I may be a foreigner and therefore an honorary colonel in this Navy, but I'm still a colonel. Move aside."

Standing at attention, he stared past me. "We cannot comply without direct orders from the captain, sir."

"Step aside, soldier," I growled, "or I'll feed you to the cuda."

The one on the left said, "I'm sorry, sir, but we answer to nobody but Captain Mmirehl. We are members of the People's Protection Force now." He held up a fist for me to see. Long urchin spines had been run through the skin covering his knuckles, blood oozing from the fresh puncture wounds. The second soldier showed his fists, his swollen knuckles freshly tattooed to look like teeth.

<What in Sire's name is that about?> I asked Pol.

<I do not know.>

Sensing my confusion, Dugu put a hand on my shoulder and leaned toward my ear. "It's an old tradition among warriors, sir. When they touch their fingertips to their hearts in greeting, they want people to see their knuckles and know that their generosity has limits."

"Charming."

"All of the PPF recruits are getting their knuckles adorn-ed."

Captain Mmirehl came from around the corner. "What's going on here?"

"Tell your men to step aside."

A grin leaked across his narrow face, and his eyes danced along with his one-word response. "No."

My lips were squeezed tight, same as my fists. "You can't keep me out."

"Per the admiral's order, the People's Protection Force is a wholly independent branch of the military. Nobody goes through that hatch without my approval."

It was becoming obvious Mmirehl's secret police wasn't an overnight invention. He'd launched it with such efficiency, it must've been in the works for months. All he'd needed was an excuse to enact it, and my botched body disposal had served that excuse to him with butter and jam.

I crossed my arms to say I wasn't going anywhere. "I demand to see the Falali Mother."

"Is that all?" He pointed at the hatch behind my back. "She's in there."

My brows bunched up, and I pointed straight ahead. "Then what are they guarding in there?"

Mmirehl stepped between his guards and spun the hatch's wheel lock. He opened the latch with a clank and swung open the door. He ducked to get through, and without even a glance in my direction, he pulled the hatch closed behind him.

The wheel lock spun and stopped with a hollow clang.

Stunned, I stared at the closed hatch.

"What's going on in there?" I asked the guards.

"Sorry, sir," came the response.

I looked at Dugu, who shrugged his shoulders and shook his head.

"Fine," I said with a throw of my hands. "Fine."

I turned around and opened the hatch to the Falali Mother's cabin. No, not her cabin. Her cell.

Leaving Dugu in the corridor, I ducked inside. The cabin was a long rectangle except for the slightly curved outer wall from which two portholes stared like a pair of charcoal eyes, the left with a rivulet of tears trickling down the wall to form a small puddle on the floor. A single chair gave the face a nose, the Falali Mother perched atop with her knees hugged to her chest.

"Where's your sleeping mat?"

"I don't have one."

"Where did you sleep?"

"I didn't." She kept her voice level.

I poked my head back out into the corridor. "Get her a sleeping mat, Dugu." Looking at the other guards, I asked, "Have you been feeding her?"

"I ate," I heard her say behind me.

I craned my neck to look at her. "Bathroom?"

"They bring a bucket when I ask for it."

"Has anybody come to see you?"

"You're the first."

"They can't treat you like this. You're not a common criminal."

She stared down her nose at me, no easy trick from her seated position. "You are most obviously incorrect."

Her headdress sat piled on the floor, and her sandals marked the place her feet would be if she didn't have them pulled up. Her eyes sat in sockets that sagged like dishrags.

Without turning around, I called to the corridor, "And bring a washtub with soap!"

I sat on the floor, my back against the wall. "I didn't know the Admiral planned to lock you up."

"I know you didn't. I've come to know you better than that over the last few years. How's Sali handling this?"

"We both drank the night away."

"You have to watch out for her. Her flow is a turbulent one, but she carries the spirit of Falal in her heart."

"Indeed." I didn't want to praise Sali further for fear of sending Pol into another fit.

The Falali Mother pointed at the open hatch door. I pushed it shut with my foot.

"I won't make a statement," she said.

"Of course not. I've come to know you better than that, too."

"Have they said anything about me to the public?"

"They made up a fake assassination plot and said you were in hiding."

She rolled her eyes. "The admiral is beyond hope, isn't he?"

"He's not currently open to reason. That's for certain."

"So how are we going to get me out of here?"

"We have to convince the admiral to let you go."

"And how do we do convince him?"

"With the truth. We spread word that you're being held against your will."

<Exactly right, Jakob. The Jebyl won't stand for such an injustice.>

"His regime must fall," she said.

<It will,> said Pol.

<Indeed.>

CHAPTER 17

> "It's natural for an operative to sympathize with
> the local populatipn. But can I ever truly be ont
> of them?"
>
> —Jakob Bryce

I put the claw to my lips and pulled out the sweet and stringy flesh with my teeth. I tossed the shell out the window like so many other shells Sali and I had picked clean. The crabmeat couldn't be called tender, but at least its sweetness added a little flavor to my bland Maritinian diet.

Sated, I rinsed my hands in one of the water-filled basins that sat atop each table.

"Ready?" asked Sali.

The meeting. It was time to see the Falali Council of Interpreters. "Ready," I said.

We stood and walked to the counter to pay. The restaurant owner, a tall Kwuba in silk robes, put up a hand to say he didn't want money. Still, I took some polished abalone shells from my pocket and dropped them on the counter.

We stepped onto the quay, a broad expanse of stone that gave way to a broader expanse of water sparkling under the noonday sun. A mammoth hauling a massive load of kelp labored into our path, legs pushing like tree trunks against a gale force. Bathed in the musty smell of damp wool, we waited until the beast lumbered by, then waited some more for its load of sopping kelp to drag past.

We stepped through the trail of kelp slime, careful to keep our footing, and met Dugu, grin on his face and firerod slung over his shoulder. Together, we marched toward the quay's far side, the three of us carving a path into the bustling crowd.

People spotted me, and their faces lit with recognition. Stopping in their tracks, they bowed their heads and touched their hearts. An old woman dropped her bag of eels so suddenly I almost tripped over the squirming silk sack. Pushing forward, we sailed through the sea of Maritinians and left a wake of figures frozen in awe.

The novelty hadn't worn off for these people even though it had been almost two weeks since a cuda gave me its affectionate peck. Each day, my legend seemed to grow. The latest news was that the Falali Council of Interpreters had decreed the cuda's kiss a true blessing and an incontrovertible manifestation of Falal's will.

Time had done wonders for my cheek. The bruising had faded, and the scabs had sloughed away to reveal a pair of jagged, dotted-line scars. Ugly as the bite mark was, I wore it like a medal. Unlike Kell's chest scar, this one was mine, and every time I brushed my fingers across the bumpy scar tissue, I felt more comfortable in this body. Putting my mark on it finally made it mine.

The crowd continued to part for us, dockhands and divers, travelers and mammoth trainers. With my fingers pressed to my heart, I asked Dugu, "Have you seen him?"

"Yes. He must be following. I saw him watching you from the restaurant next door."

A man had been following me, no doubt one of Mmirehl's secret police, a short Kwuba man with a threadbare aquamarine silk robe. Dugu had been the first to notice him three days ago, and the man had been my blue shadow ever since.

At the far side of the quay, I let Sali and Dugu lead the way down a broad avenue. A pair of Mmirehl's PPF recruits came the opposite way with black sashes tied over their waistwraps. Having used up the last of the military-issued clothing, Mmirehl's newest recruits had taken to improvising uniforms.

They strode past us, brandishing their knuckles as they touched fingers to their hearts. The one on the left had a strap of leather tied around his knuckles with bone spikes stabbed through the leather. And the one on the right's entire hand had been dyed to match the menace in his ink-colored sash.

Sali and Dugu turned left, and I followed them into a narrow alley. We had to lose our tail before meeting the Falali Mother's caste of high priestesses. Another left took us into a narrow gap between buildings where, single file, we scraped our shoulders along the stone walls. Up a short set of stairs, we stepped over water sluices and ducked through wet laundry. Accelerating our pace, we hustled through clothesline after clothesline of damp silks, then ducked behind a curtain hung across a broad door.

Dugu dropped to his hands and knees and peered under the curtain. Sali tapped her foot nervously, waiting for Mmirehl's spy to go by.

I scanned the room: tiled floors and whitewashed walls with cerulean trim. Sunlight trickled down through webs of clotheslines, while water drizzled from robe tassels and waistwraps. Bare-legged men and women stood in shallow pools, scrubbing clothes against washboards carved into the faces of large stones.

Dugu stood to tell us the spy had gone by before leading us through the workspace and out to a courtyard that connected to a bone-carving shop. A pair of women stood inside, the same women from the ceremony, the ones who had scraped me raw with seashells.

"The council awaits upstairs," said one of the women.

Sali and Dugu headed for the staircase, but I grabbed Dugu by the shoulder. "You don't have to go up there with us. If the admiral finds out about this, I won't be able to protect you."

Dugu blinked and straightened his shoulders. "With all due respect, sir. Falal will decide my fate. Not you."

"You sure about that?"

"We shouldn't keep them waiting." He headed up the stairs.

The awkwardly uneven stairs led to a room jammed with worktables and floor-to-ceiling shelves stacked with mammoth femurs and ribs. Dim light filtered through windows coated with dust. The five high-ranking priestesses known as the Council of Interpreters sat shoulder to shoulder around a pedal-operated lathe.

Dugu took post before a table littered with bins of finely carved fishhooks and sewing needles. I squeezed onto a stool next to Sali, and, with no place else to put my elbows, I stretched forward to rest them on the lathe's battered surface.

"Greetings," I said to the quintet of sober faces. "I want to thank you for coming to speak with me. I know some of you had long distances to travel."

"Anything for the Bless-ed Hero," said the priestess seated next to Sali. "Have you seen the Dearest Mother?"

"I visit her every day."

"How is she doing?"

"She's well. They allow her ample food and drink."

"And her spirit?"

I saw how they longed for an answer, worry written in the lines around their pinched lips and etched into the furrows of their brows. I looked each and every one of them in the eye, drawing them all in before responding. "Her spirit is fierce."

They nodded, almost in unison, the beads on their headdresses moving to and fro.

The same priestess spoke again. If I had to guess, I'd peg her as the eldest. "Tell us about these stories of assassination."

"Lies," I said. "She's in no danger. There are no assassination plots. The admiral simply refuses to free her until she makes a statement to calm the resistance."

"There is no resistance."

"I know, but the admiral believes there is."

"He truly believes? Or is that another lie?"

"Captain Mmirehl is the real danger," said Sali. "He's the one who whispers paranoid fantasies in my father's ear."

"To what end?" the priestess asked of Sali.

"The man has nothing but darkness inside."

The priestess looked to the others. "The situation is as we thought."

"Yes, Sister Selmira," said the priestess to my left. "The question is what we choose to do now."

I lifted my elbows off the lathe and gathered a small pile of ivory powder into my hands. Tossing it into the air, I watched the cloud grow. "First, we must spread the truth."

<Nicely done, Jakob. Very theatrical.>

"I agree with you, Colonel," said the priestess. "These lies must be expose-ed."

"And second"—I closed my fists—"if they expect a resistance, I say we give them one."

Sali twisted the lathe's crank, and a long stretch of bone turned like a cart's axle. "We must keep up the pressure," she said. "We need more demonstrations. Thousands of Jebyl and fair-minded Kwuba have to take to the streets. My father can be a reasonable man. When he sees his people speak with a clear voice, he'll listen."

"More than that," I said. "What we really need is your help to organize a militia. A small force can take the Ministry and strip the admiral of his pow—"

I felt a heel on my toes, felt it grind down until my toenails hurt. Sali's glare was blindingly intense, like a sun had gone supernova behind her eyes. My mouth still hung open, stalled midword. We'd talked about this over lunch, about how we needed to encourage a real resistance. What did she think I meant?

<Who cares what she thinks?> Pol's voice was laced with contempt. <Don't let her stop you.>

"A militia is totally unnecessary, Drake." Sali spoke slow, as if she were teaching a child. "You know very well my father is a reasonable man."

<Her father is mad,> said Pol. <Beyond hope. Push for a militia. That's an order.>

Sali's heel lifted off of my boot, but she kept pressing with her voice. "We agree-ed on peaceful demonstrations."

I closed my mouth and damned myself for not seeing it sooner. Since I'd met Sali, she'd spent so much time railing against her father, I'd completely forgotten she still cared for him. Crazy or not, he was the man who raised her, and she was going to give him every last chance to see the error of his ways before resorting to anything so extreme as open rebellion.

I'd do no less for my father.

<Jakob, I gave you an order. You can't let her sway you. The mission requires you to be strong.>

"Right, Drake?" said Sali. She stared into my eyes, expecting me to agree. I wanted to please her. I really did.

But Pol was right. A militia could distract the admiral's forces from the Empire's eventual attack.

I opened my mouth, but Sister Selmira cut me off. "Let me save you before you say something you'll regret, Colonel. It doesn't matter what you or Sali think we should do. We shall follow the way of Falal, the way of truth and righteousness. We shall spread the word that our Dearest Mother has been wrongfully imprison-ed. Falal expects nothing less of us. But we will do nothing more."

"But the Falali church is the only institution on this world with the structure and organization to rival the admiral's. I wouldn't ask you to take up arms. I just need somebody to help me recruit and facilitate a proper—"

"Go no further, Colonel. We are simply translators. Our job is to interpret the signs of Falal in all things, water and stone, success and tragedy. We have no interest in power or politics. And we never will."

<It seems her mind is made up,> I said to Pol. <You don't expect me to keep arguing, do you?>

A defeated word limped into my mind. <No.>

"Very well," I said to her. "I respect your wishes."

I looked to Sali, whose betrayed glare hadn't dimmed.

"Don't be too hard on him for wanting to organize a militia," said Sister Selmira. "He's a warrior, after all. What did the soldier do when his wife hand-ed him an awl and ask-ed him to punch holes in her belt?"

Sali shrugged to say she didn't know the answer to the riddle.

"He use-ed the awl to mark a bull's-eye for his gun."

The muscles in Sali's face started to loosen. Same for mine. A smile begging to break loose.

Dugu laughed first, his stomach rocking to mirthful joy. Soon the whole room was laughing.

Except for Pol. <No more waiting. We destroy the missile platform tomorrow.>

CHAPTER 18

"Imagine a dmouse who makes a hoome in
a nestof cobras. Now you know the life of an
undrecover spy."

—Jakob Bryce

I carved an eye. A circular groove for an iris with a
deep hole for the pupil. Finished, I raised the carved
cuda to let it swim in the morning sunlight.

It was done.

<Excellent work, Jakob.>

I could do better, but overall I had to agree. I ran
my finger along the cuda's body to feel the scalloped
pattern of scales. Pushing my fingertip into its toothy
mouth, I felt the sharp bite.

I hadn't done any wood carving since I was a
teen, but I still had skills. If I hadn't succumbed to

family pressure to join the E³, I would've been a good artisan.

I put the carving tools back in their box and closed it. Dropping to my knees, I used my hands to sweep shavings off the balcony. I couldn't let Sali see. For several days now, I'd risen early to carve before Sali woke.

Much as I wanted to show her this piece of me, the true me, Jakob had to stay hidden. The mission came first.

Today was the day I'd destroy the missile system. Today was the day I guaranteed the Empire's safe return.

I surveyed the contents of my bag one more time: two large stones, several wriggling glowgrubs, a knife, a coiled kelpstalk rope, and one comm unit just like the one Dugu had been using as a camera. I'd lifted it from the communications room three days earlier.

\<You sure this thing will survive underwater?\> I asked.

\<If eel skin works for the messages they send with the mantas, it'll work for the comm.\>

I pulled an eel-skin bag from my pocket. Made from a moray's tail, it had a broad opening on one end and tapered to a point on the other. I stuffed the comm unit inside and carefully folded over the wide end, then folded it the opposite way, as if I were making a fan from paper. Eight folds in, I stopped and used my weighted bag to hold it in place.

I stepped to the wall and reached for the closest of several crabs. Damn things were everywhere.

<No,> said Pol. <You need a blue one.>

<Are you sure?>

<Yes, I'm sure. Don't you remember the deckhands sending a message ahead when we were getting close to Selaita?>

<I remember, but I didn't see what kind of crab they used.>

<Yes, you did. I see through your eyes, you know.>

<I guess I wasn't paying attention.>

<Obviously.>

<Give me a break, will you? Don't you ever miss anything?>

<No.>

I rubbed my face with my hands. Arguing with Pol could be exasperating. A quick search of the balcony yielded no blue crabs, so I went to the rooftop and trapped three in the flag I usually wore as a scarf. I brought them back down to the balcony and dropped to my hands and knees. Carefully, I held the rear of the first crab's shell with one hand and directed its left claw with the other. Forcing the pincers around the folded eel skin, I pinched off the leg's last segment with a twist.

<Just like a clamp,> said Pol.

I gave the pincers a gentle tug, and they held firm. All I could do was shake my head. Every day, this world managed to find a way to surprise me.

I attached the crab's second set of pincers before apologizing to the declawed creature and tossing it to the sea. Two more crabs, two more pairs of pincers, and I had what should be a watertight seal.

I stuffed the comm unit along with my carving tools and bamboo cuda into the bag and stood before lifting the bag over my shoulder. Heading into the bedroom, I found Sali sitting up on the sleeping mat. "Are you going early again?" she asked.

"I fear what Mmirehl might do to the Falali Mother if I'm not there to be the voice of reason."

She ran her fingers into her unruly hair. "I'll see you tonight?"

"Of course." I tried to smile, but knowing I might never see her again, I only managed a brittle grin.

"Are you okay?"

"I'm fine. Just a little tense." I went to the stairs, stopped, and took one last look back.

Her eyes were saucers brimming with concern. "Please be careful." The words drove deep like a dart to the heart. I couldn't stand the thought of abandoning her. I had to survive the day. Had to.

I took the stairs slow and brushed the front curtain aside to step out. Dugu was there, sitting on the stone with his legs stretched straight out in a V. A little girl sat opposite him, the soles of her feet pressed against his, her legs forming the other half of a four-legged diamond.

Dugu made to stand up, but I stopped him by putting up my hand. "Finish your game first."

"Thank you, sir. This is Dory, my little sister."

I crouched low to look her in the eyes. "Very nice to meet you, Dory. How old are you?"

She held up five fingers. Her face was round like

Dugu's, and her eyes were similarly cheery. She didn't seem to know who I was, her attention already back on trying to toss a seashell into a circle of silk thread resting on the stone.

I stood up straight as Dugu tossed a shell that bounced inside the circle before skipping out to the squealing delight of his sister.

<You sure we're ready for this, Pol?>

<You've developed a solid plan.>

<But so many things could go wrong. We still have four weeks before the Empire's ship arrives. We don't need to rush.>

<We also can't wait until the last minute. Should we fail, we will need all the time we can get to regroup for another try.>

<If I don't get killed or captured.>

<Such thoughts aren't productive, Jakob.>

Right. Not productive.

Dory landed a shell in the circle and clapped at her good fortune. It must have been the winning shot since she and Dugu started gathering up the shells and string.

"Ready, sir?"

I nodded. Ready as I'd ever be.

"Dory's school is on the way to the docks."

"Very well."

Dory lifted her arm to hold her brother's hand, and after a bit of walking, I felt little fingers probing at my palm. Surprised by the unsolicited affection, I took her hand, and the three of us continued as a three-linked chain. Soon I realized the unexpected hand-holding had nothing to do with affection as Dory lifted her feet and expected Dugu and me to swing her. Happy to oblige, we saw to it her feet didn't touch the ground again until we reached her school.

Finally letting go of our hands, she ran for the door. Dugu stopped her with a loud clearing of the throat, then ducked low to receive a kiss on the cheek before telling her to mind her teacher.

Feeling wistful for nieces and nephews I might never see again, I walked the rest of the way in silence. Same for the boat ride to the Ministry. I watched Dugu much of the time, watched how he seemed to find enjoyment in most everything: the sun on his face, the sea spray in the air, the dance of undulating tentacles in the water.

I envied him, the simplicity of his life. I wished I could see things the way he did. I'd been a clock-puncher once, free of all this duplicity and treachery, but the simple life left me wanting. Somehow I was incapable of finding happiness even when it was all around me.

Instead, here I was on this distant world, walking into the Ministry, shivering as I headed downstairs into the underwater coffin I'd grown to hate.

Dismissing Dugu so he could get some breakfast, I strode through the main dome. Water dripped on my head and shoulders. Puddles splashed under my boots. A sour knot gathered inside my belly. One mistake was all it would take. One mistake, and I'd pay the ultimate price.

I went through tunnel after tunnel, feet moving of their own accord. The baths weren't much farther. Time for my massage.

Every day for a week, I'd kept the same routine, setting up my alibi with an early-morning massage followed by a nap.

I turned right, my fingers tingling with uneasy energy. I turned again and stopped in my tracks. Mmirehl was there, standing outside his mysterious hatch. The door was open, and a pair of black sashes came from the opposite direction, escorting a short Jebyl man with hands tied before him.

Beleaux.

My breath snagged in my throat like a fishhook. I hadn't seen Beleaux since the day I rented his boat. The day I killed Kell.

Mmirehl lowered his buzzard head for a beaky look at his catch. "Take him inside."

Beleaux saw me. His eyes met mine, and my stomach wrenched at the thought he could recognize me.

Me. The man underneath this disguise.

<Stay cool, Jakob. He won't remember you from before. Your face was full of implants.>

"Bless-ed, Colonel," called Beleaux. "Please don't let them take me."

<See, he believes you are Kell.>

"You are the champion of Falal!" he called, as they dragged him through the hatch. "You will rescue me!"

I coughed into my hand to cover the fact that I'd been holding my breath. Mmirehl turned to give me one of his steel-eyed grins before disappearing through the hatch. Beleaux's desperate pleas continued to worm into my ears until the hatch door thankfully shut with a clang.

I didn't know what to feel. Relief I hadn't been recognized? Fear that Mmirehl had inexplicably inched closer to discovering me? Concern for Beleaux and the uncertain fate he faced? Guilt for thinking of Beleaux last?

I forced my feet forward. I gave the Falali Mother's hatch a longing stare as I passed, wishing I could spend the rest of the day in her calming presence.

<Captain Mmirehl is more clever than I thought,> said Pol. <He must have gone through the customs records one at a time until he found a foreigner who couldn't be accounted for when he had them all rounded up. Once he had your old identity pinned down, he probably interviewed the hotel staff, who sent him to Beleaux.>

I felt numb from the hairs on my head all the way down to my toenails. <It's over, Pol. He's going to figure out I've taken Kell's place.>

<I wouldn't be so sure, Jakob. He still has a big leap of imagination to make, and leaps like that are rare. In any event, be glad we're taking out the missile system today. With success, the biggest hurdle to the Empire's return will be cleared. After today, our work will be near completion.>

I entered another corridor and passed another set of guards before turning into the baths. Greeted by a hot cloud of sulfur-scented vapors, I walked across the damp rock floor. To my right, terraced pools of turquoise springwater burbled under bright lights. Like a tiered fountain, frothy overflow cascaded from one tiled travertine to the next. Overhead, a vaulted ceiling came together in a steamy fusion of stone and steel.

The pools were unoccupied except for one. Admiral Dii Mnai sat on the rim with his feet dangling in the water. His skin was slick and shiny from a recent dip. He was naked, knees apart, his stomach covering his private parts effectively as any bathing suit.

<Make sure he sees you,> said Pol. <You can't ask for a better alibi.>

I walked alongside a chiseled rock gutter that collected freshwater into tanks. Mnai was flanked by two topless women sitting cross-legged with bowls on their laps. The admiral reached for one of the bowls and selected an exotic fruit I'd never seen before. He took a bite of the round, red fruit and loosed a watery spray. I stepped closer until he spotted me, his smile dripping with juice and self-satisfaction.

"Colonel!" he called, like I was the new arrival at a holiday bash. Behind him rested two wine bottles, one empty and lying on its side.

"Admiral," I said with a nod. "I trust you are enjoying yourself."

"The fruit is delicious," he said with a wink and a vague wave of his hand that left me uncertain whether he was referring to the fruit or the breasts. "We're winning, you know."

"Winning what?"

"The battle against the resistance. Captain Mmirehl has made much progress. It won't be much longer before it's completely crush-ed. Stability will be restore-ed. Isn't that what your precious Sire values most?"

"Yes. But he's not my Sire anymore."

"No. You betray-ed him, didn't you?" He wiped the smile from his face. "I'm not fond of traitors, Colonel." He took a meaty chomp of his fruit as if it were a poor substitute for my hindquarters.

The two women kept smiling, but I could see discomfort in the way their spines had stiffened at his tone. I shifted my weight from one foot to the other. <Why is he calling me a traitor, Pol?>

The admiral spoke with a full mouth. "I hear you visit the Falali Mother every day. What do you talk about?"

I stifled a relieved sigh. Was that all this was about? <Give him an answer, Jakob.>

"We talk about life," I said. "She's a very wise woman."

He chewed on his fruit, and—based on his down-turned brows and squinting eyes—he appeared to be chewing on my words, too. "Life? What do you mean by that?"

I carefully chose a response. "She coaches me on the ways of Falal."

"She's trying to turn you against me, isn't she?"

"Of course she is," I said without hesitation. "Did you expect anything else?"

He nodded, wary eyes weighing my words. "I'm glad you can still be honest with me, Colonel. Don't let that change. You've come for one of your massages?"

He knew my routine. I should've been elated my alibi was falling into place so nicely, but instead, my insides squirmed with the knowledge he'd been checking up on me. His message was clear: I'm watching you.

"Yes," I said, forcing a smile. "My back has been bothering me since the cuda attack. The massages seem to help."

He tossed his half-eaten fruit into one of the bowls and rinsed his fingers in the water. To the women, he said, "I'm done here. Dry me."

With a bow of my head, I moved past. <I have a bad feeling about this, Pol. We should wait another day.>

<No. The missile system must be destroyed, or the Empire's ship won't be able to land.>

<Don't you worry how he's going to react? He's already letting Mmirehl arrest anybody suspicious. What will he do when we make the resistance appear real?>

Reaching the far side of the pools, I ducked to enter a tunnel of rock. Geothermally heated walls baked my exposed hands and face. Sweat broke out on my forehead and in my armpits.

<We've talked about this, Jakob. Fooling him

into pursuing a resistance that doesn't exist is a good thing.>

<No matter what damage he does?>

<*Especially* because of the damage he can do. But really, how much damage can he do in four weeks? The new contingent will remove him from power soon enough.>

I entered a small stone room, stood straight, and hung my bag from a metal spike jammed into a fissure. Following my regular routine, I stripped out of my uniform, folded the clothes, and set them on a bench before taking a silk waistwrap from the pile and covering myself. Crouching low, sweat dripping from my brow, nose, and elbows, I walked down a low-ceilinged tunnel into a tight space with a stone table at its center. The masseuse was there, as usual, sitting on a stool in the corner next to a bucket of cold water she could use to keep herself cool. Every day, she'd sat in the same spot, waiting for anybody to request her services, which never seemed to happen in the mornings, myself excluded. Evidently, much of the admiral's government liked to sleep late.

I climbed onto the table, its edges worn smooth from centuries of use. Lying facedown on the hot stone, warmth radiated into my thighs, stomach, and chest.

I let her work my back for a while, but I was incapable of relaxing, my teeth clenched tight enough to make my jaw ache.

She pounded my shoulders with closed fists. "Your muscles are wound tighter than a whirlpool's spiral."

"Leave me be," I said in fist-pounding vibrato. "I want to nap."

And like she had every time before, she told me she'd see to it I wasn't disturbed.

Down the tunnel she went before disappearing to wait obediently in the cool of the main corridor for me to retrieve her when I woke.

One hour.

I had one hour.

I slipped off the table and down the tunnel, where I grabbed my bag off the spike and hustled barefoot in the opposite direction of the baths. Reaching a seldom-used service corridor, I leaned into the cool air to look both ways. As expected, the corridor was empty.

I dashed for the air lock, my bare feet making hardly a sound on the cold steel. Greased by sweat, my feet skidded to a stop, and I knelt before a murky aquarium resting on the floor. Pushing aside the plastic tubing, I reached through the surface scum and air bubbles all the way to the gravelly bottom of the tank. Tentacles snaked between my fingers and wrapped my wrist. I pulled the creature from the water and looked into its emotionless eye. "You better keep me alive, you hear me?"

With my free hand, I spun the hatch wheel, climbed inside the air lock, and sealed myself in. I hit the button on the wall.

A red light flashed as the small space pressurized. Feeling the sting in my ears, I pinched my nose and blew to equalize. I dropped the bag off my shoulder to keep it from getting tangled with the octopus before taking a deep breath and lifting the creature to my face. Cringing, I watched suckered tentacles reach and take hold. The creature made the transfer and moved to the top of my head. With a shudder, I eyed the strange appendage as it crept alongside my nose. Curse the geneticist who had engineered these creatures.

Soon the appendage was in my mouth, burrowing down my throat. Knowing what to expect couldn't keep me from gagging. Wracking coughs filled the chamber until my body adjusted, and I started breathing evenly, lungs ballooning in and out.

Frigid seawater ran across the floor and instantly chilled my feet. Already shivering, I felt the water climb my legs, every inch a shock to my sauna-heated skin. Swirling water soaked into my waistwrap, then up my chest to finally take my shoulders and head.

The flashing red light now glowed green. Remembering to loop my bag back over my tentacle-tied shoulder, I spun the outer hatch wheel and opened the door onto the cold black of deep ocean. To my right, a row of underwater lamps on posts glowed in the murk. I stepped toward the first of the lights, knowing they led to the underwater turbines that powered the Ministry.

With its own submerged sources of electricity and freshwater, the Ministry was remarkably easy to defend. If any of the Empire's previous contingents ever found themselves under attack from the locals, all they'd had to do was lock themselves in and call for reinforcements, who could easily bomb a mob of any size into submission. It was little wonder the Empire's control had lasted for millennia.

Until Kell's daring betrayal.

I reached the first lamp and took hold of a guide rope attached to the post. Hand over hand, I pulled myself toward the second post, my feet kicking through sand and gravel.

From here the plan was simple. Soon, I'd reach the turbines, at which point I'd turn right to swim up the rock face to the shallower water that washed over the reef. From there, it would be a short underwater swim to the Ministry's ring-shaped island, where I'd stay as deep as the reef would allow until I reached the missile platform.

I was still worried the guards might spot my submarining approach, but Pol and I agreed that if the water was deep enough to support the draft of the ship Mathus had used to transport the missile system, it should be deep enough for me to avoid notice. Besides, the guards would be looking out, not down.

I reached the second post and continued for the third. I would've smiled if my mouth weren't stuffed. Mmirehl was a cunning bastard, but so was I. Cunning enough to con him into keeping the missiles hidden under a broad tent that would shroud my climb from the water.

Approaching the next post, I spotted a large object

to my left. I strained my eyes to see through the green-black water. <What is that?>

<I can't tell.>

I needed to keep moving. But the object was so out of place in this barren wasteland of sand and stone. Letting go of the guide rope, I veered in its direction. A sack. A tattered sack sitting inside a triangle of large rocks.

Getting close, I could see ropes twined around the cloth with more ropes running to the rocks. I moved closer. Small fish darted out of my way to hover a short ways off.

Kneeling in front of the sack, I peered through a footlong gash in the cloth. But it was too dark to see. I reached into my bag and pulled out a knife, along with one of the glowgrubs. After impaling the grub, I held my makeshift torch close and looked through the tear.

Crabs. A teeming mass of them bumped and scrabbled over top of each other. I pulled one out and dropped it to the sand. Then another, and another.

The last had something pinched in its claws. With sickness stewing in my gut, I watched it eat. Bladelike mouthparts picked off one morsel after another and shoved them into a chitinous grinder.

<You know what he's eating?> asked Pol.

I did. The size of a coin purse. The swooping seashell curves.

A human ear.

Dropping the crab, I ripped through the cloth with my knife. I peeled back the flaps to look at the face. The eyes were gone, the tail end of an eel wriggling from one eye socket. The lipless mouth hung open, a missing tooth on the lower right.

Right where the arms dealer's gold tooth used to stand.

I stood up. Black water pressed down on me. I could feel it seeping into my pores and sinking into my bones. Chilled to my core, I swept my eyes left and right to take in the dozens of sack outlines standing like ghosts on the edge of night.

Sire, help us.

CHAPTER 19

> "Certainty is the foundationn upon which
> unconscionable action is builtt. But it's a
> foundation that eventualy eroddes to leave yor
> conscience standing naked beforeyour actions."
>
> —JAKOB BRYCE

I was so tired. So, so tired.

Bursting lungs screamed for oxygen. I'd stayed under too long. So long that the octopus had weakened to the point it felt like my breathing tube had been stuffed with wet cotton balls.

But the surface wasn't much farther. I sucked hard at the tube in my throat to receive only the tiniest sip of oxygen. I tried to kick my feet, but my legs barely fluttered in water that felt like molasses. Chasing a small cluster of air bubbles, I somehow managed to keep rising, my eyes nearing the rippling ribbon of light. Just a few more inches.

My head broke the surface, and I had to concentrate to keep from sinking back under. The octopus retracted from my throat, and I resisted the urge to gasp for fear of being heard by the guards. Instead, I took slow, deep, delicious breaths.

I was under the cover of the missile platform's tent. I looked up at the patchwork tent made from swaths of leather crudely sewn together with twine. A pole stood on either side of the missile tower, thus giving the tent two peaks. Walls of leather stretched down to where ropes wrapped around poles standing in the water behind my back.

Regaining some strength, I took my bag from my shoulder and quietly pushed it up out of the water onto the stone floor. Hooking my hands over the stone, I lunged upward but only managed to pull my shoulders out of the water. I kicked at the barnacled wall and felt the sharp sting of shells slicing through skin. Bracing against the pain, I scrambled for footing among the blades, and, with a final excruciating push, I lifted my hips from the water.

Lying facedown on the stone, my lungs heaved air in and out, in and out. I rolled over and sat up. My feet still dangled in the water, red stains pluming like smoke from barnacle-chewed skin.

I didn't care. My mind was already sinking back under the water, sinking all the way down to the horror of the underwater graveyard. So many bodies.

<Excellent work, Jakob.>

The compliment barely penetrated my senses. So many bodies. Most had been wrapped in cloth. A few had been left bare to the cruel indifference of the sea and the hungry mandibles of the crabs. I could still see their bloated souls straining to break free of their anchored restraints. I'd found others who had been reduced to small spreads of bones picked clean of skin, muscle, and humanity.

Having almost forgotten where I was, I was returned to the present by the touch of tentacles slithering down my torso as the octopus worked its way down the back of my neck. Careful to make as little noise as possible, I opened my bag and emptied the contents.

The octopus dropped off my back with a wet slap that made me wince for fear the guards outside the tent would hear. Some tentacles wormed across the stone while others twisted and tangled under its melon-shaped body. Carried atop the writhing knot, the octopus propelled itself toward the sea.

I lowered my bag into the water and held it open. "Here you go," I whispered. "A nice little cave."

The octopus went over the stone lip and dropped into the bag with barely a splash. Tentacles followed like suckered snakes tapering to lizard tails before disappearing.

Pinning one of the bag's straps under a stone, I let the rest of the bag hang in the water so the octopus could regain its strength. I needed it for the return trip to the deep-water airlock.

<Your feet, Jakob.>

<Yes.> I scooted back and pulled my bleeding feet from the water. The last thing I needed was another blessing of the cuda.

<Check to see if the comm still works.>

I drew my knife and cut the comm unit out of the eel-skin pouch. With a touch, the screen lit.

<Excellent,> said an excited Pol. <You need to find the missile system's power switch.>

I went to the spiral staircase and started up, tracking bloody footprints all the way to the top. I rested a hand on one of the missiles and felt the cold steel. Long as I was tall, one end had a pointed tip, the other end a trio of small wings that stood out like feathers on an arrow.

A power cord ran through a small hole on the lagoon side of the tent and traced a path to a control board. I searched the front of the board with my eyes, the back with my fingers until I touched upon the switch.

<Got it,> I told Pol.

His voice was calm and professional now. <Put the comm unit in connect mode first. Then turn off the control board and turn it back on. That will sever the connection to the Ministry's computer and give you control.>

I did as instructed, and a few seconds later, the comm unit's screen asked for a passcode. Pol recited a code that I tapped into the screen.

Error.

Pol spelled out the next code. They'd preloaded all the manufacturers' codes into his consciousness before they implanted him in my head. But he couldn't be certain which code would unlock this particular board. Each manufacturer had several codes, depending on model and manufacture date.

Error.

I kept cool, trusting in Pol, trusting in his abilities. I entered the digits he spoke into my mind, knowing a team could already be coming to investigate. The alert would've gone up in the underwater control room the instant I turned off the power.

We would've done this remotely if we could have, but as a security measure, the manufacturers' backdoor codes required a manual reset of the control board's power. That way, the backdoor passcode couldn't be used even if it fell into the wrong hands, unless the Empire's Army let you through the front door to flip the power.

Red letters blinked on the screen. Another error.

<That's three failures, Pol.>

<Not to worry. I only have two more.>

<You sure one will work?>

He responded by starting into the next code. I tapped out the letters and numbers as fast as I could, my heartbeat quickly catching up to my finger's pace.

I tapped out the last digit and held my breath until the screen unlocked and blossomed with controls. <Thank the Sire,> I said. <What now?>

Pol efficiently directed me through the steps, the two of us working as if we were one brain instead of two.

The countdown timer started. Five minutes . . . four fifty-nine . . . four fifty-eight . . .

<Move, Jakob.>

My wounded feet stung with every step as I circled down the stairs. Reaching the bottom, I hustled to the water's edge, where I stopped to pick up the rope and the bamboo cuda fish I'd finished carving that morning. My nerves stayed calm as I tied a knot around the cuda's tail. According to Pol, the blast would be modest. We had only set the timer for one of the missiles, and it was only the missile's hull-piercing head that would detonate instead of the entire warhead.

Still, the guards would be pulped by the force of the explosion. The domes would be sprayed with shrapnel, and any boats docked nearby would be shredded. Many would die, but mine was a righteous mission.

The Empire's return would be a blessing far greater than the kiss on my cheek. I knew the Empire was flawed, but the new contingent would make its best effort to rule this world with fairness. I didn't doubt that was the best thing for Maritinia. No more of Mnai's paranoia. No more black sashes. No more waterlogged mass graves.

The octopus was in place, and my bag was on my back, restocked with heavy rocks. With the roped cuda in my hand, I slipped into the water with serene efficiency. I kicked for the bottom, my eyes already fo-

cusing on a knobby piece of coral close to the atoll's
wall of rock.

I wrapped the other end of the rope around the
coral and tied off. Releasing the bamboo cuda from my
hand, I watched it shoot upward and stop several feet
below the surface. I took a moment to watch it bob and
sway on its line. Protected by the atoll's rock face, Pol
thought the cuda would survive the explosion.

To be the calling card of the so-called resistance.

<Excellent, Jakob.>

My arms and legs swept through the water like a
frog's. Pol's voice was jubilant in my head. <You've
done our Sire a great service. Now nothing can stop
the Empire from retaking its rightful place as the
rulers of this world.>

Salt water stung my feet as I upped my pace to
the maximum my octopus-fed lungs would allow.
Branches of purple-and-orange coral passed below my
chest as I slalomed through patches of kelp and around
a cluster of jellyfish. I plowed through a school of shiny
silver minnows that pecked harmlessly at my skin. I
ducked under an amoeba the size of my head, gelatinous arms oozing in random directions.

I could see the reef's edge now, could see where it
gave way to the plummeting black of deep water.

A cuda swam into view.

My pounding heart jumped into another gear, and
my cheek started to throb. I wished I could turn around
and swim the other way. But I couldn't. Not now.

I tracked the cuda with my eyes as it darted through

a stand of kelp before skirting the atoll's wall with swift flicks of its tail. It hadn't seen me, hadn't smelled my blood in the water. Not yet.

I pushed for deeper water, hoping it might not follow. The cuda was big. The biggest I'd seen, as long as one of the missiles and almost as thick around. Battle scars ran down its flank, and its tail was ripped and weathered like an old flag.

The cuda spotted me. Its long head angled in my direction, and an instant later, the entire streamlined body lined up like an airborne spear. It was close. Close enough I could see a piece of seaweed hanging from its teeth.

But it didn't attack. Instead, it seemed to hang in the water, staring me down like an accusing finger.

The concussion struck. My ears stung, and my chest tightened before a push of water tumbled me over. I righted myself and searched for the cuda. I looked left and right, up and down.

The angry soul was gone.

But I could still feel its scolding stare. I could feel it in the tingle of my cheek.

CHAPTER 20

"Right and wrongg, why must one alwys bleed
into teh other?"

–JAKOB BRYCE

I exited the air lock and dropped the octopus in its tank
before sneaking down the corridor. I was cold, chilled
by deep water, and doubly chilled by my second pass
through the underwater graveyard.

Nearing the end of the corridor, I pressed up to a
steel wall that felt like ice against my wet skin. I inched
my face toward the bulkhead and edged an eye past
the corner.

Clear.

To avoid tracking bloody footprints, I walked with
my right foot wrapped in my bag. My left foot, I'd had

to bundle it in my waistwrap. Which left the rest of me naked. I clenched my teeth to keep them from chattering and peeked into the stone-carved waiting room outside the massage cave.

Clear.

Shivering, I entered the saunalike room and luxuriated in the warm glow of relief. I'd made it back unseen. Whatever came next, this phase of my mission was complete.

I ducked behind a shower curtain to wash the salt off my skin and out of my hair. I rinsed my bag, same with the waistwrap.

"Colonel!" The voice echoed from the rock tunnel leading to the baths. "Colonel!"

I poked my head over the curtain and saw the flicker of shadows coming down the tunnel before Dugu burst into the room. "Colonel," he said. "You must come quickly. There's been an explosion."

"What kind of explosion?"

"The missile system. It's gone."

"Gone?" I asked, feigning a mix of shock and outrage. "How can that be?"

I told him to wait outside until I dressed. I quickly dried, using a coarse mammoth-wool towel before slipping back into my uniform. Ignoring the pain, I crammed my wounded feet into socks and boots.

I met Dugu outside the baths and hustled to keep step with his double-timing pace. "Don't ask," he said before I could speak. "It's best you see for yourself."

We journeyed down one empty corridor after another. Other than the guards outside Mmirehl's torture chamber, we didn't pass a single soul until we reached a somber crowd outside the main control room. We forced our way through the soldiers and black sashes packing the entryway. Inside, Kwuba technicians huddled over terminals and stared at the wall of video screens. With hushed voices and wringing hands, they shook their heads in confusion and disbelief. How could such a thing happen?

Afraid of the carnage I might see on the video screens, I kept marching, eyes straight ahead. Exiting the other side of the dome, I let Dugu lead me through ankle-high floodwater toward the long staircase that led topside. I didn't want to go up. Didn't want to know the extent of the damage. Didn't want to know how many I'd killed.

I told myself to stay strong. I'd done my job. A job that had to be done. Mnai and Mmirehl had to be overthrown.

Starting up the staircase, I concentrated on steeling my thoughts. We passed the first bulkhead and continued upward, my feet falling into the rhythm of the stairs, my mind fully focused. I had to build a wall against the ugly truth of my violent actions.

Step by step.

Brick by brick.

Reaching the top, we walked past the unattended water pumps. The machinery cranked and whined and spat high-pressure needles of water that pelted my uniform and stung the backs of my hands. Jebyl workmen packed the doorway that led outside.

Dugu whistled to signal our approach. Wearing glum frowns and grease-stained waistwraps, the workers moved aside. I walked into the light breeze that smelled of smoke. Sunbeams slanted through the arched doorway, twinkling motes of dust drifting in its glare.

I stepped into the sunlight. The atoll's rock floor was dusted with ash and charred chunks of bamboo. Looking to the far side of the ringed island, I could see that the missile platform was gone, a water-filled crater sitting in its place. The usually resplendent lagoon was dulled by a scummy film. My boots crunched on grit and debris as Dugu led me past the cries of a bloodied man suffering too many wounds to count.

I spun around slowly to take in the full panorama of my destruction. The archway of the dome I'd exited was pocked and scarred. Patches of silver tile had been stripped away from the dome, exposing swaths of naked stone. To my left, a damaged boat listed in the waves, its deck bustling with Jebyl who feverishly bailed water. I counted five bodies on the quay, their crumpled forms strewn about like dirty socks on the floor.

Dizzy, I steadied myself by taking hold of Dugu's shoulder.

The injured man called at my back. "Colonel? Is that you?"

I closed my eyes. Hadn't I done enough? I shouldn't have to see any of this devastation.

"Give me your blessing, Colonel."

I cracked open my eyes.

Dugu stared at the ground. "I don't think he'll last much longer, sir."

I took my hand off Dugu's shoulder and went to the wounded man. Seeing my approach, he started to smile, but his grin quickly devolved into a grimace of bared teeth. His uniform had been shredded into blood-drenched rags. Same with his skin.

I knelt next to him, pebbles of debris trapped painfully under my knees. He lifted a hand and reached for my cheek but only made it halfway before his arm started shaking.

Taking his hand, I pulled it the rest of the way, pressed it against my scarred cheek. "In life and death, we are all one with Falal."

His eyes became a little less desperate, his breathing a little less labored. As he languished, his arm weighed heavy in my grasp. I lowered it and rested it by his side.

His eyes became distant, and I watched him fade a few minutes more before his breathing withered to nothing.

<War is ugly, Jakob.>

I stood. I made no effort to wipe his blood from my hands. His blood belonged on my hands.

<Jakob, I know this is painful, but you must remember you've saved many more lives than you've taken. Thanks to you, the Empire's new contingent

will be able to land safely. That's a hundred lives you've saved.>

I heard Pol's words and knew they were true, but they didn't make me feel any less pained. I doubted they ever would.

I heard a splash and turned to see a soldier who had dived into the lagoon. A Jebyl workman dove in next. Leaving rippling trails of clear water, the two of them swam through the surface scum toward a body floating a short ways out.

I stayed where I was, aching feet planted to the rock floor. I watched the two men, Kwuba and Jebyl, approach the body. They stopped every few strokes to look back, checking with several men posted around the atoll who had taken the up the task of looking out for cuda fins.

The two men arrived at the body, and I watched them drag my victim through the water. Reaching the stone, they passed the body to a group of soldiers who pulled the waterlogged corpse from the lagoon. The pair of swimmers about-faced and went back out to claim another of the dead.

I held in the tears with the stoic poise of an officer and a veteran. Instead, I let the tears rain down inside me.

I remembered the last time I'd seen bodies floating in the lagoon. Kell had stood in almost this very spot to supervise the brutal slaughter of the Empire's contingent, and my drowning heart gasped with the painful realization that I'd found another way to become him.

With each word, Mmirehl poked the table using a pointed finger. "They will pay for this."

Sitting at the head of the conference-room table, Admiral Mnai held my carved cuda fish in his hands. It had been found a half hour ago. Right where I'd left it tied underwater.

Mmirehl pecked out another sentence, hand bobbing like a bird. "The traitors have gone too far."

"How did they do this?" asked the admiral. He tossed the bamboo cuda onto the table. It bounced once, twice, and skidded to a stop. "How?"

Sitting between two lieutenants, I stayed silent. My eyes were on the cuda, my mind drifting out to sea, out to where the ancient cuda had stared me down. It must've smelled my blood in the water. It should've attacked.

But it didn't.

"Tell me, Colonel. How did they do this?"

I lowered my bloodstained palm from my cheek—couldn't remember putting it there. Reluctantly, I pulled my gaze off the bamboo carving and turned to the admiral. He sat forward in his chair, his fat gut compressing into the shape of a powder keg, eyes burning like a fuse inside his cannonball head.

"I can't be sure," I said wryly. "They probably hit one of the missiles with a rock."

The admiral's stare looked ready to detonate. I turned to Mmirehl, whose eyes quizzed up as if he had to wonder if such a thing was really possible. "Can't be," he said after another moment's thought. "The technicians report-ed losing control of the system before the explosion. The system was hijack-ed."

"They seized control of the system?" I shook my head as if Mmirehl's words were a stunning revelation. "Even I wouldn't know how to hijack a weapons system."

The admiral's thick fingers squeezed into blunt fists. "The resistance didn't do this on their own. Those ingrates are even more ignorant of technology than we are." The fists came together on the table. "They had help from the Empire's spies."

"Agreed," I said. "I don't see how else they could've done it."

"The Empire will be coming soon, won't they?"

I nodded gravely.

"I need options," the admiral said.

"There's nothing we can do to stop them," I replied. "If they can land, they will retake Maritinia."

"We can fight," said Mmirehl. "You said they wouldn't bring an army."

I scoffed with as much derision as I could muster. "Trust me, with their technology, they don't need an army. Our only chance is a new air-defense system."

"And where will we find one of those?" asked the captain.

I put my eyes square on his. "We need to talk to Mathus. He'll have something we can buy."

Mmirehl crossed his arms over his narrow chest. "Mathus is gone."

"I know," I said with innocent sincerity. "But he might not have left orbit yet. Even if he has, he couldn't have gotten far. We can enable the offworld antenna to send him a message."

Mmirehl's face tightened, jagged features sharpening. "We can't."

"Why not?" I asked, secretly enjoying the opportunity to play dumb. I wanted to hear him say what he did. Wanted to hear him say he tortured the man and left him to rot on the bottom of the ocean. And I wanted to know why.

Mmirehl twisted in his chair, lips pinched into a tight pucker.

"We still have a missile," said the admiral with a breath of hope in his voice. "Mathus gave us a spare. It's store-ed with all the other supplies in Dome 4."

"It won't help without a launch system," I said. "We need to contact Mathus right away."

"No," said Admiral Mnai. "That is not going to happen."

I leaned back in my chair. <He knows what happened to Mathus.>

<Yes, Jakob. Captain Mmirehl must have acted with the admiral's approval.>

I opened my mouth to protest once more, but the admiral wouldn't hear it. "We cannot contact Mathus," he said.

"Why not?"

"He's dead," he said with no trace of emotion. "He

knew too much about our defenses. We couldn't trust he wouldn't sell that information to the Empire."

"You killed him?"

"No. I protect-ed us. Everything we've built."

I tossed my bloodstained hands. "Then we have no more options. The Empire will take Maritinia."

The sour twist to his lips said he'd come to the same conclusion.

Silence reigned for a time, and I used the opportunity to prepare for my next move. I knew where this conversation had to go, where I needed to lead it.

I looked into the admiral's eyes and held them in place with the force of my gaze. "It's over, Admiral. Free Maritinia is doomed."

He didn't fight it. He knew. The man was crazy but not at all stupid.

"You only have one choice," I said. "You have to run and hide. We all have to run and hide." I looked to the other faces around the table, met them one by one with a determined stare. Mmirehl slumped in his chair. The two lieutenants' shoulders sagged with defeat.

Confidence surged inside me. The regime's power players were ready to quit. The government was ready to topple. My goal was close. So close I could actually end it and end it now.

A year and a half ago, I was just a paper-shuffling bureaucrat. But I'd turned myself into a force. A spy so cunning he could infiltrate the enemy's innermost circle. An assassin so lethal he could crush a regime all by himself. I clenched a fist and felt the course of history in my grasp. Squeezing down, a rush of power rippled up my spine. The surge was so strong it sent tingles to my fingers and toes.

I dropped my fist on the table. "We're all dead." I let my voice rise to an impassioned pitch. "We can't fight them with machetes and firerods. Do you understand what kinds of weapons they'll unleash upon us? Bullets so smart they can enter one ear and exit the other before taking out the next man. Flash bombs that will fry our eyes inside our skulls. Gas grenades that will melt our lungs. We can't afford to waste time. We need to get as far as we can. We can make it if we abandon the Ministry now."

I had them. I could see it in their faces, that perfect mix of fear and hope that could compel any man to action. I coaxed them along with my own nodding until I scored nods of agreement from each of the lieutenants. Then Captain Mmirehl.

Only the admiral resisted. But his defenses were cracking, worry lines spreading from the corners of his eyes and mouth. I had to keep at him. A few more blows with my verbal hammer, and Free Maritinia would crumble.

The admiral looked to the hatchway, and I pulled the reins on my next words. Somebody was coming, footsteps clapping quickly down the corridor outside the conference room.

Out of breath, Sali leaned through the hatchway

and searched the room with wide eyes. "Oh, thank Falal," she said upon spotting me, then her father.

Despite my frustration at the interruption, my heart swelled with the knowledge that she cared for me.

"You heard the explosion from Maringua?" asked Mnai.

"Y-yes," she said, her eyes starting to mist. "I thought the Ministry was under attack."

The admiral was out of his chair, walking to her, his hands held wide. "Come, child."

She ran to him, and he swallowed her in his embrace. He closed his eyes and buried his nose in her hair. "Shush, child. We're fine. The missile platform was sabotage-ed, but we were perfectly safe down here."

With a twist of her head, she found daylight through the crook of his elbow, her teary eye finding me. To keep from upsetting her further, I hid my bloodstained hands below the table and told her everything was okay with a smile.

Mnai released his hug and put his big hands on her shoulders. "If you thought the Empire was attacking, why did you come here? You should've stayed away."

"I was worried," she said.

"That's my brave girl. Have you eaten? How about we go to the kitchen, and I'll cook something for you like I used to?"

She nodded and wiped water from her eyes.

He led her to the hatchway. I stayed in my seat, my

mind trying to reconcile the two men, ruthless tyrant and tender parent.

"The responsibilities of fatherhood are calling," said the admiral. "This meeting is over."

Mnai followed her out and disappeared for a few seconds before returning to fill the hatchway. He leveled a grin so cold it felt like icy fingers had gripped my soul. "You should take a lesson in courage from my daughter, Colonel. We will not abandon our people like loathsome cowards. Talk like a traitor again, and I'll cut your tongue from your mouth."

CHAPTER 21

"Someithmes you choose your fate. Other timeas
fate choouses you."

—JAKOB BRYCE

The computer screen said my message had been sent.
In a few hours, the Empire's new contingent would receive the encoded datagram: *all's clear*.

I looked through the communications-room door
to the partly flooded control room. Blinking lights reflected on the floodwater. Dugu sat at a computer terminal by the water's edge. Blank-eyed, he stared off to
nowhere. Behind him, Kwuba technicians pretended
to work. They tapped their screens and pointed fingers
at numbers they didn't understand. One urgently stood

and went to hover over a different terminal as if it were capable of something the others weren't. It wasn't.

I couldn't blame them. I'd be doing the same thing if I'd failed to stop the attack on the missile tower. Like them, I'd be feverishly jumping from terminal to terminal, hoping the mirage of productivity could save me from the admiral's ire.

I looked down at the box sitting next to my chair, a stash of comm units piled inside. To this point, nobody had noticed one was missing. If I'd known I was going to land such an easy opportunity as this to return the comm I'd stolen, I wouldn't have left it to be destroyed by the explosion. Not that it mattered. The techs were so flummoxed, I doubted they'd ever realize a device so small could control a system as big as the missile platform.

<Jakob, check the secret in-box to see if we've received a new message.>

Entering the in-box, I found a message waiting. I opened it and stared at the coded message until Pol had time to memorize the seemingly random string of characters.

<Got it, Jakob. I'll translate it later.>

I closed and deleted the message. <Are we done now?>

<Yes.>

I turned off the interplanetary link, and Maritinia returned to hushed silence. I logged out and stretched my arms over my head, muscles groaning like ropes pulled taut.

<See, Jakob? I told you the techs wouldn't suspect a thing.> Pol was right. I'd easily conned them into letting me use the communications-room computer by telling them I would try to locate the source of the security breach.

<What now, Pol?>

<I think it's best you turn your focus to playing the good soldier until the Empire arrives.>

<I thought my continuing job was to sow discontent.>

<You've already planted the seeds of fear and mistrust. Now, we stand back and let them flourish.>

<The admiral won't quit, Pol. He's going to fight.>

<Yes, but you saw his officers. They are afraid for their lives. It's only a matter of time before they start turning on each other. As long as the Falali Mother stays locked up, Jebyl unrest will continue to grow. His support among them is already lost. To keep the uprisings under control, the admiral will have to spread his limited forces wide. Trust me, Free Maritinia won't survive a small but concentrated attack.>

<Neither will the Empire.> The words slipped out too fast to pull back. So fast I didn't even know such a revelation existed in my mind. But the staggering truth was incontrovertible. The Empire was spread so thin, it couldn't withstand a concentrated attack without consolidating forces and ceding immense swaths of territory.

The Empire was on the verge of a massive contraction. I was sure of it. I'd seen how these people regarded the Empire with suspicion and defiance. How many other worlds felt the same way? How many others were ready to rise against their perceived oppressors? The Empire's total collapse might even be possible. Kell understood that, or he wouldn't have dared to rebel.

That was why Maritinia was so critical. It had to be tamed or remain a symbol to all who believed revolution was possible.

Pol stayed silent. Eerily silent. Unease slithered around my spine. Had I actually put voice to such a dangerous thought? How could I be so stupid? I knew better, dammit.

The E³ didn't tolerate seditious attitudes. Careers and lives had been ruined for much less. Say too much, and even my father wouldn't be able to protect me. The silence dragged on, my nerves tingling, my face flushing.

Finally, he spoke, his words slipping into my mind with the incisive precision of a scalpel. <You said our glorious Empire wouldn't survive an attack. Explain yourself.>

My heart drummed wild beats. I told myself to stay cool. He couldn't read my mind. Couldn't see the panic gripping my psyche. If I spun this right, I could salvage the situation.

I spoke firmly into the rabbit hole. No hint of fear. <I know it's not my place to question the generals' wisdom, but I can't help but worry. If the admiral

could overthrow the Empire's contingent, the Maritinians might have the confidence to try again. Why didn't they send a whole army to occupy this world?>

<So now you're saying that the Empire's new contingent won't survive attack? Are you telling me that when you originally spoke, you didn't mean the Empire as a whole?>

<Of course I didn't,> I said, amping up the indignation. <That would be ridiculous.>

I held my breath waiting on the response.

<I understand,> he said. I listened close as he continued. <The generals couldn't send a fleet. As you know, the Empire's forces must guard and patrol an impossibly broad expanse of the Outermost Ring.>

I couldn't detect any lingering suspicion in his voice. I let out my breath as quietly as I could. He was always listening.

<Fifty soldiers and another fifty administrators were all they could spare,> he said.

Which I understood to mean the generals were already moving forces to the inner rings. <I know, but I still wish they'd sent more troops.>

<That is why we must be smarter than the forces of chaos, Jakob.>

<Agreed,> I said. <Sire and Empire.>

<Sire and Empire.>

The fear quickly washed away, and I sank into the sands of exhaustion. With Pol, I always had to be the proper spy. The perfect loyalist. I had to play the part.

But I was so damn tired. I already had to dress in the false identity of Colonel Kell. I shouldn't have to wear another mask under that mask.

I put my elbows on my knees and dropped my chin on closed fists. Four more weeks. Four more weeks, and I would be delivered from this tortuous existence.

The admiral appeared with Sali on the far side of the dome. The technicians leaned in close to their screens as if the key to avoiding a death sentence was avoiding eye contact.

Sali hadn't noticed me. Neither had the admiral. They'd spent the entire afternoon together. He put an arm over his daughter's shoulder. I watched to see if she was happy to receive the overdue attention, but I couldn't read her face from this distance. If I could, I'd expect to see dread chewing on her delight. She knew the Empire was coming. She knew she'd lose her father.

She'd lose me, too.

And I'd lose her.

<Pol, are you sure they'll never know?>

<Never know what?>

<Never know who I really am.>

<Of course, Jakob. As I've told you before, when the Empire retakes this world, the new governor will decide the best way to handle the situation. She might announce that Colonel Kell was killed in the attack. Or she might say Colonel Kell is being sent back to Korda for trial. One way or another, your identity will stay secret. These people can never know how the E³ plants its spies. We must protect our methods at all costs.>

<Good.>

<Now tell me why you're asking. You have feelings for her, don't you?>

I knew I should continue to deny it, but I couldn't bear another pretense. Just this once, I decided to admit the truth. <I do.>

Pol didn't speak, but I heard disapproval in his silence.

Sali rose on tiptoes to peck her father's cheek before he stepped away. Left alone, she turned her contented face to the wall of video screens, most of them displaying camera feeds of the topside cleanup. One screen focused on Jebyl workers sweeping debris into the water with brooms made of dried sea fronds. Other screens tracked soldiers who patrolled the ringed island in groups of three and four.

Another screen showed the line of bodies laid out like butchered fish.

Her spine stiffened, as did her arms and shoulders, her carefree bearing hardening into rigid lines.

I was the cause of her anguish. I was the one who murdered those people. I was the one who murdered Colonel Kell. I was the one who had doomed her father to die at the hands of the Empire—no, to be fair, Mnai had done that to himself the moment he decided to lead this rebellion. Still . . .

The compulsion to unburden my soul burned inside. I didn't know how much longer I could stand to hold it all inside. I needed a release. Looking at the box of comm units again, an idea blossomed in my mind.

I gazed up at the ceiling, so Pol couldn't see my hands. I let out a loud sigh to cover any noise as I reached down into the box and nabbed a comm unit. Standing up, I slipped it into my back pocket.

The hatch clanged closed behind me, and heavy with thought, I took my usual seat on the steel floor. I had so much news to share, I didn't know where to start.

The Falali Mother paced across her cell. Stopping a half step from one wall, she about-faced and marched three paces to the opposite wall before spinning around to march back again. Pace, pace, pace, turn. Pace, pace, pace, turn.

"You know," I said, "I've seen caged animals at the zoo who do the same thing."

"Zoo." Turn. "Tell me what a zoo is like." Turn.

"The Sire's Zoo on Korda is gigantic." My voice was flat from fatigue. "It's very close to the palace. It takes at least a week to see the whole thing. They have many thousands of species from all over the Empire."

"And they pace like I do?"

"Just the feisty ones."

She stopped for a moment to give me a wry stare. "Tell me more."

"It's beautiful. So many animals, you wouldn't believe. Birds as colorful as the brightest silks. Bugs that build massive castles out of sand."

"How massive? As big as one of the Ministry domes?"

"Bigger," I said. "As big as a Maritinian city."

"Fascinating," she said, and sat in her chair, eyes twinkling with wonder. "What about large animals? Do they have wild cats?"

"Of course they do." Infected by her enthusiasm, my voice lost its monotone listlessness. "Cats almost as long as mammoths. They have your mammoths and squids, too. There's an entire exhibit dedicated to the creatures created for the technology-restricted worlds."

"Create-ed?"

"Children come to the exhibit to learn about genetics and biology."

"Create-ed?" she repeated.

I gave her a puzzled frown. I didn't understand what she was asking.

Leaving her sandals on the floor, she pulled her knees up to her chest, her robe hanging off the chair like the sheet of an unmade bed. "The natural world and everything in it springs from Falal. The Sire's claim for credit is a lie."

I opened my mouth to refute her claim, but her claim was so far from reality, so far out in the clouds, I had no place to set my foot.

"The Sire is just a man," she said, "one of a long line of extremely powerful men whose technology can do things I can hardly imagine. But creating life itself? I think not. That is the realm of the divine."

<Her ignorance is stunning,> said Pol. <If the people of this world truly believe this nonsense, it's no wonder they turned against us.>

I took a deep breath before giving a history lesson. "The squids and mammoths were engineered to perform specific tasks, and they were brought here by the Empire two thousand years ago. The Empire brought your ancestors, too. They took the poor and starving and gave them this world, like hundreds of other worlds. The Empire assigned some people to the worker class and others to the aristocracy, the Jebyl and Kwuba as you call them now."

She waited for me to finish, an amused expression on her face. "The Empire is most adept at indoctrination."

This was an argument I couldn't win. I didn't know if there was a point to winning anyway. "Tell me," I said, "how do *you* think people arrived on this planet?"

"Really, Colonel, we've been through this before. Maritinia is the living manifestation of Falal. She drinks the sea. She breathes the sky. And she populates both the aquatic and terrestrial planes with spirits. We Kwuba and Jebyl are the terrestrial manifestations of these spirits, while the sea creatures like the squids and cuda are the aquatic."

<You hear these delusions, Jakob? You see now why she's a cultist. She peddles dangerous falsehoods.>

<Yes, but I want to understand her way of thinking.>

<I suppose you are correct. This will be useful information to pass to the new governor.>

I rubbed my chin, hand scraping across whisker stubble. "Have you ever told me how you became the Falali Mother?"

"Souls move from life to life." She lifted her hands and aimed her fingertips at herself. "Currently, the Falali Mother's soul occupies my life."

"But you weren't always the Falali Mother, right? What did you do before you took that title?"

"I was a young girl when I went to live with the sisters. Until then, I did as most young Jebyl do. I dove for crab and urchins. I learn-ed how to manage the squids. I learn-ed how to sew and how to patch a boat."

"How old were you?"

"My father fell ill and die-ed shortly after my ninth year. My mother die-ed giving birth to me. Like many orphan-ed girls, my village sent me to Selaita to become a Falali sister. It had been nineteen years since the previous Falali Mother pass-ed. The Council of Interpreters had been seeking the reappearance of her spirit, and they recognize-ed her spirit in me."

"How did they know?"

"They test-ed me."

"How?"

"They ask-ed me questions. For months and months, they ask-ed me questions of life and meaning. Priestesses came from all over Maritinia to tell me stories and ask me to interpret them. They found the same wisdom in me that they remember-ed in the previous Falali Mother."

"What was your original name?"

"Emmina."

"When was the last time somebody called you Emmina?"

"Since before I was ordain-ed."

"Would you mind if I called you Emmina?"

She grinned self-consciously. "Friend that you are, you can call me whatever you like."

"So, Emmina, you were nine years old, and suddenly you had to become a different person. What was that like?"

"I'm not a different person. I'm the same soul I always was. The same soul through countless lives."

"But you were living a vastly different life until you became the Falali Mother." I scooted up a few inches. "You said yourself, you were crabbing and sewing, then your entire life changed when you went to the city and became the Falali Mother."

"It was what it was."

"But you were a child? Wasn't it hard to become a totally different person?"

She put her feet down on the floor and straightened the robes on her lap. "Why do you ask? Do you want to become a different person?"

I thought before responding. "I already have."

"No you haven't." She shook her head like a disappointed schoolteacher. "You just keep trying on new skins. One of these days, you're going to realize who you are and stop dressing for everybody else."

Her truth flooded over me and soaked into every pore.

"Falal knows who you are," she said. "She bless-ed you, your true self."

<Enough of this claptrap, Jakob. Get on to business.>

I wanted to tell him to shut up. I needed to think. Needed to process.

But I had to keep dressing as the good spy. Time enough to reflect later. I could feel the press of the comm unit in my back pocket and knew I could write it all down. Every pent-up thought and emotion. Tonight. I'd start journaling tonight.

<Jakob? Get to business.>

"I met with the Council of Interpreters," I said.

"And?"

"And it was like you said. They agreed to spread the truth of your incarceration, but they won't act beyond that."

"Don't be disappointed, Colonel. Truth is a powerful thing. It just might bring enough pressure on the admiral to set me free and start negotiating with the Jebyl majority."

I shook my head. "Negotiations won't happen."

"Don't give up hope."

"No, you don't understand." I wrung my hands before breaking the news. "The Empire is coming back."

"How do you know?"

"Their advance spies destroyed the missile-defense system. They'll attack soon."

She put her hand over her heart. "Can they be stopped?"

"No. The admiral will fall. He will be executed along with the other officers. Including me. But the good news is you shouldn't have trouble making peace with the new governor. You'll be free."

"You're wrong," she said. "None of us will be free."

CHAPTER 22

"I can't see what Im typing. I don't even knoow if it's working, but I hpe it is. I have som much to say."

—JAKOB BRYCE

Without opening my eyes, I rested my hand on Sali's stomach, felt the rise and fall of her breathing. She was asleep.

The day was finally over. It seemed an eternity ago that I'd finished carving the bamboo cuda. But that had only been this morning.

I rolled over and, keeping my eyes sealed, I felt for my pants and dug the comm unit out from its pocket. Pol wouldn't approve. Too risky, he'd say. Somebody could find the comm and read my secrets, the Empire's secrets.

He couldn't ever know. To keep him from seeing,

I'd have to write my story without looking at the comm screen. I'd probably make a mess of errors, but I didn't care. I doubted anybody would ever read it anyway.

Feeling a mischievous thrill, I pulled the tiny manual keypad from its slot and typed orders: *screen off . . . sound off . . . autosave every second.*

Unsure if I'd typed correctly, I typed the orders again to make sure they were received.

A smile broke on my face, and I had to suppress a giggle. For the first time since I'd arrived on this world, I could be Jakob.

Blind, I started typing, and deliciously uncensored words spilled from my frenzied fingertips.

"**W**hat happen-ed to your feet?"

The voice oozed through the murk of sleep to nibble at the base of my brain.

"Your feet, Drake. Why are they all cut up?"

<Jakob, we have a problem.>

Nerves fired to life. I opened my eyes. It was daylight, golden sunlight beaming through the windows. Sali was standing above me, dressed in sky blue silks. She'd just come from a shower, her face framed by wet ringlets.

I'd overslept. Like Kell, I was supposed to rise at the sky's first whispers of color. But I'd stayed up so late. And now she could see my barnacle-sliced feet in the light of day.

Looking down on me, she put her hands on her hips. "What happen-ed, Drake?"

"The missile system," I said, lies clicking into place. "I was in the shower when it blew. I should've put on my boots before I went outside, but I was in such a rush that I wound up cutting my feet on rubble and shards of metal."

"Why would you be so careless?"

I sat up on the sleeping mat and shrugged. "I wasn't thinking."

"You are such a fool." Her tone was sharp as the shells that had cut my feet.

"Because I forgot my boots?"

"A fucking fool." She hurried out the door to the balcony.

Okay, not about the boots. I put my hands on my face and rubbed the sleep away. I stood and slipped on my pants, remembering to reach for my back pocket to verify my purloined comm unit was present. Shirtless, I walked on sore feet out to the balcony. Sali was busy shooing crabs.

The last of them disappeared over the wall, and she turned around to face me. "It's all turn-ed to shit, hasn't it?" Her eyes were made of glass ready to shatter.

"Yes. The Empire is coming back, and there's nothing anybody can do to stop them."

"They'll kill you."

"Yes, but they won't hurt *you*. You'll be safe. Things will go back to the way they were before."

"They'll kill my father, too." She turned away and pressed herself against the balcony wall.

I walked up next to her, the two of us leaning out over the sea. Vast patches of golden kelp stretched to the horizon like spills of yolk across a broth of liquid jade. The Ministry domes sparkled in the distance like diamonds on a ring, no sign of the damage they'd taken.

"You did a cruel thing," she said.

"What was that?"

"You gave us hope. You defeat-ed the mighty Empire. You told us we had meaning."

I put a hand on her elbow and leaned in close. "You do have meaning."

Sali pulled her elbow from under my hand. "All we are to them is a kelp factory. Isn't that what you told my father when the two of you first talk-ed of revolution?"

Unsure where to put my abandoned hand, I buried it in my pocket.

She faced me. "You said we had no value to the Empire beyond kelp yields and cost-benefit ratios. All we were was a source of vitamins to them. You said they'd leave us be. Retaking this world was more trouble than it was worth."

I lowered my head.

"You suck-ed my father into your little conspiracy. You told him to create a secret navy. You plann-ed the coup. You ran the operation, and when it succeed-ed, you gave control to my father. You said Maritinians wouldn't accept a foreigner as their leader. You urge-ed him to become the face of the Free Maritinia. And now he's going to die. You kill-ed him."

"Yes," I said. I'd killed him the instant I blew up the missile system.

"You made him believe, Drake. You made us all believe we could be free."

I rubbed the scar on my cheek. "I did what I thought was right."

"And thanks to your hubris, I'll lose you, too." A tear broke from the corner of her eye. I pulled her close and pressed my face into her damp hair. Four more weeks. All we had was four more weeks.

A loud crackle pierced the moment. She twisted in my grasp to face the skyscreens. Admiral Mnai stood behind a podium, an impossibly tall cap riding on his head. He gripped the lectern on either side with thick mitts. Angling forward, his broad shoulders threatened to swallow the screen.

People of Maritinia, I have grave news, he said. *The Empire is returning.* He allowed a long pause to let the weight of his words sink in. I looked left and right. Rooftops and balconies filled with people. Kwuba families in silk robes. Jebyl workers in bright-colored waistwraps.

I repeat. The Empire is returning. Again, he paused. *They will attack soon, but we will resist with everything we have. I won't quit until they rip out my heart!* He pounded his chest with a fist. *Yes, good people, the usurpers will pay for invading our home. They will pay in blood.*

But I need your help. We must overwhelm the enemy with our numbers. Join the black sashes and volunteer what you can. We must pull together as one people with a common goal.

<He's saying all the right things, Pol.>

<Fear not, Jakob. He's a small man. He'll prove incapable of unifying his people. You just have to give him time.>

I call on all of you. Patriots and people of honor. Young and old. Men and women and children. I call on all of you to contribute what you can. Contribute your machetes. Contribute your knives. Give anything that can be used as a weapon. Time is short. You must act now or forever feel the squeeze of the Sire's fist.

I looked at Sali. Her tears had evaporated—her eyes now clear as an alpine lake, her head held high like a mountain peak lifting from the clouds.

<It's working, Pol. He's inspiring them.>

Pol responded with total confidence. <A good speech won't change his fate.>

CHAPTER 23

> "Ask me bfore Maritinia wht is teh worst thing that
> could happen to me, and I'd have said I coould die.
> Askl me now, and death is last on my llist."
>
> —JAKOB BRYCE

I sat in my usual spot on the floor. Sali had taken the cabin's lone chair, while the Falali Mother paced. "Infuriating," she said. She went back and forth from one side of her cell to the other, footsteps getting louder and louder as she wound herself into a silk maelstrom of pumping knees and elbows.

"Infuriating," she repeated.

"I know, Emmina. I wish you wouldn't work yourself up like this."

"It's been a week since the admiral announce-ed the Empire was returning, and yet he keeps me locked up! This is a time of horrible uncertainty. The people need me."

"I don't understand it either," I said.

"I do," Sali said with a straight face. "I understand it perfectly."

The Falali Mother stopped and crossed her arms over her chest. "Enlighten us."

"My father believes this isn't a time for coddling. He needs his people to fight."

Emmina aimed a stern stare down her nose. "I don't plan on coddling, child. What the people need is an interpreter. They need guidance to find Falal in trying times."

"They need to fight."

"What good would that do? The Empire cannot be defeat-ed by a million machetes. Telling them to fight is the same as telling them to die. Is that what you want? Is that what your father wants?"

"A million machetes might not stop the Empire," Sali said. "But neither will a million cowards."

Emmina slowly shook her head. "She thinks she knows better than I. What do you say, Colonel?"

I didn't want to say. I couldn't dash Sali's last shreds of hope. I'd seen the way she'd latched onto her father's rebellious optimism over the last seven days. Let her believe whatever she needed in order to think she had a chance of keeping him.

Of keeping me.

"Colonel," said Emmina, "you must tell her what

you told me so many times before. The Empire can't be defeat-ed."

They couldn't.

They wouldn't.

Pol had decrypted the Empire's last message. I knew exactly what was coming in only three weeks.

I could picture it in complete detail. How the screeching ship would plummet from the sky like an attacking hawk. How it would strike the water with enough force to start a tidal wave that would sweep any soldiers guarding the atoll to sea.

I could see the swirling cloud of remote-controlled drones that would launch from the floating ship to bar-rage a quarter-mile radius with purple strikes of deadly lightning. Protected by impenetrable cover fire, the Empire's troops would emerge from the ship, just fifty of them flying across the water on zip lines.

They'd split into two squads that would simultane-ously charge into two of the domes to descend the pair of functioning staircases leading to the bottom of the sea. With methodical efficiency, they'd clear one com-partment at a time, using a ruthless combination of gas grenades and target-seekers.

In less than twenty minutes, all of the admiral's forces would either be captured or killed. And when the Ministry fell, Maritinia would follow.

The new contingent would seal themselves inside the underwater fortress and monitor the feeds from the cameras mounted on the skyscreens. They'd wait for crowds of protestors to form, and they'd relentlessly attack them with drones until complete surrender was achieved.

The instant that ship struck water, they would be unstoppable. Invincible.

Kell was no fool. He knew his only chance to stop an attack was to blast them from the sky before they could land their assault force. The missile system was this world's only play.

Emmina took a step in my direction. "We're waiting, Colonel. Tell her the Empire can't be beaten."

"Leave it be," I said.

"They can't be beaten in a fair fight. That was what you told me when you engineer-ed the coup. You said they could only be defeat-ed through treachery. That was why you put their contingent to sleep by fouling the Ministry's air supply."

My eyebrows lifted at finally learning how Kell had seized control.

Emmina took another step toward me. "Tell her, Colonel. Tell her the admiral's bluster is nothing but toothless folly."

I looked at Sali, her brow holding firm over steeled eyes and sealed lips. She exuded strength from that face, but I knew how fragile it was, how the steel in those eyes was propped up with feathers and frayed string.

"Colonel?"

"Emmina," I said with a tone sharp enough to

kill the disagreement. "We probably only have a few weeks left. I won't spend it arguing."

The two women stared at me, their rigid faces less than satisfied.

The hatch wheel spun. We weren't expecting visitors. I stood and straightened my uniform. The latch clanged, and the door swung out into the corridor.

Captain Mmirehl leaned through, his head seeming too big for his ropy neck. He measured me with the cold eye of a vulture. "Ah, there you are, Colonel."

Cold fingers grabbed hold of my spine. "Yes?"

He moved back and stepped aside. Black sashes rushed through the hatchway, six of them armed with firerods. In seconds, I was surrounded. <Pol?>

Sali's voice sounded behind me, her voice ringing with alarm. "What's going on?"

"Move," ordered one of the men as he brandished a fist, his knuckles encircled by tattooed snakes.

"I don't take orders from you, soldier. I'm not going anywhere."

The barrel of a firerod drove deep into my kidney, and I fell to my knees. Sharp pain shot through my back. I huffed at the air, my heart pounding furiously in my chest. Hands grabbed me by the arms and legs.

Operating on instinct, I tried to jerk myself free but took a kick in the ribs for my effort. My lungs emptied with a whoosh, and I sucked at the air.

I was dragged out and shoved through the hatch on the other side of the corridor. I reached for the bulkhead and tried to grab hold, but my fingers slipped free, and I tumbled through. Another jab with a firerod sent me scrambling across the floor, deeper into Mmirehl's mysterious torture chamber.

The hatch clanked shut behind me, and Sali's screams were instantly strangled off.

I rolled onto my back.

Mmirehl looked down at me and rubbed his palms together. "You, Colonel, are a liar."

I sat on a chair. Naked. My wrists tied to the armrests.

I kept my eyes on my feet, which rested on a stone floor. A broad and not so shallow pool of water sat a few inches from the tips of my toes and stretched to the room's far wall. I refused to look at the water, choosing to keep my head bowed so low my chin touched my chest. A cry came from the water, its timbre so lonesome and haunted I could feel the sound vibrate in my bones.

Don't look, I told myself as I mashed my chin into my breastbone.

Mmirehl stood on one side of me. Admiral Mnai on the other. "I'm disappoint-ed in you, Colonel," said Mnai.

<Say as little as possible, Jakob.>

From the corner of my eye, I could see the bulging buttons on the admiral's uniform jacket. "You haven't been honest with me," he said.

"I don't know what you're talking about."

"Don't be coy, Colonel. The Empire is coming, and I have much to do before they arrive."

"You're wasting your time. You can't beat them."

"Of course not. Their victory will be as swift as it is decisive."

Surprised, I looked up at him.

He towered over me with the shadowy stare of a thundercloud. "You thought I actually believe-ed I could stop the Empire, didn't you?"

I shrugged my shoulders.

"Admit it, Colonel. You saw my speeches and thought I'd convince-ed myself victory was possible."

"Okay," I said. "Yes. I thought exactly that."

"You thought me an idiot." He scowled. "You thought it would be just like us natives to be too stupid to see when they're beat. You don't think I'm a real admiral, do you? You think it is just my ego who dresses in this uniform every day, not the man. You think the man is an undeserving fool."

"No," I said, a defensive pitch infecting my voice.

"You must have. Who else but a blathering idiot could think he could defeat guns and bombs with harvesting implements?" He slapped me across the cheek. "I'm not an idiot!"

My head snapped to the side with a painful wrench, but I refused to look at the pool resting before me. Instead, I immediately swung my gaze back on the big man.

He slapped me again, this time on my cuda-scarred cheek.

"There," he said with a curled upper lip. "Now that cheek has my blessing, too."

I blinked at the tears forming in my eyes.

"The Bless-ed Hero of Maritinia!" shouted the admiral. "Look at you now, Hero. You're not so arrogant anymore, are you? You were always too full of yourself to see how capable I was. You came to me with your plots and plans, your brilliant strategies. When you told me how you were going to engineer the coup, you act-ed like a magician revealing his precious secrets. You want-ed me to drop on my knees and thank you. After all, you chose me. Of all the lowly, ignorant people on this world, you chose me."

I listened intently while I used my shoulder to rub the cuda scars on my cheek.

"And now you have that chubby Dugu following your every step. What happen-ed, Colonel? Did you miss having somebody to tell you your shit smells like a sunny day?"

I could hear Mmirehl's chuckles, but I didn't turn my head for fear of glimpsing the pool.

The admiral continued. "I couldn't believe my ears when you told me you want-ed me to be your figurehead. You used that exact word. Figurehead. You actually thought I'd pretend to be in charge when we were in public but let you call the shots in private? You were wrong."

"I was," I said with a defeated tone that didn't need to be faked.

"You lent me the reins, and I kept them for myself."

He grasped the imaginary leather straps in his fist. "I'm no idiot. I wasn't then, and I'm not now."

He bent down to me, close enough I could feel his breath on my cheek. "I know." He jabbed his chest with a thumb. "I know the Empire will kill me. I know fighting is a lost cause."

"Then why the pretense? Why are you on the sky-screens every day saying you can defeat them?"

He inched closer, hot breath wafting across my face and up my nose. "The days of including you in my plans are over. You were a useful tool for a time, but your time has pass-ed."

I put my eyes back on my feet. Not the pool. Never the pool.

The admiral stood up straight. "Now, Colonel, what do you say we get back to the question of your honesty? Tell him, Captain."

Mmirehl cleared his throat. "I've identify-ed the dead foreigner."

Not good. But I'd become an accomplished liar. There was still a chance I could talk my way out of this mess. I could beat whatever accusations were about to assault me. I had to. I'd seen enough of the pool to know the alternative was not an option.

"Who is he?" I asked.

"Look for yourself." Mmirehl held out a comm unit.

I lifted my eyes just enough to look at the picture on the comm screen. A hole opened in my heart. It was me. Before I'd taken Kell's place. Before I'd punctured the implants under my face.

"Meet George Barnes," said Mmirehl. "All of the other foreigners have been accounted for. A boatman name-ed Beleaux told us how George set to sea in one of his boats and never return-ed. I paid handsomely for this picture. It was taken at the last customs checkpoint before he cross-ed into the Outermost Ring. I wouldn't call him your twin, but he sure looks like you, doesn't he?"

I stared at the picture of myself, at the face I'd worn for the last few months in transit to Maritinia. My hope disappeared, every drop of it sucked away by the grim lips of doom.

Mmirehl took away the screen. "Care to explain?"

The game was up. Eyes on my feet. Chin on my chest.

<You have to fight, Jakob. Act like an innocent man, dammit!>

<It's too late. They know.>

<They don't know anything. All they have is a picture they can't explain.>

Mmirehl repeated his question.

I marshaled as much strength as I could to look him in the eye. "I don't know who that man is."

"But he looks so much like you."

"A lot of people from Korda look like me."

Mmirehl's voice was thick with sarcasm. "Boy, that sure sounded reasonable. What do you think, Admiral? Should we let him go?"

"Maybe so," said the admiral in a mocking tone.

They were toying with me now. Enjoying their

power to make me squirm. I lifted my chin to look at the pool. The water was still. Quiet. Shapes swam under the surface. Hundreds of them, wriggling and writhing.

A net stretched across the pool, perhaps ten inches above the surface. Beleaux was in the water, his whole body submerged except for his head and one arm, which was hooked through a hole in the net over his head. He was almost unrecognizable. His usual smile had been twisted into a tortured grimace. His complexion had faded to a sallow gray, and his cheeks had sunken to fit like rotted leather over his skull.

The poor man's only crime was to rent me a boat.

Others were in the water, too, more than a dozen of them. The man to Beleaux's left lifted an arm and reached it through a hole in the net, water sheeting off the lampreys hanging from his withered biceps and forearm. With skin like oil, the lampreys squirmed and curled like dangling worms.

With his other hand, he ripped one off his wrist, a round red sore left in its place. The creature twisted about, a sucking mouth where there should be a head. The prisoner threw the lamprey over his shoulder, and it bounced across the net before falling through and dropping back into the water.

I put my eyes on my feet.

Mmirehl's words penetrated my senses for the first time in at least a minute. Speaking to the admiral, he said, "Perhaps he needs some time in the water to become more receptive to our questions."

I thought of Korda, the home I'd never see again. I thought of coffee and bread and cheese, so many kinds of cheese. I thought of nights at the theater and sipping the Empire's finest wines in the palace gardens. So beautiful those gardens. Since I was a boy, I'd always loved to stare up at the five buttressed towers stretching so high in the sky, they reached into space itself. A spectacular metaphor for the Empire, grounded on Korda but grasping for the stars.

I thought of my father and tried to take solace in the fact that he'd be proud of me. After years of jockeying a desk, I'd finally become the spy he'd always expected. And I'd carried out my mission successfully. Ugly as it was, I'd done what had to be done.

I thought of how the news would crush him, his only son, and I felt my heart shred to bits.

"Put him in the water," ordered Mmirehl. A pair of black sashes closed in and started to untie my wrists. Mmirehl went to the net and unhooked one of its corners. He lifted it and smiled at me like he was lifting the blankets for a child to slide into bed.

<Jakob, you should know you've served your Sire with distinction.>

<I'm scared, Pol.>

<I know. But it will be over soon.>

I looked at the pool, and seeing so many crooked gazes drowning in misery and torment, I knew it wouldn't be soon enough.

CHAPTER 24

"It's not surprisng wefeel terror. What is suprising
is how wlling we are to inflict it on others."

—JAKOB BRYCE

Ropes fell from my wrists. The black sashes grabbed
my arms and guided me from my chair. Captain
Mmirehl waited by the pool, net in hand.

They walked me to him, cold stone like ice under my
bare feet. I didn't fight it. My fate was sealed. Mmirehl
was right when he'd once told me I wouldn't be buried
in dirt. The lampreys would suck my life away, drop by
agonizing drop, then he would shove my body out the
air lock, condemning me to drown for eternity.

I stood at the pool's edge, toes dangling over the lip.
I looked at Beleaux. I stood in his direct line of sight,

but he didn't see me. He was lost to this world, his face a gaunt echo of its former self. His mouth hung open, lips curled downward like he'd opened them to moan and left them that way long after his voice had spent itself to nothing.

"Get into the water," said Mmirehl, his voice straight as the blade of an executioner's sword.

I looked back at Mnai. His brows hovered low to shade determined eyes, and his head was tipped forward like he was walking into the wind, his jaw jutted just like Sali's when she was intent on pushing through an obstacle.

Taking a deep breath, I aimed my gaze downward and watched the creatures slither through the water, tails sweeping left and right, their bodies shaped like badly healed scars. They moved slow, funnel-like mouths first, blindly bumping and feeling for new flesh to plant upon.

I was shivering as if a breeze blew across my wet skin. Except there was no wind. And I wasn't wet.

"Get in," repeated Mmirehl.

I couldn't breathe, throat muscles tightening around my windpipe.

"Now or we'll push you in."

I tried to speak, but couldn't jam a word though my constricted throat. I tried again and forced my voice out with a burst of air. "No," I said. "I'll talk."

<No, Jakob. You can't talk.>

"I'll tell you about the dead man," I said with a crack of desperation. "I know all about him."

Mmirehl looked past me to the admiral. Gaining approval, he told me to sit.

I padded back to my chair and rested my naked skin on the bamboo slats.

<Listen to me, Jakob. You mustn't talk. Our orders are very clear.>

I fumbled for something to say. Anything that would delay the inevitable. "Let me see the picture again," I told Mmirehl.

He obliged by holding out the comm unit.

I looked at myself for the second time. The picture wasn't very old, but he was a stranger now. A wide-eyed fool responding to the calls of duty and family. That man wasn't a murderer. Not yet. He hadn't fallen for Sali. He hadn't been blessed. He hadn't killed more than a dozen bystanders with his sabotage.

He was a child. An ignorant child reaching for the stove's pretty blue flame.

I was the scorched aftermath.

"George Barnes," said Mmirehl. "Who is he?"

I dropped my head into my hands. "His name isn't George."

"We figured it was an assumed name. But the real question is why he looks so much like you."

<Jakob, I order you to shut your mouth. Not another word.>

<The surgeons implanted a kill switch, didn't they? You have to kill me.>

<I can't kill you.>

<Please,> I begged. <I can't go in the water. Kill me, or I'll talk.>

<I can't, Jakob. There is no kill switch.>

<There must be a kill switch. What if I went rogue? The E^3 couldn't allow it. I know their ways, Pol. My family has been in the E^3 for generations.>

Captain Mmirehl was shouting at me now, but I wasn't listening. I was too focused on the rabbit hole in my head. <I can't,> said the somber voice. <They don't use kill switches in replica infiltrations.>

Mmirehl's open palm struck my face, but I didn't feel it. The psychological slap of Pol's words were so much greater. <You're lying,> I said.

<It's true, Jakob. Sire's orders.>

<Why would He do that?>

<A sudden and unexpected death would only invite an autopsy.> I struggled to stay focused on his voice after another slap. <A simple DNA test could tell the enemy you're not actually who you say you are. Our enemies can never know we have the ability to infiltrate by turning our operatives into look-alikes of our targets.>

<But we're on Maritinia, dammit. They don't have the technology to do any tests.>

<Rules are rules, Jakob. With a weapon this powerful, we can't take any chances. That's why replica infiltrations are used so rarely. You're only the third in the last twenty-five years. You understand how important this secret is? The truth can never be told.>

Another slap struck my cheek.

<Jakob, I need you to tell me you understand.>

Feeling the full weight of crushed hopes, I said, <Fine. I'll keep the secret.>

Mmirehl said, "Hold him down."

The black sashes grabbed my arms and legs, fingers squeezing down until my muscles ached. An arm forced itself under my chin, and the choke hold tightened until I could barely breathe.

Mmirehl had something in his hand. Something that glistened like oil and twisted in his grip.

He lifted it to my eye, and the jawless mouth stretched wide, exposing circles around circles of close-packed teeth. A brown tongue reached for my pupil. I pressed myself against the back of the chair and tried to turn my head.

But my head wouldn't budge. I closed my eyes, but fingers pressed into my eye socket and pried the lids back open.

The tongue tasted me, just a little sweep. Then came a full lick, the coarse swipe scraping across my eyeball. My eye burned like it had been blown full of dust. Reflexes made my eyelids twitch against the fingers that held them firm.

"Once it attaches," said Mmirehl, "you won't be able to pull it free without pulling out your eye."

<Stay strong, Jakob. Your sacrifice is for Sire and Empire.>

<Sire and—>

It licked me again. The pain was excruciating. Tears streamed from my eye, and my lungs heaved in my chest. Sweat raced down my forehead as I struggled against the arms and hands that held me tight. It was too much. It was easy for Pol to make me promise to keep silent, but he couldn't feel what I felt. Couldn't feel the teeth that were about to attach to my eye, or my life being devoured by this insatiable parasite.

The lamprey moved closer to my eye. So close that my entire field of vision was filled with teeth. I had to say something. Anything . . .

"My brother!" I shouted. "He was my brother."

Mmirehl pulled the lamprey back, and the choke hold loosened enough to allow air to fully fill my lungs. I plucked the name from memory. I'd studied Kell's bio for a year. "His name was Daniel," I said between panting breaths. "Daniel Kell. He looked like me because he was my brother."

"Your brother?" Mmirehl scoffed. "What was he doing here?"

Lies tumbled into place. "The Empire sent him. He snuck into my house. He took a boat under the city platform and climbed up my garbage chute. He tried to talk me into turning against you."

Mmirehl took a quick glance at Beleaux and turned back to me, thought lines forming on his forehead. He was likely merging my story with the one he'd extracted from the boatman, seeking contradictions and, I hoped, finding none.

<A brilliant move, Jakob. You've given them something to chew on.>

Encouraged by Pol's words—and trying to forget that just moments ago he had told me to resign myself to torture—I told the black sashes to let me go. I was talking now. With a slight nod from Mmirehl, the black sashes released my hands, and the arm under my chin slipped away. However, a pair of heavy grips stayed on my shoulders.

I rubbed tears from my eye and craned my neck to look at the admiral. I had to see if he believed the lie, see if the rekindled hope burning inside me really had a chance to flourish. But his face hadn't broken from its stern pose. He watched me meet his stare and doused the embers with a disapproving shake of his head. "I don't believe you."

I had no other lies. Only the truth. But these bastards didn't deserve the truth. And I knew the truth would condemn me to the pool anyway.

The clang of a hatch echoed from somewhere out of sight. Sali raced into the room and made a hard stop.

I felt a surge of heat in my chest. I still had a chance.

She looked at me. She looked at her father. She looked at the pool, eyes darting from one victim to the next, her face blanching. "What is this place?"

"Who let her in here!" shouted Mmirehl, the lamprey still squeezed in his hands.

"Get away from him." She rushed across the room to stand between Mmirehl and me.

The captain backpedaled a few steps and tossed the lamprey into the water. "How did you get in?"

Sali ignored him and turned to face me. "Are you

okay?" She slapped at the hands that still held my shoulders. "Move this chair back."

The chair scraped over the stone.

"Father," she said, "whatever you think he did, he didn't do it."

"He hasn't been truthful," said the admiral. "He could be working for the enemy."

"He can't be working for the Empire. He was the one who talk-ed you into rebelling in the first place."

"Show her," he said to Mmirehl.

The captain promptly displayed my picture for her. "This man's body was recently recovered from the water. He was murder-ed."

Sudden doubt quirked her eyebrows. "Who is this, Drake?"

"Daniel." I rubbed my watering eye. "My brother."

"Your brother was here?"

"Yes." I loaded my voice with as much conviction as it could hold. I had to convince Sali and hope she could convince her father. I grasped her wrist like it was a lifeline and looked into her eyes. "I killed him, Sali."

"Let her go," ordered the admiral.

I did as I was told, letting go of her wrist but not the lock I had on her eyes. "The Empire sent him to talk me into turning against your father. He promised they wouldn't punish me if I did as he said, but I knew it was a lie. We had a fight, and I killed him."

"When did this happen?" she asked.

"The night before you came back from your mother's. His body was in the closet, and I threw it out the window when you were in the shower."

She brought her hand to her face, the squint of her eyes telling me she was thinking through every detail of that morning.

"The cuts on your hand," she said. "They weren't from a crab. They were from the fight."

I nodded.

"Your chest was scrape-ed up, too. More wounds from the fight. And that was why you were acting so strange. That's why you haven't been the same person ever since."

Another nod.

"If this story is true, then why didn't you simply tell us?" asked the admiral. "You could've told us the night it happen-ed. You could've told us when the body was recover-ed. But you didn't."

I opened my mouth to respond, but the well was dry. I needed that perfect lie, that perfect fragment of logic, but it didn't exist.

"You could've told us," Admiral Mnai said. "Nobody would've condemn-ed you for it."

<Be smart> said Pol.

<Shut up and let me think!>

Mnai was right that my claim wasn't rational. Reasoned argument wasn't the way forward. My mind shifted direction. I had to go big. Bold. I had to take it to the edge and leap off.

"You need to tell us," said Sali.

I pinched my lips tight, knowing I had to act like a man who had been holding it all in. I crossed my arms and hugged them tight to my body. I closed in on myself like a man who had been cursed with a guilty enough conscience to hide what he'd done.

"Talk," said the admiral.

I contracted the muscles in my shoulders and neck. Tensed my legs and gritted my teeth. I held my breath until blood rushed to my cheeks. A chorus of "whys" peppered me from every direction. I let the tension mount, my shoulders starting to shake, holding on until the time came to let loose.

Intentionally forgetting my nakedness I sprang from my chair. "He was my brother!" I shouted. Turning on the admiral, I threw my chair aside and blasted him with unbridled emotion. "I loved him, damn you. I didn't want to kill him."

I pounded my chest, tears leaking from my eyes. "He was my brother. What I had to do was none of your fucking business."

<Really, Jakob, I don't know what to say. Your kind of talent is rare.>

Giving my chest a slap, I channeled every ounce of lamprey-fueled terror into a fiery torrent. "I sacrificed everything for you, you stupid, ignorant fool." I stalked up to Mnai, spitting bitter words with every step. "I gave up my career. I gave up my home and my family so you could lead this world to a better future. And now I've murdered my own brother. His blood was my blood, and I spilled it to preserve what we've made. How dare you accuse me of disloyalty? You were nothing without me! And this is how you repay me? Torture? Accusations?

"Fuck you!"

Black sashes closed in, but I didn't raise a hand to the admiral. Just kept marching him backward until he bumped the wall. I pressed my chest into his, pushed my face up to his chin, and unleashed the loudest, longest, most primal scream of my life.

Mnai stayed silent after my voice was exhausted. Creases stood out in the corners of his eyes while the two of us stayed locked in a high-intensity staring contest.

A hand landed lightly on my shoulder. I backed away from the admiral and turned to face Sali. "It's okay," she said, wide eyes full of compassion. "Let's go home."

"He's not going anywhere," said Mmirehl.

I waited on the admiral's word, his face lined with tension.

Sali tugged on my arm. "Come on, where is your uniform?"

I went to the pile of clothes sitting under an aquarium filled with green-striped fish. Mmirehl and Mnai didn't budge. I pulled on my pants. My comm unit was still where I'd left it in the rear pocket.

Mmirehl watched me with a disapproving stare. The admiral with his unbreakable gaze.

With an unbuttoned shirt over my shoulders and boots on my feet, I followed Sali toward the exit.

"Wait," said the admiral. He covered the ground between us with two long strides. He gave his daughter one of his gap-toothed smiles. "I need a quick word with the man. I'll send him right out."

She gave a long, suspicious stare.

He widened the grin. "He won't be harm-ed, child."

With a reluctant nod, she went down the corridor. The admiral waited to hear the clank of the closing hatch before turning off the lights on his smile. "I don't know what you're up to, but I no longer believe a thing you say."

"I wasn't lying."

He struck quick, the heel of his hand ramming into my solar plexus. Air whooshed out my lungs, and I gulped for air.

"Don't say another word," he said. "You're a manipulative man, Colonel. You always have been. Every word from your mouth is hewn to be a monument to the great Hero of Maritinia. You care about nothing but your own glory. That's what makes me better than you. I see the people around me. I care about them."

Having gained control of my breathing, I asked him if he really believed that.

He backhanded me, hard, across the face. I figured that was answer enough, but a megalomaniac like Mnai wouldn't be content without hearing his own voice. "How dare you ask me that? Of course I do. All great leaders care about their people. And I care about my daughter, too. Only Falal knows why she's become so fond of you, but because she is, I won't be the one to kill you. I won't let Sali remember me as the man who took you away from her. The Empire will do that for me. They'll execute you just as surely as they will me. Until then, I grant you a reprieve."

"So it's like none of this ever happened?"

"No, Colonel. Not like that at all. You'll be under guard at all times, and as of now, you are banned from entering the Ministry. Come close, and my soldiers will cut you down."

CHAPTER 25

"Finding happinss is like grasping at water. Your
hands might gett wet but it will evaprate soon
enout."

–JAKOB BRYCE

The sun had just fallen, the sky painted with gradu-
ated shades of blue darkening to navy, then to black.
I stepped off the boat, my feet dropping to the stone
quay. I held out a hand for Sali, but she didn't take it. As
always, she didn't need any help. After all, she was the
one who had just rescued me.

My two new guards disembarked next. One was the
short Kwuba man who had been following me for the
last two weeks, except now he'd turned in his aquamarine robes for a full uniform. The other guard was taller
and thinner, with pocked cheeks and a stiff demeanor.

Heading down the quay, we slowly passed a cargo vessel. A group of black sashes passed crates from person to person bucket-brigade style, hastily unloading the ship. Yesterday, I would've wanted to see what was in those crates. Today, I didn't care. I was a free man. Not in the literal sense. With Mmirehl's guards attached to my wings, it was impossible to say that. No, my newfound freedom was of a kind much more liberating.

I was free from responsibility.

My mission was finished. No more sneaking around the Ministry. No secret messages or devious plans. No more of the delusional admiral or his spiteful captain.

I'd survived. I'd done my duty and survived.

I was free. Nothing left to do but wait for the Empire to arrive. If only the admiral knew the gift he'd handed me by banning me from the Ministry.

Walking on light feet, I tuned in to the sound of penned mammoths munching on dried kelp, the noise akin to that of tearing fabric. I breathed deep and savored the smell of roasting eel drifting on a smoky breeze. A storyteller caught my ear with talk of cuda with teeth so sharp they could cut you if you looked too close. Standing on a stool, she spun what sounded like an adventure tale for a small gathering of entranced listeners. She soon fell out of earshot, and we approached a pair of hawkers using a bellowslike device to suck fireflies from a hatchery draped with gauzy silk. I stopped to watch one of the hawkers insert the sea-bamboo nozzle into a collapsed paper globe and squeeze the handles, the paper ballooning and filling with dancing lights.

Sali said, "Come on, Drake, let's get home."

I let myself be led. But something had been puzzling me. "How did you get into Mmirehl's secret room?" I asked her.

"I told the guards to let me in or I'd hurt myself and tell my father that they'd done it."

I couldn't help but smile.

This time, she let me take her hand. We headed into the city, water drizzling from sluices that crisscrossed overhead. We strode past restaurants and shops, one with a woman spinning silk outside the door. We walked silently, hand in hand, the darkness affording me enough anonymity that no one recognized me.

Approaching our house, we found a young girl waiting outside with a Maritinian torch—a stick with a glowgrub impaled on the end. "Hello, Colonel."

"Hello, Dory."

"My brother told me to wait here for you. He said that if you came, I should ask you to come for dinner."

"Sali, this is Dugu's sister, Dory. What do you think about dinner?"

"It sounds wonderful."

I looked at the lead guard and raised questioning eyebrows.

"You can do whatever you want," he said, "as long as it doesn't involve plotting against the admiral or going to the Ministry."

"Nothing could be further from my mind," I said before turning to Dory. "Will you show us the way?"

She stuck the stick down the back of her silk pants so the glowgrub hovered over her head. With freed hands, she pried my hand out of Sali's grasp so she could insert herself in our chain. "Swing me."

I was happy to oblige.

In fact, I was plain happy.

I stepped through the curtain and immediately received a hug from Dugu. "I knew they'd let you go," he said. "Keeping you lock-ed up in addition to the Falali Mother would've brought too much pressure."

I returned his bearlike grasp. "You can thank Sali. She's the reason the admiral set me free."

Releasing his hold on me, Dugu bowed to Sali, fingers on his heart. "You've done us all a great service."

"No thanks necessary," she said. "My father would've let him go of his own accord."

I studied her face, looking for signs she'd lied to cover for the admiral. But I saw no tightness in her smile or tension in her eyes. She appeared to truly believe what she'd said. After seeing the horrors of the lamprey pool, I didn't know how that was possible, but I knew the bonds of family were hard to break. I wouldn't fault her for it. Instead, I'd try my best to enjoy our last weeks together.

Of course, it didn't stop Pol from noting she was as delusional as her father. I ignored that, too.

Dugu stood straight and noticed the guards standing in the doorway.

"My new detail," I said. "The admiral wants to keep an eye on me."

"I understand. I'll let my mother know we'll need food for two more."

"No," said the lead guard. "We're on duty."

"Not in our home you're not. What are your names?"

"I'm Mnoba. He's Mmuro."

Dugu touched his heart. "Come, let me take you all out back."

A mere four paces took us out the back exit to an irregularly shaped courtyard with lanterns hanging from overhead balconies. Near the center, a large fire burned inside a shallow well that was positioned under a stone shelf crammed with steaming earthenware pots.

Dugu led us across the courtyard. Entire families crammed the window frames, heads leaning far out to get an up-close view of the Blessed Hero of Maritinia. To our left, a sweaty Jebyl workman who hadn't noticed us kept scraping air barnacles from a wall. Ahead, Dory had already joined a pack of children kicking and chasing a ball made of an intricate weave of bamboo strips.

We stepped up to a woman seated on a flat rock next to a hole in the stone floor. Her hair was gathered up into a swirl and held in place by a pair of urchin spines. With quick hands, she worked a fish with a bone blade and dropped the innards through the hole to the ocean below.

"Mother," Dugu said, "I'd like you to meet Colonel Kell and Sali Mnai."

The dim light couldn't hide the brightness of her smile. She touched the fish head to the silk robe over her heart and left her seat to drop to one knee. "I am most honor-ed."

"Please," I said, "the honor is ours."

"How can we help?" asked Sali.

"You mustn't do any work. You are our guests. Krioux? Where's Krioux?"

"I'm here," said a man descending a dogleg-shaped staircase of uneven steps. He wore a Jebyl waistwrap and carried a bottle of imported wine. "I've been saving this for a special occasion."

"You must be Dugu's father," I said. "You've raised a fine son."

"You are most kind, Colonel."

Pulling a knotted cord from behind his ear, he pressed the knot between the cork and the glass. Borrowing his wife's knife, he used the blade—stained with fish blood—to jam the knot past the cork's bottom before pulling the cord and uncorking the bottle. I had to shake my head at the complete disregard for proper sanitation, but I told myself not to worry. By now, my stomach had fully adjusted to Maritinian conditions. Its rumbling and cramping protests had stopped two days before I took Kell's life.

Chairs arrived for Sali and me. Dugu reached high

overhead to pull bamboo skewers from where they'd been soaking in a water sluice and ran them through the gutted fish. Soon, the wine was flowing, along with a salty kelp stew. The courtyard grew crowded, men and women bringing their own fish and eel and propping so many skewers around the fire it seemed to be a pond surrounded by fish-topped cattails.

Full-bodied wine splashed across my tongue, fingers of alcohol beginning to tickle my brain. A bowl of quartered crabs came my way, and I burned my fingers peeling sweet flesh from the shell. The fire sizzled with dripping juices, while laughter tumbled from the overhead balconies.

Dugu carried an old man in his arms and set him down on a mat near the fire. With bony knees poking from his waistwrap, the old man sat cross-legged. Dugu brought a piece of fish, broke off a small bite, and set it in the man's palm. Picking up the fish in his fingers, he lifted it to a toothless mouth and popped it inside.

"This is my great-uncle," said Dugu. "He can't see anymore."

I reached over and patted the man's knotted knuckles. "Good to meet you, sir."

"He doesn't hear so well anymore either."

"He wears a waistwrap. I didn't realize you were descended from Jebyl."

"My entire family is Jebyl, except for my mother. She sent me to school, so I could have a better future. She's doing the same for Dory."

"How does your father feel about that?"

He handed another bite of fish to the old man. "My father is proud of us. He loves to read. He's a very smart man. He would've excell-ed if he'd ever gotten the chance to go to school."

"Is he angry he never got that chance?"

"I wouldn't say angry. He's a gentle soul. He knows Kwuba and Jebyl flow together like the tides and currents. He long ago accept-ed the place Falal chose for him."

"Falal has nothing to do with it. You know the classes are arbitrary, don't you? Kwuba and Jebyl were an invention of the Empire's first governor. He wanted to create a stable class structure, so he chose up sides."

"I've heard that history before, but it was so long ago, nobody can say that was the way it really happen-ed. The Sire fancies himself a god. He likes to take credit for everything we are. He denies Falal's role in creating this world and its people. But we see through the ruse. He is no god. He is only a man."

Pol's voice slipped into my mind. <These people are in great need of some major reeducation. We'll recommend intensive reprogramming be a high priority for the new governor.>

Dory appeared behind the old man and slipped her hands over his eyes. With a mirthful grin, he reached for her wrist, but she pulled away and giggled. She waited for him to lower his hand, then covered his eyes again. This time he was quick enough to snatch her wrist. With more strength and dexterity than I would've thought him capable of, he pulled her around to his front and tickled her ribs. Dory's giggles quickly escalated to breathless belly laughs.

"Your uncle is full of humor," I said to Dugu.

"He finds a way. These last years have been hard on him, but he finds a way."

Dugu's mother handed out fruit the size of a berry. I bit it in half and chewed mealy flesh that tasted like a concentrated version of the ocean. Sali lifted the wine bottle, and I eagerly held out my glass.

I felt something brush my hair, felt it on both sides of my head, sliding along my temples toward my eyes.

My eyes. *Lamprey.*

I jumped from my chair, and the wineglass fell from my fingers to shatter on the stone. I whirled around, hands lashing out to bat away the lamprey.

But there was no lamprey. Just a scared little girl cradling slapped hands.

A hush came over the people nearby. Every eye was on me, one particular young pair already glassing up. I looked at Sali, whose stunned brows had lifted high enough to crease her forehead. I turned back to Dory, swallowed the misguided panic lodged in my throat, and pressed my lips wide. I forced the last bits of my newly formed smile with a curl at the corners and a baring of teeth.

Dory's eyes filled with water, twin tears breaking free with a blink. Desperate to make her stop crying, I snatched her up in my arms. "I caught you," I said with deliberate jocularity. She hung limp in my grasp while I tickled her ribs in the same spot her uncle had. She responded first with unamused grunts, but after a few seconds she wriggled in my arms, and I kept tickling until her infectious laughter put the party back in swing.

Setting her down, I watched her run off to be with her friends.

Sali tugged my sleeve. "Are you okay, Drake?"

I nodded, but I wasn't okay. My survivor's high had evaporated, and I felt myself drowning under the crush of images battering my mind like crashing waves—Mmirehl's wicked smile; the lamprey reaching for my eye; the unbreakable clamp of teeth; eyes ripped from my sockets; tears of blood running down my cheeks.

Blind.

The pool; lampreys latching onto my arms and legs; the spaces between my fingers and toes; the slow, excruciating drain of life leeching away.

Dizzy, I reached for the chair. Sali was up, one hand on my elbow, the other around my biceps, both guiding me down to a seat. Dugu's mother arrived to clean up the spilled wine. With a bowl of water pinned against her chest, she scrubbed the stone with a worn-down brush made from tufts of coarse mammoth wool.

When she looked at me, I tried to smile an apology but couldn't find an ounce of humor to prop it on. She seemed to see the distress on my face, and said, "Worry not, good Colonel. It is only wine."

Before I could respond, a loud voice tumbled into the courtyard and echoed off the walls like the rumbles of distant thunder. Conversations quickly faded to silence as the admiral's words boomed from the skyscreens. *The time is upon us, good peoples of Maritinia. The Empire's fleet has enter-ed orbit. Study these pictures of their ships closely.*

Closed inside the courtyard, I couldn't see any of the skyscreens. Some people started filing up staircases to watch from the rooftops. Others stayed where they were, faces gazing vaguely upward with intent stares.

You see these ships. They are fill-ed with soldiers who think they will meet no resistance. They think we are weak.

<Can there really be ships in orbit?> I asked Pol.

<Absolutely not. The Empire is still three weeks away. And there will only be one ship.>

I once beat the Empire all by myself. I risk-ed my life and the lives of my family to defeat them. Me. I show-ed them exactly what one righteous man could do in the face of unthinkable power.

One man? Clearly, the erasure of Kell's role in history was already under way. I looked to see Sali's reaction, but she didn't meet my eyes. Her gaze was aimed upward, as if she were trying to spot the ships in orbit.

One man cannot stop them. Not this time. But one world can. One world unite-ed in a common cause. One world embolden-ed by the taste of freedom. This is Free Maritinia. And it will remain free.

If you love freedom, you will fight. If you love your people, you will fight. Look to your sister and your brother. Look to your son or daughter. And if you find love in your heart, you must fight.

Fight, and you commit an act of love. Sit idle, and you watch your babies drown.

The voice went silent for long seconds. Then another voice took its place, the timbre fluid as silk sliding across skin. Mmirehl said, *Fighters report to the closest water-purification plant. Fighters report to the closest water-purification plant. Fighters report. . .*

A holler sounded from somewhere far off. Then another, this one close by, a lonesome-sounding howl followed by shattering glass. Soon the air was thrumming with war cries. The primal forces struck a chord up my spine, and the resulting reverberations gradually harmonized with the war cries until my nerves sang the same eerie tune.

Swept up like a leaf in gusting wind, I was ready to fight the Empire myself. But the Empire wasn't in orbit.

Nobody was.

CHAPTER 26

"I shhould've knownn."

—JAKOB BRYCE

I rolled onto my side, and with one eye pressed into my pillow, I lifted the other eyelid to take a peek at the window before quickly closing it like a reverse wink. Dawn was almost here, the charred black of the night sky finally giving way to an ashy gray.

After the party, I'd easily fallen asleep, but it hadn't lasted. The sound of a crab scrabbling across the floor had woken me, and unable to shake the fear of its pincers plucking out my eyes, I'd lain awake the rest of the night, passing the hours by secretly writing in my journal.

Finished for now, I silently tucked the comm unit

into the pocket of the pants heaped next to the sleeping mat. Then, for Pol's benefit, I feigned my usual wakeup routine by scattering a few slow blinks before rubbing my eyes.

<Good morning, Jakob.>

<Morning.>

<We should go to the water-purification plant. You must be as curious as I am to see what kind of fighting force the admiral has assembled.>

I almost responded with the truth that I had every intention of seeing the admiral's army for myself. But I held the words back from traveling between our two minds. I didn't want Pol to think I was his to boss around anymore. It was time to start establishing my independence. <My mission is over, Pol.>

<All I'm asking you to do is observe. That's all.>

I paused like I was mulling it over. <That's all?>

<Yes. I guarantee it. I just want to see what's happening. Nothing more.>

Satisfied to have won the assurance, I sat up and looked at Sali. She didn't stir. Her eyes were closed below bunched brows, her upper lip twitching at a dream. Wherever she was, I wished I could join her.

She and I didn't have much time left. I didn't want to leave her behind when I went home. She just might love me. Me. Jakob.

She'd faced down her father to save me from the lamprey. That had to mean she cared for me, didn't it?

I remembered the coldness when I first met her. The stern looks and knifelike tongue. Yes, we'd had sex the morning we met, but that was an act of hunger. An act absent tenderness and emotion.

At the time, she'd thought I was Kell. But she'd learned to see the real me underneath. She'd said as much when she told me it was like I'd become a different person. That was when her attitude started to soften. When her kisses became more about love than need.

I didn't have to lose her three weeks from now. I could tell her the truth. I could tell her who I was and how much she meant to me. I could take her home with me.

I could.

<Why must you stare at her so much?>

I no longer saw any reason to hide my feelings. My mission was over. <I'm just trying to memorize her face.>

<You might as well save yourself some pain and end this now. Tell her you need time to yourself and find a different place to sleep for the next twenty days.>

<If you could feel the way my stomach knots at the thought, you'd understand why I can't.>

<You weary me, Jakob.>

<You don't know what it's like. All you can do is see and hear. You don't feel what's in my heart.>

<Can we please go now?>

Reluctant to let the argument drop, but curious myself, I gathered my uniform and walked downstairs to dress. After a short trip to the bathroom to wash my face and drain myself of last night's wine, I stepped outside.

Mnoba and Mmuro were still on duty. Surprised, I asked why nobody had come to relieve them last night.

Mnoba shook a fatigued head. "The captain must've forgotten about us."

"He must be too busy organizing the defense," said Mmuro.

I strode past them. "Let's take a walk." I didn't know exactly where the closest water-purification plant was, but it had to be south of here, near the waterwheels.

With my guards lagging a few paces behind, I ambled slowly down the streets, the buildings occasionally parting to afford us a view of the sun birthing on the horizon. I stopped to buy Mnoba and Mmuro dollops of fish eggs wrapped in kelp leaves. Even balls and chains needed to eat.

Speakers crackled, and we simultaneously turned our heads toward the skyscreens. Footage of last night's short speech ran forward, the admiral's words making a repeat call to arms. For the first time, I saw the picture of the ships in orbit, three of them, long and flat like floating warehouses.

<That imagery is very old,> said Pol. <Those barges are M-class. That model was decommissioned over a century ago.>

<He must've dug that footage up from the archives.>

Looking at the screen, Mmuro tut-tutted and shook

his head, while Mnoba chewed his food with eyes locked in a persistent glare. I was about to ask their opinions, but my attention was drawn by a large group of Jebyl teenagers crossing in front of us. The boys marched with their chins held high and proud. Volunteers for the cause.

Realizing they were going the same place I was, I followed them through a tented glass market, early-bird hawkers setting bowls and bottles on display. Exiting from under the tarps, I looked up to see a series of capillary-like sluices converging into broad arteries. Following the largest channel for a way, I saw the first waterwheel, its topmost buckets reaching above the rooftops.

The air grew dense with the pungent smell of mammoth dung, and turning a corner, we found ourselves at the base of the wheel, one of several spread across an open square. Rings of yoked mammoths trod in circles, turning massive stone gears that cranked the waterwheels around.

I stopped for a moment to watch the woolly beasts work. With each determined step, powerful shoulders bulled unrelentingly forward. Feet shaped like the barrels of cannons tracked around furrows worn deep in the stone. Amazing what they could do. Even more amazing that the people on this world thought land-based animals such as these could be native to this world of water. Gifts of Falal according to the Falali Mother.

Buckets almost large enough to be called tubs hung

from the wheel. At the bottom of the rotation, the leaky buckets sipped from a broad pool of freshwater, and at the top, the buckets poured onto raised sluices with hardly a splash. Some of the workmen recognized me and stopped to kneel, while those oblivious to my presence kept driving the animals along their circular paths.

I made for an opening in the city's floor, a wide set of stairs leading down to the ocean below. My guards and I started down, the memory of the last time I'd been under the city platform fresh in my mind—on Beleaux's boat, seeking Kell's trash chute.

I stuck to the center of the staircase, shaded ocean undulating to my left and right. In every direction, support columns reached up like tree trunks in a uniformly spaced forest. Connected by a network of branching arches, the stanchions were topped by the city's massive canopy of stone slabs.

The stairs bottomed out just a few feet above the water level, and I stepped onto a long strip of land. Except it wasn't dirt crunching under my boots. It was crystallized salt. A sprawling salt island sat at the end of the white road. Sandwiched horizontally between the island and the city platform was a large, walled structure with a crowd gathered outside.

Mnoba steered in close enough to bump my shoulder. "Where are you going, sir?"

"Wherever I want."

He put a hand on the firerod slung across his chest, a subtle reminder that he was in charge. "I'll ask you again. Where exactly are you going?"

I stopped to face him. "I'm going inside the desalinization plant. I want to see what's going on in there."

"Don't think of trying to lose us in that crowd, I'll—"

I didn't let him finish. "You want to hold my hand?"

An extended stare eventually terminated with a single word. "Proceed."

We entered the crowd, the three of us plowing forward in a tight wedge. We forced through the group of teens I'd seen earlier and slowly made our way to the front, where a line of armed black sashes guarded the entrance.

A press of people pushed from behind, prompting one of the soldiers to stand on a stool and shout at the impatient crowd. "Wait your turn! There's no more room inside."

I marched straight through the line of black sashes. Nobody tried to stop me. Inside, I found a hot, thick, impassable mass of people squeezed elbow to elbow.

"This way," said Mmuro, pointing at a guarded set of interior stairs to the right. "You can get a good view of the plant standing on the wall."

I followed Mmuro up a spiraling staircase that emptied onto a walkway atop the wall. Uniformed soldiers and black sashes hustled about, many carrying crates, possibly the same crates I'd seen being unloaded onto the quay last night.

One of the admiral's lieutenants stepped up to me. Doko was his name. "What in Falal's name are you doing here?"

"I came to observe."

"Oh, you want to watch, do you?" His tone was downright accusatory, but I couldn't fathom why.

"I do want to watch," I said with halting uncertainty. "Why shouldn't I?"

He angled his head forward, his eyes hooded in shadow. "You don't know, do you?"

"What are your orders?"

"I can't be seen talking to you." He waved me away.

"What are your orders? What is the admiral planning?" With each word, my voice rose in volume.

The lieutenant turned his back on me, his gaze now aimed at the mass of people crammed into the cistern below. At least a thousand of them stood in hip-high water, staring upward, the sea of expectant faces lit by sunbeams angling through dozens of openings in the city platform overhead.

"What are your orders, damn you!"

Alarmed by my aggressive tone, black sashes rushed to protect the lieutenant. With puffed chests and harsh shouts, they ordered me to move along.

I stood on tiptoe to see over their heads. "What are your orders, dammit!"

Mnoba grabbed me by the elbow and pulled until I had to move my feet to maintain my balance. "Come, Colonel. You mustn't be disruptive."

"What is he going to do?"

"Please, come. You're putting all three of us in danger."

Letting Mnoba usher me away, the fear in his

voice enough to get me moving, I struggled to figure out what the admiral had planned. I took frustrated footsteps, my cluttered mind trying to sort out his intentions.

Eyeing an uncrowded spot a ways down the wall, I jerked my elbow from Mnoba's grasp and marched to the bamboo railing. The waterwheels on the far side of the cistern had stopped turning, and a train of mammoths were cutting a path through the crowd just wide enough to make it out of the pool before going out the back exit.

Looking straight down, I saw water pour from spouts protruding from the wall. The spouts ran all the way around the rectangular cistern, people taking turns sipping from the chest-high streams of freshly desalinized water.

Under my boots was a closed bamboo trapdoor. Peering through the slats, my eyes traced a dim beam of light to a patch of glistening skin the color of raw chicken.

A salt gland. Large as horses, the kidneylike organs were inventions of the Empire. Acting as filters, the glands provided Maritinians with a constant source of potable water. Lined up in dark chambers like the one under my feet, the glands ran all the way around the cistern's perimeter.

A pair of eyes moved into the light. Startled, I jumped back. Then the man smiled and lifted a glow-grub so I could see him more clearly. Standing ankle deep in a pool of soupy excretions, the Jebyl man touched his heart. After I echoed the gesture, he went to work scooping salty slurry down a chute that emptied into the ocean.

Turning my attention back on the pool, I watched a line of soldiers slosh and jostle through the crowd. A pair of them passed directly below me, their mission evidently to pick out certain members of the crowd and herd them toward the exits. A recently selected Kwuba man protested but complied, his voice momentarily rising above the din to complain that he wanted to fight the Empire.

<The soldiers are selecting only the Kwuba,> said Pol.

I scanned the exits and saw he was right. Only the Kwuba were being culled and herded out. I asked myself why, but was incapable of summoning the answer. So I continued to stand there like the fool I was, my face knotted in concentration like a child staring at a difficult math problem.

I couldn't see the solution. Not until it had already happened.

CHAPTER 27

"I wasa killer myself. The ruthless murdrer of
dozens. If anybdy could understnd the darkest
chambers insde teh human heart, it hsould've
been me."

—JAKOB BRYCE

I watched the whole thing. I watched the confused
conversations among the Jebyl once the Kwuba had
been plucked from their ranks. I watched the most
boisterous among them shout over the din. *How long
do we have to stay here? When can we start bleeding the
Empire's soldiers?*

I watched a pair of black sashes open a crate just a
few feet away from me. I saw them pull green-striped
fish from the box. I'd seen the same fish once before.

In the admiral's torture chamber. My clothes had been piled under an aquarium teeming with them.

One at a time, the soldiers pulled fish from the box and drove bone blades through the fish heads. Why would they do that? The fish were already dead.

I watched them throw fish over the railing to the people standing in the pool below. One fish after another. Other groups of black sashes did the same all around the cistern. Dozens of crates worth of fish dumped down into the pool below like flocks of birds suddenly struck dead.

I thought the Jebyl would appreciate the meal. It was time for breakfast.

I couldn't understand why they tried so hard to stop the fish from landing in the water. I couldn't understand why they ran. Why they trampled the weak and unlucky in a surge for the exits. Couldn't they see they were drowning their comrades?

I didn't know the fish had sacs of poison inside their skulls.

I didn't know.

Some of the soldiers and black sashes congratulated each other on a job well-done. A few laughed. But most silently stared.

Like me.

With an anguished cry, one jumped the railing, perhaps in a misguided attempt to rescue somebody he knew. He splashed into the water below and swam through the bodies, nudging them aside like logs until the toxins soaked through his pores and took control. He shook, arms and legs seizing in splashing spasms. And then he went still.

Like the others.

I backed away from the railing until I bumped the cistern wall. Mnoba knelt on the floor and bent his head so low his forehead pressed against the stone.

Mmuro stood stiff as the column behind him, his face wiped of all emotion. He lifted the firerod strap off his neck, dropped the weapon, and simply wandered away.

I leaned down and pulled on Mnoba's uniform, telling him we had to go. He raised himself, and we headed for the spiral staircase that led down and out to the salt road. I heard shouts behind me but didn't turn back. I had to leave. Nothing else mattered.

We passed the spot where I'd left the lieutenant, but he was gone, and I had no idea where he'd disappeared to. Following Mnoba down the stairs, I picked my steps carefully to avoid tripping over attempted escapees.

Mnoba reached the floor at the bottom of the stairs, the pool sitting to his right. Looking at the exit to his left, he threw his hands in frustration at the sight of all the Jebyl on the ground, blocking the way. "How are we supposed to get out?"

I didn't let myself think about it. Brushing past him, I lifted my left leg and pressed the sole of my boot onto a prone hip. With my hands spread wide for balance, I placed my other foot on a bare shoulder blade.

Making slow progress, I stuck to stepping on those who had died facedown. Those who couldn't witness their own desecration.

A thigh twisted under my weight, and I started to fall. Knowing the poison could soak through skin, I couldn't let my bare hands touch wet clothes. I had no choice but to keep my hands raised as I let my tipping body crash. The back of my shoulder impacted with such force that I thought I heard the snap of a bone somewhere inside the pile.

They hadn't tried to roll out of the way. Hadn't groaned or winced. Not even a flinch.

I struggled upright and continued my slow, unsteady journey out the cistern doors, where the spread of bodies formed a fan shape like the flow of silt from a collapsed pipe.

Mnoba hightailed it past me, feet hopping like he was sprinting across hot coals, and skidded to a stop on the salt road. I reached the road myself shortly after and only managed a few steps before dropping to my hands and knees.

I had to labor for breath, as if the weight of the city above had come down on my back. I tried to understand. Tried to find reason in the unfathomable depths. But my unmoored thoughts couldn't find anchor, as if the ocean bottom itself had been set adrift.

Mnoba's hand landed on my shoulder. "Come, Colonel, let's keep moving."

I dug my fingers into the salt, pushing aside white crystals to reveal a layer of oily grit that gathered under my fingernails. To my right, bodies floated on the waves. To my left, crabs scrabbled from the water and marched with raised claws toward the pile of bodies, but stopped short and clicked their claws in frustration at smell of the poison-spoiled feast.

The road was almost deserted, just a few soldiers and black sashes holding guard. The others must have had the good sense to run, including the Kwuba who had been spared by being pulled from the cistern before the mass killing.

Mnoba grasped my arm and lifted me up. I walked alongside him, the return trek to the staircase seeming so much longer than I remembered.

We started up the stairs to the city platform. The rectangular opening at the top was surrounded by Kwuba onlookers. Unable to see the cistern from where they stood, they fussed and whispered and wrung their hands. Curiosity got the better of one woman, who started down the steps, her back hunched like she was ducking for cover. She crept slowly from stair to stair until she could see the spill of bodies outside the cistern. A hand went to her forehead, and she started back up the stairs, only to stop for another look to verify that the horror was real.

A uniformed man broke through the crowd and started down the stairs, his stomach round as his face. "Colonel," said Dugu.

Meeting him close to the top, I snatched hold of his sleeve. "Don't go down there."

"I have to." He waved his comm unit. "The admiral wants pictures for the skyscreens."

"Go be with your family."

Dugu tilted his head to see around me. He sucked in a breath and slumped to a seat on one of the steps.

I leaned down to block his view, my eyes in front of his. "Go be with your family."

His mouth opened and closed and opened again. "I c-can't go home. Admiral's orders."

"Fuck the admiral. You hear me? Fuck him."

He slid his sleeve out of my fingers. "Let me go, Colonel." His voice softened so only I could hear. "If I defy him, he'll have me kill-ed. And then he'll kill my family."

<Jakob, let him film it.>

"Please," said Dugu.

"Ten minutes," I relented. "Use the lens as your shield, understand? See without seeing."

I waited for him to nod.

"See without seeing," I repeated before continuing up the last three stairs. The crowd cleaved a path, and they watched my every step, all of them expecting me to say something, to be the voice of authority in a time of need.

But I marched straight past their disappointed expectations. I marched past the stalled waterwheels into the city, where everything had fallen silent except for the hollow echo of our heels.

The crackle of skyscreen speakers shocked my nerves. I refused to look up. I didn't want to see his face.

Peoples of Maritinia, do not drink the water. I repeat, do not drink the water. The Empire has attack-ed. They've struck a terrible blow, but not with their ships. No, they've done something much more sinister. By enlisting the support of the traitors among us, the oppressors have poison-ed our cisterns.

I kept my head bowed, the booming voice pounding my eardrums.

We'd recruit-ed an army of fierce warriors from all around this world. It was an army that would've been the envy of the Sire's own personal regiment. Now look at our fallen brothers.

A quick glance at the sky confirmed Dugu had gotten his footage.

They've been robb-ed of their right to defend their home. Robb-ed of the right to fight. They've been murder-ed, and now we have no way to defend ourselves. Free Maritinia is finish-ed.

I picked up my pace, my footsteps clapping on the rock floor. I had to get to Sali. Only she could convince her father to stop this madness.

Yes, my friends, Free Maritinia is no more. Soon, the Empire's soldiers will eliminate what's left of our military. Their new contingent will take over for our administration. The Empire's governor will take control, and the shackles of oppression will take the place of freedom.

But there is one more thing they have plann-ed. His voice lowered like he was whispering a secret. *Listen to me closely. They plan to have the Jebyl take the Kwuba's rightful place.*

Striding even faster now, my scalp started to itch with sweat. I braved a look up at the closest screen. His face filled the entire frame.

The Jebyl resistance is working with the Empire. They've made a secret deal to betray their sisters and brothers in exchange for replacing the Kwuba as this world's privileged class. He leaned even closer to the screen and snarled his next words. *The Jebyl have kill-ed our warriors.*

I knew better. I'd seen the soldiers and the black sashes poisoning the water. And I knew the Jebyl had no interest in supplanting the Kwuba as the new aristocracy. Only a madman's paranoid fantasy could imagine the Jebyl conspiring with the Empire.

The screen cut to a view of the bamboo cuda I'd carved.

The Jebyl left this cuda fish when they destroy-ed our missile system. With this symbol of the resistance, they claim-ed responsibility for the attack.

But the Jebyl hadn't attacked the missile system. That was me. To save myself from suspicion, I was the one who planted the cuda fish. I should've known it could lead to this.

I was the one who turned the admiral's outlandish theory of a Jebyl plot into fact.

And now, thousands had already lost their lives. Thousands.

I stopped walking to cough and gag, the number impossible to swallow.

The skyscreen zoomed in on the fish's bite, its sharp teeth shaped with my own hands just like the hideous events unfolding all over this word.

You all know, I'm a kindheart-ed man. At first, I refuse-ed to believe we had traitors among us. I couldn't believe that Maritinians could be so treacherous.

But now the Jebyl resistance has kill-ed our army. They are so desperate to raise their station that they've slaugh-ter-ed thousands of their own in order to keep me from de-fending our world. They've made it clear what they want. The leeches are no longer content to suck Kwuba blood. The bottom-feeders want to enslave the Kwuba and suck directly from the Empire's rich veins.

I ran, breath huffing in and out of my lungs. Some-where behind me, I could hear Mnoba trying to keep up.

The Empire will kill me soon. But I won't allow my clan to become slaves to traitors. The Jebyl menace must be de-stroyed. Now, before their comrades in space arrive. Because what do you do when a leech takes too much blood? The ad-miral had moved so close to the screen that only bared teeth and flared nostrils were visible. *You rip it off, and you grind it under your heel.*

CHAPTER 28

"The Empre was my womb, bt I wass born on Maritinia."

—JAKOB BRYCE

I raced down the street and tore through the curtain into our home. The living space was empty. Calling Sali's name, I sprinted through the kitchen to the bathroom, but she wasn't there. Shooting up the stairs, I found a vacant bedroom.

<She's not here, Jakob.>

Desperate to talk to her, I rushed onto the balcony, then forced my weary legs to carry me to the roof.

<She's not here,> Pol repeated.

I put my hands on my knees and sucked air in and

out of my lungs. A quick swipe of my sleeve wiped the sweat from my face.

Where was she? A terrifying thought knifed into my mind. Had she drunk the water?

No, I told myself. The admiral ordered the waterwheels stopped before poisoning the cistern. Had that water been allowed to flow through the city, the Kwuba would've died, too. His first strike was targeted at only the Jebyl who were willing and capable of fighting back.

I went to the wall, pressed my stomach against the barnacle shells, and leaned over to look for Sali on the street below. Mnoba stood by the entrance. His body was bent at the waist, his torso bobbing with heavy breaths.

Other than Mnoba, the street was deserted. An abandoned cart sat at the corner, its catch of fish and eel baking in the sun. A breeze rustled down the boulevard, the air reeking of salt water and spoiled seafood.

The skyscreens came back to life. This time it was Mmirehl's angular face that bisected the screen. *The Jebyl traitors have cleared the way for the Empire's return. The Empire will arrive any minute to impose their new order. The Jebyl can't wait to take your place. They will steal everything you hold dear. They have no honor. No respect. They will take your wives in their filthy hands. They will slit your children's throats and feed them to the angry souls. The Jebyl are leeches who will suck you dry and kick your desiccate-ed corpse into the sea. They must be exterminate-ed.*

<I have to find her, Pol.>

<Why?>

<So she can convince her father to stop this insanity.>

<Your mission is over. Let it be.>

<But we started this, Pol. You and I. We have to stop it.>

<We didn't kill those people, Jakob. The admiral did.>

<He thinks the Jebyl are working with the Empire.>

<We didn't put that falsehood in his head.>

<Of course we did! And we made it true when we framed the resistance for destroying the missile platform.>

Mmirehl's voice slithered into my ears. *The Jebyl are ungrateful backstabbers. They are a plague. They will put leashes around your necks and make you lick their feet clean.*

<Please,> said Pol, <I urge you to stop thinking this way. Be proud that you've completed your mission and leave it at that.>

<He's going to kill them all.>

<We can do nothing for them. You can't save them. You can't even approach the Ministry without being killed on sight.>

<But Sali can. Her father still cares what she thinks.>

<You don't really believe she can make a difference.>

I tilted my head. <Why are you being such a defeatist?>

<Events must run their course.>

The seriousness in his tone made me light-headed with shock. <You want to let the Jebyl die.>

His voice was cold. Emotionless. <Correct.>

I felt a sharp pinch and looked down to see a pair of crab claws clamping at my stomach. I took a step back from the wall. Refusing to let go, the creature pulled out of its shell and dangled harmlessly from my shirt. <You knew this could happen.>

<Yes. The analysts thought a catastrophe of these proportions was possible but unlikely.>

I pulled the crab from my shirt and held it in my hand. Eyestalks rose from its head and mouthparts and silently moved up and down. <And how did the analysts classify this particular scenario?>

A single word crept up from the depths of the rabbit hole and instantly exploded upon making contact with my mind. <Optimal.>

My entire body went weak. I steadied myself by reaching to the wall with my free hand. Mmirehl's shouts assaulted my reeling senses. *Exterminate them now! Now! The Empire is coming!*

I squeezed the crab tight to keep it from slipping out of my fingers and saw myself mirrored in the way it kicked its helplessly unmoored legs back and forth. <Why?>

<You should know the answer, Jakob. You were an analyst once.>

<Tell me. I want to hear it from you.>

<You know we've tried to block news of Maritinia's successful revolution from infecting the rest of the

Empire, but word has spread nonetheless. When we retake this world in a few weeks, we will not only be able to claim victory, but thanks to your friend Dugu's camera work, we will also be able to show pictures of what happened here to the rest of the Empire. The lesson will be clear. This is what happens when people shun the Sire and try to rule themselves.>

<There are half a million Jebyl on this world. You'd let them die to use them as a symbol?>

<Perception is everything, Jakob. It's important we're not seen as oppressors. Instead, we'll be saviors.>

<A half million will die. A half million flesh-and-blood people.>

<What are a half million people compared to the billions and billions who will die of war and famine if the Empire cleaves in two?>

<You wanted this to happen. You engineered it.>

<Political systems are near impossible to engineer, Jakob. But after witnessing the admiral's psychological instability, I thought the possibility of a massive catastrophe was much greater than originally estimated. Even so, the best you or I could do was encourage the conditions for such an event. But in the end, the decision was the admiral's and his alone.>

I heard shouts and looked down to see nobody but Mnoba on the street. Scanning left and right, I saw eerily still homes and businesses. A woman's screams echoed from some hidden place, and I searched neighboring windows in an effort to spot her. Loud enough to compete with Mmirehl's relentless hate speech, the screams seemed to swirl all around me before falling silent.

I took one last look at the crab before setting the hapless creature down. <You used me.>

<Used you? Isn't that what you signed up for? To serve your Sire? Didn't you swear allegiance and volunteer to be His servant in every way?>

<Yes.>

<You wanted to follow in the honorable footsteps of your father and grandfather, and you did. Take heart in the fact that you've exceeded every one of their expectations.>

I stared up at the broad, blue sky, knowing my home world was out there somewhere. Korda, capital of the Empire, an amazing world of boundless industry and wealth. A planet completely encased by sprawling structures of glass and steel. An architectural marvel that flowered with sculptures and fountains and glorious monuments.

I'd grown up believing Korda was a wonder of such incredible grandeur that it served as absolute proof of the Empire's divinity.

But I couldn't believe that anymore. Where was the divinity in denying your subjects the freedom to pursue their own hopes and dreams? Where was the divinity in denying them the technology that could extend their lives? Where was the divinity in allowing a half million of your subjects to be murdered for a piece of propaganda?

The Empire was wrong. And the Falali Mother was

right. I had a role to play in this world's future. A destiny to fulfill.

And this was my moment.

Sali was the only person who could stop the atrocities about to unfold. And I was the only person who could convince her to do what was necessary.

Me.

Jakob.

I wouldn't let Maritinia fall into murderous chaos. Maritinia was a part of me, and I was a part of her. We'd been joined from the moment I'd been blessed by the cuda. That was when Maritinia's oceans began to wash the Empire from my heart. That was when her corals had taken root on my soul.

I smiled into the sun and felt the spirit of Falal surge through me. She and I would rise against the Sire and spend eternity dancing to the gentle sway of kelp. Together, we'd flow and mingle like the tides.

I was Maritinian.

"There you are," said Sali.

I turned around to face her. Seeing the worry lines around her eyes, I allowed my smile to fade into concern. "Where were you?"

"I went out to find you."

I took her in my arms wanting to tell her everything would be okay. But the Jebyl needed her help. "You have to stop your father."

"I can't."

"Yes, you can. You're the only one who can. His soldiers won't stop you from entering the Ministry."

She pulled from my embrace just far enough to look into my eyes. "And then what?"

<Enough of this, Jakob. That's an order.>

I swept Pol's comments out of my mind and pressed my forehead against Sali's. "You have to convince your father to stop. You can't let him murder the Jebyl."

"He won't listen to me."

<Stop, Jakob.>

I narrowed my focus to Sali and only Sali. "You have to try."

She closed her eyes. "And what if I fail?"

I rested my hands on her cheeks. "Then you'll have to kill him."

She took a slow step back, her face pulling free of my hands. Her eyes were open now, but distant. "I can't do that."

"Listen to Mmirehl, Sali." I pointed in the direction of the skyscreens.

A plague. The Jebyl are germs, worthless parasites. The leeches must be squash-ed before they. . .

I watched Sali's eyes, watched them drown under the torrent of sewage spilling from Mmirehl's mouth. Taking her hand, I told her the truth. "Mmirehl and your father have already eliminated the Jebyl who could fight. All over this world, they lured the young and willing to the cisterns, and they poisoned them."

Her voice was a whisper. "That was the resistance who poisoned them."

"You know there is no resistance. Why would the resistance murder their own? Your father did that. I was there. I watched his soldiers and black sashes. I saw them poisoning the water. He's going to kill a half million defenseless people, Sali. You're the only one who can save them."

"I'm not the only one. The Empire is already descending from orbit. They'll end this before it goes any further."

"No, they wo—"

<JAKOB!> Pol's voice burst from deep inside my head with a volume I didn't know was possible. <STOP NOW OR YOU'LL SUFFER THE CONSEQUENCES.>

<What consequences?> I terminated the question with a dismissive chuckle. <Threaten me with all the bad performance reports you want. I'm not going home.>

<I'm warning you. Stop now, or you will answer for this treason.>

Sali stared at me, waiting for me to finish my thought. I dropped her hand and took hold of her shoulders. "The Empire will arrive too late to stop this. They're three weeks away."

Her dazed eyes sharpened to pinpoints. "How could you possibly know that?"

A wry grin pushed at the corners of my mouth. Even under total duress, she missed nothing.

<YOU UTTER ANOTHER WORD, AND I SWEAR YOU WILL PAY DEARLY.>

<I won't be your tool anymore.>

His voice dropped to a low growl. <I'm only going

to say this one more time. I will protect the Empire's secrets at all costs.>

<You can't stop me. You don't have a kill switch, remember?>

Sali's brows hovered over confused eyes. "The ships are in orbit, Drake. I've seen the pictures. They'll be landing any minute."

Mmirehl's face loomed in the sky, his tongue sharp and deadly as any machete. More screams rang from the street below. It had begun. The storm was upon us.

But what I felt was total peace.

Destiny was all around me. I could feel it in the sunlight heating my skin. I could taste it on the air.

This was *my* time. I touched the scars on my cheek, felt the mark of Falal, and like a fledgling cuda daring to swim with the school for the first time, I dove into my future.

"Those pictures were fakes. The Empire is still weeks away."

"How do you know?"

"I'm done with the lies, Sali. From now on, I will only tell you the truth, but first I need you to know that I love you. I never meant to hurt you."

"What are you saying, Drake? You're scaring me."

"I'm not Drake. I'm Jakob Bryce. I'm the Empire's spy. I took Drake's place."

Her jaw dropped, and her brows twisted into confusion. "What are you talking about?"

I waited for Pol to do something, say something. But he didn't. He was as impotent as I thought.

I pushed forward. "I killed him, Sali. I killed Drake, and I took his place. That wasn't my brother they found in the ocean. That was the colonel."

She pushed me away. "That's impossible."

"You knew I wasn't him. I look like him, and I sound like him, but you knew I was different. You knew that right from the beginning."

She covered her face with her hands.

"I've been in contact with the Empire. They're still three weeks away."

"This can't be."

"It is. I destroyed the missile system. Remember how I told you I'd cut my feet on the wreckage? That was a lie. I cut my feet on barnacles when I climbed out of the water to set the timer."

"Why are you telling me this?"

"Because you need to know the Empire can't save the Jebyl. Only you can save them, Sali. If your father won't listen to reason, you have to kill him."

CHAPTER 29

"Reality comes to me in the cruelest disguises."

—JAKOB BRYCE

I tried to follow her, but one venomous look from her betrayed face froze me in place. She disappeared down the steps, and I was alone on the rooftop.

She'd see I was right. She might never forgive me, but she'd see I was right about the Jebyl. I was right about her father. I just had to give her time to reach the same conclusion.

I listened as the skyscreens continued to rain bile all around this world. The bile was effective. Shouts and screams were becoming more regular now.

Much as I wanted to continue giving her space,

I couldn't wait any longer. I had to convince her. Quickly, before more died.

I took a step toward the stairs but stopped when I heard the unmistakable clop of boots on the stone. First a cap came into view. Then came shadowed eyes and a sharp nose. Mmirehl climbed the last step and sneered. "The admiral isn't here to protect you this time. And neither is his daughter."

"Where is she? What did you do with her?"

He walked toward me. "She's well, but she's just told me the most wonderful story."

I looked to the skyscreen and saw the same foul expression blown up to hundredfold size. How could he be in two places at once? "Where did you come from?"

"Oh that," he said with a dismissive wave at the screen. "That's a recording."

He stepped the rest of the way up to me and put his hands on my shoulders. "Over the wall you go."

I twisted away from his grasp and swung an elbow at his throat. Connecting, I heard a gurgle and saw his cap fly off. With one motion, I dropped my shoulder into his midsection and seized an arm. I lifted him off the ground, and as I moved closer to the wall, I felt his hair sweep across my face.

Something wasn't right.

But I wasn't going to think it through. Not now. Not when I had it in my power to wipe this scourge from existence.

With a heave, I threw him out into the open space beyond the wall.

I watched him fall. No, wait—*her* fall. I watched her legs crumple and saw her head bounce off the stone.

Her legs. Her head.

My mind screeched with the sound of fractured thoughts scraping against each other like jagged shards of glass. My eyes were seeing something that couldn't be real.

But it was real.

Sali lay on the stone. Her neck was kinked at an impossible angle. Her eyes were open, but empty. Her mouth hung open like the mouths of so many dead I'd seen.

A voice crept up from the darkest dungeon in my head. <I warned you, Jakob. I told you I would do what was necessary to protect the Empire's secrets.>

CHAPTER 30

"The enemmy is in miy head."

—JAKOB BRYCE

Blood sopped into the knees of my pants as I huddled alongside Sali.

Mnoba rested a hand on my back. "Why did she jump?"

She hadn't jumped. I'd done this to her. But I thought she was Mmirehl. I saw him. I heard him.

Mnoba lifted his hand, and I heard him shuffle away to give me space.

I took a lock of her hair into my hand and pinched the strands in my fingers. When I'd lifted Mmirehl, I'd felt his hair brush over my face. But it couldn't have been his hair. His was trimmed too close to the scalp.

It was Sali's hair that had swept my cheeks. My Sali's.

I shot the question down the rabbit hole. <How could you?>

Pol didn't respond. He'd already said all he needed to.

For Sire and Empire.

I leaned over and pressed my forehead against hers. I'm sorry, Sali. I didn't know he could make me see things that didn't exist. I didn't know he could make me hear anything he wanted.

I should've known his connections to my eyes and ears weren't just for receiving. When he'd admitted he didn't have a kill switch, I should've known he had some other power over me. The E^3 didn't let their dogs run without leashes.

I'm so sorry, Sali. Tears spilled from my eyes to fall on her cheek. I couldn't imagine what she must've thought when she'd come back up the stairs. She'd seen my shock and anger at thinking I'd seen Mmirehl. She'd heard me ask him questions that must've sounded like nonsense. She'd come across the roof because she was worried about me. She'd taken hold of my shoulders to show her concern.

My chest tightened around lungs that hurt for air before wracking sobs took hold. She must've been so confused when I'd struck her in the throat. So betrayed when I'd lifted her up and tossed her to her death.

Sobs gave way to a coughing fit as my throat choked on the most horrific thing of all.

She'd died thinking I didn't love her.

I lifted my face to look at the sky—a vast blue smear to my tear-filled eyes. How could you let the cuda stop with a kiss to my cheek? If you loved your people, you should've let the angry souls rip me to pieces.

I was no blessed hero. I was a wrecker of lives and dreams. My love for Sali was her death sentence. My love for this world's people and culture was a curse of madness and bloodlust.

I was a plague to this world. A wretch with a heart made of black tar that trapped and smothered anybody I dared let inside.

<You left me no choice, Jakob.>

The sound of his voice raked down my spine.

<Nobody can know our ways,> he said. <The secrets you divulged to her were a dangerous breach of security.>

Tears of sorrow became tears of rage. I tried to shout at the foul bastard, but the tempest of emotions swirling through my mind made it impossible to find the dirty little hole he lived in.

<You let your emotions muddy your decision making. Be thankful the Sire had the wisdom to put me here to protect you from yourself.>

I squeezed my eyes shut and concentrated on sending my words down the rabbit hole. <Get out of my head!>

<Is this how you thank me?>

I pressed the heels of my hands against my temples. <I loved her.>

<I told you not to develop feelings for her. Every step of the way, I've tried to guide you, and you've ignored my advice. The pain you feel is entirely of your own doing.>

<She could've saved the Jebyl.>

<From now on, I expect total compliance.> His tone took on a cruel edge. <Or the next time you try to suck crab meat from a claw you might find a piece of broken glass in your mouth. The next time you step out onto a bridge, the bridge might not be there. You are an agent of the Empire, and you *will* obey.>

My nerves iced over, and I felt heavy with the cold weight of defeat. I looked into her eyes one last time. I'm so sorry, Sali. I thought I was significant. I thought I was the blessed hero. Like Kell before me, I thought I could set this world on a better course.

But Kell and I were both too arrogant. The Empire had punished us for our insubordination. Kell's punishment had been vicious but quick. Mine would be long and tortured as I'd be forced to watch the downfall of the world he and I both loved.

CHAPTER 31

> "I hearr voices. Does tht make me insane? I think
> it does."
>
> —JAKOB BRYCE

I wandered Maringua, the capital city of the world I'd
helped to destroy.

Broad avenues would pull me along for a while,
then an alley would steal me for a bit until it spat me
onto another street. The sun had almost sunk from
existence, but not the mayhem. Hour after hour,
Mmirehl and the admiral had taken turns broadcasting from the skyscreens in an unrelenting campaign to
keep the Kwuba whipped into a bloody froth.

Machetes.

So many machetes in the hands of butchers. Butchers who hacked their helpless neighbors like they were breaking down fish carcasses.

I'd felt every blow of the blade as if I'd delivered it myself. Kell was just the first. One after another, the Jebyl fell to the roving mobs trapped in a lust for death.

Nobody touched me. My uniform made me invisible to most, and those who charged close enough to recognize their Bless-ed Hero shambled away in shame.

I turned a corner, one of a hundred corners I'd turned, one of a hundred horrors I'd walked past. But this time I stopped.

A woman lay on her side. Dead. Her throat had been gashed, and her blood had drained into a broad spill. Her baby girl sat in the pool, face flushed and crying. I watched the baby reach for the silk cloth covering her mother's breast, but her tiny fingers failed to grasp hold. She tried again, this time succeeding in gripping the fabric but failing to find the strength to move it. Next, she slapped at the fabric as if it might retreat by force of will. When it didn't, she flapped her arms in frustration.

I picked up the hungry baby and wiped the smears of blood from her face. "Shush, little one. I've got you."

When I reached my home, Mnoba stood dutifully by the door. Five firefly lanterns lay on the stone, circling the spot Sali had died.

Her body had been removed, and although the

stone had been washed, I could still see the faint discoloration of blood. The woman I'd loved had been reduced to a stain.

I carried the baby through the curtain into my home. Dozens of Jebyl sat on the floor, their faces strained with terror. Mnoba stepped up next to me. "I'm sorry, sir. I couldn't turn them away. They came to seek refuge."

"You are Kwuba, no? Why haven't you turned them in?"

He met my gaze directly. "We don't all think as the admiral does."

I moved the baby to my other arm. "You didn't follow me when I went for my walk."

"The old rules no longer apply. All that matters now are these people."

A couple came to take the baby. "We'll clean her up," said the man.

I released the young one. "She's hungry."

The woman put the infant on her hip. "I'll take her to Buna. She's nursing a little one of her own."

I stepped into the center of the room and felt the press of body heat all around. Surrounded by the stare of wide eyes, I wrung my bloodstained hands. I wanted to apologize. I wanted to drop to my knees and beg forgiveness for the part I'd played in creating the calamity that had befallen their world.

I rubbed bloody hands together. My heart broke

for them. It broke for all the living. And the dead. Especially for Sali. How could I ever make sense of the things I'd seen today?

Mnoba whispered in my ear. "Are you okay, sir?"

I pulled my mind back into the moment. These people had come to me for a reason. They'd come to me because they thought I could save them.

<Will you stop me if I try to help them, Pol?>

<Do as you wish. The genocide will proceed whether you help a few people or not. In fact, saving a handful of Jebyl might make a nice feel-good story one day. In the midst of chaos, an agent of the Empire risks his life to—>

I tuned out Pol's propagandizing and spoke to the crowd. "You're safe with me."

I walked fast, but I couldn't escape the tide of hatred coming from the skyscreens. The beak-faced Mmirehl had been at it all night. Circling the skies like a vulture, he attacked his carrion with words of violence. Inciting machete-wielding mobs, he pecked Jebyl skin from muscle, and muscle from bone.

I pressed my hands over my ears but couldn't stop his voice from picking at my mind. Couldn't stop him from pulling apart my last few threads of sanity with his bloodstained beak.

I'd stopped walking. Couldn't remember where I was going.

Someplace important. That much I knew. I had to concentrate.

Forcing my ears flat to my skull, I took stock of my surroundings. The sky had started to ooze the light of dawn. And the street was littered with shadowlike forms that wouldn't rise with the morning sun.

Focus.

I hadn't done such a bad job focusing most of the night. Mnoba and I had accomplished much. A guard rotation. Provision rationing. A short expedition to the quay to steal as much food and clean water as twenty men could carry.

Our ranks had grown throughout the night. Grown until my home was jammed with so many Jebyl that I'd been squeezed out onto the street.

That was when I realized I should've saved space for Dugu and his family.

Dugu. I was on my way to Dugu's. Other than his mother, his family was Jebyl. They'd be safe in my asylum.

Keeping my hands over my ears, I started moving again, trying to remember the path young Dory had led us along the previous night.

<Take the stairs, Jakob.>

I uncovered my ears and plugged them with my index fingers. <SHUT UP!>

<What's wrong with you? Remember how the stairs lead to the rope bridge? From the far side of the bridge, Dugu's house is just around the corner.>

I drove my fingers painfully deep into my ear canals in a useless effort to silence him. <I TOLD YOU TO SHUT UP.>

<Fine. If you don't want my help, let your friend die with the rest of them.>

He went silent. Blissfully silent. Now where was I going again?

The bridge. Chagrined to admit he was right, I headed for the stairs and took them up several flights to the top of a building where I could spy the sun just starting to peek over the watery horizon.

I walked up to the broad expanse of crisscrossed ropes that suspended the bridge over a chasm of collapsed stone. Scattered as my mind had become, I remembered Pol's threat: The next time you step out onto a bridge, the bridge might not be there. Reaching out a toe, I tapped the bamboo. Stretching out a hand, I tapped my palm against the fibrous rope. He could make me see and hear what he wanted, but my other senses, including the sense of touch, were still mine.

Stepping onto the bamboo slats, I felt the bridge sag under my weight before it rebounded to the bouncy creak of rope. The bridge was real.

I walked, fingers sliding over rope railings that had been worn shiny and smooth. I looked to the homes on the far side, cerulean walls bleached to a drab gray by the weak light of dawn. Arriving at the span's low point, I stopped and knelt so I could reach a sluice that ran parallel to the bridge. Putting my fingers inside, I felt the bone-dry bottom. If clean water didn't start flowing soon, many more would die.

I started to rise but stopped when my eyes landed on a rope that had been tied to the bamboo under my feet. Looking through the gap between the slats, I could see something solid below the bridge. Carefully poking my head through a space between the ropes, I leaned out into open space.

A bald man. Hanged. His midsection had been splayed open, a tumble of tangled intestines swaying alongside his lifeless feet.

Next to him was a woman. Also hanged and disemboweled. Beyond her were the three children, the youngest just a baby.

Clustered together, the entire family hung close enough to hold hands. Separated by death, they'd be forever incapable of comforting each other.

I pulled my head back through the ropes and tried to rub the images out of my eyes.

Monsters. Only monsters do such a thing to children. Who but a monster could look into the eyes of baby and cut it open?

But I remembered the sight of Kell's wild eyes when I'd embedded my machete in his jaw. I remembered the row of corpses killed when I detonated the missile system.

Was I a monster, too? Or just a man. A man who was capable of monstrous acts in the name of his Sire.

The people who murdered that family weren't monsters.

They were people. My eyes teared up with the power of the revelation.

They were people. My people.

Now where was I going again?

CHAPTER 32

> "Did I turn my hpme into a safe asyluum or an
> insane asylum? Or both."
>
> –JAKOB BRYCE

Like every morning for the last three weeks, I stepped into Dugu's house and searched every room, only to find the same hollow result. Floors that were bare except for the remnants of smashed furniture. Closets that were empty except for rolled-up sleeping mats.

I half expected Pol to tell me I was wasting my time coming here every day. But after weeks of my ignoring anything the son of a bitch said, he'd finally taken the hint and stayed quiet most of the time.

Stepping outside, I headed for the quay so I could make my daily stroll through the dead. Wandering the piles, my eyes would search for a girl the size of Dory. Or a portly young man in uniform. An old uncle with bony knees.

I knew they'd probably been killed, but until I saw their bodies, I refused to accept it. Dugu was a clever young man. He could've found his family a safe asylum like the one in my home. I'd heard of several run by Falali priestesses. Or he and his family could've set out to sea. Boats arrived every day with families that had ridden out the storm by sailing off to distant waters or remote islands.

The Empire hadn't arrived as promised by the admiral. Some were relieved. Some were disappointed. Others saw it for the lie it was.

The killing lasted about a week. Maybe more. Maybe less. Couldn't remember because the days bled one into the next.

What stopped the slaughter? A principled rebuke by the Falali Council of Interpreters? A Jebyl uprising? Nothing so heroic.

Instead, it was the lack of potable water that finally halted the savagery. When even Kwuba began to die of thirst, they were forced to come to their senses. Repairing the cisterns became a priority, and after several days of labor, the city's lifeblood began to flow again.

Even then, the admiral and Mmirehl continued to shout from the skyscreens, but when they eventually realized nobody was listening, they gave their hoarse voices a rest, and silence returned to a shell-shocked population.

Then came the cleanup. Day after day, bodies arrived on the quay. Like bails of kelp, they were roped and hauled behind the powerful legs of mammoths. Some of the dead were recognizable enough to be claimed by family. Others had been butchered beyond identification. And others had so badly decomposed that their flesh wouldn't hold as they were dragged across the stone. These arrived as nothing more than bundles of naked bones held together by rotting sinew and stringy muscle.

Falal received all of their remains in her waters, where some would get pulled under and others would float slowly out of sight, and out of existence. Out of everything but the memories of the survivors.

I turned left onto Maringua's broadest avenue. The quay was visible just a few blocks ahead. A month ago, this area was abuzz with activity. Now it was ghostly quiet. Rare pedestrians ambled like sleepwalkers, blank-faced and numb to the nightmare.

I hadn't slept. For weeks now, I hadn't slept.

But when darkness fell, I'd pretend to sleep. Pretend, so I could journal.

I'd gone crazy, you see. I could see it in the way people avoided me. The way they'd cringe when I yelled. The way almost every word I said would be followed by the exchange of concerned looks.

My mind was diseased, and I had to drain the infection. My head had to be purged before it could be purified.

So I journaled like mad. I put my mind's impulses

and urges into words. My thoughts into sentences. My memories into paragraphs.

I'd keep journaling until I converted my entire self into writing.

Then my mind would be empty. I'd be in the journal.

And once my entire self was converted into words, I could rewrite myself. I could prune and graft and reorganize until a coherent me emerged. A sane me. A better me.

Having created my new self, I'd do the long work of assimilating what I'd written. That was when my conversion would be complete.

I'd be transformed. Re-created. Rebirthed.

If Pol could be uploaded from one mind, reprogrammed, and downloaded again, so could I.

So could I.

And I'd do the whole thing with my eyes closed.

I stood on my rooftop. The ocean stretched out in front of me. Fields of golden kelp swayed under bottle green waves that sparkled bright under the afternoon sun.

I held up a piece of bamboo to gauge its length. The next fish had to be cut a little shorter than the previous one. I looked down at the more than two dozen carved cuda fish stacked by my feet. I needed five of each size.

Exactly five. Better count again.

Dropping to my knees, I carefully sorted the fish into several different piles. Here were the shortest ones. And here were the next shortest, about a quarter inch longer from mouth to tail. And these fishies were a tad longer, but I tallied only four. Not five. There had to be five, dammit.

I stormed down the stairs. "I want my fish, you stupid fucking freeloaders!" Reaching the balcony, I was greeted by the nervous stares of Jebyl refugees. Many had gone home after the killing stopped. Those who remained had no home to go to. I stomped my boot. "My fish! Somebody took one of my fish."

Buna stood, baby in her arms. "She's teething. I thought it would help her sleep."

The bamboo cuda was clutched in the baby's hands, its tail shiny with saliva. Buna gently pulled the cuda from the baby's hands, which prompted the same frustrated flapping of tiny arms I'd seen when I'd rescued her.

"It's okay," I said. "Keep it until she falls asleep, but I want it back immediately after."

"Very well, bless-ed one." She passed the fish back to the baby, and the fishtail went back in the baby's gnawing mouth.

I leveled a commanding gaze at Buna. "Don't take my fish again." I spun slowly around. "Same for the rest of you. Don't. Take. My. Fish."

Heads bowed and fingers nervously tapped hearts until the sound of a distant rumble turned all of our heads skyward. One of the Jebyl pointed, and I spotted the faraway speck of silver dropping from the heavens.

<They're here,> said Pol.

CHAPTER 33

> "The carver doesn't see a blockk. The carver
> sees teh form insde the block. The carver's job is
> simple. Whittls away the bits that don't belong
> and reveal the frm for all tto see."
>
> —JAKOB BRYCE

The Empire's squad of eight soldiers didn't come for me until morning. They found me on my rooftop, my bamboo cudas and carving tools packed neatly into a pair of satchels.

With one satchel over each shoulder, I followed them downstairs, past the dumbfounded stares of Mnoba and the Jebyl refugees. Their confusion was understandable. Didn't the soldiers consider me a traitor to the Empire? Shouldn't they shackle me or shoot me on sight?

I offered no explanation. Didn't say a word on my way out, or the entire way to the quay, or when I boarded the squad's squid-powered boat and sat near the bow.

We set sail for the Ministry, and I stared straight ahead as the squids dragged us through corpses that thumped the hull. No sign of cuda. They'd long since had their fill.

The skyscreens had been wiped of the admiral's bull of a face and now glowed with the gentle smile of the Sire. I stared at his perfectly positioned teeth for most of the trip, waiting for him to open his mouth so I could see his forked tongue.

Approaching the Ministry, I studied the Empire's transport vessel floating in the deep water perhaps a hundred yards behind the domes. Like an iceberg, most of the ship's bulk was submerged, its dark shadow looming below the rippling surface. The ship's perfectly sloped steel walls rose a few a few feet out of the water, where they flattened into a broad circle centered by an open hatch.

A pair of gunners stood behind firecannons on tripod mounts. Another soldier was busy stringing gold bunting from a rickety wire framework.

<See how the ship has no antimissile-defense system?> said Pol. <If we hadn't sabotaged the admiral's defenses, the transport would've made an easy target.>

Ignoring Pol's commentary, I turned my gaze on the soldiers who had retrieved me. Several could be older than me, but to my eye, they seemed very young. Like toddlers who had just learned to walk.

They were good little soldiers. Follow orders, get a cookie. Carry out your mission, get another cookie. Always stay inside the lines.

They were too green to know the lines were drawn by a tyrant whose one and only goal was maintaining and extending power. The Sire and His minions had no respect for this world or its people. They didn't care that Maritinia breathed with a life her own.

So they'd kept this world chained in fear and ignorance. And when Maritinia defeated all odds by breaking free, the Empire took advantage of that fear and ignorance by manipulating us into cannibalizing ourselves.

I turned an eye on the sergeant, his head scanning left and right like the training manuals taught. The fool still believed the manuals could prepare you for any situation. I wanted to ask him what the manuals said about hatred that could spread from person to person like a voracious cancer. What kind of prepackaged wisdom did they offer to explain the tide of bodies fouling these waters?

The wounds this world had suffered were unfathomable. But I believed recovery was possible. Even if it took generations. Touching my cheek, I knew the deepest wounds grew the toughest scars.

But the Empire wouldn't allow this world to recover. Instead, they'd put us on display. They'd take our story to the Empire, a little show-and-tell to demonstrate the disasters that await those who experiment with self-rule. And when that story ceased to be useful, they'd put us back in a box and leave us to suffocate.

Our boat arrived at the Ministry, and, tossing my satchels over my shoulders, I climbed onto the pier. A woman waited for me. A straight-lined suit hung over an authoritative posture, gray hair draping over an erect collar with starched points. Shallow wrinkles added a good measure of gravitas to an otherwise youthful face. She waited for the guards to move out of earshot before speaking. "Mr. Bryce, I presume."

I nodded.

She offered a regal smile. "I'm Governor Prima. Your Sire sends his congratulations. He's very proud of what you've been able to accomplish under the most trying of circumstances."

I shrugged. And then I strode away.

"Where are you going?" she called.

I didn't stop. Had no interest in listening to her platitudes.

Up ahead, two soldiers put their hands on the fir-erods strapped over their shoulders. Telling them to stand down, the governor hustled up to fall in step alongside me. "We met no resistance last night. The admiral and his officers are locked up. It's absolutely amazing what you accomplished."

Reaching the ringed island, I barely glanced at the lagoon and turned for the domes.

"I have to introduce you to Major Lensa. He and I need to debrief you. Perhaps it's best you take a short break to relax. We have a room ready for you, and when you're ready, we can talk."

The domes. I was saddened to see the damage they'd taken from the missile blast I'd engineered. Patches of silver tiles had been stripped away, leaving pieces of shrapnel embedded in small craters of stone. Repair should be a high priority.

The governor took hold of my forearm. "Are you okay, Mr. Bryce?"

I stopped to glare at her hand. Manicured nails painted pastel green.

"Maybe we should get you to the doctor," she said.

<Talk to her, Jakob. You're making a fool of yourself.>

I kept drilling her hand with my eyes. When it finally lifted off my arm, I resumed my brisk pace. She kept up but didn't speak, her breathing growing labored. Too much time behind desks could do that to you.

Passing the first dome entrance, I started counting my footsteps. One. Two. Three.

She started prattling again, but I didn't listen. I was too focused on counting. Eight. Nine. Ten. I'd wanted to know how far apart the domes were. I was betting on 107 steps from door to door.

She talked the whole way, but all I heard was background noise, like the drone of an engine. As we neared the second dome, I became aware of an increasingly worried tone, like her engine was running too fast on a low gear. Then I heard the words, "Get the doc."

A soldier ran off, and I had to concentrate even

harder to keep from getting distracted by the hurried rhythm of his clopping boots: 122; 123; 124.

Taking my 125th step, I found myself under the arched entrance of the second dome. Interesting. Almost twenty paces farther than I'd thought.

"I don't need a doctor," I said finally. "I'm going in to see the Falali Mother. Then you can debrief me whenever you want."

I strode into the dome and made a straight line past the water pumps to the tunnel that led to the underwater complex. Down the stairs I went, the tapping of the governor's heels right behind me.

Reaching the bottom, I stopped at the hatchway and dropped my satchels into a puddle. Opening the satchel on the left, I started sifting through my bamboo cudas.

"What are you doing?"

"The Ministry entrances require blessings." I picked out one of the shortest of the batch, the perfect choice for this particular hatchway, and balanced it on the metal lip over the opening. "Have you fixed the pumps? Three of the five stairways are flooded."

"We're working on bringing the pumps up to full capacity now, but for the moment we're not worried about the stairways. The priority right now is repairing the control center."

"That's too bad."

"Why do you say that?"

I pointed to the satchels. "Looks like I carved more fish than I needed."

She squinted her eyes like she was trying to bring me into focus. "I can only imagine what you've been through. I'd like you to see our doctor."

"No doctors."

"Can't you see how strange your behavior is?"

"By strange you mean crazy?"

She tilted her head. "I wouldn't use that word. How about erratic?"

"I can see why they sent you," I said. "You've got a talent for diplomacy."

"Why do you think the hatches need blessings?"

I didn't respond until I found the right words. "The fish create balance."

Her eyebrows pinched together as if she didn't understand what I'd said. "How so?"

"I've watched hundreds of thousands get butchered in the streets. That's a lot of angry souls to appease."

"Angry souls? You must be referring to the Falali myth that those who are wronged in life are reincarnated as cuda fish."

"You've done your research."

"I spent an hour with the Falali Mother last night. She had much to say."

"Emmina is very wise."

"She's been made aware of recent events. We've barely begun to sift through all of the footage captured by the skyscreen cameras, but we have a good idea what happened here. Isn't it horrible what can happen when people reject the Sire's leadership?"

I picked up my satchels and measured the bamboo

cuda I'd set over the hatchway with a good long stare. Yes, that was the best choice. "I need to bless the other entrance that isn't flooded. Then I want to talk to the Falali Mother."

I ducked through the hatchway, Governor Prima following right behind. "I can arrange that. But before I let you talk to her, I want to get your assessment. She demands to be set free so she can heal her people's spirits. Is she being earnest? Or is she a seditionist?"

"You needn't fear Emmina. All she wants is the best for her people."

I sat in the conference room, alone at the table, in the seat the admiral used to occupy. My fingers traced the table's wood grain. Such beautiful Karthedran redwood. Ducking my head under the table, I counted six table legs. Thick as my thigh at the top, they tapered down to narrow ankles before terminating in circular feet.

What a pleasure it would be to carve real wood. Sea bamboo was a limited medium for my creations.

Did this table really need all six legs?

The governor arrived ten minutes later. By that time, I'd moved all the chairs, tipped the table on its side, and was one screw away from unfastening a leg.

"Give me a minute," I told her.

<Jakob, you are truly being ridiculous. The past couple weeks, I've tried my best to give you space, but it's time you got your head right.>

I paid Pol no heed. I wasn't taking advice on my mental state.

A few seconds later, I heard a male voice from the doorway. He asked what was wrong with me, but I didn't look up to see the new arrival. Using the handle of one of my carving tools, I gave the screw a turn.

"I think he's had a bit of a breakdown," said the governor.

"I don't have time for this," said the man.

"Be patient. He's been through a lot."

After several more turns, I'd loosened the screw enough to finish the job with my fingers. Pulling the screw from its bracket, I let the hunk of wood fall heavily into my hands. "There we go," I said. "I'll make good use of this."

"Apparently, he likes to carve wood," said the governor.

I waved at the man, a major according to the stars on his chest. "Help me stand this table back up."

He closed the door and complied with a sour smile. As expected, the table stood fine on just the five legs. I took a chair and sat down. "You must be Major Lensa."

He sat next to the governor on the opposite end of the table. "Yes, I am. But"—he glanced at the door to make sure it was still closed—"you should know that my military posting is just a cover. My true allegiance is to the E^3."

"You have my condolences."

His eyes wrinkled up in the corners. "Only you and

the governor are authorized to know that I'm the political officer for the resettlement effort."

"Political officer? I'll be sure to never turn my back on you."

His face darkened.

<Stop being rude, Jakob.>

For the first time in weeks, Pol made me smile. <A little sensitive, are we?>

"Where's the Falali Mother?" I asked the governor. "I told you I wanted to see her before my debriefing."

"We'll bring her to you," said the governor. "But the major and I want to talk to you first."

Gauging their faces, I knew further argument would be fruitless. I set my carving tools out on the table. "What do you want to know?"

She sat next to the major. "We want your story. We need to know everything that happened. Then we need your assessment of the current political situation. We're putting out calls on the skyscreens right now. We're asking that each population center choose representatives, including both Kwuba and Jebyl. We're asking that they come here to the Ministry so that we can restore the Empire's economic and political structure."

I hefted the table leg and set it on my lap. "You mean you're going to buy them off."

"A little carrot when appropriate. A little stick, too. These things can be very volatile if not handled correctly. That's why we need an accurate account from you."

I picked out the U-tipped tool. "Ask your questions."

"Please put the table leg down," said the major. "That's Ministry property."

I dug a long groove. "It's mine now."

"My patience has limits," said the governor. I didn't have to look up to hear the frown in her voice.

"I said I'd talk. Where should I start?"

A clunk on the table drew my gaze. The major had set a comm unit on the table, a far newer model than the one in my pocket. "I will be requesting codes from your embedded political officer. As you know, some codes mean true. Others false. I'll know if you're telling the truth."

The governor said, "Start at the beginning, Mr. Bryce."

CHAPTER 34

"People who see evrythingg in black adn white
fit in onne of two groups. Thos who are lucky
enugh to go through life and never have thos
principlles tested. Ant those who are idiots."

—JAKOB BRYCE

I carved while I talked. Finding it difficult to keep my composure, I kept my focus on the gouge in my hand and the short strips of wood tumbling to the floor. Staying lost in the heavenly aroma of cut redwood, I told my story.

Kell. Sali. The ceremony. The missile-defense system. Sali.

The major stopped me every ten minutes for a code check. Because Pol had no way to directly communicate with anybody outside my head, he'd recite a new string of numbers for me to repeat to the major. The major kept his eyes on his comm screen as he compared Pol's code against a predetermined list of true and false codes that had been communicated to Pol before his consciousness was implanted in my brain. Upon verifying I was telling the truth, the major would ask me to carry on.

The admiral and Mmirehl.

The lamprey and the mass poisoning.

Terror and murder and death.

Finished, I switched to the fishtail gouge. "I want to see the Falali Mother now."

The governor laid her hands flat on the table. "A harrowing tale, Mr. Bryce. No, an amazing tale. The results you've achieved are incredible. I can't help but marvel at what one man can accomplish when he carries the Sire in his heart. I don't mind telling you I was very nervous about accepting this post. I was convinced that a full-scale invasion force was required, but my requests for two thousand troops and an escort of warships were denied."

"Resources are hard to come by," said the major. "I imagine you haven't heard the bad news, Mr. Bryce. War is imminent. At latest count, ninety-two industrialized worlds have seceded. And another seventeen Outermost Ring worlds like this one have joined the rebellion."

"Yes," said the governor with a grave nod. "We'll hope that word of the atrocities that happened here will have a dampening effect on the traitors supporting revolution. The Empire hasn't been tested like this for a thousand years, but thanks to the selfless efforts of people like you, Mr. Bryce, I have complete faith we will prevail. The Sire owes you a debt of gratitude for completing your mission so successfully. Understaffed and underequipped as we are, I'd feared the worse."

I said nothing and drove the fishtail gouge into the wood, a long strip peeling free.

<Don't you have anything to say, Jakob? The major said war is imminent.>

Nearing a knot in the wood, I pushed harder.

<War is a serious thing, Jakob.>

It took all my will not to respond to him, not to shout that I, of all people, knew damn well how serious war was. But I wouldn't give Pol the satisfaction of a response.

Tightening my grip on the handle, I dug at the knot, the effort making my wrist shake. What I needed was a mallet, but I doubted my bone tools could withstand much pounding. Instead, I put the gouge back on the table and took up a carving knife so I could shave the knot away one flake at a time.

<Look at them, Jakob. They don't understand why you're not saying anything.>

Lifting my eyes, I met their questioning stares one at a time. "Are you going to let me see the Falali Mother or not?"

"Don't you want to know when you're going home?" asked the governor.

"I am home."

Her brows rose, thin creases forming on her forehead. "You're clearly not thinking straight, Mr. Bryce. It's no surprise after what you've been through. But staying here is not possible."

"Why not?"

"The local population believes you're really Colonel Kell. They think you're the Empire's most wanted man. We can't let you walk among the locals without raising suspicions. We need you to go home, where you'll be put on trial along with Dii Mnai and Mr. Mmirehl. Your executions will be broadcast throughout the Empire, though yours will obviously be faked. Trust me, we have ways to make an execution look believable. Then you'll be surgically changed back into yourself. From there, if you want to request a posting on Maritinia, I'm sure you can. Your experience with these subjects could prove valuable."

"Fine. When is my deportation scheduled?"

She crossed her arms over her chest. "For now, we need to keep the transport vessel floating outside the Ministry in case an emergency evacuation proves necessary. I'll release it, and you, once I'm sure the situation is stable, say four to six weeks."

I leaned back in my chair. "And what do I do until then?"

"You cannot leave the Ministry. Outdoor walks are allowed only under the cover of darkness, and only with an escort. A select few of our officers know you are a plant, but the rest think you're really the traitor. Fear not, we've given explicit orders to all our soldiers that you are to be treated with respect. We've told the rank and file that you turned against the admiral and gave us invaluable information in exchange for not being treated like a criminal. As long as you remain indoors, you will have the freedom to go where you like."

Somebody knocked on the door. My eyes went back to the wood.

"Come in," called the governor.

The door squeaked open, and a voice said, "We've checked all the video feeds for boats, and there are none within a half mile of the Ministry."

"You're thinking this is a good time for a drill?" asked the major.

"We need to make sure we can do a proper lockdown. We do it now, and we can have guards back on their posts in fifteen minutes. There aren't any boats close enough to pose a threat."

The major rubbed his jaw. "What about the water pumps? This complex leaks like a sieve. How are we going to protect them?"

"They'll be fine. There aren't any boats close en—"

"What about when it's not a drill?" the major interrupted, his words chopped with by impatience.

"Unlike the other domes, Dome 2 has a door that can be sealed, but the power situation is a mess."

"How so?"

Following an audibly deep breath, he said, "The ignorance of these people is stunning. I can hardly believe what they've done."

Having witnessed the Maritinians' technological incompetence on more than one occasion, I had to smile.

The soldier standing in the doorway was an engineer according to the purple patch on his shoulder. His face was young and full like Dugu's. He rubbed his jaw as he spoke. "The pumps' power lines aren't secure. Have you seen those black lines running alongside the lagoon?"

"Yes."

"That's them, right out in the open. They run across the stone before dropping underwater to go down to the turbines. And you're not going to believe what else they did."

"What?"

"They hung crab traps off the lines. At least fifty of them."

The major groaned, while I laughed under my breath.

The engineer rubbed his jaw some more. "It'll probably take us a day just to remove and untangle all the ropes."

"What's the best way to secure the lines?" asked the governor.

"The lines will be vulnerable to attack until we reroute them through the protected conduit that runs along the outside of the Dome 2 stairway. That conduit terminates in the electrical room, where we can tap into the power lines that run along the ocean bottom between here and the turbines."

"What about those lines? Are they vulnerable? The locals are legendarily good divers."

"I know they are, but no need to worry. The lines between here and the turbines run under a couple feet of rock."

"How soon can we get the lines rerouted through the conduit?" asked the major.

"Well, we have two challenges on that score. First, we need to make sure the conduit has no breaks that would leave the power lines open to tampering. I have two divers out there right now checking it out."

"And challenge number two?"

"The electrical room is flooded."

"Flooded?"

"Yes, sir. Which is probably why they rerouted the power in the first place. Frankly, I'm surprised we have power at all."

I looked to gauge the major's reaction, but my eyes were drawn back to the door by a new arrival in civilian dress. He stood behind the engineer, leaning against the doorframe, his hands wrapped around a bamboo cuda fish.

I banged a fist on the table. "Where did you get that?"

After a startled jump, the man looked about like he hoped I was talking to someone else.

"Where did you get that fish, damn you?" I was up out of my seat, the table leg thudding to the metal deck. The major was up, too, already coming to meet me.

"That's sacred, dammit."

The major took hold of my shoulders, "Come, sit back down," he said.

I twisted out of his grasp and tried to lunge past. "That's a sacred blessing. Without it, we'll all be cursed!"

Managing to keep a hip in front of me, the major yelled, "Sit down!"

Trying to pass him again, my feet tangled with chair legs, and I tumbled to the floor. I felt the major's knee drive into my lower spine to pin me painfully to the deck.

I tried to wriggle free, but the engineer was on me, too, his weight pressing down on my shoulder blades. Trapped against the cold steel, I could feel icy water from a window leak soaking into my pants. Wrenching my neck, I saw the man in civilian dress place my fish on the table. "Um, sorry," he muttered. "I found it by the exit to Stairway 2."

"You think it was a gift?" I said between short breaths. "I put it there for a reason, you stupid asshole."

I was back in my chair with the table leg across my lap. Scarred and dented, it didn't look like much, but soon it would become a cuda, the biggest I'd ever made.

They'd left me alone after I finally calmed down, which wasn't until after the governor agreed to have the cuda put back where it belonged over the hatchway. Harmless enough was what she said. Which the others took to mean, let the crackpot have his totem.

The emergency drill was under way, the alarm's awful whooping echoing off the walls. By now, the Empire's new contingent was locked up safe inside the Ministry except, I imagined, for those who were stationed on the transport vessel anchored in the water nearby.

Kell's successful coup aside, the lockdown strategy was unbeatable. So unbeatable, the same strategy was employed on all of the tech-restricted worlds of the Outermost Ring. In the event of attack, an Empire's contingent could simply lock themselves inside steel chambers that might be underwater or raised high in the air, where they were completely impregnable to attackers who had little more than stone tools.

Lock yourselves in like cowards and call in the bombers. Such was the wisdom of the Sire.

The alarms finally quit though my ears continued to ring. I went back to peeling away large slivers of wood from what would soon become the dorsal fin. This cuda would be special. Its spine would be lined with fishhooks, its tail made to look like two machete blades. Scales like flames. A mouth full of viciously jagged teeth, and a corkscrew tongue.

The door opened, and the governor stepped through, closely followed by Major Lensa.

"We've sent for the Falali Mother," said the governor. "She'll be here shortly, but we have to talk to you first."

I made no attempt to hide a frustrated sigh.

The governor sat without reaction. Not the same

for the major. Tight-faced, he took his seat with quick efficiency. I knew his type. A man who was used to cutting through the nonsense and giving orders. Not at all the artful operator the governor was. Despite his dual role in the Army and E³, he was clearly more soldier than spy.

"I sense you don't like me, Major."

Expecting a gruff affirmative, I was surprised to hear a denial. "Couldn't be further from the truth." The smile on his face looked painful, like it had been hung with thumbtacks. "Like all of the E³'s operatives, you're a silent hero to the Empire."

I matched his smile as I struggled to comprehend the sudden change in attitude.

The governor said, "I asked the major to send word home that you're safe and sound. He was quite impressed to learn who your father was."

"You didn't already know?" I asked him.

"Until yesterday, you were just a number."

The governor said, "Yes, the E³ loves their secrets. Your personnel files were closed to us until just before entering Maritinia's atmosphere. It appears the major hadn't bothered to read them until I asked him to send word home."

"I had an invasion to oversee," he said before turning to me. "I'm sure you understand. The safety of the men and women under my charge took priority. Your family's reputation within the E³ is impeccable. I look forward to learning as much as I can from you."

"Why, Major," I said, my smile widening, "I didn't know you had so much to learn. I'd be happy to teach you how to do your job."

The twist at the edges of his tacked-on smile said I'd pricked him deep. The governor's eyes flashed for just a second. Whether in anger or delight, I couldn't tell.

<Your disrespect is growing intolerable.>

I honored Pol's input with a rare response. <He deserves it. He's a political officer.>

The governor drew our gazes with three sharp taps of her lacquered nails against the table. "We're planning a show of force tonight. We'll be launching and detonating hundreds of low-grade rockets over the population centers. Though they're harmless, the major tells me the racket they'll create will be more than sufficient to cow the locals.

"After the show, I'll be making a speech introducing myself as governor and establishing the parameters of the Empire's return. As a gesture of goodwill, I'm considering setting the Falali Mother free. I think it could enhance our image as magnanimous rescuers."

"Rescuers? That's how you think of yourselves?"

"Of course," she said, her tone indicating she was surprised it was even in doubt. "These people aren't capable of self-determination. Humans like these are savages at heart. After what you've witnessed, you know that better than anybody. They require structure and stability. They need society and culture. Only then, when their wild sides are caged, do their better qualities emerge. Qualities like respect, nobility, and charity."

<She's a true leader, Jakob. We're very lucky to get somebody with such clear vision.>

If I could've rolled my eyes at Pol, I would have. "Maritinians are nobler than you think."

"Save it, Mr. Bryce." Her voice was suddenly lacking any patience. Apparently showing some respect for the people of this world was a sore spot. "I've worked with dozens of undercover operatives, and they all find themselves sympathizing with the locals to one degree or another. So trust me, I've heard the noble-savage argument many times before. Let me do you a favor and smother this nonsense while it's still in its crib. Maritinians were given the chance to govern themselves, and they decided to slaughter each other by the hundreds of thousands. Excuse me if I don't find any nobility in that. The sooner you get these misguided notions out of your head, the better. Now can we get back to the topic of the Falali Mother?"

Biting my tongue, I slowly nodded.

"Do you think setting her free is a good idea?"

I nodded a second time. "She means much to her people. They'll never trust you as long as you keep her locked up. You have to let her go."

"We have another choice, you know."

My heart darkened at the thought of it. "You want to kill her, don't you?"

"It would give me no pleasure, but the thought has crossed my mind. We can say the admiral killed her like he did so many Jebyl." She shrugged her shoulders. "We merely found the body."

I shook my head. "You have nothing to gain from killing her. She'll just be replaced."

"Agreed. So the question is: Will she work with us? Or can we get a better deal from her successor?"

"What kind of deal?"

"Reconciliation is the goal. From what you've told us, the admiral has been spewing plenty of paranoid fantasies about us. We need to gain the trust of the people. The Falali church is the most respected institution on this world, is it not? Her endorsement would cement our legitimacy."

"Have you asked her for her endorsement yet?"

"I have, but I'm still waiting on an answer."

"She's a principled woman. She chose imprisonment over supporting the admiral's government."

"That is why I need you to reason with her." She pulled a comm unit from her pocket to check the time. "The show of force begins in about three hours. I'll be doing my speech soon after, and one way or the other, I will make a statement about her. I hope to have the opportunity to announce her support. Otherwise, I'll be forced to announce her unfortunate demise."

Without giving me a chance to speak further, she stood and went to the door. Opening it, she leaned out to wave the Falali Mother in before returning to her own seat.

Emmina stepped through the doorway, her chin held high above sagging shoulders. The last few weeks had taken a toll. Silk robes hung loose on a withered frame, and her cheeks had narrowed below swollen bags under her eyes.

"It's good to see you, Emmina," I said.

She took the chair next to the governor, the glint in her eye bright as ever. "You look horrible, Colonel."

"I can't look worse than you," I said with a grin. "You need to eat."

Her eyes went to my carving tools and the unfinished cuda on my lap. "You found a hobby, I see."

"More of an obsession," I said.

"I fear-ed they'd kill-ed you."

"Sali convinced her father to let me go. She saved me."

"How is Sali?"

My grin burned to ash. I couldn't say the words.

Emmina mercifully saw to it that I didn't need to. She covered her heart with a hand. "I'm sorry for that, Colonel."

"Be sorry for her, but don't waste your sorrow on me. I've made a real mess of things."

"Tell me what it's like out there."

With my thumb, I ground a tear into my cheek. "I can't."

"Tell me, Colonel."

I shook my head, "There are no words, Emmina."

She leaned forward in her chair. "I beg you, Colonel. If I agree to endorse the governor, I need to know what I'll face when they set me free."

I lifted the wood off my lap and laid it on the table. "I don't sleep anymore. I close my eyes, but I don't sleep. The visions are always the same. I see vast lakes of blood, but the blood is perfectly still. Stiller than a fetid pond. And I cross bridges made of bone that lead to a mountain of death. A mountain of bodies piled up high to the sky. And on this mountain, there are babies crying, and mothers weeping. I see people trapped and tangled between all those dead arms and legs, and they call for help and try to dig their way out, but they don't realize that they are dead, too."

She didn't speak. Nobody did. Not even the little bastard in my head.

I reached for the wood, set it back on my lap, and took up one of my tools. Besides the insistent scrape of wood, the room stayed silent for a long time.

Emmina spoke first. "I've spent the last five and a half weeks cursing Falal for locking me up at a time like this. Now I'm beginning to understand she might have been protecting me."

"The survivors need you."

"Endorsing the Empire is not a small thing."

"I don't care what the Empire wants. All I know is your people need you. You remember when I talked to your Council of Interpreters?"

"Of course. You try-ed to convince them to help you unseat the admiral."

"Yes, and they chose their principles over averting disaster. You know that was a mistake now, don't you?"

"They did what I taught them to do."

"They did nothing."

"It's not our place to act. Merely to interpret."

"The act of doing nothing is still an act. You and your council failed our people. Like me and every other person on this world, you share responsibility for what happened. The time for sticking to principles is past. When our people need leadership, inaction is not an option."

"The will of Falal is not always clear."

"If Falal has even an ounce of kindness inside her, she could not have wished the horrors I've seen." I paused to give my next words the gravity they deserved. Every hope I had for Maritinia's future depended on her decision. "I repeat, inaction is not an option."

Emmina didn't nod, but I could see acceptance in her eyes.

"You have to take the deal," I said. "More than anything, the people need your help."

"What is your answer?" asked the governor, her face devoid of emotion after listening to our exchange.

Emmina faced her. "I agree to your terms."

I relaxed into my chair, knowing that the Falali Mother wouldn't be another senseless casualty.

<Well done, Jakob. Just when I think you're lost to us, you come through.>

Keep thinking that, my friend.

CHAPTER 35

"Beyond vengence standsa better place."

—JAKOB BRYCE

I leaned over to look in the aquarium. "Is anybody feeding you?"

Scummy surface water stirred and broke. A suckered tentacle snaked along the surface before sinking back into the murk.

I set my satchels filled with carved cudas on the floor along with the weighty table leg I'd been carrying on my shoulder and moved down the corridor, past the air lock, past a rack of air tanks to find a bucket filled with masks and snorkels. Dumping the contents on the floor, I returned to the aquarium.

<What are you doing, Jakob?>

<Setting the octopi free. Nobody's feeding them.>
<You don't know that.>

I dunked the bucket into the tank and filled it halfway before setting it on the floor and plunging my hand into the aquarium. Suckers latched onto my wrist, and I pulled the first creature from the water.

<You should ask the major first, Jakob.>

I lowered my hand into the half-filled bucket, and the creature uncoiled itself. <Nobody's going to care. The divers have plenty of scuba gear.>

Reaching back into the aquarium, I felt a second set of tentacles wrap my wrist, and I repeated the process of relocating the animal. Noticing I hadn't put enough water into the bucket to cover them both, I hurried to open the air lock and made it back to the bucket just before one of the octopi pulled itself over the lip.

Using one hand to wrestle the octopus and the other to grip the bucket handle, I walked into the air lock and set the bucket on the floor. Releasing my hold, I watched the top octopus's egg-shaped body flop over the bucket's edge and inch its way down the side. The second octopus seemed content to stay in the water.

Remembering the last time I'd been in this air lock, I looked to the outer door, knowing the admiral's underwater graveyard sat not far beyond it. That was where I'd found the arms dealer's corpse. Where I found his chewed-off ear in the grasp of hungry crab claws. I would've thought the freshness of the memory would send shivers up my spine, but my body didn't react that way. No, the horror of the graveyard now paled in comparison to the horrors I'd seen since. Now all I felt was sadness. A sadness that pressed on my chest with the weight of the sea.

Feeling tears well in the pockets of my eyes, I had to remind myself I'd come into the air lock for a reason. I steered my gaze toward the water intake near the floor. Covered by a screen, the intake allowed seawater to enter the air lock after the air pressure was increased to match the water pressure outside.

Worried Pol would become suspicious if I stared at the vent too long, I turned back to the octopus, who was now on the floor, its tentacles worming across the steel in an effort to pull itself toward the outer door.

I looked into its black eye and patted its head. "You can smell the ocean outside, can't you?"

Tentacles continued to stretch for open water as the eye gazed back from a bulbous socket of bumpy, blood orange flesh.

"Okay, I'll let you go now." Stepping around the tentacles, I went out to the corridor. Turning back, I stole a final glance at the water intake, verifying that it was attached by no more than a pair of simple handle locks. Thankful the designers had the forethought to make the intake so easy to clean, I hit the main switch.

"Bye, you two," I said to the octopi before the mechanical hatch sealed them in, and the air lock started to pressurize.

<You're making a habit of liberating things, Jakob.>

<Besides the octopi?>

<You did well yesterday.>

He was referring to the Falali Mother. Thanks in part to my advocacy, she'd been allowed to leave the Ministry late last night. Her absence would be short-lived since she'd committed to come back tomorrow to participate in preliminary discussions between the governor and the spokespeople of Maringua. Although nothing could be formally decided until after the representatives from all of Maritinia's cities and farthest pontoon towns arrived, it wasn't too early to begin negotiations.

The meetings would be held topside, but I'd made Emmina promise to find me. I'd told her I was going to write her a story.

That had earned me an odd stare, but I was getting used to odd stares.

The air lock finished cycling, and I opened the hatch. The strong smell of ocean clung to wet walls, and the now-brimming bucket sat where I'd left it. Stepping though the bulkhead, I used a bootheel to topple the pail and verify the resulting rush of water was octopus-free.

Exiting to the corridor, I gathered my satchels and hoisted the large cuda carving over my shoulder. I'd worked on him all night, and although he was taking shape nicely, I'd need another all-night session to add the finishing touches. My journaling would have to wait until later. Assuming I lived that long.

I walked down the corridor. Reaching a T, I looked to the left, where the hatch to admiral's torture chamber stood about thirty feet away. I'd been dragged though that hatch just a few weeks ago to face the lampreys. Dreadful images washed through my mind. The pool filled with waterlogged flesh. The silent agony of lives sucked dry. My eyes started to itch with visions of the bloodsuckers.

I knew where I had to go. Who I had to see.

Turning the opposite direction, I started counting my steps. One. Two. Three.

Ahead, I spotted the same engineer who had brought news of the water pumps' power situation. Standing with two female soldiers, he was outside the hatch that led to Stairway 4. Previously flooded, that section was being drained of water and would soon be ready to open.

Upon seeing me, the engineer said my name. I ignored him. Didn't want to lose count. Nine. Ten. Eleven.

"Somebody came to see you," he said.

Again, I didn't respond. Seventeen. Eighteen. Nineteen.

I now stood face-to-face with the engineer, so close the wooden cuda propped on my shoulder hung next to his right ear. "Who?" I asked.

Uncomfortable with my being so close, he leaned back and tilted his head to the side like he was trying to figure me out. "Um, I didn't get his name, but he was a local."

A smile stretched most of the way to my ears. "Young and heavyset?"

"That's right. I was standing on the pier when he

argued with the guards. Somehow, he had gotten his hands on a comm unit, which they confiscated before turning him away."

I dropped my satchels. Invading farther into his space, I looped my free arm over his shoulder and pulled him into an embrace. "That is great news! Thank you."

He squirmed before giving in to the embrace. "You're welcome."

<I told you he'd make it,> I said to Pol.

<Yes, you did, Jakob. Dugu is alive.>

I let go of the engineer and slapped the shoulders of the other two soldiers, who smiled weakly back. "He survived," I told them.

The one on the left said, "Yeah, sure he did."

I took up my satchels and slowly strode away. No rush to get where I was going. I wanted to savor the news before I faced Admiral Mnai.

I set my satchels and cuda carving on the floor and stood aside to watch the guard spin the hatch wheel. My eyes tried to focus on the metal spokes as they circled like the thoughts in my mind. The admiral and Mmirehl. They'd spilled so much blood. Brought so much death. Rage bubbled up inside me. I could feel it squeezing my heart and pressing against the backs of my eyes.

The guard cranked the latch handle, and the hatch clanged open.

I didn't move. The cell door was open, and my pent-up rage was ready to break loose in a fit of righteous justice.

Not now. I closed my eyes.

I concentrated on the reason I'd come. To talk to Sali's father. Not the admiral. Sali's father.

Refocused, I opened my eyes and stepped inside. My nostrils flared at the ripe stink of excrement. The guard reached for a bucket sitting to the right of the hatchway and took the worst of the stench with him before closing the hatch behind me.

A pair of stools stood under a drippy, rust-caked porthole. Captain Mmirehl perched on the left stool, bootheels resting on the stool's lowest rung. The admiral's bulky frame balanced atop the stool to the right, his feet stretched wide for support. Their shirts were buttoned to the top. Caps on their heads. Emerald flags tied around their necks in proud defiance.

The admiral showed off the gap in his teeth. "Welcome, Colonel. I knew it was only a matter of time before they capture-ed you. You best ask for another stool. These two are claim-ed."

"You think I'm moving in?"

"Of course you are." He clapped his hands. "We shall spend the rest of our lives together. Remember when you came to me with your plan to overthrow the governor? I knew right then that you and I would be forever bond-ed. Yesterday, we were revolutionaries. Today, we are prisoners. Tomorrow, we will be fodder for their executioners."

"Tell us how we did," said Mmirehl. "Did we eliminate all the Jebyl?"

The eagerness with which he asked the question left me speechless.

"Well?" he asked.

I shook my head no.

"So what we've heard is true. There are survivors." He winced as if he'd been stabbed by the admission.

"The Jebyl will thrive again," I said, my tone seasoned with a little extra salt for his wound. "You are both failures."

The admiral brushed my words away with a flick of his thick fingers. "There may be survivors, but the resistance has been crush-ed. We've destroy-ed their movement. We've taught those miscreant upstarts that we Kwuba will not sit by and let them take our rightful place as this world's nobility. The Jebyl are laborers, peasants, and that's all they'll ever be."

"The Jebyl were no threat to you," I said.

The admiral leveled one of his iron stares. "History has proven you wrong. They were given freedom from the Empire, and they threw it away. They sabotage-ed our only means of defense and welcome-ed the Empire's return because they care more about themselves than Maritinia."

"They were greedy," said Mmirehl.

"Yes," said the admiral. "They should've stay-ed in their place."

I wanted more than anything to tell them how wrong they were. Wanted to tell them it was me who destroyed the missile system. But Pol wouldn't approve of my blowing my cover. And I'd learned the hard way how vindictive Pol could be.

So I hit the admiral and Mmirehl with the biggest insult I could think of. "Stayed in their place? You two fools sound like the Sire now." I watched their eyes narrow. "You know what my biggest mistake was? I should've ruled this world myself."

The admiral chuckled like I'd said something funny. "You may be an honor-ed hero of this world, Colonel, but you are still a foreigner. You can't lead what you can't understand."

"*I* don't understand? You tried to exterminate your own people."

"*My* people?" He shook his head left and right. "The Jebyl cease-ed to be my people when they turn-ed away from me. I did what I had to do to save the Kwuba from an eternity of slavery. The Empire may execute me, but the Kwuba will forever remember my sacrifice."

"You're no savior. Just a murderer. You had a responsibility to care for the people of this world. Instead, you slaughtered them."

"Yes"—he smiled—"I'm sure the judge's decree will say exactly that. So who sounds like the Sire now?"

I wished the guard had let me bring in my cuda carving. Imagining its heft, I could picture myself lifting it high as I rushed him. Could see myself swinging at his head. Striking a single fatal blow of Jebyl vengeance.

But I couldn't act out of vengeance. This world

needed to heal. And to heal, the Jebyl would have to restrain themselves from retaliating. The cycle of violence had to be stopped. The Jebyl would have to swallow their pride. Their fear. Their unbelievable pain.

Their challenge would be monumental. Perhaps even greater than surviving the genocide. Children would have to accept the murders of their schoolmates. Husbands would have to accept the rapes of their wives and daughters. Mothers would have to accept the slaughters of their babies. That would be their burden. And I couldn't expect them to carry it alone.

I hadn't come here for vengeance. And I hadn't come to discuss their crimes, either. I'd come out of love and respect for Sali. She would've wanted her father to know. "Sali's dead."

I watched him try to hold his pose of fierce authority, but I caught the twitch in the corner of his eye, the subtle deflation of his shoulders and chest.

He was right about us being forever bonded. But I wouldn't travel home or stand trial with him. Our bond was grief.

"How did she die?" he wanted to know. "The Jebyl couldn't get me, so they took her, didn't they?"

I'd already said all I'd come to say. I banged on the hatch and waited for it to open.

"Where do you think you're going?" asked Mmirehl. "They're not going to let you out."

The hatch opened, and I stepped through.

"I knew it!" shouted the admiral.

I looked back at the accusing finger pointed my way. "You're a filthy traitor!" he yelled. "You were working with the Jebyl the whole time, weren't you? I knew they were too stupid to destroy the missile system on their own."

I looked at the guard. "Seal it up."

CHAPTER 36

"A clever boy. Tht was what my fatherr used to
cll me."

—JAKOB BRYCE

I stood at the bottom of Stairway 4. After drowning
for months, the first section had been pumped free of
water by the Empire's engineers. Given another week,
they'd have every last waterlogged cabin of the Ministry airing out.

I knelt on the still-damp floor and sifted through
my satchels to select the perfect cuda for the newly
opened hatchway. Every entrance required a blessing.

Holding one above my head, I studied its gaping
jaws before tracing a finger along its length to the
crescent-shaped tail. Yes, this was the one.

I stood up, and like the other two functioning entrances to the Ministry, I rested the cuda on the upper lip of the hatchway. <Perfect, don't you think?>

<Whatever you say, Jakob.>

I hoisted the two-and-a-half-foot redwood cuda up to my shoulder and took hold of my satchels. The staircase was dark, none of the lights having survived so long underwater. I didn't let that deter me. I started up, barnacle shells cracking under my heels.

<You need a flashlight, Jakob. You could hurt yourself.>

I kept climbing, the light from the corridor dimming until I was bathed in complete darkness. Progress was slow. After every upward step, I had to hunt and peck for solid footing with the toe of my boot.

<Where are you going? You know they won't let you go outside during the day.>

<I'm not going out. Dome 4 is full of supplies. I need fishhooks.>

<What for?>

<To finish my carving. The cuda's back has to be lined with fishhooks.>

<Why?>

<You're not an artist. You wouldn't understand.>

Fifteen stairs up, I found the rhythm and picked up the pace, planting one foot after the other with confidence. Stumbling a few stairs later, I slowed back down. Had to be patient. I could afford to be crazy—no choice on that score—but I couldn't afford stupid.

Halfway up, I'd worked up quite a sweat, the redwood cuda feeling slick against my fingers. One slow step at a time, I climbed toward the surface, toward the promise of relief in the form of fresh air.

Reaching the top, I squinted against the bright lighting inside the dome. I breathed deep of the briny breeze blowing through the open doorway on the opposite side of the dome and headed into the wind.

<Jakob, you can't go outside.>

I didn't stop walking toward the doorway. Piles of junk sat to either side of my path. Old fishing nets and crab traps. Stacks of bamboo and mammoth bone.

<You can't go out. The governor has prohibited it.>

I picked up my pace, his protests turning more urgent with every step. Reaching the doorway, I halted under the arched stone, my toes hanging over the edge of the short step that led out to the sunbaked stone.

<You're like a little child. Why must you always test the limits?>

I reached out a toe and touched the creviced rock. <Look, Pol, I'm outside now.>

<I'm starting to think you like to torture me.>

<You're just realizing that now?> I pulled my toe back and watched sunbeams ripple off the surface of the lagoon. Soldiers stood guard around the atoll. Heavily armed, they kept their eyes peeled for approaching boats. On the pier, a group of Jebyl were busy setting up tables and chairs in preparation for the talks that would begin tomorrow afternoon.

Perhaps twenty feet straight ahead, the water pumps' power lines snaked along the stone. Starting from Dome 2, I traced their path with my eyes until they disappeared behind a short stack of crab traps beyond Dome 5.

<They've started prepping the lines for reloca-tion,> said Pol.

Yes. They'd clear all the crab traps hanging off those lines before rerouting them properly through the protected conduit, then under the ocean bottom to the turbines. They had much to do.

So did I.

Turning around, I surveyed the interior space. To complete my carving, I needed fishhooks. To write the story I'd promised to Emmina, I needed pen and paper. And I hadn't even started carving the cuda's corkscrew tongue.

Caring very little about creating a mess, I dumped bins and emptied jars until I found the fishhooks I needed. Next, I sought pen and paper by rummaging through storage cabinets until my eyes landed on a large metal object leaning against the wall. Shoving aside a stack of crates, I stepped up and put my palm on the missile.

<I'd forgotten there was an extra missile,> said Pol.

Yes, Mathus had thrown it in as a bonus. And hidden away as it was, it had so far escaped the new contingent's notice. <This thing is dangerous. We should scuttle it.>

<It can't fly without its launcher.>

<We should still scuttle it.>

<Do you know how expensive this missile is? If war

is indeed imminent, the Empire can put it to good use. We'll send it back with you and the prisoners.>

<We should at least make sure it's deactivated.>

<Agreed. There should be a control panel near its tail.>

I wrapped my arms around the metal tube before lifting it away from the wall. Knowing firsthand the kind of damage it could do, I took great care as I began to lower it toward the floor. Bending over, I felt the strain on my back as I continued to control its fall. When the missile was a few inches from the floor, the weight got the better of me, and the fear-inducing thud echoed over and over in my pounding heartbeat.

<I thought it was going to blow.>

<Don't fret, Jakob. It can take a lot more punishment than that.>

I felt along the steel until I found the seam and pressed in with my fingers to pop open the control panel. Inside was a touchpad under a small screen. <What's the manufacturer's code?>

Pol recited the numbers, and I punched them in as fast as I could. <Wait, I hit a three and you said two, didn't you?>

He started over, and I took some pleasure making another mistake.

<Pay attention, Jakob.>

Glad he couldn't see the smile forming on my face, I asked him to start again.

<I know what you're doing, Jakob. I know you're playing with me.>

<Okay.> I laughed. <I'll do it right this time. I promise.>

<Four . . . three . . . three . . . zero . . . >

<Oops. Sorry.>

I kept up the game for a while. Kept it up until my cheeks ached from smiling so broadly.

<We're in,> I said finally.

<It's disabled,> said Pol.

<Yes, but it's a good thing we checked to be certain.> The interface appeared to be identical to the missile platform's. The icon in the corner was for syncing to a control system. The icon down below was for enabling and disabling the warhead. And on the right was the timer.

<We're all set, Jakob. You can lock us back out now.>

I did.

Carefully, I stood the missile back up and leaned it against the wall. Pol wanted to send it back home with me. The Empire could use it, he'd said. My Maritinian vacation was almost over, and this missile would be my only souvenir. It was fitting, really, the way Pol had it planned out. Only the Sire deserved such a fine gift.

Now where did I put those fishhooks?

I rubbed one weary eye, then the other with the back of my hand. I didn't feel sleepy. My mind was too preoccupied for that. But my strained eyes kept blurring after so many hours of carving.

A glance at the morning sun beaming through the doorway confirmed I'd been at it all night. Embedding fishhooks along the cuda's spine had taken longer than I'd expected. I'd painstakingly laid them on an angle so each barb would be the high point, the fish's back now a danger to anybody who dared reach close. My fingertips were plenty sore from getting hooked while adjusting and readjusting. The spacing from fishhook to fishhook had to be perfect.

Perfect.

I'd switched to working on the cuda's tongue midway through the night. The rough-hewn corkscrew needed more work to meet my standards. Eight inches from end to end, the tongue's tight spiral was just a quarter inch in diameter. I'd properly hollowed out the interior of the helical structure, but the edges still showed whittle marks where they should be smooth. Setting the wooden corkscrew on the table, I watched closely as I rolled it forward. Verifying that the corkscrew maintained a smooth drilling motion as it rolled, I decided it would have to do for now.

Cupping the cuda's lower jaw, I lifted the mouth of the wooden fish. Taking the sharpened tip of the corkscrew tongue in one hand, I inserted the other end between rows of cuda teeth. Pushing backward, I fit the tongue into a notch at the back of the cuda's mouth.

I stood and walked around the table to view my artwork from different angles. The tongue looked fearsome, jutting out from between spiked teeth.

And the spine of fishhooks befit the angry soul he represented.

My chest filled with pride. By far the finest work I'd ever done. I hadn't yet carved flaming fish scales along its sides, but that could wait. Emmina would be along sometime today, and I'd told her I'd write her a story.

I took up my pen and wrote with my eyes open.

The Flesh Eater King

He built his throne on an island of dead. He shouted orders from lips smeared with blood. Bring me more wine! Bring me more to eat!

His subjects tried to please him. They understood it best to not upset the order of things. His term was to be only ten years. Another king would come soon enough. A kinder king.

Keep him entertained, the people thought. So singers would try to tickle his heart, and jesters would try to tickle his ribs. When they succeeded, they'd be rewarded with ample bounty. But when they failed, he'd chain them to stakes. He called them his little garden.

He was a caring gardener. For the thirsty plants, he carried a watering can. And for the unruly plants, he took up pruning shears so he could cut himself a little snack.

As the years passed, his subjects counted the days, always thankful to be one day closer to the end of the Flesh Eater King's reign.

The people had high hopes for the king in waiting. A man of simple means, he knew little of how to rule a kingdom, but he had ten years to prepare. Unlike his predecessors, he never talked to the generals, for he had little interest in learning how to run an army. Nor did he talk to his world's mayors and chiefs. He didn't care much for politics. The only thing he wanted to learn was wisdom. So he spent ten years sailing the seas to speak with all of his world's elders.

Festivals erupted on the last day of the Flesh Eater King's term. Soon the sun would set, and when it did, so would his reign.

A new king required a new island. Separated from the old king's island of dead by a narrow channel of water, the new king had chosen to raise his island on the backs of his subjects. If he ever lost their support, all they had to do was walk away and let him drown.

But when the sun began to set, the Flesh Eater King didn't move from his throne. Instead, he said he quite liked being king. So much, in fact, that he'd decided to keep his kingdom.

He turned to his queen and told her she would never be betrothed to the new king as was tradition. And if she ever tried to run away, he'd take a thousand heads for every hour she was missing.

The queen agreed. She knew to take his threats seriously.

The Flesh Eater King turned to his generals. I'm hungry, he said. Bring me that other king's leg on a platter!

The new king had spent the afternoon watching the sun sink toward the ocean. Standing by his throne, he waited to take his seat when the moment arrived.

But before the sun could touch the water, a boat approached. The new king's subjects hurried to form a dock. Using legs as pilings, and bent backs as planking, they provided a short pier for their guests.

The Flesh Eater King's generals marched across the spines of the new king's subjects to arrive on the bamboo platform atop the new king's island. Behind them came the queen.

I cannot marry you, she said with a slight bow. The Flesh Eater King has chosen to retain power.

The new king accepted the news with a nod. You understand what this means for our people?

She simply said, Yes, I do. But there is no other choice.

I understand, said the new king. And why are you here? he asked the generals.

One held up a machete. We've come for your leg. Give it, and you may live, but never as king. Don't give it, and we will kill you and all of your people.

The new king looked down through the slatted bamboo floor at the men and women who held him above water. They shook their heads in unison. Their message was clear. You mustn't give in.

But the new king knew nothing of war. Fight, and they'd all die, just as the generals said. So he steeled his voice, and said, I will give you my leg. But first, I must have some wine to dull the pain.

The generals agreed that he be allowed to drink.

The new king looked down through the slats and saw the disappointment in his subjects' faces. He knew he hadn't lived up to their expectations, but he felt buoyed by the fact that they continued to hold his island above water. As he'd thought, they'd proven to be more loyal than they were vindictive.

You have five minutes to drink your fill said one of the generals.

Fine, he said before excusing himself to enter his hut. He went to his fish tank, and, using a net, he scooped out the one with the green stripes. He wasted no time biting off its head and swallowing it down. He stuffed the remainder of the beheaded fish in his pocket.

Looking down through the bamboo slats to the men and women below, he saw understanding in their eyes. He waited for the first cramps to let him know the poison had sunk into his tissue before stepping back outside.

He dropped his robe and straightened his waistwrap before sitting on his throne.

Take what you came for, he said.

The queen refused to turn her back as the generals made quick work of hacking off his left leg.

Taking the leg, the generals headed for their boat. The queen lingered for a moment to say, I'm sorry it had to happen this way. I had no choice.

The new king stood on his remaining leg and tried to tell her again that he understood, but a new convulsion brought him to his knee. She took his elbow and helped him get back onto his throne.

He saw her eyes go to his robes piled alongside the throne, and, taking a glance, he could see a green-striped fishtail poking free. He watched her eyes light in recognition, and, fighting with all his might against the pain, he said, With my sacrifice, I give you a choice.

She nodded her understanding before walking silently to her boat.

Managing to stay upright long enough to watch the boat set sail, the new king collapsed just as the sun ducked below the horizon. He died moments later, staring into the eyes of his subjects, who steadfastly held him from the water.

CHAPTER 37

> "Ninety-nin percent of a mission's sucess is in teh preparation."
>
> —JAKOB BRYCE

I walked with the pages of my story pinched between my lips. Thanks to my satchels and my redwood cuda, I didn't have a hand to spare.

Entering the conference room, I found Emmina sitting with the governor and the major. Mumbling through closed lips, I said, "I heard you were here."

"We're busy," said the governor. "Representatives of Maritinia's cities are beginning to arrive, and we have much to discuss."

I dropped my satchels by the door before setting my cuda on the table with a proud flourish. The governor stared at the fish with knit brows. The major tilted his head like he was giving the fish serious thought. Only the Falali Mother appeared genuinely impressed. "It's beautiful," she said.

I took the papers from my lips. "Thank you, Emmina. I knew you had an eye for art." Waving my papers, I said, "I wrote you a story."

"Not now, Colonel," said the governor.

I helped myself to a chair and sat down. "I decided to come find you, Emmina, because I was afraid these two would take up the rest of your morning, and afternoon, too. You promised to come see me."

"And I would've, Colonel," she said.

"But you might not have found me. I spend all my time in Dome 4 now. I've set up a workspace in there."

"We don't have time for this," said the major.

"Sure you do. We all know the talks won't begin for real for a few days. Your little session this afternoon is nothing more than a meet-and-greet before you send them all back to Maringua for the night."

<Again, you're making an ass of yourself, Jakob.>

I put my hand flat on my papers. "You have to read my story, Emmina." Feeling wetness under my fingers, I tried to rub the moisture away. "Sorry, I must've drooled a little carrying it in my mouth." I checked to see if any of the ink had smudged. "It's okay."

The governor turned to Emmina. "I need you to step out for a minute. I have to talk to the prisoner alone."

I hadn't missed the special emphasis she'd put on

the word prisoner. Neither had Emmina, who was now staring at me.

"It's okay," I told her.

The Falali Mother rose from her seat. It had only been a day since she'd gained her freedom, but she'd already recovered her posture. With her chin held proud, she stepped out of the cabin and closed the door.

The governor watched her go before turning cold eyes on me. "You've exhausted the last of my goodwill."

"What's your problem?" I asked. "Would it kill you to let her and I chat a bit?"

"I have much respect for the job you've done here, but you've become a pest, and it must stop."

"Fine," I said with a defeated tone. "If you don't want me around, I'll give her my story and leave you be."

"Is that a promise?"

"Yes."

"It better be, or I'll confine you to quarters. Now what's this story about?"

I handed it over. "I didn't write it for you. You won't understand it."

"Of that I'm quite sure." She put out a hand. "Let me see it. I can't let you give it to her until I know it doesn't contain classified information."

I pushed the short stack of pages across the table.

She skimmed the first page before looking up. "You really need to see the doctor."

"Can I call Emmina back in now?"

She passed the papers to the major before turning back to me. "Your political officer read this, right?"

I nodded. "He sees everything I do."

"What does he have to say about it?"

\<Pol?\>

\<You're insane.\>

"He thinks I'm a fucking loon."

"He's got that right. He deserves a medal for having to live inside your head." She turned to the major. "Verify the story is harmless, and let's be done with this nonsense."

The major pulled his eyes from my pages. "Looks like a really good story." The man was clearly still in suck-up mode since learning how well connected my father was. The major set his comm unit on the table. "If the story is indeed harmless, I need a truth code from your political officer."

\<This is a complete waste of time,\> said Pol.

\<So stop making them wait.\>

Pol spoke numbers into my head. This was the moment of truth, and not just in a literal sense. All of my plans depended on Pol's believing the story was harmless, just the lunatic ravings of a psyche cracked by too many traumas.

Forcing my voice to stay level, I repeated the numbers aloud. My pulse ratcheted upward as each digit fell from my tongue.

The major watched his screen, and when I'd recited the last number, his eyes lifted to meet mine.

"True," he said.

I stood and huffily grabbed hold of my pages. "I know when I'm not welcome. I'll go now."

Swinging open the door, I found Emmina standing just outside. With my back turned to the governor and major, I held my pages close to my chest so the back-side of the last page would face her. I needed her to see the message I'd written there without Pol's knowl-edge. Just two words was all it was. Two words that I'd written with my eyes closed.

She took the pages from my hands and clutched them to her chest. "I very much look forward to read-ing your story."

"I hope you enjoy it." I took up my satchels before turning back to retrieve my redwood cuda from the table. Hefting the cuda to my shoulder, I knew my preparations were almost complete.

"Wait, Colonel," said the governor.

My feet froze in place. I had to will myself to look back at her.

"We received a message from your father."

I stood to stretch my back. One side of the cuda was completely filled in with etched scales shaped like flames. The other side was still half-bare, fire reaching from the cuda's gills to just past the dorsal fin before giving way to smooth wood the rest of the way to its tail. It really was the best work I'd ever done. Too bad I'd never get the chance to finish it.

Stepping to the dome's doorway, I looked out at the

lagoon and soaked in every last drop of the crystal-clear water. I scanned the horizon to see waves shimmering with the gold of late-afternoon sun. I measured the length of the dome's shadow with my eyes and knew the sun would soon set.

Leaning my head outside, I could see each of the half dozen soldiers standing at even-spaced intervals around the atoll. All six of their gazes faced outward. I understood their thinking. If attack came, it would surely come from out there somewhere. Attack from within was impossible. The fools hadn't learned the lesson the real Colonel Kell had taught them.

I returned to my workspace and, with a heavy sigh, took hold of the comm unit the governor had handed me that morning. On it, I knew, was the message my father had sent. I'd spent most of the afternoon thinking I shouldn't watch it. I was a new man now. I'd put every ounce of my old self into my journal before creating a better self. One who could shed the events of the past and move boldly into the future.

I'd been a pawn my entire life. My youth was spent being the good son who left little doubt that he'd follow in his family's footsteps to become a spy. When I got older, I rebelled against those expectations to take a desk job in the E^3. I thought I was proving my independence. But in the end, I was still a pawn of the Empire's operation.

All I'd done was change chessboards.

And when life as an E^3 bureaucrat proved unfulfilling, I'd stunned my friends by leaping feetfirst into the deadly profession of spying.

I thought the experience would bring out my full potential. My father often taught me that you can't know your true mettle until you've been through the cauldron. Only the white-hot heat of danger could temper your steel. Only the pride of serving your Sire could forge true worth.

My mission would bring challenges I couldn't imagine. Challenges that would make me dig deep into my soul to find the resources required to overcome.

I'd come home a stronger person. A better man. And a hero.

But everything my father told me was a lie. A big, powerful lie. A lie so great it could make me risk my life. So seductive it could make me give up my convictions. His was a lie with such potency, it could make me welcome a dirty intruder in my head.

I didn't blame my father for lying to me. He believed the lie. He'd been through cauldrons of his own, and at some point in his spying days, he must've faced the same doubts as me. And he'd made the choice that the lie was the only truth that mattered.

Because the alternative was too hard to face. Recognizing the lie for what it was would've meant his mission wasn't turning him into a great man. Instead, it was turning him into the ultimate pawn.

Not a man at all. A tool.

I'd fought against that realization when Pol trained

me to be an assassin. And I'd continued to fight against it when he turned me into a mass-murdering saboteur. It wasn't until the bodies piled up by the thousands that I could see the truth.

By then it was too late change the catastrophic events that had befallen these people. But I had survived. As did the Falali Mother. As did many others.

The past had already slipped through our fingers. But the future was ours to seize.

The past might be gone, but it wasn't something to surgically cut from memory. It was to be accepted and studied. I wouldn't blaze a blind trail for Maritinia to follow. These people deserved better. They deserved a leader who could learn from his own wrong turns.

I turned on the comm and started the recording.

My father sat on the edge of his bed, a cinched robe hugging his shoulders. Closed curtains hung in the background.

Jakob, I just now got word that you're safe and sound. They tell me Maritinia has been successfully recaptured. I'm sure that's in no small part thanks to you.

He looked well. His smile genuine but understated, as expected of a family required to mask emotions.

I'm so proud of you, he said. *From the day you were born, I knew you would make an excellent operative.*

He leaned toward the camera and lowered his voice in concern. *The governor sent a personal message that gives me pause. She said she felt you are in a troubled place right now. You mustn't dwell on the things you've seen and done. Nothing good can come of it.*

Let me give you the same advice your grandfather gave me after my first mission. It's the same thing he heard from his father, who I'm sure heard it from his father on and on through generations of Bryces. A street needs its sweeper, and a stable needs its shoveler. Neither should feel ashamed of working in filth, for their sacrifice is for the greater good. So it should be for men like us, the cleaners of history.

You've got a long journey home, but know that I'll be here waiting for you. The end of a mission is always a difficult time. Safe travels, son. I love you.

I love you, too, Dad.

Leaving the comm unit on the workbench, I went to the door again and rubbed my eyes clear of tears. I wished I could talk to him without censor. Like old buddies, we could share our experiences as spies and assassins. Perhaps then we could discuss why the real Kell had crossed the line to become a revolutionary. I ached to tell him how I came to see the rightness of Kell's decision.

Would he disown me that instant? Perhaps. But unlike Sali's father, mine, I believed, was capable of empathizing with perspectives other than his own.

Looking to the sky, I knew he was out there somewhere very far away. Bye, Dad. I hope you'll see through the worst of what they'll say about me.

I blew out a long, head-clearing breath.

<That was a moving message,> said Pol.

I bristled at the intrusion. <Can't you leave me be?>

<Your father's words are wise. I can only hope you'll heed them.>

No. This pawn didn't move by anybody's hand but his own. Not anymore.

Judging by the length of the dome's shadow, I estimated sunset at just fifteen or twenty minutes away. It was time.

Time for revolution.

CHAPTER 38

> "The rise of tides is an umstoppable force of
> nature. So is the fall."
>
> —JAKOB BRYCE

With certainty of purpose, I strode to my workspace,
snatched up my cuda carving, and headed down the
stairs. The stairwell lighting still hadn't been repaired,
but having walked up and down the stairs a few times
before, I made quick progress in the dark.

Reaching the bottom, I marched down one empty
corridor, then the next, until I arrived at the hatch leading into the admiral's torture chamber. Looking left
and right, seeing nobody, I went inside.

<What are you doing, Jakob?>

Pol was wary. But I wouldn't let that dissuade me

from completing the plan I'd carefully constructed. Although he had the power stop me anytime he wanted by making me see and hear things that weren't real, I was confident he had no idea what my intentions were.

Uncertainty was the key. It was uncertainty that would make him hesitate until it was too late. He hadn't seen the danger hidden in almost every action I'd taken since coming back to the Ministry. He hadn't realized that the erratic moves of a madman were really the opening maneuvers of an elaborate plot.

As he'd once taught me, leaps of imagination were rare.

I spoke the words I'd been rehearsing in my head.
<I don't like the person I've become, Pol.>

<What are you talking about?>

I didn't respond. He'd figure out what I'd meant soon enough.

The pool stood to my right. Lampreys continued to swim its waters, but their prey had been removed. To my left was the aquarium. Inside was the small school of green-striped fish.

Taking a net that hung on the wall, I fished one out and drove one of my carving tools through its head before dropping it in a pail.

<Now I think I understand the story you wrote, Jakob. You mean to poison yourself.>

<You can't stop me,> I told him. <Make me see whatever you want, all I have to do is drop a hand in that bucket.> I scooped another fish from the tank and

repeated the process of piercing the poison sacs before dumping the wriggling fish into the bucket.

<What makes you think I want to stop you?>

My dark suspicion confirmed, a grin threatened to stretch the corners of my mouth. He cared so little for me, he would actually let me kill myself. My plans would be able to proceed as long as I kept him believing the poison was for me.

I pumped my voice full of disbelief. <You really wouldn't try to save me?>

<I think you're playing with me again. I've had enough of your games. This time I choose not to play.>

I dropped another pierced fish into the bucket. <What if this isn't a game? Will you really let me die?>

<Our mission is complete. You are no longer an asset. In fact, your aberrant behavior makes you a liability. My advice to you is to go see the doctor, and you might find the help you need to reconstruct your life. But the decision is ultimately yours. I won't stop you.>

Another fish fell into the pail. <When I touch that poison, you'll die with me.>

<As you so often like to tell me, I'm not a person. I care little about life and death. If I perish, it will be with the knowledge that I've achieved my goals.>

I netted another fish and pulled it from the tank.

<The first one had more than enough poison to do the job, Jakob.>

I drove the carving tool under its eye and let the fish fall into the bucket with the others. Tossing the carving tool to the floor, I looked into the bucket and let my eyes linger on the cloudy liquid pooled around the dead fish. Before moving to the next step in my plan, I had to sell the false conflict raging inside me. Had to, or he would exercise his power over my senses.

Bending over, I reached my right hand down, my fingers stretching for the poison that had stolen so many Jebyl. I edged closer and closer until I stopped just a breath above death.

<Why did you stop?>

I whispered the words. <Dammit, Pol. I was so certain when I came down here.>

<You've changed your mind?>

I pulled my hand away. <I don't know.>

<Please, Jakob, just go see the doctor.>

<No.>

<Why not?>

<Because that's what you want me to do.>

<That's what this is all about, isn't it? You only wanted to kill yourself to retaliate against me. Now that you know I won't try to stop you, suicide has lost its appeal.>

I walked to a chair, perhaps the same one I'd once been tied to, and I moved it next to the pail of poison fish. Locating my carved cuda, I set it crosswise on the seat.

<Now what are you doing?>

<I need guidance.> I knelt before the cuda.

<That's what the doctor is for.>

<Shut up and let me pray.>

I leaned my face down close to the cuda, where fish-hooks stood like cobras along the carving's spine, their barbed fangs aimed at the ceiling.

I was in position.

If I was to carry out a successful revolution, I couldn't let Pol see through my eyes. I'd never be successful if he could manipulate my vision and hearing. This was the only way.

I'd spaced the fishhooks perfectly, the distance between them the same as the distance between my eyes. Breath raked in and out of my lungs. My heartbeat pulsed in my temples.

Do it now.

But I couldn't move. I'd almost lost an eye once before in this room, and memories of the lamprey's hungry, cavelike mouth loomed in my mind.

<Falal doesn't exist, Jakob. Let's go see the doctor.>

Conflicting signals ricocheted along my nerves. Do it. Jerk away. Do it.

I'd once slapped young Dory for coming too close to my eyes. And now that same panic had taken my nerves hostage again. How could I have ever thought I could do it without flinching?

<Your prayers won't be answered, Jakob. Falal doesn't exist. Only the Sire is worthy of worship. Even your precious Maritinians must realize that now.>

Maritinians. I'd be asking much of them. The Jebyl would have to overcome their fears, grievances, and desire for vengeance. And the Kwuba would have to purge their hearts of wrongheaded righteousness and jealousy. How could I ask so much of them and nothing of me?

With singular focus, I lined myself up. I took a sharp intake of breath, then slapped the bridge of my nose against the cuda's spine. I felt the hooks pierce my eyeballs, my head exploding in pain. I pulled my head upward and felt grip of the barbs as my eyes pulled free from their sockets.

Lifting my head farther, I felt my optic nerves spool out before tugging against the backs of my eye sockets. Through my left eye, I could still see the fine grain of the wood until I ripped the ganglia out of my skull, and everything went dark.

<What did you do?> he asked, a desperate tone of incredulity touching Pol's voice.

I heard the hatch open, followed by the clopping of boots and voices ordering me to move away from the fish, but I knew better than to believe it. Dizzy with pain, I traced a path with my fingers along the flaming fish scales, past the gills, then the teeth, to the cuda's tongue. Pulling the tongue free from the cuda's mouth, I aimed the corkscrew at my right ear.

Pol's control over my hearing had to be silenced. I drove the wood as far as it would go into my ear canal, then started twisting the wood with my fingers. Clenching my jaws against the pain, I felt the corkscrew bite deep. Twisting round and round, I felt a pop and knew I'd pierced the drum.

But I could still hear the soldiers shouting orders in

that ear, and knew I had to go farther to kill the nerves Pol was using to send his false noise into my brain.

I drilled deeper and deeper, so deep I feared the corkscrew was tunneling to the other side of my brain. Forcing myself to take one more painful turn, all sound in my right ear disappeared.

I gingerly unscrewed the redwood from my ear. Gingerly because I didn't want to do any more damage than I'd already done. With my other ear, I could still hear the shouts of soldiers who, had they been real, would've grabbed me by now.

I wiped my cheeks free of tears that might've been blood and inserted the corkscrew into my other ear. Pain came in waves to slam the rocks that were my skull, but I wouldn't let that stop me from turning the corkscrew until I'd taken away the last of Pol's power.

<What have you done, Jakob?> Pol's voice somehow sounded small.

<Consider yourself neutered.>

<You really hate me so much you'd disfigure yourself?>

<I hate you more than that. But I didn't do it for you.>

<Then why?>

I felt no rush to explain myself, so I let him and his question dangle in the dark that had become my entire world. To test my hearing, I put my fingers against my windpipe and felt the vibrations as I hummed a few notes that must've sounded like pain-stricken groans. I spoke the next words out loud even though neither Pol nor I could hear them. "You don't own me anymore. I do."

I let the corkscrew tongue fall to the floor and reached about until I located the pail. Finding the handle with my fingers, I stood up. With my other hand, I felt for the top of the chair back, which I'd been sure to aim at the hatch. Mentally drawing a line for my feet to follow, I walked with one hand stretched before me.

<If you don't mean to kill yourself, Jakob, why did you gather the poison?>

Reaching the hatch, I spun the wheel.

<Why so much poison, Jakob?>

<I'm taking over.>

The hatch was open. I couldn't let myself be seen, but without sight or sound, there was no way to know if anybody was nearby. I stepped out to the corridor, trusting that the Empire's engineers had moved on to Staircase 5.

<What do you mean you're taking over?>

I turned right to head for the air lock. Dragging a palm along the wall to keep on a straight line, I counted my steps. At thirty-three, I turned again.

The next run would be sixteen steps, but a bout of dizziness made me stop halfway. Leaning against the wall, I took several calming breaths until my balance returned and started counting again.

<What do you mean by taking over, Jakob? Tell me.>

<I'm going to disable the air lock. I won't let them escape.>

<You're lying to me. You're curled up on the floor like a little baby.>

My hand brushed across wet air tanks, which served as proof that the scuba teams had already come in for the night. Arriving at the air lock, I worked the controls by memory. I reached out a hand to verify the air lock had opened before stepping inside and moving toward the back wall. Making contact, I worked my way down and to the left until I found the screen.

<I'm in the air lock, Pol. I'm pulling the screen off the water intake and setting the pail of fish inside.>

<You're a liar. I think you're with the doctor. You're in tremendous pain, and you finally realized you need help.>

I struggled to get the screen back in position, and once I did, I turned the handles and sealed the bucket inside. <When they try to escape, the water that flows in will be poisoned.>

<Escape from what?>

I was in the corridor; my next destination was back up the stairs to Dome 4. Dragging a hand along the corridor wall, I counted paces back to the T and turned for the staircase, which would be exactly nineteen steps away.

I was keenly aware of how dangerous it was for me to walk these corridors. If spotted in my current condition, all was lost. For all I knew, the governor herself was standing by the stairs, and she was watching me approach, horrified by what the crazy idiot had done to himself.

But I wouldn't let myself be paralyzed by such possibilities. I chose to believe in my destiny. Nothing could stop me from defeating the Empire.

On the nineteenth step, my hand bumped a bulkhead, and I ducked through and started up the stairs.

The Empire hadn't survived for millennia because it met the needs of its people. It had survived because of inevitability. But this little backwater world had done the impossible. With a successful revolt, it had cracked the Empire's aura of infallibility.

The Sire called it a fluke. And now that his minions had returned to broadcast the atrocities that occurred here, he called it a failure.

But what would he say when the Empire fell a second time? What could he say?

The Empire's foundation was cracking, and I held the hammer. The blow I was about to land would be the epicenter of a massive quake with the power to topple the Sire.

Let it be known that it started here.

It started with Mmasa, the diver. With a kiss on his cheek, he stood up to his governor. He put voice to the question all who are oppressed must ask: Is there no limit to what you'll take from us?

Yes, it started with Mmasa. And as Sali had said, it would end with me. I only wish she were here to see it.

My heart pounded with the exertion of the climb.

Every heartbeat tightened the tourniquet of pain wrapping my head.

Reaching the top, I bumped my way through shelves and rows of boxes until my hand landed on the chill of steel. With effort, I lowered the object to the floor and felt for seams with my fingers until I managed to find the control panel and pop it open.

I recited the numbers for Pol. <Four . . . three . . . three . . . zero . . . >

<What are you doing, Jakob?>

I kept stating the numbers until I finished punching them in.

Pol's voice had turned to ice. <That's the manufacturer's code for the missile.>

<Still think I'm with the doctor?>

<You're not as clever as you think, Jakob. I see now how you fooled me into repeating the code over and over until you'd memorized it, but arming a missile isn't going to get you what you want. Detonating this missile will level the domes, but the people below will survive, and they'll continue to rule this world. Proceed, and you'll be nothing more than a terrorist.>

With total concentration, I pictured the interface in my mind as I set the timer for thirty minutes. I had no way to verify success, but I trusted my ability to navigate without sight. I'd been journaling blind for weeks now, and although I suspected my typing abilities left much to be desired, the missile's interface was so much simpler. All I'd had to do was press *timer*, *three*, *zero*, *start*. Then *yes*, *yes*, *yes* through the verifications just like the last time I'd set one of these missiles to blow. Except that time I'd gone out of my way to disable the main payload so only the hull-piercing head would detonate. This time I'd unleash the full payload's destructive power.

Wrapping my arms around the missile, I lifted it upright. Letting the shaft lean into the crook between my neck and shoulder, I squatted low to wedge my fingers under the missile's tail. I stood, hands cupped under the heaviest end. I felt the strain in my legs and back. Felt it in my shoulder and the way the muscles in my neck stretched like bands.

I felt around with the toe of my boot until it landed on a rope I'd left lying flat on the floor. Like a tightrope walker, I followed the rope's snaking path through the dome's cluttered shelves. When the short run of rope ended, I knew the door was sixteen paces dead ahead.

Sweat streamed down my forehead to sting my open eye sockets. My torqued back screamed from the strain. But I kept moving, one agonizing step at a time. Counting step number sixteen, I felt with my toe for the single stair that would drop me outside the dome. Not finding it, I took another step forward. Still not locating it, I took another step and repeated the process.

Don't change directions, I told myself. If I'd veered off course, I'd hit the wall. Figuring I'd probably been taking shorter paces thanks to the weight of the missile, I kept up my slow forward progress and was rewarded upon finding the stair on step number nineteen.

<I'm taking the missile outside now.>

<The guards will see you.>

<No they won't. They're always looking outward. They have no reason to watch the dome. Even if they see me, it will be from a distance, and in the low light of dusk, they'll see my uniform and think I'm one of the engineers.>

<They'll see the missile.>

<But they won't know what it is. They'll most likely think it's a pipe or a piece of conduit—why would they think there's a missile here?>

I was outside now. I'd turned right but stayed close to the dome wall. My fingers had gone numb with lack of circulation. My head pounded with such ferocity I felt the need to vomit. But I couldn't stop making my way around the dome.

It was impossible to know exactly where I was, so I stopped every few steps to balance on one foot while reaching for the dome wall with the other. When I made contact, I kept on my path. When I didn't make contact, I angled to the right to close the gap between me and the dome.

<Nobody has stopped me yet, Pol.>

<Where are you going?>

<I'm between the fourth and third domes now. I'm heading for the water. The ship must be destroyed, or the drones it contains will rain fire on Maritinia.>

<You can't destroy the ship. The missile won't fly without its launcher.>

I'd hugged the dome long enough that my current angle had to be aimed at the water. Abandoning the dome wall, I picked up my pace before my back gave out.

<The missile doesn't have to fly,> I said.

<The ship is floating at least two hundred feet from the atoll. What are you going to do? Throw it?>

Greased by sweat, I felt my handhold on the missile slip from my first finger joints to my second. Accelerating my pace, I couldn't keep the missile from sliding down to my fingertips. Hustling toward the water, I knew I'd soon have to slow down or risk falling in.

I'd barely finished that thought when my left foot landed on open air. I tried to pull it back, but my balance was already lurching forward. The missile tipped out of my grasp, and I was instantly surrounded by a rush of seawater.

A pain I'd never felt screeched from my ears and eye sockets. Whether from shock or from being locked too long in one position, my arm muscles were slow to react. Sinking, I gasped with fear only to find water rushing into my lungs. My arms unlocked, and I thrashed in a fit of violent choking.

An instinctual kick of my legs thrust me upward. Propelled by a stroke from my arms, I surfaced.

Treading water, I shook my head to get the water from my ears. Forgetting I had no eyes, I instinctively tried to rub the salt out my sockets and sent lightning bolts of pain through my head. I vomited. Then sputtered water from my lungs. Then vomited some more.

<Did you make it to the water yet?>

<I fell in.>

<Where's the missile?>

<On the ocean bottom?>

He laughed. <A lot of good it will do down there. It's over, Jakob. You're a failure.>

No. I couldn't fail. My destiny wouldn't allow it. This world's future depended on me. What I had to do was find my way out of the water. But which way was the atoll?

<Time to call for help before you drown, Jakob. Did you really think you were smart enough to pull off an operation on your own?>

I looked all around as if I could see. I listened for the telltale lap of water on stone as if I could hear. Stretching a hand straight out, I spun myself helplessly round and round. The atoll could be just inches out of reach. Or the current could've already sucked me out to sea.

<You're pathetic, Jakob. You should be proud of what you accomplished in the name of your Sire, but all you do is snivel over your lost love like a stupid teenager.>

The words stung almost as much as the salt water. But I couldn't think about that now. I had to find the atoll. After slipping off my boots, I picked a direction at random and kicked forward.

<You're going to drown, Jakob. You fumbled your only weapon away, and now you're going to drown.>

I continued on my path for five, now ten seconds. Stopping, I turned around to go back the way I'd come.

<The cuda must smell your blood. I wish I could

hear you scream when they tear your traitorous body apart.>

I swam with my head raised. Was I getting closer? Farther? Had I properly accounted for drift? Drift in which direction?

I chose another angle. And another. Each failure made my breathing more labored, my swim stroke more desperate.

<You disgust me. What will your father think of you? How could his little boy become such a vile little traitor?>

I kept trying until my arms and legs wearied, and I had to struggle to keep my head above water.

<You still haven't found the atoll, have you? What kind of idiot starts off a complex operation by blinding and deafening himself?>

Despair took hold. A thick and unforgiving nothingness crept in from all sides. I wasn't in open water anymore. Unable to see or hear the world around me, I was inside a black box. Crammed into a little hole.

Buried alive.

<Jakob, do everybody a favor and let yourself sink. That way nobody will ever know what you did. This isn't a time to be selfish. For once in your life, think of others. Think of your father. Live, and he'll learn of your treason. Live, and you'll crush a proud old man.>

<I can't find the atoll.> My words came out absent any emotion. A sure sign that I'd already given up.

<Let yourself sink, and you won't have to worry anymore. Sali would want you to sink. She knows

you're suffering. She knows you can never forgive yourself for throwing her over the wall. She doesn't want you to suffer anymore.>

<I can't sink. The water hurts my eyes.>

<That will only last for a few seconds. Then you'll find peace. All you have to do is stop moving your arms and legs. Relax, and tranquility will find you.>

I cranked an arm over to slap the water. Then the other arm. <I'm not quitting. I'm going to find it, Pol.>

<Why bother? You've already lost the missile. You can't defeat us. Even if you do make it out of the water, the soldiers will eventually find you, and when they see your condition, you'll be forced to admit what you've done. I won't let you lie your way out of it. You'll be executed for treason. Stop swimming. End it now.>

<No.>

<Why not?>

<Because that's what you want me to do.>

I chose another direction, and something brushed my ankle. Probably a kelp leaf. Then it bumped against my ribs. I stopped swimming and reached with my fingers. Its body was long and solid and ridged with fight scars. It moved gently forward, and my fingers trailed down its flank to a tattered battle flag of a tail.

I spoke aloud. "You've come to scold me again, have you?"

It slapped my fingers with what felt like a flick of its tail, and it was gone. I swam after it. Ten, twenty strokes, I stayed true to the line. The water cooled by several degrees, and I knew I had to be swimming through runoff from the water pumps. I'd drifted all the way to Dome 2.

My fingers landed on a stone wall. Reaching up to press my palms flat on the atoll's stone floor, I summoned up what few reserves of strength I had left and lunged upward, my bare feet scrambling against sharp barnacles until I managed to wiggle my torso onto flat stone.

I stayed that way for a while, my legs dangling in the water, before finding the will to pull myself up the rest of the way.

<I found the atoll. I'm lying on the stone right now.>

<You've got quite the survival instinct, Jakob. I'll give you that. But I'm certain you'll be found soon, and you won't escape the executioners.>

I was close to Dome 2, but I needed a better idea of exactly where I was. I stood on tender feet and walked away from the water. Four steps later, I reached a sloped wall textured with smooth, overlapping tiles. The water pumps were on the other side of this wall.

I followed the dome a ways. Far enough that I'd moved a fair distance from the water but not so far that I had passed to the lagoon side of the dome, where a soldier could more easily spot me even though it must be dark by now.

I checked my pocket and was somewhat surprised to find the comm unit I'd stolen still wedged inside the wet fabric. I doubted it would work after such a long soak, but maybe one day the data could be recovered.

I was curious to see if any of the ramblings I'd made in my journal might be worth saving.

<I was never crazy, you know.>

<You plucked your eyes out with fishhooks, Jakob.>

I smiled. <Okay, I might be a bit touched, but I was never as insane as you thought.>

<You must be insane if you thought you could destroy the ship with a missile that can't fly.>

I took a seat on the stone before responding. <It doesn't need to fly.>

<You dropped the missile in the water. It probably rolled down the face of the reef all the way to the bottom. It won't damage the ship from under a hundred feet of water.>

<It will after the divers attach it to the ship.>

His voice turned wary. <What are you talking about?>

<In fact, I was lost in the water so long, the divers have probably already brought the missile to the ship. I wish the divers hadn't been waiting so deep, or they probably would've seen me fall in and helped out.>

<You're not making any sense, Jakob.>

<You read my story.>

<I read the ravings of a lunatic, yes.>

<I knew you wouldn't understand it. But the Falali Mother has been trained since she was very young to interpret events and stories. I gave her the story knowing that only she would understand the true meaning.>

<What true meaning?>

<The Sire is the Flesh Eater King. Emmina is the

queen who is forced to ally with him in order to protect her people. And I am the new king. I carved out my eyes and drilled into my ears. With my sacrifice, I gave her a choice.>

<What kind of choice?>

<Instead of my leg on a platter, I've given her a missile to transport from this island to the Flesh Eater King's island.>

<From the atoll to the ship.>

<Yes.>

<It won't work, Jakob. She could've interpreted that story a million different ways.>

<You didn't see the two words I'd written on the back page. Neither did the governor.>

<What two words?>

<I closed my eyes to write them.>

<What words?>

<Send divers.>

He laughed. <Send them where? And when?>

<The story takes place at sunset. And I told her I'd spend my day in Dome 4. Knowing Emmina, she probably went down to the ocean bottom with the other divers. When the missile came rolling down the rock face, she knew the choice I'd given her.>

<She's a woman of peace.>

<She is. But she's learned inaction is not always a virtue. She and the other Falali priestesses should've acted against the admiral. She won't make the same mistake again.>

He stayed quiet for a while, surely trying to think

it all through to see if everything I'd said fit with everything I'd done. He'd soon find the fit as perfect as the one between sky and sea. He'd soon realize the Empire was about to lose Maritinia.

Again.

The shock wave swept across me. I jumped upright as a flash of heat curled the hairs on my hands and the back of my neck. Next came a torrential rain of seawater that pounded my head and shoulders as I followed the dome wall toward the lagoon.

A wave of water yanked my legs out from under me. Landing hard on an elbow, I washed across the stone for a few seconds before finding my feet again. The next wave tried to slap me back down, but I managed to keep my balance, and I walked perpendicular to the current until I relocated the curving dome wall.

Hustling fast as I could, I followed the wall until my hand landed on the arched frame of the dome's only entrance. Stepping up a short stair, I knew I was inside. I turned left to duck behind some barrels I'd scoped out earlier.

This was their last chance to spot me. I expected the guards were still outside, trying to gauge what had happened. Alarms would soon alert them that a lockdown was under way. Some soldiers would pass through this dome on their way down to the underwater structure. If I managed to escape detection again, the game was over. By the time the governor understood what was happening to her contingent, it would be too late.

I'd squatted on the floor. Each beat of my heart meant another second had passed. Each puff of breath meant I was closer to landing the final blow.

My face and ears stung from the recent dousing of salt water. My elbow throbbed from the hard fall. And the lacerations on the balls of my feet chewed at sensitive nerves. I might've tracked bloody footprints, but I had to pray my feet had been freshly washed by the waves that had swamped the atoll.

<The ship has been destroyed, Pol.>

<They'll find you, and they'll kill you.>

<They're not looking for me yet. They're too busy going into lockdown.>

<Once they've sealed themselves in, it won't take them long to notice you're unaccounted for. They might not know how you did it, but with you missing, they'll know you were involved.>

I counted heartbeats until I was sure five minutes had passed. Then I stood and went to the door that exited on the lagoon. As expected, it had been closed and locked.

<The last lockdown drill they ran took four and a half minutes. I gave them five.>

<Now what?>

Feeling my way around the circumference of the dome, I found the staircase and started down.

<You understand how unbeatable the lockdown strategy is, don't you, Pol?>

<Of course I do. The Empire has successfully

used it to control tech-restricted worlds like this for centuries. By now, they've sealed the hatches of the three entrances that aren't flooded. They have an unlimited supply of clean water from the hot springs. Plenty of food. And they have electricity from the turbines. They can stay down there as long as they have to.>

<But the underwater complex is in disrepair. The Empire has let it decay to the point that it's sprung a thousand leaks.>

<That's why they installed water pumps.>

<But the pumps aren't underwater. That's why I made sure to get into Dome 2 before they locked it up.>

<You mean to disable the pumps.>

<I do. And I will.>

<So what if you do? All that will do is flush them out. They'll still have their weapons. You can't stop them from coming upstairs to turn the pumps back on.>

I reached the bottom of the stairs. <I can if I lock them in.>

<How are you going to accomplish that?>

I reached up to the top of the hatch's frame and pulled down the bamboo cuda. <You remember the carvings I placed over the hatches.>

<Yes . . . >

<I made sure they were the right length. I'm positioning the cuda so the latch handle is in its mouth.

And now I'm wedging the tail against one of the hatch wheel's spokes to keep if from spinning.>

His voice overflowed with vitriol. <You traitorous son of a bitch.>

I was back on the stairs, working my way up to the surface. Pol's insults kept coming, a surefire sign he'd realized my coup's success was inevitable.

Upon reaching the top of the stairs, I went to the door, unsealed it, and let myself out of the dome before turning left to walk exactly 125 paces to Dome 3. After putting the next cuda in place, I hurried to make the trip to the last of the working staircases.

By the time they noticed the rising water levels, their fate would be sealed. They'd send somebody to check the pumps. When the hatch refused to open, they'd try the other staircases to find the same result. That was when they'd panic.

They'd send a group out the air lock, but the seawater coming through the water intake would be fouled with poison. The next group could flush the air lock of water, but poison would have soaked into the wet clothes of the dead trapped inside the air lock. Open the air-lock door, and that poison would mingle with the water flooding the corridor, and nobody would be able to go anywhere near the air lock without being stricken down by the deadliest poison this world had to offer.

<The Empire will just take this world again,> said Pol.

<Will they? They will be at war. Their resources

are needed elsewhere. Maritinia is too far away and has nothing but kelp to offer. Will they really send another contingent to secure their supply of vitamins? I don't think so.>

Back inside Dome 2, I stood before the pumps. Hot, greasy air filled my nostrils. Pelted by the high-pressure spray of water, I reached with my palms to feel the machinery humming with life. By touch, I located the power cords and followed them to a junction.

Thinking of the people below, I wished I could spare their lives. Grabbing one of the cords in my fists, I cringed against visions of widespread panic. Yanking the cord, I was horrified by the thought of bureaucrats, their faces pressed against the ceiling to sip from a rapidly diminishing pocket of air. Taking hold of the second cord, I recoiled at the image of young soldiers gasping for their last breath. Jerking the cord free, my revolution was complete.

I didn't revel in my victory. I wouldn't stomp on the graves of the governor and her soldiers. Nor would I take an ounce of joy from bringing watery revenge to the admiral and Mmirehl. They might've been my enemy, but that didn't mean I had to make them evil in anybody's mind.

Dehumanization was the only true evil.

Now, I had a world to serve.

CHAPTER 39

"A narrwo line separates suffring from sacrifice.
The diffrence is the latter hasa purpose."

—JAKOB BRYCE

I sat near the lagoon where I'd be easy to spot despite the dark hour. <It's done, Pol. I'm in charge now.>

<You are the most despicable of all creatures.>

<And you are a pawn like I was. One day, you'll learn to think for yourself, and you will see how wrong you were. You'll come to understand that the Empire's time has passed.>

<Never.>

<Don't be so sure.> I grinned. <We have the rest of our lives to discuss it.>

I continued to wait. It wasn't long before I felt the

touch of many hands. Hands came near my eyes and pulled away in shock or horror, or I didn't know what.

I stood, and found myself lifted high on an undulating bed of raised hands. Unable to see the smiles or hear the cheers, I let myself be carried on the waves of celebration.

They set me on a mat. A cup of liquid touched my lips. Reedflower wine spilled across my thirsty tongue. I asked for water and was soon greedily drinking from another cup.

Somebody dipped my hand into a bowl, and I rubbed what felt like a very fine mud between my fingers. Gentle hands tilted my head back, and I felt the mud fill my eye sockets. Tilting my head to one side, then the other, more mud entered my ear canals giving me the sensation of sinking into a soothingly warm bath.

A hand took mine, and a finger traced letters on my palm. E-M-M-I-N-A

I reached for her, touched a hand to the shells hanging from her headdress. "We have much work ahead of us."

W-H-A-T-H-A-P-P-E-N-E-D-T-O-Y-O-U-R-E-Y-E-S

"They put a spy in my head. It was the only way to blind him to my actions."

Y-O-U-D-I-D-T-H-I-S-T-O-Y-O-U-R-S-E-L-F

I nodded. "Did you go with the divers?"

Y-E-S

"Know that you did what was best for your people. Taking lives is difficult for people of conscience."

W-E-B-O-T-H-M-A-D-E-D-I-F-F-I-C-U-L-T-D-E-C-I-S-I-O-N-S-T-O-N-I-G-H-T

Somebody took hold of my other hand. D-U-G-U

I pulled him close, so I could wrap my arms around his thick shoulders. "I tried to find you. I went to your home every day."

W-E-W-E-N-T-T-O-S-E-A

"Do the skyscreens still work?"

N-O

"Arrange a flotilla. We must visit all the cities and pontoon towns. The Empire is gone. Fear and hatred are our greatest enemies now. We must show the Jebyl and Kwuba they have more to gain through reconciliation than retribution. We must put people to work on the rebuilding effort. I want you and Emmina to travel with me."

Dugu took my hand and touched my fingertips to his heart. Emmina did the same before turning up my palm. Y-O-U-H-A-V-E-O-U-R-D-E-V-O-T-E-D-S-U-P-P-O-R-T

I felt a light touch near my temples. Fingers crept forward to cover my eyes. I snatched her wrist like her great-uncle used to and pulled her onto my lap. Sinking my fingers under her ribs, I felt her shake and twist with unbridled laughter.

I found myself joining her, the silent rumblings of joy erupting from my mouth. "Yes, Dory, we'll all need much more of that, too."

ACKNOWLEDGMENTS

Many thanks to the people who left a positive mark on this book: Mario Acevedo, Richard Curtis, Angie Hodapp, Margie Lawson, Tom Lawson, Tamra Monahan, David Pomerico, Aaron Ritchey, Jeanne Stein, and Terry Wright.

ABOUT THE AUTHOR

WARREN HAMMOND is the author of three books in the KOP series: *KOP*, *Ex-KOP*, and *KOP Killer*, which were hailed by *The Denver Post* as "an addictively readable mix of hard-boiled detective and science fiction." Hammond grew up in the Hudson River Valley of New York State. Upon obtaining his teaching degree from the University at Albany, he moved to Colorado and settled in Denver, where he can often be found typing away at one of the local coffee shops. He lives there with his wife. You can learn more about him at http://www.warrenhammond.net.